DENISON AVENUE

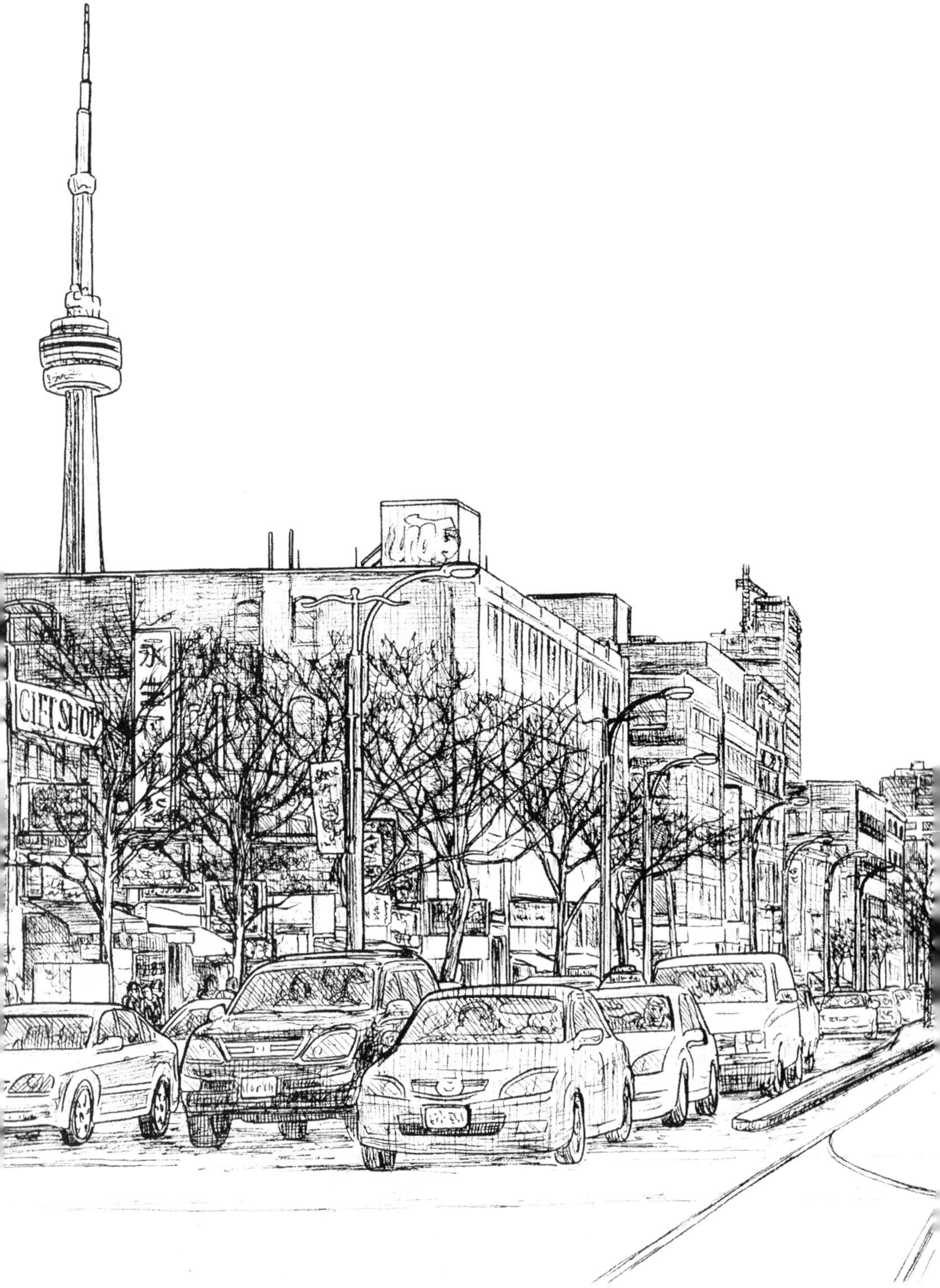
GIFT SHOP

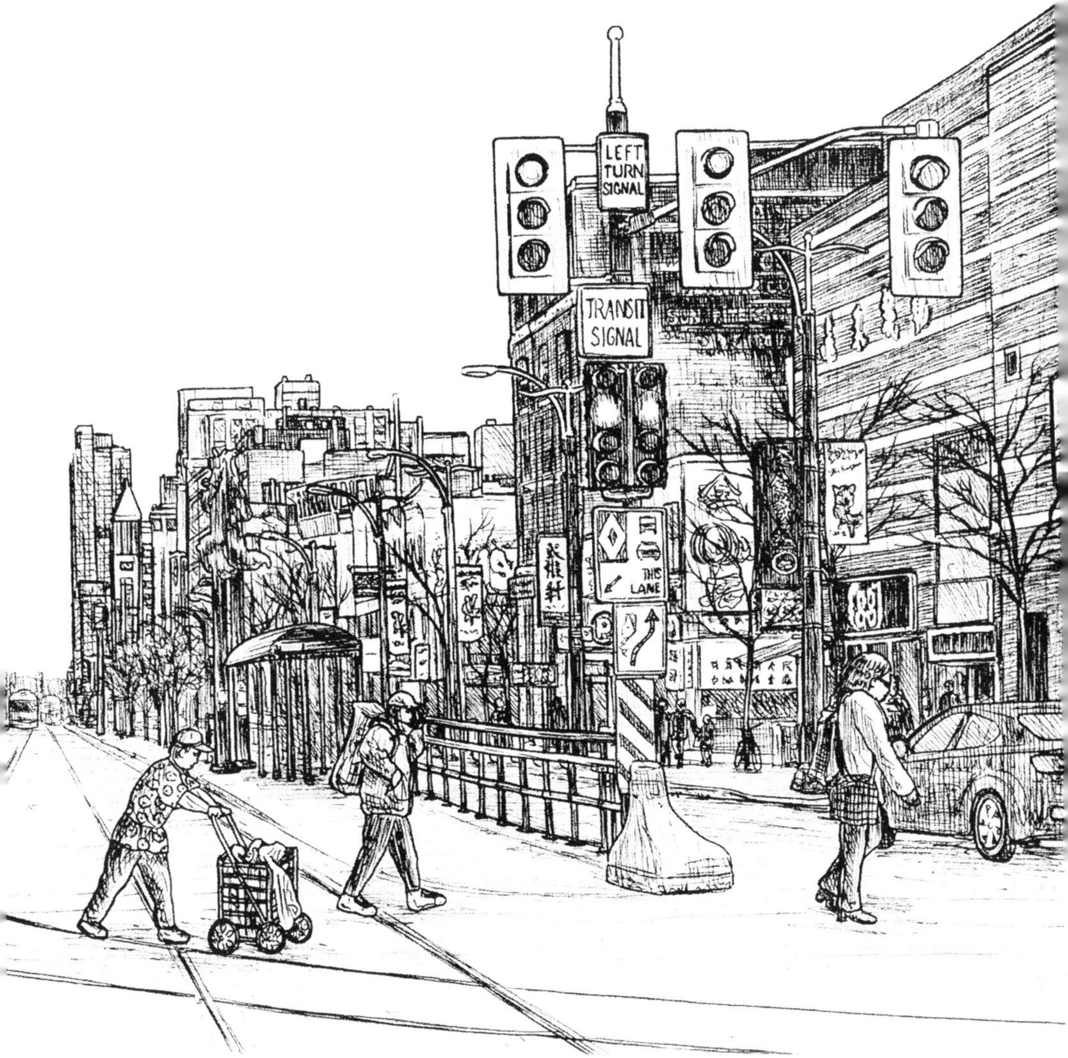
LEFT TURN SIGNAL
TRANSIT SIGNAL
THIS LANE

A NOVEL BY CHRISTINA WONG

DENISON AVENUE

This book is also available as a Global Certified Accessible™ (GCA) ebook. ECW Press's ebooks are screen reader friendly and are built to meet the needs of those who are unable to read standard print due to blindness, low vision, dyslexia, or a physical disability.

Get the ebook free!* *proof of purchase required

Purchase the print edition and receive the ebook free. For details, go to ecwpress.com/ebook.

Published by ECW Press
665 Gerrard Street East
Toronto, Ontario, Canada M4M 1Y2
416-694-3348 / info@ecwpress.com

Editor for the Press: Jen Sookfong Lee
Copy-editor: Crissy Calhoun
Cover illustration and design: Daniel Innes

LIBRARY AND ARCHIVES CANADA CATALOGUING IN PUBLICATION

Title: Denison Avenue / Daniel Innes and Christina Wong.

Names: Innes, Daniel, artist. | Container of (work): Wong, Christina (Christina M.). Denison Avenue.

Description: Artwork and text issued separately, back-to-back and inverted. | Title from cover.

Identifiers: Canadiana (print) 20220483019 | Canadiana (ebook) 20220487391

ISBN 978-1-77041-715-1 (softcover)
ISBN 978-1-77852-099-0 (ePub)
ISBN 978-1-77852-100-3 (PDF)
ISBN 978-1-77852-101-0 (Kindle)

Subjects: LCGFT: Graphic novels.

Classification: LCC PN6733.I56 D46 2023 | DDC 741.5/971—dc23

This book is funded in part by the Government of Canada. *Ce livre est financé en partie par le gouvernement du Canada.* We acknowledge the support of the Canada Council for the Arts. *Nous remercions le Conseil des arts du Canada de son soutien.* We acknowledge the funding support of the Ontario Arts Council (OAC), an agency of the Government of Ontario. We also acknowledge the support of the Government of Ontario through the Ontario Book Publishing Tax Credit, and through Ontario Creates.

ONTARIO CREATES
ONTARIO ARTS COUNCIL
CONSEIL DES ARTS DE L'ONTARIO
an Ontario government agency
un organisme du gouvernement de l'Ontario
TORONTO ARTS COUNCIL
FUNDED BY THE CITY OF TORONTO
Canada Council for the Arts
Conseil des arts du Canada
Canada

PRINTED AND BOUND IN CANADA

PRINTING: MARQUIS 5 4 3 2

MIX
Paper from responsible sources
FSC® C103567
FSC www.fsc.org

For all the poh pohs, the gong gongs, the ngin ngins, the yeh yehs in Chinatowns around the world, and for all the lo wah kiu.

ACKNOWLEDGEMENTS

Thank you to Jen Sookfong Lee.

Thank you to Shannon Parr and Jennifer Gallinger.

Thank you to Jessica Albert, Crissy Calhoun, Jennifer Knoch, Claire Pokorchak, and the whole ECW Press team.

Thank you to Kelvin Kong and K2 Literary.

Thank you to Lesley Wong.

Thank you to Tracy Wong and Irene Kent.

Thank you to Annie Koyama.

Thank you to Ruth Gabriel, Laura Kim, Aaron Leighton, Libby Ruberto, Donna-Michelle St. Bernard, Donna and Henry Wong, and Otto Wong.

Thank you to Shawn Micallef, Satchie Raudzus, Robert Ruggiero, Brenda Wong, and Crystal Yeomans.

Thank you to the Toronto Arts Council, the Ontario Arts Council, and the Canada Council for the Arts for funding support during the creation of this work.

Our story primarily takes place in Toronto's Chinatown–Kensington Market — a neighbourhood we consider home, one we feel connected to, and one we want to pay homage to before much of what we know disappears. While we were working on this book, many of the shops mentioned closed, or were forced to close.

As the area faces pressures of urban renewal and gentrification that make it largely unaffordable for the working class, we are reminded that the displacement of communities, traditions, language, culture, and people is nothing new.

The neighbourhood sits on the ancestral and traditional territories of many nations, including the Mississaugas of the Credit, the Haudenosaunee, the Anishinaabeg, and the Huron-Wendat. And as settlers, as second-generation Canadian and second-generation Chinese Canadian, we acknowledge the original caretakers of this land and share a responsibility that we, too, must take care of the land.

We hope our story acts as a catalyst for you to remember the colonial practices that continue to exist in this city and that contribute to the ongoing displacement and inequities not just in Chinatown–Kensington Market but in Toronto, and the ongoing erasure of the histories and stories of marginalized communities.

1

"Lay mang mang, ah See Heeei," Mrs. Wong's voice rang out. (Take your time.)

I peeked from my second-floor bedroom window. Next door, Mr. and Mrs. Wong were working on their front garden. Mrs. Wong had one hand on top of a shovel and the other on her hip as she stood next to Mr. Wong, who was sitting on a wooden stool with his back hunched over. They aren't my actual grandparents, but I call them Gong Gong and Poh Poh and they call me "Koh-lee," which is how they pronounce my real name, Chloe. I think I like their version better. My parents say they do too.

Aside from the two white plastic chairs that always sat on their porch, our houses were mirror images of each other. In our front yard, we had a tall tree growing by the front gate, with grooves that criss-crossed into diamond shapes on its grey bark. When the leaves were full, the top reminded me of a broccoli crown.

Gong Gong and Poh Poh had a wondrous garden both in the front and in the back filled with all kinds of vegetables like bok choy, garlic chives, goji leaves, green beans, melons (bitter, fuzzy, and winter), and tomatoes. Oh, and they also grew honeysuckle and peonies. The honeysuckle was my favourite because it gave off this jasmine tea smell in the evening, especially in August.

I watched Gong Gong take a deep breath, then slowly get up from the stool. He returned to untying the strands of navy-blue fabric and red plastic twine that held the remaining trellises together. He gathered all the broom and mop handles and wooden sticks and set them near their makeshift rain barrel, a large grey plastic garbage bin. He unfolded the blue tarp and wrapped it tightly around everything. It was a meticulous job he did every year in mid-October, sometimes in November. And at the end of May, or early June, he put the trellises back together.

Afterwards, Gong Gong took the fork and poked the soil that Poh Poh had just dug up and turned over. The left patch of the garden was left alone for the time being as the baby bok choy was still growing. We were experiencing an unusually warm October, with days that could easily be mistaken for summer ones.

Gong Gong admired the three winter melons that Poh Poh had harvested earlier and left on the steps to the house. "Geem nen gor dee doong gua gee digh gor wor! Joong digh gor go Seto Seem!" (The winter melons grew so big this year! I think even bigger than Mrs. Seto's!)

"Ahh, chaa mm or. Hor see kwuy day joong ngay sip thlay bong wor!" (They might be about the same. I think they grew some that were twenty-four pounds!)

"Geem sigh lay!" (That's incredible!) Gong Gong shook his head in disbelief as he picked up one melon at a time. "Knee joon high ngay sip thlay bong wor!" (This has got to be twenty-four pounds as well!)

"Lay mang mang ah," Poh Poh said.

"Ngggggggggg."

The screen door closed behind him.

And for a moment, it was just Poh Poh left outside.
Her hands clasped behind her back.
She surveyed the garden and took a deep breath.
She looked towards the front door, as if in anticipation.

Gong Gong came back out, left a bowl of food scraps on the steps, and quickly returned inside. Poh Poh took the bowl and scattered the egg shells, lemon and orange peels, and onion skins on top of the soil. From the second floor, the oranges, whites, and yellows speckled the dirt the way stars dot a clear night sky.

The screen door opened slightly and Gong Gong stuck his head back out. "Ah Cho Sum ah, lay heck far sang ma? Gnoi how hun." (Would you like to eat some peanuts? I'm getting cravings.)

"Gee ehm ah?" (What time is it?)

He looked at his watch. "Thlay ehm." (It's four o'clock.)

"Ah, jor lay heck fahn wor." (But it's almost dinner time.)

"Che! Ja far sang naaah!" (They're just peanuts!)

"Ahhh, okay, okay. Gnoi heck siew siew. Lay yew mor sigh dee mai ah?" (I'll have a few then. Have you washed the rice?)

"Yewww! Gnoi da geem jor gor deen fahn bow!" (I have! And I even pressed the button on the rice cooker!)

"Wah, geem nget yew gee sing." (Your memory is great today.)

"Cheee! Gnoi may mo yoong jee! Eh, eh, eh, lay bigh gor doh! Gnoi ut joon sigh." (I'm not useless yet! Leave those there! I'll wash them later.)

Poh Poh then lay the fork and shovel next to the recycling bin and wiped the dirt from her hands onto her pants. She grabbed hold of the railing; chips of paint fluttered to the ground. She stopped for a moment, then went up the steps, one at a time. The screen door closed softly behind her.

2

Ding! Ding! Ding! Ding! Ding! Ding!

Car racing.
Tires screeching.

3

The streetcar dings.
The car honks.
The sound of my heartbeat.
The faded white lines.
The pale yellow lines.
The metal from the streetcar track.

Everything was spinning.
And then
it stopped.

Dundas. Dun da.
This familiar street.
This street I've walked on almost
every day
is now on its side.
The pavement feels cold and grainy
against my face.

"Sir . . . sir."

It . . . it is . . . hard . . . to move.

"Has someone called 9-1-1?"

Voices suddenly come from all
directions, but I can only make out
fragments.

"Sir, what's your name?"

Hen ry
Henry

See
Hei.

See Hei.

Wo ng. Wong.

My words can't be heard.
I cough.

"It's gonna be okay."

The sound of my heartbeat starts to
drown out the sounds around me,
then quiets as the voices around me
return.

And again.

"An ambulance is on its way!"

I try to move my fingers,
my hand,
my arm,
my head.

"Sir . . . sir . . ."

"Sir,
try to stay still."

Toong, I try to say. (It hurts.)
Everywhere, pain.

Eyes searching.

Ah Cho Sum, lay high nigh ah?
(Where are you?)

Breathing.

"It's going to be okay.
The ambulance is coming."

I close my eyes.

Breathing.

   Drifting.

A light.

Mama.BaBa.NingNing.YehYeh.PohPoh.GongGong.Hoyping.Guongdong.

Moving.Running.

HongKong.TheviewfromVictoriaPeak.

Redtricycle.Firstbikeride.Firstcatch.

Goodbye.Hello.Goodbye.

Firstplaneride.Flight006.VancouvertoToronto.Startingover.SeeHei.Henry.

WaltonStreet.

MongGok.SaiWoo.LicheeGarden.NankingTavern.ElizabethStreet.

Citizenshipcardinhand.Canadian.Voting.Apologies.

TheWongs.LoWahKiu.Oldandnewbridges.CityHall.

Writingyou.Youwritingme.Meetingyou.Youmeetingme.

Ourwedding.

Banquets.SittinginKimMoon.Eggtarts.EatingcongeeatKing'sNoodle.Dimsum.

Forestview.HongFatt.

ChinaCourt.

TheBlueJays.WorldSeries.

Ourgarden.Thegreens.Theyellows.Theflowers.Thebirdschirping.

Thecicadassinging.Thejoy.

Sweetpotatoes.Persimmons.Freshmantou.

Snowfalling.

Starsshining.

Reflections.

Oldrecordsplaying.Dancing.

MoviesonSundays.

Ourwalksaroundtheblock.

Theparks.Thelibraries.

Thesilences.

Chinatown.KensingtonMarket.

DenisonAvenue.Home.

You.

Yoursmile.

AhChoSum.

YourlaughwhenIsaidyournameislikethevegetable.

Yoursmile.

AhChoSum.

You.

Ourhearts.

AhChoSum.

You.

Fading.

My eyes snap open.
A blur.
Shadows move around me.

Ah Cho Sum,
high mwuy nay ah? (Is that you?)

Breathing.

Gnoi hwuy migh fan see. (I went to
buy sweet potatoes.)

Breathing.

Yeet bong, teet hor giu seen. Ho leng
ah. (Seventy-nine cents a pound. Nice
ones too.)

Breathing.

Thlay gor ahn tat. Ngeem ngeem
gook hor. Hoong muy thlay gor jee
jigh bao. Lay juw joong yee. (Four
egg tarts. They're freshly baked. And
four Vietnamese bread rolls. Your
favourites.)

Breathing.
   Breathing.

And then
a different kind
of light.

Breathing.
   Brea
      thing.

"Sir,
try to stay with me."

"The ambulance is coming."

10

Is this it?

Eyes closing.
Brea   *thing.*

Please

don't
let it
be.

Let me stay awhile longer.   A siren wails in the distance.
Please.

Gnoi mm seng hang knee geen low jee.
(I'm not ready to walk this road yet.)
Gnoi yew hor dor yeh joong may
do. (There are still so many things I
haven't done yet.)

Breathing.
          Hoping.

Feeling hot,
cold,
numb.
Pain. So much pain.

Eyes opening.   Approaching.
Droplets trickling down.

Ah Cho Sum, gnoi ho geng ah. (I'm
so afraid.)
Geng lay wuy deem yeng. (Afraid of
what will happen to you.)

Inhaling.
Exhaling.

Eyes closing.

Ah Cho Sum . . .
Gnoi yew seem gay. (I have the will.)
Gnoi mm hwuy jee. (I won't go yet.)
Gnoi yew seem gay.
Gnoi yew seem gay.
Gnoi yew seem gay.

Inhaling.
Exhaling.

Gnoi geng ah. (I'm scared.)
Gnoi wuy deem seem lay. (I will
worry about you.)

"Sir, can you hear me?"

Eyes opening.

Ah Cho Sum, high mwuy nay ah? (Is
that you?)
Reaching
             out.

"We're taking you to the hospital,
                         okay?"

Eyes closing.

I stretch out my hand,
grasping,
holding on.

Holding on to your smile.

"Sir, stay with me."

12

Eyes fluttering open briefly.

I think I'm staring at the sky now.
There's a speck of blue.
Like the colour of a blue jay.
And then shadows around me again.
Like a dark curtain coming down over
my eyes.

My eyes get heavy.   "Sir, try to stay awake, okay?"
My body starts to feel light.
My breaths begin to soften and
shorten even more.
It feels like I'm getting further
and further away.

Dwuy mm jee. (I'm sorry.)

                                                 "Sir . . ."
Ah Cho Sum.
Ah Cho Sum. Gnoi mm hwuy jee.

Ah Cho Sum.
Ah Cho Sum. Gnoi mm hwuy
Ah Cho Sum. Gnoi mm
Ah Cho Sum. Gnoi
Ah Cho Sum.
Ah Cho
Ah

Two of the eight fan see rolled out of the white Hua Long Supermarket plastic bag and made their way to the middle of Dundas Street West. The small white cardboard box that contained four fresh ahn tat from Kim Moon Bakery was now crushed. A black fur trapper hat and a silver cane lay not far from the scene.

It happened at 4:17 p.m.

A series of dings came from the streetcar, each one more urgent than the last. But it did not matter.

The driver of the car passed the open streetcar doors and continued speeding east along Dundas, ignoring both that the light had turned red and that a man had started to cross the street.

"Man in 70s critically injured after being struck by a vehicle in downtown Toronto"

"Vehicle flees scene after seriously injuring elderly pedestrian near Chinatown"

"Senior in life-threatening condition after hit and run by Kensington Market, police say"

The suspect's vehicle would later be described as a black Porsche SUV, 2010 or 2011 model, with probable front-end damage. The police would urge the driver to seek legal counsel and come forward. Investigators would also ask the public to contact police or Crime Stoppers with any information.

Following this, officers would remind pedestrians to exercise caution when walking and to be aware of their surroundings, particularly at night, and that dark clothing should be avoided.

The story and its variations have become all too familiar in this city. Some garner more coverage than others; some are forgotten.

And what is left is not always known.

Thlump!

It was the sound of recycling bin lids opening and closing out on the street that woke me up.

I lifted my head abruptly off the kitchen table. "Geem haak." (It's so dark.) I let out a loud yawn, stretching my arms up in the air, my eyes adjusting to the darkness.

"Say ah! Gnoi foon jor gow. Ah See Hei?" (Oh no! I must've fallen asleep.) My stomach grumbled softly.

What time was it?

I got up and turned the light on in the kitchen.

The fluorescent tube flickered once before lighting up the room.

The clock on the wall read 6:05. "Ai ya, luk ehm?!" (It's six o'clock?!) I glanced at the kitchen table: the two bowls of plain rice, the two bowls of winter melon soup, and the plates of stir-fried green beans with fermented bean curd, steamed spare ribs with preserved black beans, and steamed pork patty with salted fish remained untouched.

"Ah See Hei? See Hei ah? Lay fahn jor gwuy may ah?" I called out. (Are you home yet?)

No answer.

I looked at the coat rack; the space beside my coat was still empty. "Joon high may fahn? Mo lay wor." (You really aren't home yet? How can that be?)

My stomach growled again.

It shouldn't take this long to walk home from Hua Sheng, or from Hua Long, or even from Hua Foong.

Maybe you went to Kim Moon too?

Or maybe you ran into a friend?

Or a quick visit to the Wong See to see if Peter was in?

Did you have a book to return to Sanderson? Or maybe you went to Lillian Smith instead?

Where could you have gone?

"High, mo deem seem. Mo see, mo see." (Don't worry. Everything is okay, everything is fine.)

Deep breaths. In and out. In and out. In and out.

I took the bowls of rice and scooped the grains back into the rice cooker, poured the soup back into the pot, and covered the other three dishes with the small plates used for scraps and bones. I started running the tap to wash the bowls.

Hiiiiigh, I should've just gone with you! But you said it would be fine and I wouldn't have to worry.

Creeeeeaaaaaak.

I quickly pushed the lever of the faucet down and stared at the front door. "Ah See Hei?! High mwuy nay ah? High, knee gor say giew uk. Ah See Hei?" (Is that you? This damn old house!)

I wiped my hands with the towel and called out again, "Ah See Hei?"

I stood still, careful to not make a sound.

No answer.

I headed to the living room. Blue and red flashing lights leaked through the beige lace curtains and illuminated the room in intervals. I parted the panels and peeked through. Something must have happened down by Dundas, but it was hard to tell from here.

I grabbed my coat and hastily put it on and went outside. The storm door slammed behind me. I stood on the porch, then walked down the steps and stood in the yard just before the gate. I looked in both directions, hoping to catch your familiar shape coming up, or down, Denison.

Nothing.

I looked towards the corner and counted at least three police cars parked there. There was yellow tape surrounding the intersection, the ends flapping as the wind blew. I wondered what had happened.

A sudden gust of wind made the front gate swing back and forth. I clasped it shut.

I shivered and wrapped the coat around me tighter. I glanced up and down the street once more before going back into the house, bringing in the cold, crisp air with me, and then I gently closed the storm door.

"Aiiiiii, joong gee doong." (It's still very cold.) I hung my coat back on the rack.

Even though it was almost two weeks into spring, the warmer weather never seemed to arrive until the middle or end of May.

Right before you left, I handed you your winter gloves and fur hat, insisting. "Joong doong ah. Mo gam taam leng ah." (It's still cold. Don't be so vain!)

You protested, "Swuy moot ahhh! Gnoi wuy hor figh nah. Mm high lay geem yeng, hang gor Chaan Lau yeet, lerng gor joong tow!" (What for! I'll be so quick. I'm not like you who walks around Honest Ed's for an hour or two!)

"Cheee! Geng lay seng foong ah." (I'm just worried you'll catch a cold.)

You finally agreed and begrudgingly placed the Blue Jays baseball cap on the kitchen table and put on the thick hat and the gloves.

I muttered under my breath "Ah sor jigh" as you went down the porch stairs. (You silly man.)

You shouted over your shoulder, "Gnoi may yee loong jee!" (I'm not hard of hearing yet!)

I leaned out before closing the door. "Mo lam koh oah yeh ah! Heng mm heng geen ah?! Swuy gnoi mang lay gor ngee jigh ah?" (Don't buy too much! Did you hear me? Do I need to pull your ears to remind you?)

"Hiiiiiigh! Gnoi heng geen! Mm swuy deem seem naaaaaaaah!! Hiiiiiigh!! Figh dee saang moon naaaaaah! Ut joon doong chun laaay! Hiiigh!" (I heard you! Stop worrying!! Now go and close the door behind you! You will catch a chill if you don't!)

I retorted, "Cheee. Lay gong mm doong." (Thought you said it wasn't cold.)

You lifted your right arm and gave a slight wave with the cane.

That was at 2:45 p.m.

I returned to the sink. "High, ah See Hei, lay hwuy nigh ah?" (Where could you have gone?)

Knock.

Knock.

Knock.

A cloud of steam rose as I carefully unwrapped the foil. I brought you a fan see today. Steamed — the way you like it.

"Lay juw joong yee. Na, joong ngit ah." (It's your favourite. See, it's still hot.) I placed it on the bed and broke it in half. I unpeeled the dark purple skin slowly, blowing to cool it down at the same time.

"Ah See Hei. Laaay! Fan see!! Ngeem ngeem jing." (Look! A sweet potato!! I just cooked them.)

I glanced in your direction.

Your nose always knew that sweet smell. Wherever you might be in the house, you knew. And you'd come to the kitchen and hover around the stove before I even took them out of the pot and put them all in the bowl. You'd try to reach for one and I'd brush your hand away, fearing you'd scald your hand.

You did this every time.

But this time, there was no hand reaching, no scolding, no coming to the kitchen.

I took one half and held it under your nose and sang softly as if you were a baby just learning to eat. "Joot joot seng, joot joot seng." I took a small bite, hoping the familiar chewing sound might wake you.

But it was just stillness as you lay there in that light blue patterned hospital gown.

Your wiry hair now matted.
Your chest moved up and down.
An IV taped to your arm, your hand, a tube ran through your nose, and another in your mouth, all connected together somehow.
A clear plastic bag with liquid hung from a metal pole.
A machine made a steady beeping noise.

Another machine made sounds like heaving sighs.
Lines moving on the screen.
Numbers changing.

And I wondered
if you knew
I was here,
in the same way
you were there
for me
that day.

7

"Gnoi high how been chor," you reassured me. (I'll be sitting at the back.) "Mm swuy deem seem nah." (You don't need to worry.)

My heart was beating so fast and I could feel myself getting anxious as I fiddled with the jade bracelet on my left wrist.

We rode the subway to get to the Citizenship Court at 55 St. Clair Avenue East. We walked up the stairs to the second floor, our heels clicking and clacking on the staircase with each step we took.

We sat on the wooden bench just outside the room and waited.

You wore your charcoal-grey suit with the tan oxfords, the black fedora nestled on your head, and the Minolta 35mm camera around your neck. You loved to document everything.

I wore my short-sleeved white polyester dress with a forest-green paisley print that had a bit of a sheen to it, paired with a mohair cardigan, its rose pattern a mix of purple, mauve, and grey. And black loafers. I gave my straight hair a slight wave using the rollers you gave me for Christmas last year. I clipped both sides with bobby pins. And I wrapped my hair with a lilac chiffon scarf to keep the style intact. Respectable. And pretty. I felt like a movie star.

"Lay yew mo mui ah?" (Do you have any preserved plums?)

You patted your jacket pockets. "Lay mo meh?" (You don't have any?)

I gave a sheepish look. "Gnoi mm gee duck." (I forgot.)

"Wah! Lay mm gee duck? Siew geen wor!" (You forgot? That's so rare!)

"Hiiigh. Mo gong siew gnoi yee ga nah!" (This isn't the time to tease me!)

"Aiii mm swuy deem seem! Na, ngeem ngeem yew lerng gor," you said. (Stop worrying! Here, I just happen to have two.) And you handed a mui to me.

We unwrapped the familiar crinkly blue-and-white wrapper and let the preserved fruit sit in our mouths, savouring the sweet, salty, and sour, before we spit the seeds into the wrappers. We chewed our mui in silence, sinking into a temporary space of comfort.

Soon other people's footsteps echoed down the long, narrow hall.

I unclasped my black leather handbag and took out the letter and reread it. I had already memorized its contents, but I wanted to see it again, to be sure.

CANADA

DEPARTMENT OF THE SECRETARY OF STATE
SECRÉTARIAT D'ÉTAT
Court of Canadian Citizenship,
55 St. Clair Avenue East,
TORONTO, Ontario M4T 1M2.

Dear Sir or Madam:

Your application for Canadian citizenship has been approved by the Judge of this Court, and will now be forwarded to Departmental Headquarters in OTTAWA for final consideration.

When your Certificate of Canadian Citizenship is received at this Court, you will be notified to appear before the Judge again. At that time, you will be required to take the Oath of Allegiance to Her Majesty Queen Elizabeth the Second, Queen of Canada.

The OATH OF ALLEGIANCE, which you will be required to repeat orally, is worded as follows:

X "I SWEAR THAT I WILL BE FAITHFUL AND BEAR TRUE ALLEGIANCE TO HER MAJESTY QUEEN ELIZABETH THE SECOND, HER HEIRS AND SUCCESSORS, ACCORDING TO LAW, AND THAT I WILL FAITHFULLY OBSERVE THE LAWS OF CANADA AND FULFIL MY DUTIES AS A CANADIAN CITIZEN. SO HELP ME GOD." X

If you wish to apply for children under 21 years born outside of Canada, please bring with you the passport on which the children's names appear. Children 14 years and over, but not yet 21, must accompany the parents in order that they may take the Oath of Allegiance.

Finally, a word to those husbands whose wives have not yet applied for Canadian Citizenship. When you become a Canadian citizen, your wife may apply for citizenship, provided she is a landed immigrant and has one year's residence in Canada. When coming in to apply, your wife should bring along your Certificate of Canadian Citizenship, her own passport, and the marriage certificate.

Manager, Registration Services.

It had arrived in a manila envelope with the words ON HER MAJESTY'S SERVICE / SERVICE DE SA MAJESTÉ on the bottom of the envelope and FIRST CLASS stamped across in red. I showed it to you right away and had you read it to me. You shook your head as you skimmed the letter. "Wah, mm ser lay gor meng!" (They didn't even bother to write your name!)

After dinner that night, we sat in the kitchen as you enunciated each word and I repeated after you.

"A-pli-kay-shun."
"Ah-pli-kay-shun."

"Ci-ti-zen-ship."
"Ci-ti-zhen-ship."

"A-proo-ve-d."
"A-proo-a-proo-ve-d.
High. Ho lan ah." (It's very difficult.)

"Lay mang mang la," you said gently. (Just take your time.)

When you first arrived in Toronto, you started writing in a small black pocket notebook all the words you learned or weren't familiar with. And next to them, the Chinese characters. You had the most beautiful penmanship. The notebook was always found tucked inside your shirt pocket on the left-hand side, along with a blue medium-point Bic pen and a small black comb. You brought them everywhere with you.

When it was time, someone in a uniform came out and opened the double doors and welcomed us into the room. I looked around the space; there was nothing special about it. There were six rows of chairs and in the corner was a potted palm tree that could have used a bit of watering.

You took a seat at the back, just like you said you would, where all of the guests were, while I took my place at the front along with the others waiting to take the oath.

The chairs had wooden backs with square seats that were upholstered with a dark green fabric. They didn't look comfortable in the slightest, but when you sat down, the cushion had just enough plush. I chuckled to myself, realizing my dress matched the chair. I briefly closed my eyes and imagined the hundreds, thousands even, who had each sat in this very chair waiting to become Canadians.

The citizenship judge arrived. His black, white, and red robe swung as he walked in, and we were instructed to stand up. I removed the chiffon scarf and adjusted my hair. I looked over my shoulder but did not see you.

"Cho Sum ah."

I glanced in the direction of your voice.

"Smile," you said. I beamed.

Click.

And then you quietly darted back to your seat.

I glanced at those around me; this was it. Each one of us sharing this moment. A moment we'd prepared and waited for. My palms started to sweat. I wiped them on the sides of my dress, forgetting that I had a handkerchief in my purse. I took a deep breath and closed my eyes.

Thirty voices
     in unison.

    "I swear that I will be faithful and bear true allegiance to her majesty
                  Queen Elizabeth the Second."

At 12:35 p.m. I, Wong Cho Sum, became a Canadian. With a slight bow, I shook the judge's hand firmly and received my certificate.

And by 1 p.m., we were ushered out of the room so the next group could take the oath. There was no reception to celebrate. But it didn't matter; I held that paper tightly, feeling the dreams of those before me.

And yet I also wondered how many of those dreams came true.
How many would remain only a dream.
And how many were quietly forgotten and never spoken about again.

Rrrrrrrrrring.

   Rrrrrrrrrring.

      Rrrrrrrrrring.

"Hel-lo?
Hel-lo?
Woon been gor? (Who do you want to speak to?)
Huh?
Yes . . . I am Mrs. Cho Sum Wong.
Ah swuy ah? Who's calling?

Huh?"

"Ai ya, kwuy gong geem figh. Gnoi mm sik heng." (She is speaking so fast. I don't understand.)

"Meh wah? (What?)
Move?

I-C-U?

ICU. Second flo-or.
Fell? . . . Fell meh?
Meh?

Ah, ang jun, ang jun. (Hold on a second.)
One se-cond."

"Hiiigh, gor jee beet high been ahhh?" (Where is that darn pen?)

Scrambling.

"Hel-lo?
Okay.
T?
P? Uh huh. A-V-I-L-I-O-M? No M? N?
Oh.

Huh?
Fa-mi-ly?
Fa-mi-ly mee-ting?"

What is that?
I don't know what that means.

"Gee see ah? (When?) What day?
Oh.
Okay . . . Okay.

Ng.

Ng.

Bye.

Ng.

Bye-bye."

Phone rested back on the cradle.

I clutched my chest.
Deep breaths.
In and out.
In and out.
In and out.

What did I say okay to?
I don't know.

I stood in the hallway, staring at the calendar.

Closing eyes.

Tick.
    Tick.
        Tick.

Opening eyes.
    Scrambling.

Where is my bag?
What else do I need?

I can't remember.

Clutching the piece of paper.

PAVILION

FELL

Reciting.

I-C-U.
Second floor.
Fell
Pa-vi-lee-yun.

9

The minute I stepped out of the elevator, I was greeted with pale yellow walls and the gurgling sound of an aquarium-like tank that glowed like a lava lamp. The sound reminded me of that tank — crowded with tilapia, sea bass, lobsters, and crabs — we would pass on our way into that restaurant that used to be in the basement. On Dundas, by Spadina. The one near the laneway. Now a bargain store. Hiiigh . . . it's been so long now, the name escapes me, as things do as we get older.

But how the red-carpeted staircase used to feel beneath the shoes, the mirror along the stairwell, and the chatter and sound of porcelain bowls and cups that could be heard as soon as we opened the double glass doors that led us downstairs. All those things I remembered.

In the waiting room, there was a small television mounted on one of the walls, in a corner tucked away, set on a news channel. The volume was at a comfortable level: not too quiet and not too distracting. A row of pink chairs with grey floral backing. The kind of chairs you'd often find on sale in the flyers for Leon's, the Brick, or Bad Boy. And off to the side was a small room fitted with an olive-green chair and a maple laminate desk, with a courtesy telephone on top.

A stack of complimentary *Toronto Star* newspapers was piled neatly on a stand where you check in.

The sign "ONLY ONE FAMILY MEMBER ALLOWED AT A TIME" sat precariously at the edge of the reception desk, in an acrylic frame, the top corner chipped. And another sign in a sheet protector taped haphazardly with frosted Scotch tape beside the double doors to the Intensive Care Unit: "Did you sanitize your hands?"

Once through the doors, the sound of the tank disappeared, and everything became muted. I was now in a space where the family members who came in shared a collective pain and sadness. We nodded slightly to one another, as if to say *I know. I understand.*

The ward you were in was split into six different sections, each divided by a white faded paisley curtain. The room felt cold, stark, and grey that afternoon, despite the warmth of the sun.

It had been three days since you were moved here and still no change.

Your eyes fluttered open, then closed, time and time again. I got my hopes up each time, but I was always met with disappointment that you did not wake up.

I patted your leg and caressed the beige-and-white-striped blanket. One hundred percent cotton, the washed-out tag read.

"Lay nun muh?" (Are you warm?)

I tucked in the sides of the blanket so it was now taut against your body. Maybe I should ask the nurse for another blanket? Do I have time? I looked at my watch: 2:15 p.m. "Wah, kwuy day koi ang geh." (They are so late.) I was about to get up when several feet appeared from under the curtain. The curtain was parted cautiously, and one by one, four people trickled in. I noticed the young hongngin nwuy first. They drew the curtain behind them, though not all the way; the rings rattled against the rod.

A young man with a black beard and gold wire-framed glasses took the clipboard that was slipped into a taupe acrylic holder at the end of the bed and quickly scanned it. "Mrs. Wong? I'm sorry for running late. It's been really busy this afternoon. Thank you for being here for this family meeting. These are my colleagues, two of whom are resident students. I'm Dr. . . . ."

His mouth continued to move fast.

Words
        swirled
    here
        and
                there,

                        . . .
            . . .   .
            . . .   .
        . . .   .
    . . .   . . .

ebbing and flowing like a tide along the shore.
Around my ears, but never in.
Never in.

I don't understand.

. . .
. . .   .
. . .   .
. . .   .
. . .   . . .

Letters jumbled.
Sounds.
Just sounds.

. . .
. . .   .
. . .   .
. . .   .
. . .   . . .

    I put my hands in the pockets of my quilted vest and felt inside. I clutched a mui; I had forgotten I put one in there. I wanted to unwrap it and put it in my mouth to ease my anxiety. Can I do it with one hand without the wrapper making too much noise?
    I grimaced.
    He paused, then continued.

. . .
. . .   .
. . .   .
. . .   .
. . .   . . .

I took my hand out of my pockets and placed them on my lap, then on the edge of the bed, then back on my lap.

"I don't think she understands what you're saying," the Chinese girl interrupted.

The doctor, whose name I didn't catch at the beginning, suddenly had a look of annoyance. First at the student for making that suggestion, and then at me. His expression said *Why don't you know English? This is Canada!* without having to say it.

His mouth moved again, speaking slightly slower and louder.

I squeezed my eyes shut, as if by doing that, I could will my mind to understand, shaping these sounds into words I would be familiar with.

months
. . . we don't know . . .   . . . wake up . . .
. . . weeks . . .   . . . years . . .
. . . keep him on this . . .   . . . never . . .

. . . machine . . .   . . . wake up . . .
. . . hard to say . . .   . . . decision . . .
. . . days . . .   . . . difficult . . .
. . . wake up . . .   . . . we know . . .
coma

But the words
would not all go in.
Deflecting.

I opened my eyes and stared at the floor while he spoke. The Chinese girl wore black ballet flats. I wondered how comfortable they were as they didn't seem like they had much support. She should be wear running shoes like the ones I had. I liked this brand — Reebok. They were very comfortable. You had a pair as well. My eyes moved to the doctor's feet. He was wearing bright red socks — like the colour of a ligh see — paired with pointed caramel brogues that looked freshly polished, although scuffed at the top.

You always liked to polish your tan oxfords every week, even though you didn't wear them as regularly as you used to. You'd sit on the small wooden stool that you built yourself, perched near the kitchen window because throughout the day that was where the best natural light was in the kitchen. And when it was nice out, on the front porch. It didn't matter that the tops were creased, the bottom heels were getting worn, and the soles were losing a bit of traction, you cherished those shoes. But now you only wore them to the Wong See's annual summer banquet (the Christmas one, too, if it wasn't snowing), and on other special occasions.

"Do you understand, Mrs. Wong? . . . Mrs. Wong?"

I stared at him blankly. I wanted to say no, but all that came out was "Shoes. Nice-ee. Henry. Almost same," pointing to his shoes.

The doctor closed his eyes for a moment, then opened them again.

I took a deep breath and whispered, "Sorry. My English, my English is no good. I don't understand."

There was nothing in the doctor's face that showed empathy, or offered any form of apology, or condolence. Instead he released a sigh that hissed like the ventilator and shook his head. He said, to no one in particular in the group, "How come she didn't tell us earlier she needed a translator?"

You never asked.

The doctor turned to the Chinese girl. "You speak Chinese, don't you? Can you make sure she understands what's happening? We don't have a lot of time. She needs to make a decision as soon as possible. Either that, or we need to book that translator. And who knows when they can accommodate us."

The Chinese resident looked flustered. "My Cantonese isn't the greatest. I don't know enough to translate medical terms."

"That's better than nothing. Please, just try."

I could see there was a combination of hesitancy and panic across her face. I asked her, "Lay hongngin? You Chinese?"

She nodded. She brought an extra chair that was just outside the curtain and placed it across from me. She smoothed her black chinos before she sat down. "Ah Poh Poh. Gnoi giew Lesley." (My name is Lesley.)

"Les-ley," I repeated. "Lay sing meh?" (What's your family name?)

"Gnoi sing Choy." (I'm a Choy.)

"Ahhh, Sing Choy. Gnoi sing Wong . . . Wong Cho Sum. Hor see gor dee choy geem yeng." (Oh, you're a Choy. I'm a Wong . . . Cho Sum Wong. Like the vegetable.)

"Gum duck yee gum yeng gong." (That's a cute way of putting it.)

I grinned. "Lay high knee doh chut sigh mor?" (Were you born here?)

"High ah." (Yes.)

"Ho la. Lay dook gun shee?" (That's good. Are you studying right now?)

"Ng, joong dook gun." (Yes, I still am.)

"Ho dee. Ah siew jeh, dwuy mm jee. Gnoi yingmun mm ho. Mm high gee sik heng. Mm high gee sik gong. Ping see, ah See Hei bong gnoi. Lay bong gnoi toong gor yee sang gong la." (That's good. I'm sorry, miss. My English isn't very good. I don't really understand. I don't really speak it well. Usually See Hei helps me. Can you please tell that to the doctor for me?)

She nodded. "Kwuy jee." (He knows.)

"Kwuy jee ah ho." (That's good he knows.)

"Ah Poh Poh, dwuy mm jee. Gnoi gong Gwongdong wa mah mah deh. Gum gnoi mm sik gong Toisan wa." (I'm sorry. My Cantonese is so-so. And I don't speak Toisan.)

"Gnoi sik heng Gwongdong wa." (I can understand Cantonese.)

I watched her take a deep breath.

"Okay, gum gnoi try la. Gor yee sang gong lay gor seen sang . . . " (I'll try then. The doctor is saying that your husband . . .)

She then relayed to me slowly, in Cantonese, what the doctor had said. This time, the words reached my ears. According to the doctor, there was no hope. That in his medical opinion, the best thing to do would be to take you off of life support.

"Lay ming ming bak ah? Gnoi geng gnoi gong mm high geh ho." (Do you understand? I'm worried I didn't translate very well.)

I looked at her, then at the doctor.

I wanted to ask questions like:

How do you know he won't wake up?

How much time do we have?

Hours? Days? Weeks? Months?

How do you know?

Can we wait?

Why can't we wait?

What else can you do?

Why are we giving up?

Is there no hope?

Is there nothing else you can do? Really nothing?

Can he still hear me?

Will he feel any pain?

All these things I wanted to ask,

but again, I couldn't find the words.

"Maybe we should give her more time. It's a lot to process," Lesley suggested to the doctor. "Ah Poh Poh, do you have any family — ga tihng — here? Sons? Daughters?"

I closed my eyes briefly, then shook my head.

"Ah Poh Poh, lay ming ming bak ah? Gnoi jee yee ga ho lan num knee dee yeh. Lay seng dor dee see gan ma?" (Do you understand? I know it must be hard to think about these things right now. Would you like some more time to think about this?)

I opened my eyes and turned to look at you.

If there's no hope, then there's no hope.

But how can we be so sure?

I took a deep breath. In and out.

And another. In and out.

As if they read my mind, everyone stepped out to give me space. They drew the curtain around. It jostled until it was still again, moving only with the air blowing from the vent in the ceiling.

The room was back to just you and me.

I watched your chest rise as I took the mui out from my right pocket and unwrapped it.

I placed it in my mouth and kept it there for a moment before I spit the seed into the wrapper.

I put the wrapper back in my pocket and chewed in silence.

A beam of sunlight came and went.

Your face covered in shadow.

Ah Wong See Hei.

Henry Wong.

I never really understood why you preferred the English name.

I preferred the Chinese one, but you insisted on Henry.

"See Hei.

Ah See Hei ah, lay hay soon. (Wake up.)

Hay soon lor. (C'mon, wake up.)

Lay foon geem noy geh. (You've been sleeping for so long.)

Ah See Hei, lay yew hay soon." (You need to wake up.)

Nudging you.

"Hay soon lor,

See Hei.

Lay hay soon lor!

See Hei, mm ho siew ah. (This isn't funny.)

Hay soon, nah, hay soon.

Figh dee hay soon!"

Nudging harder.

"Laaaaay.

Lay heng geen gnoi ma, See Hei? Lay gong lay mm yee loong. (Can you hear me? You said you were never hard of hearing.)

Lay heng geen gnoi geem lay yook gor dee jee, dee siew, dee siew bay, dee gek, gor how la. (If you can hear me, then move your fingers, your hands, your arms, your legs, or how about your head.)

Ah See Hei . . .

Gnoi mm seng nam knee dee yeh. (I don't want to think about this.)
Gnoi mm jee deem yeng do." (I don't know what to do.)

I moved the chair closer; its legs made a deep rumbling sound across the floor.

I closed my eyes.

I will count to ten.

"Yeet

. . .

ngay

. . .

thlam

. . .

thlay

. . .

ng

. . .

luk

. . .

teet

. . .

baht

. . .

. . .

giu

. . .

. . .

. . .

ngw"

I held my breath and released it slowly.

I opened my eyes one at a time,

hoping

you opened yours.

                                                            I glanced over.

I closed my eyes.

"Yeet
. . .

ngay
. . .

thlam
. . .

thlay
. . .

ng
. . .

luk
. . .

teet
. . .

baht
. . .
. . .

giu
. . .
. . .
. . .

dp

. .

I opened my eyes one at a time.

I took a deep breath. In and out.

And another. In and out.

One more. In and out.

I looked out the window.

The weather channel had said it was going to be sunny all day, but it was overcast now.

I moved the chair back, its legs rumbling again, and got up. I opened the curtains slightly. They were all gathered not too far away. Lesley came to my side. Staring at the floor, I nodded. “Okay.”

They know best. Who am I to argue, to question?

“Ah Poh Poh . . .”

I said quietly, “Gor gor yew hang knee geen low.” (It’s a road we all must walk.)

“Ah Poh Poh, lay seng yiew dor dee see gan num ma? ” (Would you like more time to think about this?)

I wanted to say yes.

Yes, please give me more time.

Please.

I stared at the floor and shook my head.

She turned to the doctor and nodded to him.

"Ah, ah siew jeh?" (Miss?) She turned. I thought, Am I making the right choice? What I'm doing . . . is it wrong? "Ah . . . Ah mo yeh. Mor yee see wor." (Never mind. Sorry to trouble you.)

I closed the curtain and sat back on the chair.

I looked out the window again.

And then I turned to look at you.

I brought the chair closer.

Your chest rising up and down. The hissing sound of the ventilator. The monitor beeping. The machines humming and sighing. The lines moving. The numbers changing.

Your eyes remained closed.

10

I woke up to the familiar smell of freshly steamed mantou and Taster's Choice instant coffee. The aroma of mantou reminded me of childhood, when Poh Poh woke up at 4 a.m. to make them for the family. After you were let go from Hat Moon Low, you made these plain buns on the last Sunday of the month. And on the second Sunday of the month, I rotated between cooking four different kinds of dumplings: faan sor, tay doy, fan see tay doy, and, your favourite, hom sui gowk.

The short hand pointed to the six and the long hand pointed to the five on the twin bell alarm clock. I reached out from under the blanket and turned off the alarm before it could sound at 6:30. I sat up and slipped on the golden knitted cardigan with beige buttons that lay on the arm of the La-Z-Boy before I realized I was still in yesterday's clothes. I rubbed my eyes, still feeling half-asleep, then took a deep breath, taking in that sweet bun smell.

I stretched my arms into the air and launched into my daily morning routine. I took my right hand and patted my left arm up and down. I did this three times. Then I switched to my left hand and patted my right arm up and down. I then shook my legs, got up from the bed, and stepped into my slippers.

I called out as I headed downstairs, "Ah See Hei? High mwuy nay ah? Lay jor meh ahhh? Bing ing bang an." (Is that you? What are you doing? All this clambering about.)

"Jor siiiiin, jor siiiiin!" you bellowed out. (Good morning!)

"Lay seng haak ngin mor?" (Are you trying to scare someone?)

I came into the kitchen and you were puttering about, keeping an eye on the steamer pot, while stirring something in the small saucepan humming and singing a recognizable tune that I couldn't place.

"Da da, da daa, da da, da daa, da daaaa da daaaaaa da da . . ."

You were wearing your charcoal-grey suit, the tan oxford shoes, and the Blue Jays baseball cap. Underneath the jacket, I could see the light blue hospital gown. It was as if you were planning on sneaking off somewhere.

"Lay hwuy nigh ah? Jeck geem yeng geh? Di gai lay jeck high ngip been geh? Ut joon jing lat tat." (Where are you going? Why are you dressed like that? How come you're wearing shoes inside? You're going to get everything dirty.)

"Meh ah? Mm leng gah?" (What? It doesn't look nice?)

"Mm high." (No, that's not what I meant.)

"Gnoi seng jee gor doh taan geem gnoi hwuy hang lor." (I wanted to make you breakfast before I went for my walk.)

I took a seat at the table. "Swuy moot ah." (You don't have to do that.)

I watched as you took the three-prong plate lifter out of the drawer and latched it carefully onto the shallow stainless-steel dish.

You continued to sing. "Da da, da daa, da da . . ."

What was it?

"Da daa, da daaaa da daaaaaa da da . . ."

"Gor Teng siew jeh?!" (Miss Teng, isn't it?!)

You nodded and continued humming and singing.

Yes, you always preferred that version.

You lifted the plate of mantou from the steamer, brought it to the table, and poured me a cup of coffee. You also mixed a cup of boiled water with a bit of cold water from the tap and set it down.

"Da da, da daa, da da, da daa, da daaaa da daaaaaa da da . . ."

"Wah, lay joon high sor." (You really are acting silly.)

"Da da da daaa . . . Mak pei joong may duck . . . Da da daa da da da daaaaaa." (The oatmeal isn't ready yet.)

I looked at the calendar hanging by the telephone. It was Tuesday.

"Geem nget mm high thlin kay nget wor." (Today isn't Sunday though.)

"Mm swuy ang lai by, high migh ah? Heck la, heck la. Mm swuy ang gnoi." (We don't have to wait until Sunday, right? Eat, eat. Please don't wait for me.)

I took a few sips of the water before sipping the coffee. I blew onto the pillowy bao before taking a bite. "Aiii, ho heck, ho heck. Knee chee jing gee ho heck." (It's very good. You've outdone yourself this time.)

"High migh ah? Joot joot seng?" (Really?)

I nodded and put half the bun in my mouth. "Wooooo, joong ngit!" (It's still hot!)

"Wah, lay yew mang mang!" (You should eat it slowly!)

"Ho ho heck ah mah!" (But it's so good!)

The oatmeal was bubbling. In a minute or two, it would be the perfect creamy, thick consistency, that moment just before burning and sticking to the bottom of the pot like noong. You always got the timing right. You also added 2% milk at the end, along with a heaping spoon of condensed milk to sweeten.

You placed a steaming hot bowl in front of me and one for yourself.

You cautioned, "Joong ngit ah!" (It's still hot!) as you sat down and removed your baseball cap and put it on the table.

I chuckled to myself. You and that Blue Jays cap. You loved to watch baseball and bought it just before the big game in 1992. "That Joe Carter!" you said with a huge grin when they won. You tried to get into watching sports as you'd seen others do; baseball was the only one you seemed to like. You even bought a baseball glove at Chaan Lau. Though I don't remember you using it often.

Almost in unison, we both took small spoonfuls of the oatmeal, lifted the spoons close to our mouths, and blew to cool it down before slurping.

We rarely spoke when we ate. And when we did, it would be to comment on the food.

"Ho heck." (It's delicious.)

"Ng . . . gee ho heck." (Yes . . . it's very delicious.)

Both our heads nodding as we gulped another spoonful.

I glanced in your direction. Whenever you ate, the lines on your forehead creased, your eyebrows furrowed, your eyes narrowed, almost squinting. You had the same look whenever you read the newspaper. So focused.

"Ah See Hei ah." You looked up. "Ah, mo yeh, mo yeh . . ." (Never mind, it's nothing . . .)

"Ah Cho Sum." I looked up from my bowl. "Ho heck ma?" (Does it taste good?)

"Gun high la!" I exclaimed. (Of course it does!)

You nodded.

"Ah See Hei ah." I wanted to ask, Did I do the right thing? But nothing came out.

I stared back at the bowl of oatmeal as I stirred it a few more times. I looked up from the bowl and scanned the kitchen and everything was where it should be, and yet it wasn't. You were no longer sitting at the table and I was left alone.

I opened my eyes.

The sound of the alarm clock pierced the silence.
I reached my arm out from under the sheets and turned the alarm off and lay on my back.
I listened for slippered feet or the thump of the cane on the old hardwood floors, the carpeted staircase, or on the old linoleum tiles in the kitchen.
I sniffed the room; there was no smell of freshly steamed mantou.
Instead, it smelled of mothballs.

You had one of the beds by the window and the view looked towards Chinatown. It was as if you each wanted to see the other one last time.

The sky was clear; it was a bright blue. Like the colour of a blue jay, as you would say. The afternoon sun was beginning to shine, warming the room.

I brought the chair closer to your bed. "Ah See Hei, lay nun nun muh?" (Are you warm enough?)

You have lost weight since you came.

Your cheeks, no longer rosy.

Your face, paler.

Your hair, even more dishevelled.

Bruises and cuts still visible.

But if you woke up now, I know you would say, "Gnoi hor gnor." (I'm so hungry.)

And you would ask for fan see, hom sui gowk, far sang, or maybe ahn tat.

Then with a playful smile, you would pat my hand and say, "Ah Cho Sum, laaaaaay, mm swuy deem seem. Gnoi mo see." (See, there's no need to worry. I'm okay.)

It's not too late.

I looked to the foot of your bed where a beam of sunlight shone. And in that beam of sunlight, I could see the dust motes floating ever so slightly.

The invisible made visible just right then.

All the things we want to say
remain left unsaid.
We were never ones with words.
We would sit in silence, eating our mantou, how sa bao,
sipping our hot water, our coffee, bo lay cha, at home, at Kim Moon,
slurping congee at Fwoo Hor,
attending the Wong See's banquets at Chwuy Hor Ting.
Surrounded by the sound of porcelain spoons hitting against porcelain bowls,
plates clattering around us as tables were being cleared and set,
orders being called and prepared,
the sizzling of the woks,
the smell of ahn tat, char siu, ahp, gai, you ja gui,
the sound of newspaper pages turning.
We were comforted by one another's presence
even though each of us was in our own little world.
It was enough.

I take your left hand and clasp it.
I then hold it with both of mine.

Your hands still rough to the touch from decades of labour.
Fingertips stained yellow from the years of smoking.

I take a deep breath.

   In that moment, I realized I hadn't held your hand since we had our portrait taken by your friend David Wong. You used to talk about his studio on Chestnut Street, quite near where the original Wong See used to be. Many of your friends and colleagues would get him to take their portraits so they could send them back home along with their letters and the money they earned. To let their families know they were okay.
   His studio was filled with various backgrounds and props; you could be anyone and anywhere. You could be the person you'd always wanted to be, even if that dream never came true. But in that moment, in that studio, it

was true and your family back in the village would see it and that was what mattered the most.

There was a glisten in your eyes whenever you told that story.
And I often wondered if you ever believed that you had made it here too.

We decided to go with the grey floral background with its billowy clouds. The background was lit from below and behind so it looked like we shone like the sun's rays. We posed for the camera, side by side, holding hands, which you insisted on.

"Ready?"

We cast a sideways glance at one another, gleefully smiling with our mouths and eyes, and squeezed each other's hands.

"Okay. We are ready," you announced to David.

"Okay. Yeet-ngay-thlam . . . Cheese," David said.

Click.

Flash.

A moment captured, frozen in time.

It's as if the photo officially signified our new life ahead in Toronto.

The eight-by-ten version came in a cardboard folder with a raised gold seal of David Wong Photography at the bottom. It sat on the dresser in our bedroom. The four-by-six versions, with their scalloped borders, were in that small photo album — the one with the waves and rocks — I bought at Chaan Lau during its ninety-nine cent bargain days. You kept the wallet versions.

All printed on thick Kodak paper.

I take a deep breath. In and out.
And I try to match my breath with yours.

I take your left hand and press it against my right cheek.
I close my eyes.

Writingyou.Youwritingme.Meetingyou.Youmeetingme.Ourwedding.
SittinginKimMoon.Eggtarts.EatingcongeeatKing'sNoodle.Dimsum.Forestview.
Banquets.Oldrecordsplaying.Dancingandsinging.Makingdoong.Yourmantou.
MoviesonSundays.Ourwalks.Home.Ourgarden.You.Yourlaugh.You.AhSeeHei.

Ah See Hei, will you take me with you?
What am I going to do without you?

Another breath.

The distance between us
grows further
and

further

apart.

It's
almost

time.

I can feel you leaving soon.

I open my eyes.

The movement of your chest becomes slower
        and
                slower
                        and

                                        slow
                                        er.

Breaths shorter,

   sparser,

and

further

                                                       apart.

A minute passed.

And then another.

And then
something about the room
changed.

I didn't notice the nurse come in, nor did I see her make note of the time on the clipboard. She had already turned off the heart monitor. I guessed that it was easier that way.

She placed her hand gently on my shoulder. "I'm sorry, Mrs. Wong. He's gone now."

But all I heard were muffled sounds.

Just sounds.
Deflecting.

Not because I didn't understand this time.
But because I had hoped what she said wasn't true.

I glanced up at her.
"Is there anyone I can call?" she asked.
I looked down at her feet, speckled-grey running shoes, and shook my head.

"Take as long as you need, Mrs. Wong. And I brought you some hot water. It's on the table if you want some. And if there's anything else you need, just press the button," she said.

She made a slight movement to give me a hug, but instead gave my right shoulder a sympathetic squeeze and a pat and then she left.

I wondered how many times she had done this.
I sat up, not knowing what to do.
I shifted in my seat.
The clock above the bed read 12:06 p.m.

Your face looked calm.
The way you do when you are fast sleep.
And the way you do right before you wake up.

I closed my eyes and remained where I was, still holding your hand.

All I could hear now was the sound of my own heartbeat, my own breath, the whirring of the overheard fluorescent light, the swoosh of the air blowing from the vents, announcements made on the overhead speakers, and the shuffling of feet from the nearby patients and nurses.

1 x well-worn black fur trapper hat
1 x silver foam-grip walking cane
1 x forest-green winter coat, slightly torn, from Simpson's
1 x pair of black cotton twill pants
1 x pair of navy-blue-and-grey running shoes, Saucony
1 x pair of black leather gloves
1 x charcoal-grey knitted scarf
1 x watch, Seiko
1 x weathered black leather wallet, within it a red-and-white health card,
a business card for Rooster Bakery, for Kim Moon, and one for Super
Electronics, one old receipt for a pair of prescription eyeglasses from Public
Optical, two twenty dollar bills, one five dollar bill, one green neatly folded
five cent Canadian Tire bill, loose change, and a photo tucked inside
1 x small black tattered pocket-sized notebook
1 x blue Bic pen, medium, 1.0 mm
1 x small black comb
1 x small handwritten note:
      MY NAME IS HENRY SEE HEI WONG.
      MY EMERGENCY CONTACT IS CHO SUM WONG.

All contained in a white plastic drawstring bag,
with "Patient's Belongings" printed in blue big letters on the outside.

Objects and memories are all that we leave behind.
Artifacts, evidence of a life lived.
The things we cared about,
the things that mattered most to us,
the things we held onto
tell others who we once were.

The walk home took longer than usual.

One foot shuffled after the other, softly.
Where the sidewalk ends and the street begins.
Step after step.
Each one feeling heavier than the last.

And then,
there I was.

I stood there,
gazing up at the house.

This two-and-a-half-storey old brick house
that came with its own past.
It needed a lot of work, but you made sure it felt like home.

He looked up at the black-and-white sign.

Denison Avenue.

Walking up this tree-lined street.
Black locust. Honey locust. Hickory.
Horse chestnut. Pine. Spruce. Dogwood.
A mixture of houses. Bay and gable, bungalows, two storeys, two-and-a-half storeys.
A park in the middle of the neighbourhood.
Once filled with sycamore and maple trees.

It was old and it needed work, that much was true.
The overgrown grass and dandelions peeked through the green wire fence.
But Henry knew the minute he laid eyes on that two-and-a-half-storey old brick house, it would be their home for the rest of their lives. Although he had the same thought about the house they shared with the Mahs on Walton Street, this one on Denison felt different. It would be one to call their own.

The reddish-orange-hued bricks.
The attic with its pointed roof.
The bay windows.
The bedroom's curtains drawn open.
The sky-blue diamond pattern on the porch fence, now faded.

The reddish-orange brick facade.
The attic and its pointed roof.
The bay windows.
The vibrant sky-blue diamond pattern on the porch fence.

I looked at the two white plastic chairs that we kept out on the porch all year round.
When it was warm out, we sat and watched people walk by, chatted with neighbours, admired each other's gardens.

He pictured himself sitting on the porch with Cho Sum in the summer months, listening to the radio, watching people walk by.
Speaking in different sounds and words that spoke to them.

I opened the gate and let my hand rest there.

I took a deep breath taking in all that's left.

Everything about the house suggested two people still lived there.

And I hold on to this thought.

I took another deep breath.

I never thought we would leave Walton, but everything around us was changing.

He never thought they would leave Walton, but there was little that could be done.

One by one, the Chins, the Stanleys, the Kwans, the Greens, the Takedas, the Yens, all took the offers and sold their houses to the City, to Midtown Parking. Their neighbours and his friends called him foolish for holding out as long as he did, but he did it out of principle and pride. He knew they were being offered less than what the houses were worth, or that there was no point to what he was doing, but he wanted to try. That maybe this one time, he would win.

I didn't really understand at the time.

And then I began to see the signs.

But the signs of "Closing," "For Sale," and "Sold" popped up more and more.

"Closing."
"For Sale."
"Sold."

Rumble!

Boom!

Smash!

They told you they were signs of progress to come, but we knew it was progress that wasn't meant for us.

The same sounds as when parts of Chinatown were demolished for City Hall could be heard as the neighbouring houses and shops were knocked down, paved, and the parking lots began to take their place.

It started to snow lightly.

Very little of what he knew of their home, the neighbourhood, of Chinatown was left.

The kind of snow that didn't stick
on the ground but instead vanished
within seconds.

False hopes.
Broken dreams.
Another lost battle.
Again.

I watched a snowflake land on my
hand and melt.

*By then most businesses relocated west
to Dundas and Spadina, and the Wong
See followed suit once they secured a
building for their headquarters. Other
family associations also made their way
west, while the Lums remained.*

I took my hand off the gate and
closed it behind me.

I looked down on Denison.
The bare branches of the black locust
trees shook as the wind howled.

*He examined the front yard, the backyard.
Cho Sum could plant as much as she
wanted in these spaces. On Walton, there
was no backyard, growing vegetables only
in styrofoam boxes they got from Mong
Kuo that they put out on the front steps.
Rows of houses crowded around each
other here, coloured in palettes of
grey, dirt, and grime that saw years of
neglect, and yet it was their home and
home to many like them.*

I knelt down in the front garden.
The ground still frozen.
It will be ready soon.

I closed my eyes.

Home.

*Henry opened the gate and closed it
behind him.*

*He looked down on Denison once more.
He imagined the canopy and shade the
trees would provide in the sweltering
summer months.*

He stared at the house again, reciting the address quietly to himself, smiling.

He closed his eyes.

Everything they need would be here.

It would feel like home again.

I opened my eyes and took a deep breath.	*Henry opened his eyes* *and took a deep breath.*
I walked up the front steps, steadying myself with the railing.	*Henry walked up the concrete steps, his hand on the railing.* *Flakes of paint fluttered to the ground.*
One step after another.	*The railing will need to be repainted.*
I took another deep breath. Is this it?	*He took another deep breath.* *Is this it?*
I turned the key and opened the door.	*He turned the key and opened the door.*

I left my hand on the doorknob and stood there quietly.

I watched my breath materialize in the air and disappear. Another deep
breath.

And then
one
    foot
        after
              the
                    other.

I gently shut the door behind me. My right hand moved to chain it but
stopped midway.

I turned on the porch light.

I steadied myself against the wall as I took my shoes off, one by one, and
then slipped my feet into the slippers that lay next to the doormat.

I placed my coat on the rack, brushing away the droplets of snow.

I noticed the cuff of the right sleeve was slightly frayed.

And for a moment, it was quiet inside.
It was as if the life of the house
had been sucked dry of its marrow.

I took a deep breath.
In
                                 and
                                                    out.

The sound of the refrigerator humming softly.
The sound of the clock ticking in the kitchen.
Each footstep seemed louder on the old hardwood floors.

I twisted the cap off the thermos and poured some hot water into the mug that still contained the jasmine tea leaves from this morning and drank two big gulps.

Everything was still as it was: the Blue Jays baseball cap on the kitchen table and the A section of the *Sing Tao* newspaper you were reading left folded.

The sound of the clock was deafening now.

I went into the living room and sat down on the sofa, arms by my side.
The photo album with the cover of a meadow with pink flowers and a mountain in the distance was left open on the table.
I picked it up and placed it on my lap, flipping through the pages like you did with the Consumers Distributing catalogue. Looking, but not looking.
But then my eyes landed on the portraits we sent to one another.
Our eyes filled with hope, confidence, and pride.
I pushed it gently aside and glanced out the window.
It stopped snowing then.
And then I watched the sunlight shift from one side of the room to the other, until the darkness surrounded me.

Two photographs separated by an ocean.

Carrying generations and histories on their backs.
Making their way to a country that did not want them.
Armed with suitcases, steamer trunks, bags filled with aspirations and sacrifices.
Letters exchanged, laced with hope and promise.

Geem san.

A dream of a better life,
waiting to be fulfilled.
New memories and stories,
waiting to be written and lived.

Until the time
    the photographs would be reunited.

Dor-run-dor.

Wearing his charcoal-grey suit, one of the few suits he owned, bought with
the money he had earned. Along with his tan oxfords, a gift from his yeh yeh
and his uncle.
His black fedora.
His navy-and-crimson striped tie.
He pushed his glasses up that kept on falling.

He glanced at his watch.

Any time now.

His heart pitter-pattered.

He glanced at the bag of mantou he had steamed that morning. Judging by the cloudy appearance of the bag, they were still hot, and he was relieved.

He stood tall, as if he belonged all this time, and held the sign he had made.

WELCOME TO
TORONTO
CHO SUM

On our evening walks home from Chaan Lau, the lights from the Kromer Radio sign used to illuminate the street, the sidewalks, the window panes across the street, and our faces with a deep violet hue. Under the sign was another sign that wrapped around the building, now covered with bright blue paint. Though you can still make out the words "Home Theatre," "Audio," and "Security."

Most of the windows have been boarded up and painted over in broad black brushstrokes. A development proposal sign was now affixed to the wall, with details of an upcoming meeting, partially scribbled over with black spray paint spelling an unrecognizable word and squiggly shapes resembling happy faces.

When I arrived at the crosswalk at Bathurst and Nassau, I could hear the sound of bottles and cans hitting against one another not too far away.

Just past the parking lot, by the church, was a shopping cart full of them, with two bulging clear bags, also filled with cans, stacked on top of the cart, coming towards me at a steady pace. And peeking above the bags, I could see a pink toque's pompom swaying along.

"Ai ya!" a voice cried out.

It wasn't until one of the bags fell that I saw it was Li Seem behind the cart! I hadn't seen her since November when the qi gong classes in Alexandra Park ended for the season. I hurried over to help with the bag and retrieve a few of the cans rolling away.

"Ahhh, oow de nay ah," she said without looking up. (Thank you so much.)

"Ah Li Seem! May geen lay gee noy ah!" (I haven't seen you in so long.)

She looked up. "Aiii, ah Wong Seem! Geem haak gnoi da mm jee high lay! Lay heck jor fahn may ah?" (It's so dark I didn't even realize it was you! Have you eaten yet?)

"Gnoi heck jor! Lay ne?" (I have eaten! Have you?)

"Gnoi heck jor." (Yes, I've eaten.)

"Lay hwuy nigh? Lay yew koh oah gwoon hoong muy jun geh?" (Where are you going? How come you've got so many cans and bottles with you?)

"Gnoi hwuy be jow por. Lay wan dee gwoon, dee jun, geem lor dee ngan ah mah." (I'm going to the Beer Store. You find cans, bottles, then you can get money in return.)

"High meh?" (Really?)

"Lay deem yeng ah? Lay gor seen sang deem yeng ah?" (How are you doing? How is your husband doing?)

I fiddled with the plastic bag I was holding before I finally said, "Oh. Kwuy . . . Kwuy gwor jor." (He . . . he passed away.)

Li Seem nodded. "Oh. Gee see ah?" (When?)

"Thlam ngit." (In March.)

"Ngeem ngeem wor. High, yew hang knee geen low." (That was pretty recent. We all will walk this road.) As she tightened the top of the bag, she asked, "Lay fahn gwuy mo?" (Are you going home?)

"High ah. Gnoi ngeem ngeem hang ha Chaan Lau." (Yes. I just came from Honest Ed's.)

"Yew mo yeh migh peng ah?" (Was there anything on sale?)

I opened the plastic bag and showed the contents to her. "Wah, Wonder Bread."

"Yeet moon ah!" I exclaimed. (It was one dollar!) "Thlin kay thlam gor dee mean bao seen my peng wor." (The bread is only on sale on Wednesdays.)

"High meh? May hang Chaan Lau gee noy ah. Jip knee doh, jip gor doh." (Really? I haven't been to Honest Ed's in so long. I've been working here and working there.)

"High ha hor sin foo!" (It looks back-breaking!)

"Jup gwaan jor. Gor see yee sang gong gnoi gek mm hor. You hang ah mah. Geem gnoi high gor dee ngin jip jun, geem gnoi hwuy jip jun lor. Koi see, hor see ng gor, luk gor nen wor." (I've gotten used to it. But the doctor said my leg isn't good. That I need to walk around. Then I saw some people collecting cans and bottles, so I started to do the same. Now it's been maybe five or six years.)

"Geem noy?" (That long?)

"High ah, hor noy lor. Yew dee ngin da giew gnoi 'bot-tle lady.' Ah, lay loi la?! Mo pah chew. Mo nam kwuy yook sheen. Har go thlin kay thlam lor? Ho ma? High luk ehm? High go gor park gnoi day do qi gong, gor doh ang gnoi lor." (Yes, it's been a long time. Some people even call me the "bottle lady." How about you come along?! Don't be shy. Don't think of this as embarrassing! How about next Wednesday? Sound good? Six o'clock? Let's meet at that park where we do qi gong.)

"Oh, gnoi mm jee." (I don't know.)

"Loi la." (C'mon.)

I shifted the bag from one hand to the other. "Aiiiiii, okay, okay-la."

"Migh ho la. Lay uk kay jor meh? Yew yook ah mah. Geem jaan cheen. Mm ho meh? Mm wuy moon uk kay." (It'll be good. What else would you do at home? It's better to move around. Earn some money. Isn't that better? It's good to not be restless at home.)

"Okay. Gnoi mm jor lay lor." (I won't keep you then.)

"Har go thlin kay geen." (See you next week.)

"Ng. Bye-bye."

"Bye-bye."

Li Seem added over her shoulder as she continued up Bathurst, "Aiii, mo pah chew. Mm yook sheen. Gnoi da jor. Jor gee noy." (Don't be shy. It's not embarrassing. I do it. And for so long.)

I stared after Li Seem as she carefully manoeuvred the cart so as to not drop the bags again.

The light changed and I crossed the street.

I looked back, but I could no longer see Li Seem or her pink toque. It was as though she blended into the buildings, gone unnoticed by passersby, until she emerged from the shadows as she passed under a streetlamp.

16

I reached my arm out from under the sheets and switched the alarm off, then turned to lie on my back. I brought the blankets up to my chin, not yet ready to get up.

A deep breath.

I stared at the swirled pattern on the cream-coloured ceiling and wondered how long it took to paint that. In the far right corner, I noticed peeling flakes of paint, hanging as if they would fall any day now. What was holding them up? Still on my back, I looked towards the door. The brass knob was scratched and losing a bit of its colour. And along the wall, next to the telephone, a thin jagged line, the length of my palm. Was that crack always there?

I took another deep breath before sitting up. I grabbed the golden knitted cardigan, now slightly pilled and smelling of Man Geem Yiew I use for my joints, and put my arms through the sleeves slowly. I turned slightly to the right, feeling that side of the bed, patting it gently, as if to say *It's time to wake up*. I swung my legs to the side of the bed, feet barely touching the scratched hardwood floors. I looked closely. I had never noticed the circular grain on the wood before; it reminded me of the rings of a tree trunk. I slipped my feet into the slippers and sat there for a moment, letting the stillness wrap around me like a padded quilt on a cold winter's day.

The sound of the clock, the creaks on the floor,
and the silence
all seemed more pronounced
when it was just me in the room.

I sat there, hands clutching the edge of the bed.
My eyes began to water.

I sniffled softly.
A tear landed on the wooden floor.
And then another.

What have I done to deserve this?
What did I do wrong in my past life?

I felt my body shake, finally giving in to the reality that was before me.
A sound emerged that I didn't think I was capable of.
I covered my face with my hands.
The tears kept coming.
I could not hold back any longer.
My voice cracked open and my sobbing echoed in the room.

And slowly
        the sobbing became softer and softer.
And then
        stillness once more.

    I wiped the tears with the back of my hand. "Hiiiiigh, mo ham, mo ham.
Gnoi okay. Gnoi okay. Gnoi okay. Mo sor, ah. Mo sor, ah. Heng tien high."
(Don't cry, don't cry. I'm okay. I'm okay. I'm okay. Don't be silly, okay. Don't
be silly. Look ahead.)
    Deep breaths. In and out. In and out. In and out.

Another day.

                        Another
                        day.

                                            Another

                                                day.

17

I'd been sitting on the bench in the middle of Alexandra Park for about fifteen minutes. I got there ahead of the 6 p.m. meeting time, perhaps out of anxiousness and restlessness. I looked at my watch: exactly six o'clock. I scanned the park. No sign of Li Seem yet.

I held the bottom of my winter coat between my hands, straightening it, then unsticking and sticking the velcro patch.

I had spotted this coat hanging in the children's section at Chaan Lau; the deep purple and seaweed-green colour block caught my eye. I found a youth size 14 and tried it on, modelling it in front of the mirror. To my surprise, it fit perfectly! I looked up at the handwritten sign: "$9.99 Ed's Bargain!" A very good price for a winter coat! I zipped and unzipped the coat a few times — the zipper worked fine. I touched the material, inside and out: it felt well made, it was insulated and water resistant. I put my hands in the pockets — they were deep enough that a small wallet and a few mui could fit. And it had a removable hood. The coat must be twenty years old now. Aside from a slightly frayed sleeve and a couple of holes, it has held up very well. They certainly don't make coats like this anymore.

I looked at my watch again: 6:03.

Still no Li Seem.

I stared at the ground by my feet. There were peanut and sunflower shells, gum wrappers, and cigarette butts scattered around. I counted eighteen tiny holes on the tops of my shoes.

I started to rotate my wrists, then my feet, tilted my head from side to side, then twisted my upper body back and forth.

Between April and November, we came to the park daily for qi gong exercises, before going to Sanderson library to read the newspapers. You always liked to get there when it opened at 9 a.m. so you could be the first to read the *Ming Pao* and *Sing Tao*, that is, if Ng Bak didn't get there first. It was always a race between the two of you. If the papers weren't ready, you'd sit on the chair in front of the reference desk and patiently wait until one of the staff members brought it out to you. I'd browse the films and the books in the cooking section while you waited. And then we'd sit at the table and take turns reading the paper. You would exchange a few words here and there with Ng Bak, grumbling about politics, taxes, and no good Mayor Ford and how David Miller was actually okay in comparison. But mostly you read in silence with that concentrated look on your face, your forehead creased.

It was now the second week of May, but a chill still lingered in the air — winter's final grip on the city. I sat on my hands to keep them warm and swung my legs back and forth, feet just grazing the ground. I took a deep breath and sighed. Maybe Li Seem forgot? Maybe I should go home? But then from the corner of my eye, I noticed a figure in the distance rushing towards me. I squinted my eyes; it was Li Seem! You could hear the swooshing of her grey and lilac ski jacket and the wheels from the shopping cart as she approached. The pompom swayed as she hurried over.

"Aiiiii ya dwuy mm jee Wong Seem, dwuy mm jee ah. Yew mo ang hor noy ah?" Li Seem apologized, catching her breath. (I'm so, so sorry. Were you waiting long?)

I shook my head, waving her apology off.

"Lay heck jor fahn may ah?" she asked. (Have you eaten yet?)

"Heck jor, heck jor. Lay ne?" (Yes, yes, I have. Have you?)

"Heck jor."

"Gnoi lor yeet gor doy hoong muy knee gor," I said. (I brought one bag and this too.) I took out the plastic bag from my left pocket and showed her the stick I had picked up earlier.

"Waaaah, ja yeet gor doy?! Koi thligh! Ahhh lay mm sik. Gnoi day yoong knee ga chay joong ho dee." (Just one bag?! It's so small! Well, you didn't know. It's better if we just use this cart.)

The cart had cardboard pieces that lined the bottom and sides, and within it, a new black garbage bag. Looped around the handle were two well-used reusable shopping bags from Metro.

Over the sleeves of her coat were another two clear plastic bags — the type you'd put your produce in at the supermarket — tied around with elastic bands. Li Seem noticed my puzzled look and said, "Mm wuy lat tat ah mah." (So they won't get dirty.)

I stretched out my arms. "Gnoi mo jeck doy wor." (I'm not wearing bags though.)

"No problem! Gnoi wuy lor." (I'll grab them.)

Li Seem came prepared. I made a mental note to wrap my sleeves for next time, assuming I would be joining her again.

Shortly after we started walking, she stopped and stared at the ground. She picked up a longer branch — about the length of a metre — that had a bit of heft to it. She inspected it then handed it to me. "Ho dee." (This is better.)

I took it from her and tossed the other stick aside.

She pressed the button at the crosswalk and looked up at the lights to see if they were flashing. She looked to her left, then to her right, and immediately stuck out her left arm.

"Yew high ha seen. Lay mm geem yeng jor, gor dee chay mm ting. Knee koi pigh, gee dor chay mm ting." (You have to look first. If you don't do this, the cars won't stop. These days, cars don't seem to stop anymore.)

Just as we stepped off the sidewalk, a black BMW sped past, nearly missing us.

Li Seem yelled in the direction of the car, "Ahh yew mo gow chor ah! Ah swuy ngin tow!! Heck see ah!!" (You've got to be kidding me! Bastard!! Eat shit!!)

My eyes widened. She looked back at me. "Moot ah? Yew lau kwuy ah mah. Knee dee ngin joon high ho swuy ah. Lay mm lau kwuy, kwuy joong geem yeng jor." (What? You have to yell at them. These people are so evil. If you don't yell at them, they'll keep doing it.)

It wasn't until we reached the sidewalk on the other side that she put her arm down. She muttered under her breath, "Gee baht sip chee gor dee chay mm ting. Cheeee." (I've counted so many times that these cars just don't stop.) Li Seem then gestured back towards the temple and asked, "You mo hwuy gor doh bigh seen ah?" (Do you go there to pray?)

"Yew see. Seen nen gor see." (Sometimes. Usually for the Lunar New Year.)

"Yew mo high gor doh heck ah?" (Do you stay to eat?)

"Yew. Ho heck. Bay gee dor fahn." (Yes. It's good. They really fill the plate.)

"High ah. Lay ngim ga fe ma?" (They do, don't they? Do you drink coffee?) I nodded. "McDonald, moot Tim Horton-ah?"

"Gnoi uk kay bor. Yew see wuy ngim high gor mean bao por. Yeet moon thligh bwuy." (I make it at home. But sometimes I'll get coffee from the bakery. One dollar for a small.)

"Yew see, ga fe yeet moon high McDonald wor. Ho ngim. Lay heck McDonald ma? Gnoi yew coupon!" (Sometimes you can get a small coffee for a dollar at McDonald's. It's good. Do you eat McDonald's? I have coupons!)

I shook my head. "Mm heck. Ho siew heck lo fan yeh. But gwor, yew see migh frenchie fry bay gor nwuy nex-see door heck." (No. I rarely eat Western food. But sometimes I'll buy French fries for the next door neighbour's daughter.)

"Oh. Whoo mm whoo ah?" (Then do you want them?)

"Ahhh, lay mm yoong sigh kwuy, geem gnoi oi yeet gor la." (Well, if you won't use them all, then I'll take one.)

She stopped and took out quite a few folded slips of papers, receipts, McDonald's napkins, and even a packet of ketchup from her jacket pockets, sifting through the items until she saw what she was looking for and gave them to me. "Na." (Here.)

"Ahhh, yeet gor migh ho la." (Just one is fine.)

She shook her head. "Ehhh, lor naaah." (Take it.)

I reluctantly took the booklet of coupons and stuffed it in my right coat pocket.

When we reached Dundas, we crossed over to the north side and continued west. The sunlight was now in our eyes. Our shadows projected in front of us made us look six feet tall.

We headed north on Markham and stopped at the first house to our right. There was a black metal fence, that came up to our chest, that surrounded the property and the front yard was paved with pink cement tiles. There was a large recycling bin, a medium recycling bin, and a large garbage bin.

"Lay jee ma, knee gan uk gor see yew gee leng baak gwo por shee. Geem gnoi wuy whoo gor dee baak gwo. Gor dee ngin goo gnoi chee seen. Kwuy day mm hiew. Geem gor ngin hor see gwor jor. Geem gor gan uk migh jor. Geem gor dee sun ngin chaat jor gor tien been. Hiiiiigh." (You know this house, they used to have this beautiful ginkgo tree. I would come here and pick up the ginkgo nuts. Some people thought I was crazy. But what do they know? And then, I think the owner must have died. The house was sold and the new people removed the front yard.)

I looked up and pictured a ginkgo tree in place of the concrete slabs.

"Lay jee UT?" (Do you know U of T?)

"Ah, gor digh hock." (The university, yes.)

"Gee dor baak gwo por shee high neng. Gaan jee gor Queen Park gor tow. Gnoi day hwuy lor! Ho mm ho ah?" (There are lots of ginkgo trees over there. Right by Queen's Park. Let's go together! Sound good?)

I nodded, then watched her open the gate and walk through. "Wah, lay hwuy ngip bin?" (Wait, you're going inside?)

"Gun high la! High knee doh deem high oh ah? Mo hat hay la! Kwuy day jee gnoi day geem yeng jor." (Of course I am! How can we see from here? Don't be shy! They know what we're doing.)

She walked over to the first recycling bin and lifted the lid. She used her stick to poke around. I looked up at the front window of the house to see if anyone was looking through the curtains. Nope. I glanced around us to see if anyone was watching. No one.

I could hear Li Seem muttering to herself. With each can she found, she threw it over the fence so it made a loud sound as it hit the sidewalk.

Yeet.
> *Clink!*

      Ngay.
>   *Clink!*

            Thlam.
>   *Clink!*

I was about to retrieve them when she cried out, "Eh, eh, eh mo dow jee ah." (Don't touch them yet.) It was as if Li Seem had eyes at the back of her head.

      Thlay.
>   *Clink!*

Ng.
> *Clink!*

She closed the lid and then moved to the next recycling bin.

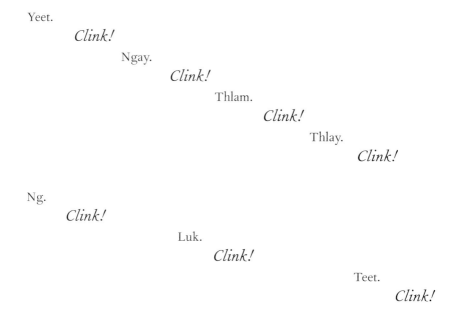

Yeet.

Clink!

Ngay.

Clink!

Thlam.

Clink!

Thlay.

Clink!

Ng.

Clink!

Luk.

Clink!

Teet.

Clink!

"Seep ngay? Koi siew geh? Ping see yew dor dee wor." (Twelve? How come there's so little? Usually there's more.) She quickly looked into the garbage bin and scanned it. "Hi cor lor." (That's it then.) She hoisted her stick and left the yard, closing the gate after her. She gestured back to the closed gate. "Mo mm gee duck geem yeng jor. Mo jing lat tat." (Don't forget to do what I just did. And don't make a mess.)

She then picked up the cans and shook out any excess liquid and put them into the cart. Li Seem was very methodical in her approach.

I was relieved to see there was no gate at the next house and the bins were closer to the sidewalk. We both lifted up the lid and peered inside.

"Yeet gwoon!" I cried out. (One can!) I didn't mind putting my arm in, so I grabbed it. I shook the can of its excess liquid just as Li Seem did and dropped it into the cart.

"Aiiiiii, migh cor lor. Ho easy. " (See, just like that. So easy.)

The next few houses already had the cans and bottles set out beside their blue bins so that made our job easier. We added them to the cart and kept going.

After a few more houses, Li Seem crossed the street to quickly check on those bins, while I stayed with the cart. I watched her dart from house to house, armed with the knowledge of which houses drank and which houses to skim over on the west side of the street. She also pointed out that this stretch between Dundas and College usually went by pretty fast because she avoided the houses that kept their bins further into the backyard.

She had two rules: don't go on someone's porch if that's where their bins were located, and don't go into someone's backyard unless she knew them or they gave her permission. If the bins were at the side of the house, she would still have a peek. If I decided to collect, then it was up to me if I wanted to follow the same rules.

I tried counting in my head the number of houses on each side of the street, plus the blocks to cover. There must have been hundreds! This was going to be a lot harder and take a lot longer than I originally thought.

When she came back with a full bag of cans, I said, "Wah, lay kwuy figh geh! Hor see gor ai may see geem yeng!" (You were so fast! You were like a squirrel!)

Li Seem burst out laughing. "Ai may see?! May heng geen geem yeng wor. High. Gnoi jo jor luk gor nen. Lay da wuy geem yeng." (A squirrel?! I haven't heard that one before. I've been doing this for six years. You will be like this too.)

Once we reached College, we walked west to Palmerston and continued on south, lifting up the lids on the recycling bins and poking and rummaging through with our sticks. I began to feel more comfortable and entered a steady rhythm with Li Seem.

She suggested the following schedule:

> between 4 and 5 p.m. for the evening round,
>
> after 8 p.m. for the late evening round,
>
> and between 7 and 8:30 a.m. for the early morning round.

"Lay yew high ha Chow Seem hoong muy kwuy gor seen sang. Lay wuy jee kwuy. Kwuy day wuy yew gor digh shopping cart. Lay goo gnoi figh, kwuy day joong figh gwor. Kwuy day ho joong yee high knee doh jip. But gwor, kwuy mm lay gnoi knee doh jip. Che, gnoi jo jor noy dee. Koi see, gee dor ngin jip, geem gnoi yew jor dee hang lor." (Look out for Mrs. Chow and her husband! You'll recognize them! They will have a huge shopping cart with them. If you thought I was fast, they work faster. They really like collecting in this area. But they don't mind if I collect here too. I've been doing this longer. And now that there are more people doing this, I have to leave even earlier.)

I noticed Li Seem liked to remind me that she'd been doing this for a long time. It gave her much pride when she said that, but I think it was also her way of saying I had a long way to go and much to learn.

Once we reached Palmerston and Dundas, we walked over to Euclid. And we continued in this pattern of going up and down the streets, stopping at Clinton, detouring through Claremont and Mansfield, streets I was walking on for the first time.

"Ngit teen gor see, go gor Trinity Bellwood, go gor park, yew gee dor jun hoong muy gwoon. Gee dor ngin ngim jow. Yew see gnoi ang ha, geem moon kwuy day wuy bay gnoi. Hang gnoi see gan geem mm swuy high gor lap sup geem ha. Gor gor park high geem yeng." (In the summer, you know that Trinity Bellwoods, that park, there are so many bottles and cans. So many people are drinking. Sometimes I'll wait around and ask them if they'd give them to me. It saves me time from picking through the garbage. All the parks are like this.)

When we got to the corner of College and Clinton, Li Seem turned to me and asked, "Yee ga deem yeng ah? Gwuy mm gwuy ah?" (What do you want to do now? Are you tired?)

"Da gee gwuy." (I'm pretty tired.) I tried to hold back a yawn.

"Baht ehm gee la. Gnoi day fahn gwuy la? Da gee doong." (It's around eight now. Maybe we should go home? It's pretty cold out.)

I nodded.

On our way back, Li Seem suggested we take the laneway that ran parallel to College. She liked walking through laneways because they were quieter and sometimes more cans could be found. In the one between Euclid and Palmerston, we were met with another laneway.

Li Seem stopped in her tracks. I gazed in the direction where she was looking. The lights were blinking red on the CN Tower. Everywhere you looked in the city, there it was. Sometimes with clear sightlines, other times hidden behind buildings and trees. But it was always there.

"Seng gor may ah?" she asked. (Have you gone up?)

I shook my head. "Geem gwuy." (It's so expensive.)

We actually have a gold-coloured plastic replica of it on our fireplace that you bought at Chaan Lau. It was about as tall as a standard ruler and light as a feather.

"Lay ne?" I asked. (You?)

Li Seem shook her head. "Gnoi day high knee doh jee gee dor nen gnoi day lerng gor joong may seng hwuy." (We've been living here for so many years, and yet neither of us have gone up.)

We stood for a moment longer just as the street lamps in the laneway flickered on. We continued our walk home in silence.

Before we parted ways at the northeast corner of Dundas and Bathurst, Li Seem filled one of her reusable bags with as many cans and bottles that could fit and handed it to me. "Lay lam mm lam dor ma?" (Will you be able to carry this?)

I objected, but she dismissed it with wave of her hand. I took the bag from her and nodded. "Oow de nay." (Thank you.)

"Hi cor la. Geem digh ngay chee la. Lay mang mang hang ah," she said. (Okay, that's it. Until next time. Walk safely, okay.)

"Ng. Lay dor high." (Yes. You too.)

"Ng."

I watched Li Seem cross Dundas. I turned, carrying the bag over my shoulder, and cut through the driveway outside the hospital's emergency department to head home.

When I reached the front gate to the house, I noticed a white plastic bag on one of the chairs. When I got to the porch, I untied the handles. "Gor dee chaang? Digh thlam chee wor. Gwigh gwigh deh." (Oranges? This must be the third time now. How odd.)

I had no idea how long they'd been sitting there, but they had certainly not been there when I left. I looked up and down the street, but I didn't notice anything unusual. I thought I saw movement in the window next door, but then thought nothing of it. I opened the storm door, then took my keys out of my right pocket.

I called out as I stepped inside, "Gnoi fahn jor gwuy la." (I'm home now.)

The daily wall calendar that we bought from Sun Wah every year hung just above the phone in the hallway.

Its pages felt like thin rice paper.

The monthly calendar from Kyu Shon Hong hung on the wall over two nails. The year of the snake.

The vegetable oil, the used vegetable oil, the sesame oil, and two soy sauce bottles — light, dark, stained on the outside — all on a styrofoam plate wrapped in foil sat on the counter next to the stove.

Oil-stained sheets of newspaper folded to the side of stove that were placed on the floor when we cooked.

The stovetop rusted and chipped. The oven used as storage for other pots and pans.

Coffee, jam, pickle, and roasted peanut jars repurposed to hold black and white pepper, corn starch, five spice, star anise, dried orange peels, and slabs of brown sugar cane.

New jar labels written on scrap pieces of paper taped over the old labels.

The sixteen-ounce container of chicken broth granules next to a small plastic container of white sugar, with a white plastic spoon inside.

The metal spatula, ladle, and bamboo strainer hung off white plastic hooks above the sink.

The five-cup National rice cooker sat on the counter. Its cord wrapped with electrical tape.

The kitchen table always covered, never bare. Flyers from Metro, Canadian Tire, No Frills, Price Chopper, Shoppers Drug Mart, the Brick mixed in with old issues of *Ming Pao* and *Sing Tao* and their weekend supplements that the library saved for us, *Shing Wah Daily News*, the *Toronto Sun*, and the *Kensington Market Drum* all piled on top of one another, edges discolouring.

Next to them, a phone book from 2010, a Yellow Pages from 2012, a *New Lexicon Webster's Encyclopedic Dictionary* stacked.

Receipts from Hua Foong, Hua Long, Hua Sheng, Hong Fatt became scraps of paper for me to write grocery lists on the back.

Pencils too short all lined up with the receipts in an old Ferrero Rocher box. I'd protest when I saw your hand reach for the stubs to throw them out. "Eh, eh, eh, joong yoong duck ah!" (You can still use them!)

A small pile of notebooks I used to write down recipes from the library cookbooks.

A mooncake tin from Kim Moon filled with loose change; pins; a couple of dollar bills; staples; grease pencils; old Christmas cards from the Kwans, the Takedas, and the Greens; an old pair of eyeglasses; a commemorative TTC token from the opening of the Bloor-Danforth subway line in 1966; your old bank book from Imperial Bank of Canada on Elizabeth and Dundas; a flyer from Chinese Printing & Advertising that used to be on Brunswick Avenue; two old catalogues from Y.Y. Company in San Francisco from February 1965 and June 1966; an instruction manual for the Seabreeze Stereo 720; and a manual for the Kodak Pocket Instamatic camera.

A crystal bowl meant for serving punch now used to hold elastics, a handful of paperclips, shoelaces, batteries, a few blue medium-point Bic pens, a letter opener, my change purse, and a Ziploc bag filled with old keys.

The old cardboard barrel of Ajinomoto MSG tucked in the pantry to hold the rice, always a full cup ready to be taken out.

Drawers filled with coupons; napkins from McDonalds and Kentucky Fried Chicken; packets of ketchup; packets of sugar; packets of moist towelettes; and disposable spoons and forks.

Cupboards lined with calendar pages from 1993 from Lien Phong Trading and Hong Fat Seafood Market. Also yellowing at the edges.

And on the side of one of the cupboards, I maintained your habit of collecting the stickers from the fruits. Just as you got annoyed with my too short pencils, I got annoyed with your fruit stickers every time I found them stuck on the kitchen sink, on the faucet, on the counter, on the table, and sometimes on the side of the fridge.

The popular ones:

#4167, red delicious apples

#4428, Fuyu persimmons
#4011, bananas
#4133, gala apples
#4013, navel oranges
#4021, golden delicious apples
#4046, avocados
#4022, seedless green grapes
#4407, Asian pears

You said the stickers brought colour to the kitchen and that it was interesting to see where our fruits and vegetables had come from and how they were grown. How far they travelled and the journey they endured to get here.
Mexico, South Africa, China, California, and Ontario.

Like stamps on a passport.

It was warm enough now to not have to wear a heavy winter coat anymore, but the early mornings still carried a cool breeze. I wore the same black polyester pants, a long-sleeved denim shirt, and added the magenta zip-up fleece vest with the yellow trims.

It had been a couple of weeks since I first went out with Li Seem. I did not mind that walk so I agreed to another. Today she wanted to show me a morning route.

I looked in the mirror and put on one of your baseball caps. This one was green and white and said "Franco and Leona's Regal Grill Café" on the front. I think you may have gotten it for two dollars from that clothing shop on Kensington that had mannequins displayed on its balcony. I adjusted the snap back strap so it fit more snugly.

I made sure I had everything I needed: two big reusable bags and an old curtain rod that I'd found in the main floor closet. I tucked in my inhaler and a pair of old dishwashing gloves into the vest pockets just in case. I passed your photo in the frame and said aloud over my shoulder, "Gnoi chut hwuy la." (I'm going out now.)

I closed and locked the door, putting the keys into the black fanny pack.

Aside from the house sparrows that could be heard high up on the black locust trees that were starting to become full again, it was still quiet at this hour. But by 8:30 a.m., Dundas, College, and Bathurst would be filled with the usual traffic noise you would expect from these busy main streets.

I walked down the steps and filled a small pot with water from the plastic garbage bin we used as a rain barrel. I started to pour it into the garden plots when Li Seem bellowed from afar, "Jor sin, jor sin." (Good morning.)

I turned around. "Ah, jor sin."

"Lay heck jor doh taan may ah?" (Have you eaten breakfast yet?) She handed me a small plastic bag. "How sa bao." (They're red bean paste buns.)

"Wah, lay jing?" (You made them?)

She nodded.

I untied the handles. "Gee leng wor. Gor see ah See Hei jing gor dee mantou gee ho heck." (They look wonderful. See Hei used to make the most delicious plain buns.)

"High ah, gor dee mantou ho heck wor. Gee bow teem! Gor gan mean bao por — meh meng ah — Maheng? Gor gan, gor dee mantou gee digh ah! Lerng gor yeet moon!" (Yes, those are tasty. Very filling too. That bakery — what's the name — Maheng? That one, their plain buns are so huge! And they're two for one dollar!)

"Gnoi may ging gwor. Ang ah jun, gnoi bigh ngip bin." (I haven't gone in there yet. Hold on a second, I'll bring these inside.)

I quickly opened the door and dropped the buns on the kitchen counter. "Ah Li Seem jing how sa bao ah. Gnoi hwuy la." (Li Seem made some red bean paste buns. I'm going now.)

"Ho la, gnoi day hang la," I said as I came out the door. (Okay, let's get going.)

Li Seem asked, "Lay jung moot ah?" (What are you growing?)

"Doong gua, fwoo gua, mo gua, fa kay sum, bok choy, giew choy, yin choy, gow gee, luk dou." (Winter melon, bitter melon, fuzzy melon, tomatoes, red amaranth, goji leaves, green beans.)

"Gnoi dor high." (Me too.)

"Gnoi gee duck lay jung high gor tien been." (I remember you use the front yard to grow.)

"High ah. Tien been, ya meh." (Yes. The front yard, the backyard.)

As we walked up Bellevue, smells of scrambled eggs and bacon coming from the open windows of people's houses wafted in our direction. At Nassau, it smelled like coffee.

Li Seem took a deep breath. "Ga fe may ho heng ah." (That coffee smell is strong.)

"High wor." (Yes, it is.)

"Lay hiew Moonbean ma?" she asked. (Do you know Moonbean?)

"Moon-bean? High nigh ah?" (Where is it?)

"Laaay, high gor St. Andrew gor tow. Gun jee gor gai por." (You know, on St. Andrew Street. By the poultry shop.)

"Ahhh, gnoi ay tui." (Yes, I know the one.)

"Kwuy gor ga fe may ho heng ah." (The smell of their coffee is really nice.)

"High wor." (Yes, that's right.)

"Yew mo ngim gwor?" (Have you drank it before?)

"Mo. Mm jee kwuy high mm high gwuy." (No. I wasn't sure if it was expensive or not.)

"Oh. Gnoi da may ngim." (I haven't had it either.)

When we reached Bathurst, we crossed over to the other side. Li Seem stopped in front of the development proposal sign that was secured to the wall of Kromer Radio. "Gnoi heng ngin gong kwuy day seng bigh gor Walmart high knee doh." (I heard from other people they're thinking of putting a Walmart here.)

"Walmart?"

"Cheap see-dor. Hor see Chaan Lau." (It's a cheap store. Similar to Honest Ed's.)

"Ho see-dor muh?" (So a good store?)

"Ahh mm chor. Chaan Lau ho dee. Hoong muy gor see-dor high Kensington. Sa-see-Mart. Yew meeting teem." (It's not bad. Honest Ed's is better. And that store in Kensington. Sasmart. There will be a meeting too.)

"Oh. Lay hwuy mo?" (Will you be going?)

"Da mm ming baht." (I wouldn't understand.)

"Gor see, See Hei gee joong yee hwuy chaam ga knee dee yeh." (See Hei used to love going to those kinds of things.)

"Na, knee gor high gor be jow por." (Now this is the Beer Store.)

Li Seem led me to the fence, that was currently locked with a chain, next to the entrance of the store and pointed to the Chinese sign affixed to it. Behind the fence were tables and black sorting bins under a long and narrow white tent. "Lay ngip knee doh, geem bigh knee dee jun high knee doh, gor dee jun high gor doh. Be jow. Luk sik. Joong sik. Jow jun. Luk sik. Gwoon. Ho easy." (You enter here, and then you put these bottles here, those bottles there. So here's the beer. Green. Brown. Wine bottles here. Green ones. Cans. It's so easy.)

I nodded, rereading the sign. "Be jow jun. Jow jun. Gwoon." (Beer bottles. Wine bottles. Cans.)

Li Seem's voice dropped to a whisper even though there was no one around us. "Yew see, yew dee jor goong gor dee ngin, kwuy day high gee dor jun, kwuy day ho lau ah. Gor see mm high geem yeng." (Sometimes, when some of the employees see so many bottles, they get annoyed with you. Before they weren't like that.) She shook her head before continuing, in a louder voice, "Thligh gor jun, sip seen. Digh gor jun, ngay sip seen. Gwoon, sip seen." (Small bottles are ten cents. Bigger bottles are twenty cents. Cans are also ten cents.)

I repeated, "Thligh gor jun, sip seen. Digh gor jun, ngay sip seen. Gwoon, sip seen."

"Thlin kay yeet hoong muy thlin kay thlay, gee dor ngin ah. Heng geen gee dor jun hoong muy gwoon. Bing ing bang an. Da gee ho heng ah. Hoong muy hoy moon gor see, da gee dor ngin! Mm sor wigh. Hoong gor dee ngin da jiew foo. King ah guy. Hor see lun doy geem yeng." (On Mondays and Thursdays, there are so many people! You can hear all the bottles and cans clattering about. It sounds pretty nice, actually. And right when it opens, there are lots of people. But I don't mind. You can talk with the people. Catch up. It's like lining up for a sale.)

"Hor see lun gor for gai high Chaan Lau!" I replied, laughing. (It's like lining up for a turkey at Honest Ed's!)

"Ahhh, high ah! Lay yew mo hwuy lun ah?" (Yes, that's right! Have you lined up for that before?)

"Gor gor nen." (Every year.)

"Gnoi dor high!" (Me too!)

After a few minutes of silence, Li Seem then offered, "Ahhh, gnoi nam, gnoi day fahn lay knee doh hing dor la. Lay lor gor dee jun gnoi bay lay gor maan haak. Geem gnoi lor geem nget gnoi day jip gor dee jun. Ho mm ho ah?" (I was thinking, how about we come back here tomorrow. Bring that bag of bottles I gave you the other night. And I will bring the ones we collect today. How does that sound?)

I nodded. "Ho la." (Sounds good.) I breathed a sigh of relief that she made this suggestion.

We left the parking lot of the Beer Store and continued north on Bathurst.

I suddenly realized I knew very little about Li Seem. I knew she was a regular at the qi gong class in the park. I knew she lived with her husband behind the park, in one of those houses on Augusta across from those tall buildings. And I knew she enjoyed gardening. We exchanged a few words here and there at the qi gong classes, but we usually went our separate ways once class ended. I wanted to ask more about her, about her life, about why she does this, but I couldn't find the right words.

Sometimes we ask too many questions; other times we don't ask enough.

I started, "Ah Li Seem ah . . ." She looked over. I paused for a moment. "Geem nget gee hor teen hay." (It's a nice day today.)

She nodded. "High ah, dee gee hor." (It is, isn't it?)

We fell silent again. But the sound of the cart going over the uneven sidewalk made our silence feel more comfortable.

We stopped at College and waited for the light to turn green.

In the silence, she leaned in and lowered her voice. "Lay koi see yeet gor ngin high gor gan uk lay yew siew seem dee wor!" (You know you have to be more careful now that you're living on your own!)

When you live on your own,
the days feel longer,
and the sounds become more noticeable.

I wanted to say this but kept silent and just nodded. "Gnoi ay tui. Gor dee ngin nex-see door high hor ngin." (I will. The people next door are good people.)

She nodded, then pointed past the Shoppers Drug Mart. "Gor see, gnoi jigh nwuy seng gnoi day migh gor condo high neng. Geem thligh da koi gwuy. Hiiigh." (Before, our children wanted us to buy a condo unit over there. But for something so small it was very expensive.)

"Da wuy gee ho. Hongngin guy, Chaan Lau joong gee kun." (It wouldn't have been so bad. You'd still be close to Chinatown and Honest Ed's.)

The light turned green and we walked across. The crossing guard was ready, holding his stop sign and tooting his whistle, not once but twice.

Li Seem continued, "Hiiiigh. Gnoi ay tui gnoi day high lor la. Yew see, mm jor duck gor dee yeh. Hiiigh. Lay goo gnoi seng geem yeng meh? Geem gnoi jor knee dee yeh lor. Jip jun. Yook ha, hang ha. Mm seng ma fahn gor dee jigh nwuy. Mm seng kwuy day sin foo." (I know we're getting old. Sometimes, I can't do things. But do you think I want to be like that? That's why I started doing this. Collecting bottles. Get some exercise, walk around. I don't want to make things hard for my children. I don't want them to suffer.) Li Seem took out a McDonald's napkin from her jacket pocket and dabbed her eyes. "Bay kwuy day hoy seem seem." (I just want them to be happy.)

We stopped at the corner for a moment by the makeshift seating area just outside the church as Li Seem wiped away her tears. I felt my pocket and took out a mui and offered it to her.

I let the silence rest there for a few moments as she chewed on the mui. She then spit out the seed into the wrapper and put it in her pocket. "Hiiigh. Gnoi sor ah. Dwuy mm jee ah." (I'm being silly. I'm sorry.)

I waved off her apology.

Once she regained her composure, she said, "Jee gor gan uk geem dor nen. Seng say high gor doh, da mm duck. Uk gor suy nen nen hay ga. Moot da koi gwuy. Lay jee koi see gnoi day gor dee uk — geem thligh — migh kwuy lor doh yeet man moon. Yew mo gow chor ah?" (We lived in the house for so many years. We'd like to die there, but we can't. Property tax keeps increasing every year. Everything is so expensive now. Did you know the houses in our area — so small too — are selling for more than one million dollars? Isn't that crazy?)

"High migh ah? Lay gong siew nah." (Are you sure? You must be joking.)

"High ah." (It's true.)

I couldn't believe it — a million dollars for where we lived? I repeatedly heard how rundown and dirty our neighbourhood was, so it was hard to believe that the houses there would be worth that much.

We resumed our walk up Bathurst and collected cans here and there.

I fell a step behind Li Seem for a second and observed how she walked. The heels of her blue, orange, and white running shoes were worn on the outer edges. She wore tapered black-and-white checkered pants that were rolled up at the hem, an ivory-white knitted sweater that I only just noticed had embroidered strawberries all over, plastic bags on the arms, and the pink toque on top.

Just like the first night, she pushed the shopping cart while looking from all sides, stopping at each house and apartment building she knew would have bottles and cans. Light or heavy, the load in the cart never seemed to be a burden for her.

I started to mimic her stride and movements before catching up to her.

When we reached Harbord, we turned right. It started to get busy on the streets. People gathered at the streetcar and bus stops on all four corners, students getting off and heading to school. Cars were bumper to bumper.

When we got to a laneway called Croft, Li Seem pointed for us to walk down. "Knee gor low gee ho." (This street is a good one.)

Croft Street, lined with colourfully painted garage doors, ran from Harbord to College. There were murals of raccoons, birds, flowers, shapes, one of a streetcar, and one dedicated to a black and white cat.

It was definitely much easier collecting the bottles and cans from here. The road was narrow and the distance between the bins was smaller. Not too many had cans beside their bins, so we rifled through them with my curtain rod and Li Seem's bamboo stick.

Midway through the street, I noticed some garages had two storeys to them, and some were actual houses. "Wah, gnoi mm jee yew dee uk high knee doh." (I didn't know there were houses here.)

"High ah. Kwuy dut yee wor. Yew yeet gan yew gor greenhouse. Oh, oow koi." (Yes, there are. They're cute, aren't they? There's one that even has a greenhouse. Here it is.)

We looked up at the house made up of concrete blocks. And on the roof was a small greenhouse.

Li Seem exclaimed, "Hor see ngay bak moon ah!" (I think it's two million dollars!)

"Ngay bak moon?! Been gor yew geem dor ngan ah?" (Two million dollars?! Who has that kind of money?)

"Gnoi yew geem dor gnan, gnoi wuy hoong gnoi lo gong hwuy loy hang. Lay ne?" (If I had that much money, I would go travelling with my husband. How about you?)

"Mm jee . . . bigh gor ngan hong." (I'm not sure . . . probably put it in the bank.)

"Che!"

"Moot ah? Hiiigh, geem gnoi hwuy Kim Moon migh hor dor ahn tat la! Eh, gnoi day lerng gor seng gor CN Tower!!" (What?! Okay, I would go to Kim Moon and buy lots of egg tarts! No wait, we'll go up the CN Tower together!!)

In that moment, we laughed like we were school kids.

By the time we finished Croft Street, the cart was half-full.

Li Seem asked, "Hang Borden ma?" (Should we go up on Borden?)

We stopped at the corner and had a look. The recycling trucks hadn't come through yet.

Just then the Bellevue clock tower rang eight times.

I replied, "Ho la!" (Sure!)

"Geem gnoi day hwuy hongngin guy ngim ga fe high gor mean bao por la? Ho ma?" (Then we can go to Chinatown and have a coffee at one of the bakeries? Does that sound good?)

"Ho la."

And we continued on our way to Borden.

20

There was a community meeting being held in the church at the corner of College and Bathurst to talk about the future of Bathurst Street. I had received a notice about it in the mail a month ago and stuck it on the fridge as a reminder.

For many years, you attended these kinds of meetings about Chinatown and Kensington. You looked for updates in the *Ming Pao* and *Sing Tao* and in the *Kensington Market Drum* when it was still around. Any time we got a notice from the City about changes, you would do some research. You reminded me it was important to know what was going on. Otherwise changes would happen without you even noticing it, making you think they were always there. You did not want to fall for the City's tricks again.

You tried to get me to come, encouraging me by saying it would be a good way to practise my English. But the words proved to be too difficult for me so I stopped accompanying you.

Deep down, you knew that people didn't listen to people who spoke the way we did, and yet you went anyway. But each time you went to these meetings, you would come home exasperated. Why call them community meetings if you don't listen to the community, you'd say. It was rare to see you angry, but anything about politics or changes in the neighbourhood riled you up.

I opened the door to the church apprehensively and looked around to see where the meeting could be.

A young lady wearing chestnut-brown loafers with tassels greeted me at the door. "Hi there! Are you here for the meeting?"

"Meeting. Yes," I replied.

"Wonderful. Just sign in here." She handed me a pen and pointed to the line on the sheet of paper. I took it from her and stared at the sheet in front of me as she helped the next person.

Black letters and lines were all I saw.

I think she noticed my hesitation because she came back and said, "You don't have to. It's only if you want to keep up to date with what happens at these meetings and be informed of future ones."

I nodded and left the pen on the table.

I walked through the doors. The large room was basked in a warm glow as the late afternoon sunlight shone through the venetian blinds that faced Bathurst, brightening the white linoleum floors. Several round tables were spread throughout the room; I took a seat at the one closest to the doors. It was like I was at a Chinese banquet hall or going for dim sum, except there was no food or tablecloths.

On the table, stickers with "Hello my name is" printed on them were placed in the middle, along with five pens, three black markers, and five large sheets of paper. There were also leaflets about the proposed study. All written in English. I picked one up and brought it closer to my face, trying to study the words.

I took one of the markers and wrote my name and pressed it against my shirt. A few others joined me shortly after, nodding and smiling to one another. There was a mix of people in age but mostly white people — that's what you always noticed as well.

I glanced around the room; it was starting to fill up. Our names written on stickers stuck to our shirts. We were strangers, friends, neighbours gathered on a Sunday afternoon, concerned about our community.

The meeting began with introductions from the local councillors.

"Okay everyone, we're about to get started. Can everyone hear me? At the back, can you hear me? Yes? Good. Okay. Thank you all for being here and for taking the time out of your busy schedule, on a Sunday no less, to talk about the future of Bathurst Street. A lot of development has or will be happening along this street, so it's important we do it right. First we'll have a presentation about Bathurst, looking at its history, what it's like now, and where we see it going. After the presentation, we'll do something called a design charrette, where everyone in the room will have a chance to shape the future of Bathurst. For those of you unfamiliar with the term, a charrette is like a brainstorming session where we try to get all the stakeholders involved and come up with a solution together that benefits everyone and the neighbourhood. There will be a series of meetings throughout the summer. And finally, in the fall, we'll present to council the recommendations made from these meetings. Remember, your opinions matter. So be as honest as possible. And if you haven't already done so when you checked in, please leave your contact info with us to get updates and notices of upcoming meetings."

Once more, the words did not enter my ears. But I listened, trying to understand.

The lights dimmed.
Old photos beside new ones.
  History alongside the present.
    Looking ahead.
      Looking at the past, only briefly.

When the lights flickered back on, a warm murmur of excitement spread throughout the room. The councillors then asked us to write our wish lists for Bathurst on the sheets provided.

The person to my right wore thick black-rimmed glasses and a white short-sleeved shirt buttoned to the top. I looked at the name on his shirt: R-O-B-E-R-T. Robert. I silently practised saying his name in my head. He took the lead, grabbing one of the black markers and wrote:

BATHURST WISH LIST:

He asked, "So what's important to everyone here?" He started to jot down the words as those around the table called them out.

Scale
Transit
Heritage
Preservation
Humane building
Walkability
Streetscape
Parking

Robert turned to me and asked, "How about you? What do you value . . . Cho . . . Sum? Sorry, I hope I said that right."

I suddenly became flustered; I was not expecting to be asked anything. I nodded, then repeated, "Val-ue?"

"Yes, what is important to you?"

What is important to me?
Home.
Community.
Somewhere I can speak my language and people can understand me.
A place where I can find food that I like to eat.
A place to buy necessary things.
Living somewhere I recognize and know.

I could feel everyone's eyes around the table on me.

My cheeks felt warm. Butterflies crept into my stomach.

I chose my words carefully, knowing how I spoke would betray me as it so often did. I took a deep breath and began. "You know . . . before . . . my husband and I, we live in old Chinatown . . . Long, long time ago. Then . . . the City . . . tell us we have to move. So we move. And we start again."

(As I spoke, I felt like another version of myself. A version that wished this was how people saw me.)

"Now here . . . here is better. But so many changes. But also good to remember the time before . . . And everything too much money now." I breathed a sigh of relief and felt a sense of pride for having spoken. But the feeling dissipated as soon as everyone at the table commented so quickly, one after the other, that I could not follow.

"Yes, things are getting expensive."

"I agree. We have to preserve a part of the past, or at least acknowledge it," said Robert.

"But the present and the future are more important, don't you think?"

"Well, we can have both. It can be a compromise between the two."

"Sometimes things disappear in this city. Or they need to disappear."

"We definitely need affordable housing."

"Oh and no big-box stores. Write that down."

"Did you hear about the proposal of Walmart coming in?"

"I thought this meeting was about Walmart."

"What's gonna happen to all the mom and pop shops?"

"If we had a Walmart, where's everyone going to park? There's going to be way too much traffic."

"We don't need a Walmart here!"

Then an older lady with salt and pepper hair, seated across from me, R-U-T-H, piped up, "What's wrong with Walmart? I've lived on Bellevue for over forty years. Why can't I have a Walmart here? The closest one to me is Dufferin Mall. I have to take the TTC there and back and carry all those groceries home. Do you know how crowded that Dufferin bus is?! I want somewhere that I can walk. I deserve the convenience too!"

"But you live so close to the market. You can shop there!"

"I can't afford to buy half the things they sell there."

"You're also close to Chinatown. So cheap!"

"I would never shop there. Chinatown is dirty. It's smelly and disgusting. There are huge rats and garbage everywhere." She looked at me, half expecting me to nod my head in agreement. But I scowled in return.

Robert quickly said, "You shouldn't say stuff like that."

"But it's true."

"So you want the convenience, but not that kind of convenience."

"And Kensington . . . it used to be so much better. Now it's full of tacky bars, take-away shops. It makes me mad."

"Well, you could move."

Ruth's voice became defensive. "Why do I have to be the one who moves? I've lived in this neighbourhood for forty goddamn years. I should be able to stay here and not be forced to leave." And it went on like this for the next few minutes.

My eyes darted from person to person around the table. People were talking over each other, and no one was really listening anymore.

No longer focused on what our vision of Bathurst Street could be, the group erupted into opinions on how Kensington Market should be. The sound of people's voices soon became angry in tone and escalated into residents throughout the whole room asking the councillors why a Walmart was moving into the neighbourhood.

The councillors tried to calm everyone down and reminded us that the meeting about the Kromer Radio site was in July and today was solely about Bathurst.

I got up from the table, amidst the commotion, and left.

There was nothing for me there.

And I wonder if this was how you felt.

21

The navy-blue metal shopping cart hung inside the front hall closet. I opened the closet door and peered inside and sighed at the number of things stored: the snow shovel, three ten-kilogram bags of road salt, a green and white plastic bucket that used to contain twenty litres of pickled ginger now used to hold some gardening tools, two badminton rackets, the tan baseball glove, your navy-blue chore jacket and your ivory-white chore jacket you used for painting the house and one of your white cook's jackets, a broom, a metal dust pan, and a handheld Black and Decker grass trimmer still in its box. I was never sure why you bought that in the first place since we never had much of a lawn.

I lifted the cart from the hook and took it out and wiped the layer of dust with my sleeve. The cart was folded together with pink plastic packing string, edges fraying. I rolled it to the kitchen. I untied the string, opening the cart, and moved it back and forth. The back wheels made a slight squeaking noise. I brought out the two cardboard boxes I had retrieved from the side of Hua Long a couple of days ago and held one of them against the cart, eyeing how best to fit them inside. I grabbed the box cutter and made careful cuts and then placed the pieces along the bottom and sides of the cart and fitted it with a black garbage bag, just like how Li Seem fixed up her cart. Then I looped a reusable grocery bag around the handle bar.

I looked at it from all angles. "Hor see high geem yeng." (I think this is how it's supposed to look.) But I felt like there was something missing. After much thought, I looked back in the closet. "Gnoi jee high knee doh wor. High been ah?" (I know they're in here somewhere. Where could they be?) After a few minutes, I finally located the old election signs: Chow, Layton, Marchese, Ianno, Innes. They never came back for them and we held onto them for some reason. They were much sturdier than cardboard and would probably withstand the weather better. I bent them, creasing their faces and smiles in half, and inserted them around the cardboard pieces. "Na. Ho dee." (There. That's better.)

I put on my running shoes — the black Reeboks — that I purchased at an outlet shop in St. Jacobs. The Wong See, along with the Lem See, organized a day trip to St. Jacobs Market last year. With taxes, the shoes cost $56.49, still expensive, but I saved close to fifty dollars! It was definitely the most I've spent on shoes. When I first wore them, Chloe saw and pointed at them and then to her own Reeboks and exclaimed, "We're matching! You're so cool, Poh Poh!" I smiled, secretly beaming inside. Shortly after, I noticed other young people in the neighbourhood wearing similar shoes.

The shoes were now scuffed at the top and slightly torn by the mouth on the left, revealing a mustard-yellow cushion. But they were still wearable and comfortable.

I wore those black polyester pants, a floral short-sleeved shirt, and a light long-sleeved shirt underneath. I thought about wrapping plastic bags around the arms to avoid getting the sleeves dirty but decided to try that another day.

I thought of the route aloud, mapping it in my head and decided to stay around here. "Hwuy ah Bellevue, College-gee, geem Bata-guy . . . Ho la."

I put on your Blue Jays baseball cap and adjusted it on my head. The brim was now lined with a stubborn sweat stain that refused to be washed off, no matter how much bleach I used.

I added the white curtain rod to the cart and felt my pocket to make sure my inhaler was there. I glanced at the mirror and stared at my reflection. I tucked a few stray strands of hair into the cap and nodded.

I was ready.

22

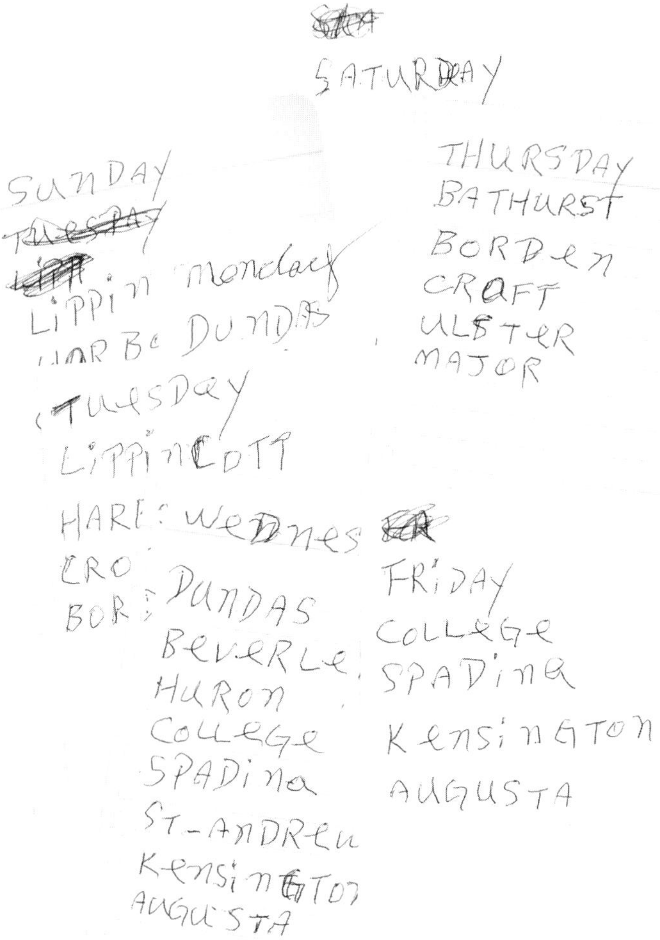

~~SA~~

SATURDAY

SUNDAY
~~TUESDAY~~
~~LIPP~~ LIPPI'n monday
HAR Bc DUNDAS

Tuesday
LIPPINCOTT

HARF: WEDNES ~~BA~~
CRO:
BOR: DUNDAS
BEVERLe:
HURON
COLLeGe
SPADina
ST-ANDREW
Kensi ngTon
AUGUSTA

THURSDAY
BATHURST
BORDen
CROFT
ULSTeR
MAJOR

FRIDAY
COLLeGe
SPADina
Kensington
AUGUSTA

23

The smell of freshly baked goods hit you as soon as you pushed open the glass door. Even though Maheng Mean Bao Phong opened on Spadina a couple of years ago, the red vinyl sign that reads "Grand opening. All day special 3 for $1.00" in yellow still hung outside. Aside from a few small tears, the sign looked relatively new. The bakery itself was slightly smaller than Ding Dong but similar to Dai Loong Phong Beng Ga with its narrow aisles. I hadn't had a chance to come since it opened, and Kim Moon was our first choice. But today I decided to stop in before heading to the Wong See.

I grabbed a pistachio-green plastic tray and a pair of tongs that were at the front, just under the microwave. My eyes stopped at each offering in their acrylic display cases. "Wah. Ahn tat koi thligh wor. High, thlam gor yeet moon, high geem yeng la." (The egg tarts are so small. Well, what do you expect when they are three for one dollar.)

I picked up three cocktail buns, six egg tarts, three pineapple buns, and three barbecue pork buns. I took a quick glance towards the kitchen, in hopes someone would bring out a fresh batch from the oven.

I saw the mantou that Li Seem spoke about. She was right: they were very big.

I got in the line to pay. When I got to the counter, the young lady behind took my tray and began adding up the cost of the pastries under her breath in Mandarin, then swiftly put them in little clear plastic bags.

"Ahh siew jeh, yew mo gor hap?" (Excuse me, miss, do you have a box to put them in?) I was accustomed to boxes at the other bakeries.

She let out a loud sigh, quickly putting together a box, and placed all the baked goods in there. "Wushi kuai. Five dollars."

I handed her the money. "Ng moon. Wah, gee digh wor." (Five dollars. That's a pretty good deal.) The lady gave a half smile.

I noticed clear bags filled with an assortment of buns at the counter and pointed to them. "Gee ooh ah?" (How much is this?)

"Liang kuai." (Two dollars.)

"Oh . . . gnoi oi yeet bow." (I'll take one.) I handed her a toonie. She put everything in a bag and immediately motioned the person behind me to approach the counter.

"Mm goy sigh. Bye-bye." (Thank you.)

"Bye-bye."

I left the bakery, pleased with my purchases.

I was about to go up to the Wong See when a handwritten cardboard sign of "4 for $1.00" at Hua Sheng caught my eye.

Wah! That's a good price! Last week they were three for one dollar and I bought six.

I walked towards the oranges, all stacked up neatly in the green wooden bin.

I squeezed one gently and nodded, and another, and another. These were going to be sweet and juicy.

I tore two plastic bags from the roll and started to fill them up. "Yeet, ngay, thlam . . ."

Shortly after, a bak stopped next to me, looking at the oranges, squeezing one of them.

"Ah Bak, thlay gor chaang yeet moon. Gee digh. Ho ho teem ah." (Four oranges for a dollar. That's a good deal. And they're really sweet too.)

He replied, "Oh. High meh?" (Really?)

"Serng gor thlin kay migh jor luk gor." (I bought six last week.)

"Lay joong migh mor?" (Will you be buying more?)

"Ng. Gee digh wor!" (Yes. It's really a good deal!)

He looked at them. "Lay sik gahn ho dee." (It's good if you know how to pick them.)

I nodded.

We both crowded around the bin, searching for the perfect oranges, feeling the ones that looked good and squeezing them to see how firm they were. Another lady came around to look as well. I picked up eight oranges: three I'd keep for myself, and five I'd leave at the Wong See. I quickly glanced at the bottom of the green wooden display bins in the next aisle to see what vegetables were marked down: eggplants, cucumbers, tomatoes. I took a bag of eggplants and went inside to pay.

I came back out and looked at my watch; it was just after 11 a.m. More people should've arrived at the association by now.

I opened the door from the street and held the railing as I went up the narrow brown tiled staircase.

Each step I took echoed in the stairwell.

As I passed the second floor, I could hear the sound of hair dryers coming from the salon and a waft from freshly permed hair drifted into my nostrils.

I stopped for a second to catch my breath.

One more flight.

When I reached the third floor, an unassuming door greeted me. I rang the bell and waited to be let in.

From the outside, I could hear the clicking and clacking of mah jong tiles, the animated chatter, old friends catching up on last week's gossip.

Once inside, I stood in the hall for a moment, gathering myself, and took a deep breath before I entered the main room. "Jor sin, jor sin." (Good morning.)

Around the mah jong table were Ava, Jenny, Rita, and Irene.

With a quick glance up but not missing a beat in the game, Jenny exclaimed, "Ahhhh Cho Sum, may geen hor noy wor! Gee ho ma?" (We haven't seen you in a while! How are things?) Her hair was a deep blue-black with hints of dark purple. She always liked to colour her hair to cover her greys and was known to sing karaoke duets with her husband at banquet dinners.

"Ah Cho Sum, lay deem yeng ah?" Ava asked. (How are you doing?) She was proud of her greying hair, though she did like to get her hair permed downstairs every so often.

"Da mah dek ma?" asked Irene. (Would you like to play a game of mah jong?) She liked to keep her thick hair short and got copper highlights every so often. She was the youngest of the group and taught the weekly line dancing classes here.

I shook my head. "Gnoi lor dee bo lo bao, gai may bao, char siu bao, ahn tat, hoong muy chaang." (I brought some pineapple buns, cocktail buns, barbecue pork buns, egg tarts, and oranges.)

"Wah, swuy moot ah? Lay sor wor. Gnoi day da yew bao high knee doh," Rita chimed in. (You didn't have to do that. You're so silly. We've got some buns here already.) She never dyed her hair and enjoyed making nor mai gai, the sticky rice wrapped in lotus leaf, every few months for the association on Sundays.

"Geem yew dor dee heck lor." (Well, now there's more to eat.)

Jenny scolded, "Mor sigh ngan ah mah." (You shouldn't waste your money.)

I removed the box of pastries from the bag and opened the lid. "Gnoi mm jee go gor Maheng mean bao por, gor dee ngin gong Gwokyee." (I didn't know at Maheng bakery, they speak Mandarin.)

Ava nodded. "High ah. Koi see gee dor por tow hoong muy taan gwoon high Gwokyee ngin hoy." (Yes. Many shops and restaurants are now opened by Mandarin speakers.)

"Yee ga heng gnoi day gor henghow wa gee lan la," Rita added. (It's getting harder to hear our mother tongue these days.)

Irene sighed. "Geem gnoi day lor ngin ga jor lay hwuy. Hor figh mor ngin gong." (And us old folks are dying. Soon there will be no one to talk to.)

Jenny chided Irene. "Cheeeeee! Mor geem yeng gong!" (Don't talk like that!)

"Hiiigh. Mm high meh? Mm jee deem sheen," lamented Irene, shaking her head. (It's true though. I'm not sure what will happen.)

We all sighed at the same time and did not say anything for a moment as the game continued.

It was as if we were nostalgic for a time when Toisan wa was spoken loudly from the streets of all Chinatowns.

A time long gone.

Ava then asked, "Ah Cho Sum, lay ngim ga fe muh? Ngeem ngeem bor jor." (Do you want some coffee? We just made it.)

"Oh gnoi hwuy lor." (I'll go get some then.)

"Gnoi hwuy lor bay la!" offered Rita. (I'll go get it for you!)

"Ah mm swuy, mm swuy, gnoi hwuy." (No, it's okay, I'll go.)

I left the room and went down the corridor, the mint-green walls graced with old photos, mainly black and white, of past events and members of the organization. Some were taken here and some were taken near the old headquarters on Dundas by Bay. One photo had the address of 111A Dundas written at the bottom.

I stopped and looked at one from 1954. A thin layer of dust had collected on the black frame. "Ah, ah See Hei wor!" I looked closely, squinting my eyes, face almost pressed right up to the glass frame, to see if it was really you. It was! "Kwuy how sang!" (Look how young you are!) Strange how the many years I'd been here, I'd never spotted you, or really looked at these photos.

I stared at the other photos more carefully as I went down the hall, pausing at each one. Photos from the annual summer civic holiday picnic at High Park, where a two-dollar ticket got every child a box of Kentucky Fried Chicken, usually two pieces of chicken, fries, and coleslaw. For the parents and grandparents, there were boxes filled with har gow, siu mai, char siu bao, and ahn tat.

Newspaper articles from the *Toronto Star* about the organization and plaques from the dragon boat races also decorated the walls along the corridor and in the main hall.

When I entered the kitchen, I saw Sam, wearing his usual faded Montreal Expos baseball cap, sitting in his regular spot at the corner of the table next to the small television, reading the *Sing Tao*. With a cup of coffee to his left. "Jor sin, jor sin."

He looked up from the newspaper. "Aiii, ah Cho Sum. Lay ho ma? May geen lay gee noy wor." (How are you? I haven't seen you in a very long time.)

"Gnoi ho. Lay ho ma?" (I'm well. How are you?)

"Gee ho." (I'm doing pretty well.)

The sounds of another mah jong game were rattling from a room past the kitchen. I quickly poked my head in and said hello. They greeted me without looking up, extremely focused on their game.

I poured coffee into a styrofoam cup and added a few drops of evaporated milk and walked back to the main hall, where I ran into Shawn, one of the Wong See's younger board directors, who always liked to wear a bowtie.

"Ah Wong tai. Lay ho ma?" (How are you doing?) "It's been a long time."

I had forgotten that he liked to mix English and Chinese, to show off his language skills. Although his Chinese sounded disjointed.

"High ah. Gnoi ho. Lay ne?" (Yes, it has. I'm doing well. And yourself?)

"Okay la. What have you been up to?"

"Ah, mo yeh. Hang ha, high deen see, high bo jee." (Not much. Just walking around, watching television, reading the newspaper.)

"What a life! That must be nice."

I smiled. "Lor high geem yeng. Lay Ba Ba deem yeng ah?" (It's like that when you get old. How is your father doing?)

"Kwuy ho." (He's good.) "He'll be here in an hour or so, if you'll still be here."

There was a pause that filled the air. The kind of pause that suggested there was something Shawn wanted to say but could not find the words. He then said gently, "If there's anything we can do, make sure to let us know. Gnoi Ba Ba gong Henry did a lot for the Wong See back then."

I nodded. "Lay yew seem." (Your heart is in a good place.)

We fell silent again.

You were the glue,
the connection to everything and everyone.

From the hall, I could hear the ladies shouting and starting a new game.

"Listen to them, they get so into it! Mm jor lay la." (I won't keep you.) "I'll see you next time."

I nodded and returned to the clacking and chatter; the ladies were basking in the sunshine that beamed through the skylight in the middle of the room. When it was sunny, the warmth from the sun made the room feel like a sauna.

I looked around. The main hall carried history: statues, plaques, photos, and words written on pieces of paper. Old scroll paintings of birds and chrysanthemums.

An altar was near the front of the room where offerings of oranges, apples, and baos were placed. On both sides were money trees. You could see that dust had collected on the dark green leaves.

The smell of incense hung in the air.

Those light pink closet doors.

The tiled floors mixed with the lacquered wooden floors that led to the two offices that looked out onto Dundas.

I carried one of the metal chairs and brought it to the mah jong table. I unfolded it and took a seat.

Irene asked, "Joon high mm da?" (Are you sure you don't want to play?)

I shook my head and took a sip of the coffee.

"Ah! Wong See wuy yew gor class-ee hok ewu. Lay loi ma?" (We're going to start a class to learn the erhu. Will you join us?) Jenny spoke as she took a tile from the centre of the table.

"Wah! Hok ewu?" (Learn the erhu?)

Irene nodded enthusiastically. "High ah. Hok knee dee sun yeh wuy jing lay gor nor joong hor." (Yes. It will be good to learn something new. It'll make your brain even sharper.)

Rita added, "Gor gor mm hiew ewu. Gor gor beginner." (None of us have ever played the erhu. We'll all be beginners!)

"High ha seen." (We'll see.)

Ava gently took hold of my arm. "Loi la. Lay high uk kay jor meh? Lay knee doh hok yeh, king ah guy, da jiew foo, mm ho dee meh?" (C'mon. What will you do at home? Isn't it better to come here, learn, chit-chat, and socialize?)

"High see. High . . . ho la." (That's true . . . okay then.)

Jenny clapped her hands together. "Wuy hor wan!" (It'll be so much fun!)

They continued playing.

Tiles hitting against each other.

The table worn from years of playing.

The middle of the white tabletop scratched, revealing the natural wood.

I took another sip of the coffee, listening in on their gossip.

Staring at the fuchsia tiles as they were shuffled around, then thrown down, like discarded peels and bones.

The sun had set, but the air still felt thick. It was one of those summer nights when it was still warm out past 9 p.m. and people would be out late into the early hours.

There were times when I preferred it quiet. I could walk around at a slower pace without bumping into anyone on the sidewalk. Nights when I could just hear my own footsteps, the wheels from the cart, and the family of raccoons looking for food in the green bins. And yet when those voices and sounds filled the streets, their presence kept me company and my mood lifted.

I wore my usual pieces of clothing for collecting: black polyester pants and a light long-sleeved shirt. The past few weeks, I added an old navy-blue apron on top. And tonight I brought out the sleeve protectors I had sewn. I noticed a few of the workers at Hua Long wore something similar. Rather than wearing plastic bags, I used scraps of purple rayon with a cherry blossom print that felt like silk, left over from a small blanket I had made a couple of years ago. I added an elastic band inside at the top and bottom so they would stay up and would be easy to slip on and off. I also made a pair for Li Seem.

I tucked my feet into the running shoes and put on the Blue Jays baseball cap.

I glanced at the mirror and noticed the liver spots on my left temple had become more prominent. "High geem laaah. Mor faat jee." (Well, that's how it is. There's not much you can do about that.)

Monday nights usually consisted of heading south on Denison to Dundas, east to Beverley, north on Beverley to College (sometimes alternating north on Huron), west along College, then south on Spadina, passing through Kensington Market.

I walked down Denison at a moderate pace. The neighbours were mostly in T-shirts, tank tops, undershirts, short-sleeved shirts with the buttons open. Some wore white socks to their knees, with slippers or fancy shoes on their feet. All fanning themselves while speaking in various languages.

"Mrs. C!" one of them called out. A couple of doors down lived a group of university students who rented the upper floors of a house that was similar in style to ours. They had moved in last spring and almost immediately set to work on the small garden at the front of the house. For some reason, they shortened my name and called me by my first initial and it stuck ever since.

I turned and saw it was Calvin. I smiled and waved. "Hello. How are you?"

"We'll have some cans for you later! Do you want us to put them on your porch again?"

"Okay! Thank you, thank you. Tomato looks good!"

"Thanks. I'm surprised the raccoons haven't gotten to them. Your garden is looking great."

I beamed. "Thank you."

"You going out again?"

"Yes. I go to Dunda, College-gee."

"Sounds good! Hope you have a good night!"

"You too."

I looked side to side, up and down, the way I've seen Li Seem do; I was getting accustomed to the search for recyclables. I spotted a can just underneath the back wheel of an old baby-blue Chrysler Plymouth parked just north of Dundas. I only recognized the make because you talked about it endlessly. I would catch you flipping through brochures for months, looking at car advertisements in the newspapers. "Gnoi ja high ha naaah." (I'm just looking, don't worry.)

You ended up buying a dark green bicycle, which was still chained to the fence in the front yard. You rode it a few times, sometimes with that cigarette sticking out of your mouth. I shook my head every time you did that.

I reached under and shook the can, then dropped it into the cart.

It may not make sense to include Dundas on the route, as the majority of the restaurants sorted their own recycling, but there was another reason why I walked this street. A few of the supermarkets often left bags of produce that were starting to go off in boxes destined for the compost collection. These were normally sold for a dollar a bag during the day but were free for the taking at night. If you had the patience to sift through them and you didn't mind some of the mould or that some sections had gone mushy (which you could cut off), you could bring home a few bags of tomatoes, peppers, eggplant, and potatoes.

I found a small bag of eggplants that were bruised and had started to turn a bit rusty in colour and a bag of slightly wilted watercress. I thought of all the dishes I could make: fried eggplant with egg; fried eggplant with shrimp paste; stir-fried eggplant with soy sauce and fermented black beans; stir-fried eggplant with ground pork, salted fish, and garlic; watercress soup with egg; stir-fried watercress with garlic and fermented bean curd. I started getting hungry thinking about all these combinations.

Beverley was full of houses where many university students lived, and I noticed they seemed to drink a lot as I would often find several cans in their bins, left in plastic bags, or in cardboard cases at the edges of their yards. Most of the people on this street were outside on their porches and balconies, sitting on their stoops, steps, or on chairs they'd put out. Music was blaring from the windows, as stifling warm air breezed through them.

College went a bit quicker as there weren't any houses that fronted onto the street. When I passed the Lillian H. Smith library, I noticed a few people standing outside, next to the bronze lion and eagle sculptures, with their phones out.

Every now and then, we would come to this location to borrow books and films as their Chinese collection was much bigger than Sanderson's. We also came for their Lunar New Year celebration, which included a lion dance, musicians playing the ewu and the yangqin, and at the end, everyone was given a small cardboard box filled with three spring rolls and two small ahn tat.

When I reached Spadina, I turned on Oxford and headed down the laneway towards the back of one of the noodle restaurants. The light from the kitchen shone onto the alley. Sounds of oil sizzling, the scraping of the metal spatula against the wok creating that perfect wok hei, the chopping of broccoli and garlic, the scrubbing of pans, and the shouting of food orders drifted out the window. The smell of the food made my stomach growl. I knocked softly on the storm door.

One of the dishwashers, Lem Seem, saw me and waved. She recently told me she got promoted on some days to help chop the vegetables, although the pay increase was only slight, and sometimes they forgot to pay it.

She wiped her hands on her apron and opened the storm door. "Aiiiiii Cho Sum, lay ho ma?" (How are you?)

"Gnoi ho. Lay ne?" (I'm well. How about you?)

"Mah mah la. Geem nget hor ngit wor. Yew mo foong seen ah?" (I'm doing all right. It's very hot today. Do you have an electric fan at home?)

"Yew. Yew see yoong. Gnoi joong yee hoy cheng. Ho dee ah." (I do. I use it sometimes. I prefer opening the windows. It's much better.)

"High see. Lay heck jor fahn may ah? Ah, ang ah jun ah." (That's true. Have you eaten yet? Oh, hold on a second.) She went back to the kitchen and returned with a plastic bag of empty beer cans and another plastic bag with two styrofoam containers. "Yeet gwor high ngow yook hor fun. Yeet gwor high chow fahn." (One is beef ho fun noodles. One is fried rice.)

"Wah, di gai ah? Mm swuy wor. Gnoi heck jor la. Lay heck la." (How come? There's no need to do that. I've already eaten. You should have it.)

"Migh bigh sheet gwigh lor! Hing dor heck da duck." (You can put it in the fridge then! You can eat it tomorrow.)

"Lay ne?" (How about you?)

"Gnoi wuy yow. Lor nah." (There will be some for me. Please, take it.)

"Aiii, lay yew seem. Wuy heck duck gee dor chaan." (That is very thoughtful of you. I can get several meals out of these.)

"Lo bang jor lay loi la. Gnoi mo geem dor see gan king guy geem maan." (The boss is coming soon. I don't have much time to chat tonight.)

"Geem mm jor lay lor." (I'll leave you to it then.)

"Ah. Gnoi heng geen gor dim sum taan gwoon — high thlam lau go gor, high Dunda — yew ngin sigh woon." (I heard that dim sum restaurant — the one on the third floor on Dundas — is looking for a dishwasher.)

"High meh? Gnoi hwuy moon. Digh ngay chee gnoi day hwuy ngim cha la." (Really? I will go and ask. And we'll have to go for dim sum next time.)

"Ho la. Lay mang mang hang ah." (Sounds good. Take your time walking now.)

I held up the bags. "Oow de nay ah. Gnik yue gen. Bye-bye." (Thank you very much. I'll see you next time.)

Lem Seem watched me walk away for a bit, then closed the door.

I continued down the laneway until I reached Nassau and headed towards one of the bars in the neighbourhood that always had a lineup.

People were still standing outside the patio, waiting to get in. A few at the front had their arms crossed and looked impatient. The burly looking security guard was on watch tonight; he shook his head and stood his ground. "We're at capacity. There's no standing. If you're not sitting, then there's no room. Simple as that."

The young woman who stood first in line was annoyed and yelled to her group of friends who were sitting at one of the patio tables, ensuring the guard also heard her. "Hey Cindy, he's not letting me in. He said there's no room."

"But there's room right here beside me."

"Hey, my friend said there's a seat beside her."

The security guard repeated firmly. "We're at capacity. You're not getting in unless someone leaves."

"He's not letting me in!"

I passed the guard and we nodded to each other. If they were busy, they would tell me to come back around 1 or 2 a.m., or in the early afternoon the following day. I pushed the cart and left it in front of the instrument shop. There was little room to walk on the sidewalk because of the line, but also because of the small group of people smoking. I returned to the bar and asked the security guard, "Is okay? I come back?"

"No, it's all good. I'll call one of the guys to bring them out."

A young man wearing black-and-white running shoes — I think his name was Adam — came out with two small cardboard boxes. I noticed his moustache had grown since the last time I saw him. I made a motion to take them, but he declined and said, "No, no, where do you want them?" I pointed to my cart by the shop and he walked them over. I waved goodbye to the security guard.

"Take care. See you next week," he said.

I walked back to the cart, lifted up the bags of food and cans, as he placed the boxes into the cart. The young man said, "Have a good night."

I asked, "Noodles? Rice?"

He shook his head and waved. "I'm okay. Thank you though."

"Thank you, thank you," I said as he turned, "good night."

I placed the food and cans on top of the boxes. I glanced at the cart from all sides, ensuring nothing would fall, then slowly made my way home, leaving the commotion of people chattering and drinking behind me.

I turned the opener around the oval-shaped can, labelled with the familiar canary and crimson colours, and dropped its contents into the pan. Usually I would've steamed the ow see leung yee in the rice cooker, or eaten it straight out of the can, but I wanted the fish to have extra crispness to it.

That aromatic smell of ow see mixed in with the salted fish hung in the air as it cooked.

There were now seven cans left in the pantry from the last time you bought them. You used to bring home cans of these when you saw them on sale, which was rare. "Yew pigh heck la," you'd say. (That'll last us for a while.)

I drew the yellow shower curtain that separated the kitchen from the hallway before the smoke alarm had a chance to go off. I heard a noise that sounded like a knock.

"Eh? High swuy ne?" (Who could that be?)

I looked through the peephole and didn't see anyone. I opened the door slightly, chain secured. I still didn't see anyone. I removed the chain and opened the door, followed by the storm door. There was no one on the porch.

Maybe it was the wind?

But then I noticed a grocery bag on the chair. I stepped out onto the porch and peered inside. "Luk gor chaang. Thlam gor fan see. Lerng gor ping gwor." (Six oranges. Three sweet potatoes. Two apples.) I looked up and down the street to see if there was someone I recognized, but there was no one I knew.

I brought the bag in and put it on the kitchen counter. "Gwigh gwigh deh geh. High been gor ne?" (How odd. I wonder who it could be?)

Just then the button clicked and the light went off from the rice cooker. Steam rose as I lifted the lid. "Heck fahn la!" (Time to eat!)

As I began to scoop some rice into a bowl, my right hand cramped up and turned into a claw. I quickly put the bowl down, but the ladle dropped onto the counter, along with the rice, and then onto the floor.

"Ai ya, geem dum mm duck." (I can't even do something as simple as this.)

I tried to stretch my fingers out, but the tingling sensation was still there.

"Hiiiiigh. Knee gor swuy siew! Mo geem yeng naaah." (This stupid hand! Don't be like that!) I continued to stretch my fingers, then hit my hand against my thigh as if I could get rid of the stiffness.

Once the cramp was gone, I picked up the ladle and removed a few specks of dust and returned it to the rice cooker. I crouched back down, picking up the grains of rice and blew any dust away, before putting them in my mouth. I then rinsed the towel that was on the counter and wiped away any stickiness the rice left on the floor.

"Hiiiiigh. Heck lor high mo yoong laaah." (Once you get old, you become useless, don't you.)

I placed the bowl of rice on the table, then removed the dace and put it on a plate. I took the oil and the remaining ow see from the can and poured a bit of it over the rice, and sprinkled a bit of sugar on top.

I picked a small piece of the dace and added it to the bowl of rice and brought it up to my mouth. I stared at the pile of newspapers, the *Ming Pao* supplements, the notebooks, and the box of receipts as I chewed. I then noticed the fruit sticker, #4021 golden delicious apples, on the box. I chuckled softly, shaking my head.

The silence felt different. As it had for quite some time. But it was a silence I hadn't gotten accustomed to yet.

26

I walked up the staircase, lined with the familiar caramel-brown tiles found in a few buildings in Chinatown, one step at a time, to the third floor where Chwuy Hor Ting was located. It was one of the few banquet halls and dim sum parlours remaining in Chinatown, and one that still had traditional cart service. When we first moved to the neighbourhood, there must've been at least six or seven banquet halls; now there were only four. I held the wide wooden railing as I went up. My knees were bothering me again today, but I did not want to ride the elevator as it would take too long. And it was good to get more exercise.

I stopped for a moment at the top of the stairs to catch my breath before I opened the door where I was greeted cheerfully by a host wearing a black vest.

"Jor sun. Gay dor wigh ah?" (Good morning. For how many people?)

"Jor sin. Ah siew jeh, mor yee see ah, gnoi yew yeh seng moon lay gor lo bang." (Good morning. Miss, I'm sorry to bother you, but there's something I would like to ask your manager.)

"Lay yow meh see, ah Moo?" (Is there something wrong?)

"Mo yeh, mo yeh. Gnoi ja seng moon yeet gor yeh." (Oh, it's nothing. I just want to ask a question.)

"Dang ah jun la. Lay high gor doh chor la." (Please just wait a moment. Why don't you have a seat over there?)

I looked to where she pointed and took a seat on one of the chairs generally reserved for those waiting to get a table.

I had a quick look around. More than half the tables were full. On the weekends, there was always a lineup to get in, which would wind down the staircase. We used to come here about once a month, usually on a Monday, sometimes on a Sunday. When it got really busy, it was hard to move your chair without hitting the person behind you. And sometimes tables were shared between groups.

The tables were now draped with white tablecloths, no longer the plastic ones.

We'd always ask for bo lay cha.

The murmur of conversation.

The clinking of teapots being refilled.

The clinking and clanking of spoons, dishes.

Before, the waiters would gather all the dirty dishes and cutlery to the middle of the table, then fold up the edges of a white plastic tablecloth, and gather everything into a grey bin with such ease.

Underneath, already on the table, would be a new clean plastic cover.

Then they'd press out the creases.

They'd set the clean plates and bowls, teacups, porcelain spoons, and chopsticks with such speed. All adorned with that pinkish-red floral pattern.

And just like that, everything would be ready for the next seating of customers in a matter of minutes, seconds even. I always marvelled at the speed of these waiters. I wondered if I could be one of those seems who pushed the carts around shouting the names of the dishes. I could be loud when I wanted to be. I nodded to myself at this thought.

I closed my eyes for a moment and imagined myself donning a crimson-red vest with a black satin backing and a white hat with ruby-red lining, pushing the plastic grey cart. Back then, they were made of metal.

"Har gow, siu mai. Har gow, siu mai."

"Ha cheung. Ho heck, ho heck."

"Pai gwoot fahn. Ngeem ngeem jing hor. Ho heck."

Hands would wave me over, or people would come up to the cart, pointing and inquiring.

I'd lift the bamboo lid and add the dish to their table. I'd then take the pen from behind my ear, or from my shirt pocket, circling or writing an X in the small, medium, or large categories on the slip of paper.

And then calling out again:

"Har gow, siu mai. Har gow, siu mai."

An order here!

An order over there!

Another over here!

I would sell out in minutes of leaving the kitchen.

"Ha cheung. Ho heck, ho heck."

"Pai gwoot fa —"

"Ah Moo, lay yow meh see ah? Ah Moo? Hello Ah Moo ah?" (Is there something I can I help you with?)

I quickly snapped out of my daydream. In front of me stood a middle-aged woman wearing black flats with a slight heel, a black blazer, and matching black knee-length skirt. Her hair was tied back into a ponytail.

I got up from the seat. "Jor sin! Cheng moon lay high gor lo bang? (Good morning! May I ask if you are the manager?)

"High ah. Lay yow meh see ah?" (Yes. How can I help you?)

"Wah lay geem how sang geh!" (You look so young!)

"Ah Moo, mm how sang la!" (I'm not that young!)

"Mor yee see ah, gnoi gor pang yiew gong lay yew gor faan gong sigh gor dee deep, gor dee woon." (I'm sorry to bother you, but a friend told me there was a dishwashing job available here.)

"High ah. Lay jee yet gor yun mor?" (Yes, that's right. Do you know someone?)

"Migh gnoi lor. Gnoi seng wan gor faan gong." (Me, actually. I'm looking for work.)

"Meh wah? Lay high migh gong siew ah? Lay high gor lor yun wor. Deem duck ah? Lay yiew lor ho dor choong yeh. Lay yow mm yow lick wor?" (What? Are you being serious? You're a senior! How could we hire you? You'd be lifting so many heavy things. Are you strong enough?)

"Che, gnoi lor duck dor! Gnoi gee hor lick ah! Gnoi bay lay high!" (Of course I can lift things! I'm very strong! Let me show you!)

"Ehhh, mm sigh, mm sigh." (Ahhh, there's no need.)

"Gnoi joon high yew lick. Gnoi mm high gong siew. Gnoi joong jor duck yeh." (I really am strong. I'm not joking around. I can still do things.)

"Lay mo jigh nwuy mor? Kwuy day mm take care lay? Mm sigh lay gum sun fu." (You don't have any kids? Won't they take care of you? That way you don't have to work so hard.)

My gaze returned to the ground, then shifted to the shoes she was wearing. They looked comfortable.

Perhaps this was a bad idea.

Perhaps it was easier to see myself the way others seemed to see me: old, unskilled, uneducated, and a burden.

I shook my head. "Dwuy mm jee wor. Mor yee see ah, ah siew jeh." (I'm sorry, I shouldn't have asked. Sorry to have bothered you, Miss.)

"Ehhhhhhh, okay, okay. Lay ser digh lay gor cellphone. Yow gor fun gong bay lay, gnoi wuy bay gor deen wa lay la? Ho mm ho ah?" (How about you write down your cellphone number. If something comes up, I will give you a call. How does that sound?)

"Gnoi ja yew uk kay gor een wa." (I only have a home phone number.)

"Wah! Mo cellphone? Ho dee wor. Peng ho sigh lay wor." (You don't have a cellphone? It's so much better. It's so much cheaper.)

I wrote down my number on their pad of receipts and handed it back to her.

"Oow de nay ah. Mor yee see ah." (Thank you very much. I'm sorry to have bothered you.)

"Mm sigh. Lay mang mang ah." (No need. Take your time, okay.)

"Lay yew mo gor jeng card ah?" (Do you have a card?)

"Na." (Here!)

I took the business card and put it in my pocket. "Okay, bye-bye."

"Bye-bye."

I could sense her staring after me as I pushed through the double doors and made my way down the stairs one step at a time.

Somehow I knew that the call wouldn't come. I stopped at the landing for a moment, watching Dundas.

27

A place of belonging
that was only temporary.

Deputations, speeches were given this time.
But part of the community's soul was still wounded, conflicted.
Most of us moved.
Some of us remained.
West we went.
Occupying a space left vacant by another.
Again.

With its many layers, the hustle and bustle stretched for blocks.
Shops on all levels: basement, street level, top floors.

Where at least twelve grocery stores and supermarkets could be found
dotted along Spadina, Dundas, and Huron.

Names like:
Hong Fat
    Tai Cheong
        Hua Long
            Hua Foong
                Kim Sun
                    Lien Phong
                        K&K Specialty
                            Hing Long Chiew Cup See Cheng

Waxed and unwaxed cardboard boxes, milk crates, or wooden crates
piled on top of one another; the produce stacked neatly.
The red-and-yellow umbrellas advertising Vitasoy wide open.
Yellow-and-white awnings outside Tai Cheong rolled out to the middle of the
sidewalk.
Handwritten cardboard signs displaying the price, in Chinese characters and
in English, but mostly in Chinese.
Workers, wearing ivory-white long chore coats, rubber boots or running
shoes, strip away
wilted bok choy leaves or gai lan into the cardboard box at their feet,
while simultaneously calling out bargains of oranges, apples in rapid-fire
succession,
enticing passersby with their bargains.

"Luk gor chaang, leng mun ah!! Ho teem ahhhhhhh!!"
(Six oranges for two dollars!! They're so sweet!!)

"Ng gor ping gwor yut mun ah!! Ho digh ahhhhhhh!!"
(Five apples for one dollar!! What a bargain!!)

As we passed Nam Me, we could hear Cantonese opera coming from the
speakers of the portable stereo from the vendor selling sunglasses and watches
who sat at the bottom of the steps
just outside the shop.
Its intense singing accented with cymbals and wooden blocks
could be jarring to the uninitiated.
But it reminded us of the live performances and film showings at the Casino
Theatre on Sundays.

The soothing voices of Anita Mui, Teresa Teng, George Lam, and Andy Lau
drifted from salons, mixed in with the whirring of hair dryers, some clients
mouthing the words as they waited for their hair to be done.
A time when these salons were all along Huron, Dundas, Grange, Sullivan,
Spadina, Kensington.

Film posters adorned the pink facade walls of the Far East Theatre,
of Golden Harvest (before, the Standard, and before that, the Victory).

A video rental shop on the second floor on Huron carried the latest films from
Hong Kong; its walls and shelves brimmed with choices from floor to ceiling
in its cramped space.

Across the street was Hong Fat market. And above it, a fortune cookie factory
that made the surrounding area smell sweet, the way Wing Hung did up on
Dupont.

If you didn't already know he was there, you would miss him.
Tucked in the alcove at the entrance of Hat Moon Low was a bak,
sitting on a milk crate from early morning to early afternoon,
selling the day's *Sing Tao* newspaper, all rolled up with an elastic band,
ready to go.

Containers of dried tangerine peels, dried goji berries, dried shiitake, ginseng-
filled barrels and clear plastic containers outside of herbal shops.
Each with its own use,
yet daunting to those unfamiliar.

Char siu, siu gee gnuk, for ahp, see yow gai, bak chit gai
hung from steel hooks,
their juices and skin glistening as the sunlight shone through the windows.
Eyes shut the way we closed ours when we wanted to remember something.
A way of life that was misunderstood by others when inspectors tried to shut
them down.
We returned with placards, protests, and speeches,
the way the rioters once came for us,
telling us to leave.

Instead we stood our ground.
We would not be silenced again.

Vertical signs.
Horizontal ones too.
Remnants found on Elizabeth.
But now mostly found on Dundas
from Beverley to almost Bathurst.
On Spadina from Phoebe to College.

Neon signs that lit up at night.
These beacons.

Always looking up.

Blocks filled with stories,
with people,
a community.

A past,
a present,
a future.

Here.

28

As soon as I stepped outside into the backyard, the song of cicadas built then lingered in the air before it slowly fell and everything was still again.

I looked around the garden to see what I could sell today. "Giew choy. Mo gua. Fwoo gua." (Chinese garlic chives. Fuzzy melon. Bitter melon.)

I took the scissors and ran my hands through the first patch of giew choy.

I inhaled deeply. "Gee ho meh." (They smell so good.) You always liked it when I added them to the pan-fried dumplings or to the faan sor.

I snipped a few more and placed them in the basket.

I went to the melons and snipped a few of the fuzzy ones and the bitter varieties from the vines.

I divided the giew choy into smaller bunches and tied them with twine and placed them back gently in the basket.

I wrapped the melons with newspaper and added them to the bucket.

This should be enough.

I went back inside and placed the basket and bucket on the kitchen floor.

I took out the shopping cart from the closet and placed the bucket, the basket, a few more sheets of newspaper, a couple of plastic bags, a bottle of water, the stool, the seat cushion, a milk crate, and two baking sheets inside. I would have to grab cardboard boxes from the supermarket on my way.

The weather channel said it was going to be hot and sunny all day, so I put on the farmer's hat and tightened the string at the bottom.

I buckled the black fanny pack around my waist. "Okay. High ha migh gee dor." (Let's see how much I can sell today.)

By 11:30 a.m. the intersection of Dundas and Spadina was bustling.

Workers calling out the daily bargains outside of Hua Foong.

Pedestrians walking hastily across Spadina with five seconds left or darting across to catch the 510 or 505 streetcars.

Cars honking.

And amidst all this, the plaintive melody of the ewu could be heard outside Loong Sing. Donning his customary faded grey baseball cap, sometimes an indigo-blue conductor hat, and white windbreaker, Gao Bak sat on a tiny brown lacquered folded stool, playing "The Moon's Reflection on the Second Spring" repeatedly. He maintained his posture as he played, just barely swaying his body in rhythm with the tune.

Some days, if the keyboard player was already at that corner, Gao Bak would play across the street by the entrance of the National Bank, usually on the Spadina side. If you really honed your ears, you could hear him play from any of the corners.

He revealed to me once he used to play in the Shanghai Symphony Orchestra before moving to Canada, and he liked to imagine they were behind him when he played at the corner. He mentioned he applied for a licence to play in the subway stations the previous year but was told he did not have enough presence. So he returned to playing on the street corners. He preferred playing in Chinatown, but sometimes he would set up at Bay and Bloor. He didn't seem to care as much that people didn't always stop to listen; he was happy he got to play at all. He confided he usually made enough to get a coffee and a few coconut and pineapple buns at the bakery.

I turned left at the corner and walked up north on Spadina.

I saw that Hui Seem, a fashionable middle-aged woman who liked to dye her hair red or dark purple, had already opened up her kiosk, located in front of Scotiabank. She sold an array of clothing. T-shirts with the Canadian flag, ones with Toronto across the chest in huge block letters, or just solid coloured ones. Patterned dresses displayed on mannequins. Skirts. Shorts. Pyjama sets. And bucket hats.

"Ah Hui Seem, lay ho ma?" (How are things?)

"Ah Moo. Gee ho. Lay ne?" (I'm doing well. How about you?)

"Gee ho. Geem nget gee hor teen hay wor." (I'm doing well. It looks like it'll be nice weather today.)

"High ah. Wuy hor ngit. Gnoi ho joong yee." (Yes. It's supposed to be really hot! I like that.)

"Gnoi dor high." (Me too.)

I casually felt the sleeve of the floral button-up shirt hanging on the half mannequin.

"Migh bay lay ng moon. Ho ma?" (I'll sell it to you for five dollars. How does that sound?)

"Gnoi ja hiiigh." (I'm just looking.)

"Knee geen ne?" (How about this one?) She showed me a leopard pattern long-sleeved button-up shirt.

"Che, gong siew mor. Koi mor dan." (Are you serious? It's too stylish for someone like me.)

"Lay high mor dan wor!" (But you are stylish!)

I looked down at what I was wearing: a black-and-grey long-sleeved floral shirt, black polyester pants, the fanny pack around my waist, and scuffed white running shoes. I tugged at the bottom of the shirt. "Knee geen? Jeck hor noy wor!" (This shirt? It's so old.)

"Joong ho dee!" (Even better!)

We chuckled just then, the kind of chuckle that made the eyes smile.

And I realized I hadn't laughed in a while.

"Lay migh yeh mo?" (You're selling things today?)

"High ah. Gnoi jung gor dee yeh." (Yes. The vegetables I grew.)

"High. Lay hor lucky wor. Yew day foong joong yeh. Gnoi day moot da mor." (You're so lucky that you have space to garden. We don't have anything like that.)

"High, mor geem yeng gong. Yew gor poon, lay jung da doh!" (Don't talk like that. If you've got a pot, you can grow something!)

"Mwuy lay geem hor." (It won't be as good as yours.)

"Na, digh ngay chee gnoi lor gor gow gee nay. Ho easy. Chup kwuy high gor nigh, geem hi cor la." (How about I bring you a goji plant the next time I see you. It's so easy. You just stick it in the soil, and that's it.)

"Geem easy? Ho la."

I suddenly noticed a few people going through the pile of T-shirts and eyeing the Hello Kitty pyjamas on display. "Oh. Yew ngin. Geem mm jor lay jor sang yee. Bye-bye." (You have customers. Well, I won't keep you from making some business.)

"Okay. Bye-bye."

I walked a few steps before I stopped again.

To my left, a roasted pig hung in the window of Fwoo Hor, along with some BBQ duck, soy sauce chicken, and squid. In the other window, steam rose as three cooks hovered over the stove and grill.

I removed my hat and wiped the sweat that had accumulated in the short walk with the back of my hand. I closed my eyes for a brief moment, breathing in. I opened my eyes, and there you were.

You walked ahead and held the door open and gestured for me to go in first.

The smells of the BBQ meats and the sizzling sound of the wok confronted us as soon as we walked in.

The cashier, donning the familiar canary-yellow polo shirt, greeted us. "Ah Wong tai, ah Wong seen sang, lay ho ma? Hum migh yeet woon jook ah?" (Hello, Mr. and Mrs. Wong, you're doing well? One bowl of congee, is that right?)

"Wah! Lay ho gee sing wor. Hoong muy lerng tiew you ja gui." (You've got a good memory. And two sticks of the fried doughnuts.)

"Hoong muy yeet deep ma cheung foon," I added. (Oh, and an order of the steamed rice noodle roll with fried doughnuts.)

She nodded and showed us to a table against the wall. I sat on the booth side while you sat across.

We went in for lunch almost every Tuesday to share an order of the plain congee and a side order of you ja gui and a plate of cheung foon, either plain, with ha, or with you ja gui inside.

We would sit there for about an hour and a half or so, as it took that amount of time to finish the jook. The bowl came in a very generous size.

I wiped two white porcelain cups with the napkin and poured the tea — always bo lay — into them. "Joong ngit ah," I warned. (It's still hot.)

We brought the cups to our mouths, blowing a bit on the hot tea before taking a sip.

The plate of cheung foon arrived first. We dipped our chopsticks into the tea before taking some pieces onto our plate.

"Hor watt ah," you said. (They're so slippery.) The piece kept getting away from your chopsticks.

When the bowl of jook arrived, you ladled the rice porridge into my bowl, then into yours. I patted the you ja gui with another napkin to soak up some of the oil, then ripped one of them into smaller pieces and placed them in your bowl, and then did the same with mine. I added a drizzle of soy sauce.

"Heck la." (Go ahead and eat.)

You nodded.

We sipped and slurped our congee in between the silences, our faces just above the bowls.

"Geem nget jing ho heck." (It's very good today.)

"Ng." (Yes.)

"Joong yew. Lay heck la. Mor sigh kwuy." (There's still some more. You have it. We shouldn't let it go to waste.)

"High ah. Mor sigh ah." (Yes, that's right, we shouldn't.)

I took out a small piece of paper tucked in my pant pocket and looked at the items we needed to buy. "Hwuy Kim Moon seen, geem hwuy migh sloong high Hua Foong, geem hwuy Yow Tai Gai. Ho ma?" (We'll go to Kim Moon first, then we'll get groceries at Hua Foong, then we'll go to Kensington Market. How does that sound?)

No answer.

"Ah See Hei?" I glanced up in your direction; you were slowly fading as Spadina Avenue filled the room.

"Ah Moo ah, lay seng yup hwuy ma?" another moo asked. (Are you waiting to go in?)

"Huh? Oh. Mm ngip ah." (What? No, I'm not.) I quickly got out of the way. I didn't realize I was blocking the entrance.

I glanced once more at the restaurant and put my hat back on before going to my usual spot to sell.

"Ah Wong Seem, ah Wong Seem ah!"

I turned. It was Chan Seem, who lives at the corner of Huron and Sullivan, towing her cart of vegetables behind her. We usually set up our stands next to each other.

She liked to wear those matching top and pants sets in the summer because they were light in material and could help with the heat. Today she wore a purple-grey set with a paisley print.

Soon everyone was manoeuvring themselves around us.

"Aiii, ah Chan Seem, may geen hor noy. Knee koi pigh gee ho ma?" (I haven't seen you in so long. How are things these days?)

"High ah. May geen gee noy. Gnoi gee ho. Lay ne?" (Yes. It has been a while. I'm well. How about you?)

I answered, "Da gee ho." (Pretty well.)

She asked, "Geem nget migh moot ah?" (What are you selling today?)

"Giew choy, mo gua, fwoo gua. Lay ne?" (Chinese garlic chives, fuzzy melon, bitter melon. How about you?)

"Gnoi da migh giew choy. Hoong muy doong gua, gow gee, yin choy." (I'm also selling Chinese garlic chives. And some winter melon, goji leaves, red amaranth.)

"Ah, mor gnui chee gua?" (No shark fin melons?)

"Geem nen mor geem digh wor." (They didn't grow that big this year.)

"Oh. Yew see high geem yeng. Gnoi day hang la." (It's like that sometimes. Shall we get going?)

We stopped in front of the bicycle stands in front of that big grey building, with a pharmacy and DVD store on the street level and medical and immigration offices at the top.

Most days there were four of us selling our vegetables and plants, but so far it was only us.

There was a period when we used to set up outside the CIBC on Dundas, but the City or the bank didn't like that we were there. A metal sign in English and Chinese was installed on the wall of the bank stating the area in front was private property and no vendors were allowed. There was also a brief time when police officers patrolled through Chinatown telling us to pack up and leave or risk getting a ticket.

Chan Seem asked, "Lay yew box-see ma?" (Do you need boxes?)

I nodded and she went to retrieve some from Hua Foong. The workers were always willing to give us empty cardboard boxes when we didn't bring any or didn't have enough.

I started to take things out of the cart: first the stool, then the cushion. Then the bucket. I held the newspaper while I took out the milk crate and lay one sheet of newspaper on top.

Chan Seem handed me a few boxes of varying sizes, some labelled garlic in huge letters, others bok choy, and a couple made of styrofoam. "Na." (Here.)

I placed one box upside down, and then the next right side up, stacking them on top of one another. I placed one baking sheet on the very top and put the chives on it. Next came the melons. I unwrapped them one by one and put them on the milk crate.

I looked over at Chan Seem's display; it fanned out like a crescent moon. She had the melons in front; to the right were the giew choy; and to the left were the gow gee and the yin choy. She also brought her own trays, but they were made of styrofoam lids and had red and yellow duct tape around the edges to prevent them from tearing. Some days, she sold succulents for five dollars, or two for nine. They were quite popular with young people, selling out most of the time. And on other days, we both sold some of our melon seedlings, but they weren't as popular.

Rain or shine, we would come out here and sell. If it was needed, she brought her huge rainbow-coloured umbrella and placed it in one of her buckets and positioned it between us.

When it got really busy, we'd be competing with the calls from the workers at the supermarket who were yelling out five oranges for a dollar, adding they were sweet and juicy.

"Ah, knee pigh gee ngit wor," Chan Seem observed. (It's been very hot these days, hasn't it?)

"High wor. Gnoi da yew jeck knee dem mo." (It has. I even have to wear this hat.)

"Ho dee. Yew mo swuy ah?" (It's better to. Do you have some water as well?)

I double-checked my cart. "Yew." (Yes.)

"Yew mo hoy lang hay ah?" (Did you turn on the air conditioning?)

I shook my head. "Koi gwuy! Mor sigh deen. Yew hang cheen. Yoong go foong seen joong hor dee." (It's so expensive. It's a waste of electricity. I need to save money. It's better to use an electric fan anyway.)

"High ah." (It is.)

"Ah, lay yew mo heng gwor? Chaan Lau migh jor wor!" (Have you heard? Honest Ed's has been sold!)

Chan Seem looked alarmed. "Huh? Migh jor? Saang moon mor?" (It sold? Does that mean they're closing?)

"Gor news-ee mo gong." (The news didn't say.)

She shook her head. "Chaam lor. Geem deem sheen ah? Gnoi day been doh hwuy lun doy ne?" (That's a shame. What will we do? Where will we line up for bargains now?)

"Gnoi pang yiew gong, yew gor Walmart wuy high Bata-guy hoong muy College-gee." (My friend told me that there will be a Walmart opening near Bathurst and College.)

"High meh?" (Really?)

"Mm jee high mm high." (I don't know if it's true or not.)

"High. Joon high chaam ah. Gnoi gee joong yee hang ha Chaan Lau." (It really is a shame. I really liked walking around Honest Ed's.)

We fell silent for a moment before I asked, "Lay seen sang yee ga deem yeng ah?" (How is your husband these days?)

"Aiii, koi see kwuy nor mm tor. Kwuy ya mm gee sing. Moong cha cha. Yew high ha kwuy. Joon high ho deem seem." (He isn't all there in the head right now. He's always forgetting things. Everything seems so foggy. So I have to keep an eye on him. I'm always worried about him.)

"Gor see See Hei high geem yeng. Yew see gee duck, yew seem mm gee duck." (See Hei used to be like that too. Sometimes he remembers things, sometimes he doesn't.)

"Hor chaam ah." (It's terrible, isn't it?)

"High ah." (It is.)

"Yew gee duck, gnoi day yew mang mang, hay mong geen hong, geen fook, choong sow." (We have to remember we have to take things day by day, and hopefully we're able to be healthy, happy, and have a long life.)

I nodded, straightening the vegetables.

Yes. One day at a time.
That is what we have to do.

We both let out a sigh and sat in silence for a moment, fixing our displays. We then each called out, one after the other — we never spoke over each other.

"Giew choy. Yeet moon. Ho leng, ho leng."
(Garlic chives. For one dollar. They're very nice, very nice.)

"Doong gua, fwoo gua, ho leng, lerng moon, gee peng ah."
(Winter melon, bitter melon, very nice, two dollars, so cheap.)

Despite our boisterous voices, we knew that many of the passersby weren't really listening to us. They were too busy getting to wherever they were going, rushing past us, running to catch the light at the intersection, or the Spadina streetcar, or walking while texting on their phones. A few gave casual glances but were never curious enough to come over.

I saw lots of white running shoes — some dirtier and more worn than others. Sandals.

Clogs.

Not too many heels.

But then I saw a pair of off-white slip-on canvas shoes turn and point towards me. I looked up.

A young lady with chin-length, flat hair, parted in the middle, carrying a big camera around her neck, holding a cellphone in one hand and a shopping bag in the other, came over. She pointed to the vegetables on the milk crate. "Hi! Excuse me, what is that?"

I answered, "Furry melon."

"Oh. I don't think I know it."

"Very good for you!"

"What does it do? Why is it good?"

"I don't know how to say in English. I know good for you. Make in soup! Fry! Very good!"

"Okay. How much?"

"Two dollar."

She pursed her lips, the way you do when you're wondering if you're getting a good price or not. I wanted to add that she was getting a good deal for a vegetable grown in the garden. Some of these supermarkets here might sell it for double and by weight, and not even the whole melon.

She bargained, "How about one dollar?"

How ridiculous! She wants it for one dollar? Two dollars is already a good price!! I looked back down at her shoes. There was a tear on the side and it looked like there was a tissue, or maybe a receipt, stuck at the bottom of the sole. Hiiiiiigh. I guess one dollar is better than nothing, isn't it.

No.

I shook my head and repeated, "Two dollar."

She smiled. "Hmm . . . It's okay then. I don't really know how to cook it anyway. Maybe next time."

"I grow."

"No, it's okay. But can I take a picture? Pic-ture?" She made a motion to her camera. I nodded and pointed to the vegetables.

I watched her take a photo with the camera and then with her phone. She then pointed to me and asked, "You? . . . Pic-ture?"

I shook my head, waving my hand.

She looked at the vegetables again and casually walked away, looking disappointed, but at the corner of my eye I saw her raise her camera to take a photo from the driveway of the building. I looked away and held the melon in front of my face.

Another passerby paused to look at my vegetables, then drifted to Chan Seem's display, but then walked away as well.

And it went like this for the rest of the afternoon. But by four o'clock, I had sold two fwoo gua and one bunch of giew choy. And Chan Seem had sold two bunches of yin choy and one doong gua. It was definitely a slow day for us.

Chan Seem got up and stretched. "Gnoi fahn gwuy, ah Moo." (I'm going home now.)

"Oh. Gnoi da hwuy." (I should get going too.)

We started to pack our things as the evening rush hour descended upon us.

"Geem hing dor geen la. Lay mang mang ah," she said. (I'll see you tomorrow then. Take your time getting home.)

"Ng. Hing dor. Bye-bye." (Yes. Tomorrow.)

"Bye-bye."

By 5 p.m., the workers at Hua Foong were no longer calling out their bargains.

The supermarket lines were snaking in the aisles again as the after-work crowd bought their groceries for the night.

The 510 streetcars were packed by the time they arrived at the Dundas stop.

The chaos of commuters scurrying to get on to the already packed vehicle.

A flock of pigeons flapped overhead as they circled the intersection before returning to the side of D'Arcy Street.

Hui Seem was still in her kiosk as I passed, eating something steaming from her tin thermos, reading a magazine that lay on top of a pile of flannel shirts.

I got her attention and we both gave quick waves.

Gao Bak was already gone; the only sounds I could hear were cars honking relentlessly, wheels whizzing by, the screeching of brakes, and the dinging from the streetcars.

I turned the corner, leaving the loud traffic noise at Spadina and Dundas behind me.

My eyes winced, adjusting to the blaring sun. Its rays cast a beautiful marmalade-orange hue on the buildings, the street, and the sidewalk. I felt the warmth on my face as I walked towards it. My shadow on the sidewalk made me look as tall and looming as the CN Tower.

29

I pressed the wheelchair accessible button. There was a slight pause before the door slowly swung open.

Whirrrrrrrrrrrrrrrr . . .

And then the second door.

Whirrrrrrrrrrrrrrrr . . .

I looked around, taking in what had changed and what remained the same.

By the main window that looked out onto Dundas were four mustard-yellow armchairs with a white polka dot print. Were they always there? They looked new.

The wall by the entrance was always decorated by the staff on a monthly basis. Paper butterflies and peonies bordered the rectangular display that included a grinning sun and the words "Summer Reading Club." A clear acrylic holder contained pamphlets for this month's events.

The security guard was now stationed near the computers, monitoring those coming in and out. A notebook and pen lay on the small desk in front of him.

Whenever we walked in, depending on who was there, the staff would either greet us with "Mr. Wong and Mrs. Wong, how are you both doing?" or "Jor sun."

I would smile and you would answer with "We are good. How are you?" In these last few years, you would ask, "Any passes left to the zoo or the art gallery?" The answer was almost always no. They did not mind that you asked every week, although I sometimes detected a slight annoyance in their responses. I looked quickly at the sign for free passes to the galleries and museums; all of them were crossed out.

I glanced at the front desk: some familiar faces and a couple unfamiliar. That was one thing we liked about this location: most of the staff remained unchanged for the last twenty years and that gave us comfort.

"Oh! Mrs. Wong, how are you? We haven't seen you and Mr. Wong for a very long time. Is everything okay?"

My mind suddenly drew a blank. Was her name Libby? Laura? Crystal? No . . . Donna. It was Donna.

There was a warmth to her whenever she spoke. She had greying hair, but she kept it in an elaborate coiffed style, the way I used to when I first arrived here. She wore red-rimmed plastic glasses that hung around her neck with a thin gold chain. She almost always wore pinafores, or crisp shirts with high-waisted pants or wide-legged ones, paired with black or brown clogs. And a brooch always pinned either to the left collar of her shirt or just over the bust. Her mannerisms reminded me of the famous actress Fei Fei.

I politely nodded at all those questions. "I'm fine," trying to place emphasis on the "fine," and returned the question. "How are you, Donna?" I hoped that was right.

"Oh you know, the same. It's so nice out, isn't it?"

She did not correct me so I must've gotten the name right. Unless she was being polite.

"Yes. Is sunny. Very nice."

"It certainly is. You're here on your own today. How is Mr. Wong doing?" Donna then whispered, "The *Sing Tao* and the *Ming Pao* are still on the table. Mr. Ng hasn't come in yet."

She looked at me, expecting a response.

I wanted to say, "Henry has gone. In March. A while now." Instead I just smiled and said, "Thank you. I go read newspaper."

I quickly turned and walked a few steps towards the Chinese section. I overheard whispers behind my back, but I couldn't bring myself to tell them. Another time.

I took a seat at the table in front of the Chinese magazines and brought the *Sing Tao* closer and unfolded it. I turned the pages, eyes skimming. Headlines about the damage the flood caused earlier this month, another heatwave in the coming weeks, housing prices going up.

You would read the paper from front to back. The *Sing Tao* first, then the *Ming Pao*.

Your arms crossed, elbows on the table, or hands on your lap.

When you turned the page, you did so very gently. But at home, when you read the paper at the kitchen table, you would scrunch up the right corner, and then turn the page.

I started to pat my legs and continued to skim the paper.

Just then a seem with short black hair peppered with strands of grey took a seat across from me.

She pointed at the newspaper. "High migh geem nget ah?" (Is that today's?)

"High ah." (Yes it is.)

"Ut joon bay gnoi high ah?" (Can you give it to me when you're done?)

I nodded. I refolded the newspaper and handed it to her. "Gnoi mm high lor." (I'm not reading it anymore.)

"Oh, mm goy." (Thank you.)

I got up and made my way to the Chinese fiction section. The shelves used to be crammed with books; they were so tight that if you took a book out, the ones next to it would fall to the ground. Now they looked spacious.

The movie section also seemed to have shrunk. There were no more VHS tapes, only DVDs. Did the Lillian Smith library still have tapes? I looked at the bottom of the spines of them: MAN, MAN, MAN. "Geem dor Gwokyee geh." (So many in Mandarin now.)

I went over to the cookbooks and glided my right finger across the spines to see if any piqued my interest. I picked one out about dim sum and flipped through the pages. "Wah, geem dor jee jeen jor geh!" (There are a lot of pages cut out!) I then noticed the fluorescent-pink note taped on the cover that pages were missing and a reminder to patrons to not cut out pages.

I placed it on top of the shelf. I looked at another book about dim sum cooking right next to it and quickly flipped through; this one had all its pages intact.

I opened the red binder where the lists of new materials were inserted; it hadn't been updated since May 2013.

I brought the dim sum cookbook over to the desk with my library card on top. "Hello."

The clerk was someone I didn't recognize, who had reddish-brown hair that was tied up into a very high bun. She looked up and said, "Are you checking out? There's a self-checkout there. Just follow the instructions."

I turned around to where she pointed.

I walked over and pressed the option for Chinese on the screen. I scanned the card.

Che. I went back to the desk.

She asked, "Is it not working?"

I shrugged and shook my head. "I don't know."

The clerk took my card and scanned it. "It says your card expired so you need to renew it."

I gave her a confused look. "Renew?" Did we have to do this before? I don't remember.

"Yes. Do you have any ID with your Toronto address?"

"ID?"

"Yeah, like a driver's licence."

"No."

"How about the Ontario photo card? The purple one?"

Ontario photo card? What is that? I shook my head.

"Do you have *anything* with your address? It could be on your phone. It doesn't have to be a paper copy."

I unzipped my purse and removed my wallet and looked through. I became flustered as I could sense a line had started to form behind me. My hands began to shake and for a moment my memory lapsed and I forgot what I was looking for. Finally, I took out my health card and showed it to her.

"No, this is a health card. You should really get the new one. They might not accept this anymore."

Everything sounded so complicated.

I then showed her the photo of us — the one that was in your wallet. I had removed it and slipped it into mine. I pointed to myself in the photo.

"No. That doesn't count. Okay, I'm going to make an exception this time so you can borrow this book. But the next time you come in, you need to bring something with your name and address, like a bill that's within the last six weeks, like a utility bill, a cell phone bill, or a credit card statement. And something with your photo. Okay?"

Aiii, she's speaking so fast. I didn't want to ask her to repeat anything so I just nodded.

Just as I was about to leave, Donna called out, "Oh Mrs. Wong, did you or your husband still want the copies of the *Ming Pao* or *Sing Tao* or any of the supplements after we're done with them? We've been recycling them these last few months because we hadn't seen either of you. I know we should've asked, but we can't really keep things here for very long."

I thought about the stacks of newspapers currently piled in the kitchen and on the coffee table in the living room. "No. Is okay. Thank you."

"Okay. See you soon then."

I walked a few steps to the exit that led to Scadding Court, the community centre attached to the library, but stopped short a few feet from the door. I returned to the desk.

"Sorry. Can you keep?"

"Of course. But remember to pick them up, okay."

I gave a thumbs-up. "Okay. Thank you. Bye-bye."

"Bye-bye now."

A few more stacks couldn't hurt.

30

The sidewalks at the top of Borden were stained blue and purple from the serviceberries and mulberries that fell from the trees. These last few weeks, I have watched them fall and rot as they've been left unpicked by the owners. I don't understand why they don't pick the fruit. Such a waste! The berries do, however, become a feast for the neighbouring birds and squirrels.

The first tree was south of the restaurant with the large patio; a section of its branches extended over onto the sidewalk. Despite the many berries that had already fallen, the branches were still plentiful with the sweet fruit. I picked one berry and popped it in my mouth. I nodded. "Joong teem." (They're still sweet.) I took out the clear plastic bag I had in my pocket and picked until it was a quarter full. I took just enough but still left enough for others to take.

The showers from early this morning offered a temporary reprieve from the summer heatwave. But by mid-afternoon, the pools of water that had formed from the storm had dissipated. The temperature had risen to 25 degrees Celsius and, with the humidex, it felt more like 35 degrees. The blazing sun made the sidewalks gleam white and warmed my back as I pushed the cart along, both hands on the handle. I could feel beads of sweat start to trickle down my back.

My route this afternoon was a modified one: through Borden, Ulster to Major, to College, then down Augusta, through Nassau, then finally back home.

The rain brought out the fragrance of the honeysuckle as I passed the corner of Borden and Ulster. Although the scent was stronger in the evenings. In the spring, the neighbourhood smelled of magnolias and lilacs.

A few of the apples had already fallen from the tree at the corner house that wrapped around Major and Ulster. They were small and clustered on the sidewalk and beside the curb. Most of them were bruised, and some had tiny bite marks on them. I spotted a couple that looked like they could be found in a supermarket and picked those up. I rubbed them on the side of my pants to get the dirt off before putting them into a separate plastic bag, which I hung around the cart's handle.

"Hiiigh. Mor sigh! Sigh ah kwuy, geem kwuy mm lat tat lor?" (Don't let them go to waste! There's nothing like a good washing to get the dirt off, right?)

I crossed the street. On the opposite corner, there was a house that was split into a few apartments. I looked from the sidewalk; the door to the shed was open. It was the first time I'd seen it open; usually the latch to the door was locked. Since it was to the side and visible from the sidewalk, I assured myself that it would be okay to look. I left my cart on the sidewalk and took the Metro bag and stick with me. I went through the arched trellis gate and around to the shed. I placed the bag at my feet and lifted the lid of the large blue bin with one hand, using the stick to search with the other.

"Wah! Koh oah gwoon hoong muy jun wor!" (There are so many cans and bottles in here!)

To make things go quicker, I dropped them into the bag, without shaking any excess liquid.

Yeet.
  Clink!
    Ngay.
      Clink!
        Thlam.
          Clink!
            Thlay.
              Clink!
Ng.
  Clink!
    Luk.
      Clink!
        Teet.
          Clink!

Baht.

    Clink!

        Giu.

           Clink!

               Sip.

                   Clink!

Honk! Honk!

A car door slammed, followed by footsteps and muffled noises. "Hold on. Let me call you back."

Sip yeet.
Sip ngay.
Sip thlam.
Sip thl—

I felt a drop of water and looked up. "Mo yee wor." (It's not raining.)

Then a stream of water hit my face and shoulders. I cried out, putting my arms out as a barrier.

The water then stopped.

"What do you think you're doing?! This is private property!"

I wiped the water from my eyes and looked from the side of the bin. Standing a few feet away in the yard was a young woman wearing black loafers, a black tweed blazer and matching skirt. She had a garden hose aimed at me. Her hand wrapped around the nozzle, the index finger ready to push the lever again. I suddenly gripped my stick. We stared at each other like they do in those Chinese films before their balletic fight in the air.

The lines on her forehead creased and her nostrils flared as she screeched, "This is private property! Can't you read?! Get out!"

But I knew there was no sign. I always made sure to look.

She continued, "DO. YOU. UNDERSTAND? This is private property. PRI-VATE PRO-PER-TY! You and all the other old ladies always make a freakin' mess here."

The slowness of words, the volume at which they're spoken, the exaggerated gestures, the way people like her talked to people like me. There was always that assumption: you can't read or speak English. Just nod and smile and everything will be okay. "Sorry. Very sorry. No problem," I said, smiling, trying to lighten the situation, speaking the words we have been taught to say.

Without hesitation, she pressed the lever underneath the nozzle and a more continuous spurt of water came out.

I threw my arms in front, shielding my face, quickly retreating to the sidewalk. She followed me out and kept spraying with the hose. I pushed the cart around the corner, disappearing behind the overgrown hedges, almost running into a woman walking her dog.

"And if I see you again, I will call the goddamn police on you for trespassing!" she shouted as she hurled the bag of recyclables onto the sidewalk. It made a loud thud. The door slammed.

Even though she wouldn't have heard me, I channelled Li Seem's energy and yelled at the top of my lungs, "Lay heck see ahhhhh, baht por!!" (Eat shit, you bitch!!)

I heard some snickering. I turned around and saw a small group of kids across the street with their phones out, laughing and pointing, but I ignored them.

My heart was beating fast.
My breathing even faster.

I sat on the edge of the concrete tree planter at the corner.
My fists clenched so tightly that my nails dug into my palm.
I took out the inhaler from my pocket and brought it to my mouth.

I took a deep breath and pressed down the top.
In and out.
                    In and out.
                                        In and out.

The water dripped from my shirt and pants.
The drips became blobs on the cracked sidewalk.

I used the only dry bit of the right sleeve of my shirt to wipe the water from my face.

I then wrung out the water from the bottom of my shirt.

I closed my eyes.

Deep breaths.
In and out.
In and out.
In and out.

I opened my eyes and stared at the ground.
Blurry, then in focus, then blurry again.

I wiped my eyes with the back of my hand.

Another deep breath.

"Lay heck see ah."

I wiped my eyes again.

Sounds of children squealing in the park, playing in the splash pad,
footsteps, coming and going,
the bird calls,
the chorus of cicadas,
all seemed louder in that moment.

I took another deep breath.

    I put the inhaler back into my pocket. I got up and went back to pick up the bag, retrieving the cans that had spilled out. My heart sank when I saw that three of the wine bottles had broken; shards of glass were in the bag and on the sidewalk. With my foot, I swept the pieces to the side of the curb on the street.

I looked over my shoulder to make sure there was no car coming and I walked into the middle of the road and retrieved three of the cans that had rolled away.

I felt a stinging in my eyes again. I quickly wiped them with the back of my hand, but the tears kept streaming down my cheeks and my nose started to run.

Another deep breath.

When I got back to the cart, I placed the bag on top. "Hiiiiigh. Mo ham, mo ham. Mo sor ah. Gnoi mo jor chor yeh high migh seen. Kwuy mm hor ngin." (Don't cry, don't cry. Don't be silly, okay. I haven't done anything wrong. She's the bad person.)

I wiped my eyes again with the back of my right hand.

I took a deep breath once more.

I continued walking, retreating to a space filled with memories that gave me comfort:

eating an ahn tat from Kim Moon,

going for dim sum or jook with you,

working on the garden,

steaming fan see,

eating mantou,

the berries and apples waiting to be eaten,

that moment in the portrait studio before the camera clicked, when you took my hand and the warmth and reassurance that came with it.

Yes, I will think of all those things.

31

We sat in front of the television in our usual spots: you sat on the brown plaid La-Z-Boy, reclined, while I sat on the sofa. On the coffee table was a bowl of boiled peanuts and an empty bowl beside it for the shells. Next to it was a plate of sliced fruit: two slices of orange, three slices of red delicious apple, and five grapes.

Apples and oranges all year round. Grapes when they were on sale.
Bartlett pears in the fall.
Asian pears, Fuyu persimmons, and pomelos in the winter, or during Lunar New Year. Kiwis, sometimes.
Summer months included cantaloupe, cherries, mangoes, nectarines, peaches, plums, and watermelon. Sometimes strawberries.

The apple slices had the skin and core removed, cut with precise angles. You'd nibble on the peels and whatever was left of the core. If any of the fruit was bruised, you'd carefully remove the imperfections with the knife. You'd eat the browning pieces yourself, but if they were really bad, you would discard them. Once you were done, you would wrap the trimmings in a newspaper sheet folded like an envelope. You found the *Toronto Sun* worked best for this. You turned the paper at an angle so it ended up looking like a diamond. You'd fold the left side, then the right. Then you'd bring up the bottom and roll it until it could be tucked in. And finally you'd put it in the garbage. But after we got the green bin delivered, you would put the peels and scraps in there.

The theme song for *OMNI News* came on, signalling that the program was about to start.

I inserted a new VHS tape into the VCR. "Deem look ah?" (How do you record on this?)

"Lay look moot ah?" (What are you recording?)

You took the remote control and set it up for me. You fast-forwarded the tape a bit so it wouldn't record on the blank spots that were at the beginning. "Moot channel ah?"

"Knee gor." (This one.)

"Gor news-ee? . . . Lay look gor see, geem knee gor hoong muy knee gor." (The news? . . . When you're ready to record, press this and this one.)

You took a peanut and cracked the shell with your teeth. You motioned for me to take some.

I shook my head. "Yeet joon." (Later.)

You took another and opened the newspaper in a dramatic fashion, settling into the chair.

I took a bite of the apple, wiped my hands on the Kleenex, and then picked up my knitting needles.

"Lay jick moot ah?" (What are you knitting?)

In my lap was a new ball of charcoal-grey yarn. "Hmmm, gor geng gun." (A scarf.)

"High migh bay gnoi ah?" (Is it for me?)

"Mm jee ah," I said with a slight smirk. (I don't know.)

My ears perked. I put the needles down and grabbed hold of the remote control. I pressed record and increased the volume just a tiny bit.

You lowered the newspaper slightly and took another peanut. "Di gai lay seng look ah?" (How come you want to tape this?) "You think they mean it?"

I didn't answer. I actually didn't know why I wanted to tape it, but I felt like I should.

You continued, "Gnoi high geen gor see . . . gor jeng jee. Gor swuy jeng jee. Gnoi uncle, gnoi ga hing, gee dor ga hing. Gnoi mm seng gee duck knee dee yeh la. Gnoi mm lay la." (I saw what this did back then . . . that paper. That stupid paper. My uncle, my family, so many families. I don't want to remember these things. I don't care anymore.)

You had said before it didn't matter, what's done is done, but I knew that look on your face. That it did. That all of it mattered.

"Hiiigh. Mo ngin giew lay high." (No one said you have to watch this.) I looked over: the newspaper had returned to covering your face.

I increased the volume again.

From the corner of my eye, I saw you lower a corner of the newspaper.

You were silent throughout the clips.

There was no channel that aired it live.

". . . an unfortunate period in Canada's past."

In total it would've been just over seven minutes.

Seven minutes to erase decades of pain, humiliation, loneliness, isolation, betrayal.

". . . the stigma and exclusion experienced."

The separation of families.

Decades reduced to a symbolic gesture.

To correct and acknowledge the historical injustices.

A reminder that we lived in a nation of equal opportunity.

"No country is perfect."

There would be compensation to some families.

For some, it would be too late.

But no amount of money could erase or undo what had happened.

When the segment finished, you brought the newspaper back up, covering your face.

"High migh geem knee gor?" (Do I press this button now?)

You peered around the side of the newspaper and nodded.

I ejected the tape and slid it back into its case. On the back, I wrote the title so I wouldn't forget and returned it back to the bookshelf, along with the other VHS tapes. I turned the VCR off and put it back to channel 4 on the TV.

I sat back down on the sofa and picked up an apple slice.

I glanced in your direction to see if I could read your expression.

Once again, you were hiding your wounds from me and everyone else.

You were always a man of few words and I wondered if it was because you carried this pain, or if it was because no one listened to you.

Sometimes silence could mean cowardice.

And yet it was this silence that gave you your strength.

I took the remote and lowered the volume and slowly chewed on the apple.

32

I lifted the green tarp covering the shopping cart, folded it neatly, and placed it on the chair with a brick on top. I wanted to wander over to Alexandra Park today. There had been a recent spurt of warm weather, which meant there would be people in the park as if it were a regular summer day. As Li Seem observed, hot weather always brought people out to drink.

Since I didn't know how long I'd be out for, I wore the old purple, mauve, and grey mohair cardigan on top of the long-sleeved shirt in case it got colder. I put on the Blue Jays baseball cap and the navy-blue apron on top and slipped on the sleeve protectors. I brought out the bamboo stick that I bought recently from B & J Trading and added it to the cart. It was much sturdier than the curtain rod. And because they were four for a dollar, I bought a few more for the garden.

As I closed the gate behind me, I heard a voice.

"Poh Poh!" It was Chloe calling out from the porch. She dashed over to the front of her yard, in front of the tree, and rested her arms on the fence. I could see the girl's eyes wander to the cart and to my outfit. "Poh Poh, where are you going?"

I paused for a moment before I answered. "Hwuy gor park."

"The park? With that?"

"Ng."

"Okay. See you later."

"Bye-bye."

I could feel Chloe's gaze as I walked along Denison down to Dundas so I quickened my pace. I didn't want her to see what I was doing, or want her to think differently of me.

It was just after 5:30 p.m., well into the rush hour.

It had become a force of habit to glance at the corner now. The flowers were still taped to the pole, although there seemed to be fewer of them.

Zhang Bak, the crossing guard at that corner, explained to me when they first appeared that the flowers were something that people did as a way to remember a life.

I didn't understand because they only reminded me of the absence of one. They never found the driver.

If they did, perhaps I could have directed my anger, my pain, but there was no one to take it out on, except on myself.

I crossed the street to the south side of Dundas.

A few families were out in the schoolyard, taking advantage of the weather, sitting on the picnic tables and benches. A few of the children were running around, trying to sit on top of the gorilla statue in the middle of the playground.

By the basketball courts, a bak was practising with his tai chi swords. And on the opposite side, a young girl was dribbling a ball.

The way the sunlight warmed Dundas at this time — bathing the trees, the sidewalk, and the blue-tinted glass on the side of Scadding Court — it cast a warm persimmon glow. I could feel it on my face.

The fragrant scents of chicken, beef, fried noodles, and potatoes from the food stalls along Dundas made my stomach growl.

I was relieved I brought a small mooncake, two of the fan see tay doy I made a few days ago, and a drinking box of Vita lemon tea with me to have in the park.

I cut through the side of Scadding Court, passing the indoor pool. The shades were down; it was rarely visible from the outside. I thought about going in for the classes after Li Seem had mentioned an exercise program that many older people went to.

This side of the community centre used to be strewn with garbage and abandoned furniture. But now it was a vibrant space, populated with community garden plots filled with vegetables and flowers. The kale, green beans, and tomatoes were the only vegetables still growing. Everything else looked like it had already been harvested. There were more plots and even a greenhouse next to the library.

I heard the sounds of wheels rumbling against the smooth asphalt and boards slamming as I approached the skateboard park.

I walked towards the overgrown bushes next to the wooden bleachers by the outdoor rink and poked around with the stick. "Yew mo gwoon ne?" (Any cans here?)

I prodded some more and then I hit something!

I bent down and used the stick to bring it closer.

"Ahh, yew yeet gor! Migh ho la." (There's one! That's good.)

I shook the can; a few drops trickled out. I dropped it into the cart.

I walked along the grass and saw there were quite a few people gathered at the skateboard area. A few of them sat on the wooden boardwalk that bordered the area, and a few sat on the benches. Some had cans in their hands, while others had them inside plastic bags beside them. Sometimes police officers rode slowly on their bikes, patrolling through the parks, looking around.

I stopped and watched the people in the rink for a moment.

Going up and down the ramps.

Focused.

Determined.

Sliding.

And with such speed.

I glanced over at the group beside me and wondered how best to approach them. I tried to eye them in a way that implied I wanted their cans.

One of the young men sitting on the ground looked up and acknowledged me with a nod and a slight wave. "Hold on. I'm almost done."

I nodded.

He wore a navy-blue toque. The back of his black T-shirt was marked by a huge sweat stain. A large plastic water bottle lay at his feet. His running shoes were grey and well-worn and looked comfortable.

"Cool hat."

I pointed to my hat with a quizzical look on my face and he nodded again.

"Yeah. Pretty old school."

"Old school?"

"Yeah. Like cool."

I didn't know what to say so I just smiled. "You . . . ?" I made a motion with my hands trying to resemble a skateboard.

"Yeah. I'm not that good though."

"Soon . . . Keep . . . going."

He laughed. "Yeah . . . you new?"

"New?" I wasn't sure what he meant.

"Yeah. Like, have you been doing this for very long? I've seen another lady around your age who comes by, but it's been awhile." Immediately I thought he meant Li Seem, or maybe I had entered someone else's area and they would not be happy. "Sometimes she would give us little things she found. Like once she gave me a basketball. I couldn't believe she found that! Another time she gave my friend a spider plant!"

I nodded. That could be Li Seem! I responded, "Yes, I am new. Maybe May."

"May. Okay. So about six months then."

I nodded.

"How come?"

How come?

To exercise.

To make money.

To help me . . .

    pass the time.

To help me . . .

    move on.

To help . . .

    how to say in English . . .
    to help make gnoi seem, my heart, not hurt as much.

To help me . . .

    not remember the pain.

"You don't have to an—"

"To make money," I finally said. Yes. To make money. It is easier to say that.

He nodded. "It must be hard."

"Yes . . . yes. Very hard."

"I'm Daniel, by the way. Or Dan."

"Dan. Dan-ni-el . . . Cho Sum . . . like vegetable."

"Cho Sum . . . like the vegetable. Got it . . . Hey, you guys done?" His friends shook their cans and guzzled the last drops before they dropped the cans into the bag. He then came back and handed it to me.

I gave him a thumbs-up and took it from him. "Ahh, thank you. Bye-bye."

"No problem. See you around."

I tied the bag and added it to the cart.

I pushed the cart and continued along the sandy dirt path.

A young man sitting on the bench along the side of the rink motioned me over.

At first I wasn't sure if he meant me. I looked around before I pointed at myself.

He nodded. He also wore a baseball cap, a black, purple, and red one with a dinosaur embroidered on it. He wore black shoes with white soles that also looked quite worn.

I went over and he gave me two crushed cans. "Oh. Thank you, thank you."

He nodded.

I pointed to his hat. "Cool hat."

He laughed. "You too."

For fear of saying "old school" incorrectly, I left it at that.

From the corner of my eye, I saw another young man who wore an olive-green jacket and white running shoes with a stripe, locking his bike. A plastic bag hung on the handlebars. I approached him from the side, waving. "Hello. Cans?"

He chuckled. "I just got here. Later, though."

I nodded, feeling slightly embarrassed for asking.

I then continued walking through the park. "Wah, geem nget, gor dee ngin gee hor." (The people are very nice today.)

I scanned the area, and there were several people sitting at the picnic tables, on the benches that lined the path, and on blankets spread out on the grass.

I stood back for a moment, then took one of the Metro bags off the cart. I went up to a group of six sitting on a grey plaid blanket. Spread out in the middle were plastic and styrofoam containers of chicken wings, dumplings, spring rolls, cheese, and a loaf of bread. Five of them had a can in front of them; one had a coffee cup.

I took a deep breath. "Hello! Can?" I think I took them by surprise as they seemed startled by my question.

"Oh, sorry. Not yet."

"Okay. Thank you."

I posed this question to a few more groups, but I soon realized everyone had either just started on their drinks, or perhaps they wanted to bring them to the be jow por themselves. I returned to the cart empty-handed.

My stomach grumbled again.

I pushed the cart to the bench closest to the area where we did our morning exercises.

I brushed off the sand and dirt that had collected on top before sitting down, and I placed the cart in front of me.

I swung my feet, looking around.

Everyone seemed to be enjoying themselves.

I closed my eyes, feeling the sun on my face, although it wasn't as strong as it had been earlier.

The sound of people chatting, laughing, beer bottles clinking: it was comforting.

My stomach growled again.

I took out the mooncake but then decided to eat one of the fan see tay doy instead. I removed a paper towel from my pocket and patted the oil from the pastry before taking a small bite.

33

Knock, knock.

I looked up at the clock in the kitchen: 3:35 p.m. Who could that be? I put down the small pencil and left it on the page of the library book I was copying a recipe from.

Knock, knock, knock.

"Ah, ligh la, ligh la. Hiiiiiigh." (I'm coming, I'm coming.)

I crept to the door and peered through the peephole; it wasn't anyone I recognized. There was a stout man standing on the porch, an older gentleman with white hair and specks of grey, thinning at the top. He wore a navy-blue lightweight jacket, beige pants, and white running shoes with a blue stripe. In his left hand was a white plastic bag.

I opened the door slightly ajar, chain still intact. "Yes?"

"Hello! Good afternoon! Sorry to bother you." He had a slight lilt as he spoke.

I remained silent.

"Is Henry home?"

The question took me by surprise. Who was he? I'd never seen him before here, or at the Wong See banquets, or at any of their events, or anywhere else. How did he know you, See Hei?

I replied cautiously, "He is busy."

"Oh. Okay. Well, every year I come around this time and he buys a pen from me." He opened the plastic bag and in it were boxes of blue medium-point Bic pens, some with a clear barrel, and some with a white one.

"He buy pen from you?" I asked.

"Yes. Usually he's the only one on this street who does. And there's a few who do on Kensington as well."

"Gnoi da mm jee lay geem yang jor geh," I said under my breath. (I didn't know you even did this.)

"Would you like to buy a pen. You don't have to."

"How much?"

"One dollar."

One pen for a dollar?! Ah See Hei, you paid a dollar for a pen? You knew these packages of pens always went on sale for ninety-nine cents at Chaan Lau in September.

I patted my pant pockets.

He was about to say something, when I said, "One second."

I closed the door and went to get the clear plastic bag that contained some of the change I made from collecting. I stood still for a moment before reaching in.

I opened the door; his back was towards me. He turned when I rapped against the screen of the storm door. I handed him the loonie.

He removed a pen from the package. "Thank you so much. It is very kind of you. Have a nice day. And I hope Henry is doing well. Please say hello to him for me."

I nodded.

I watched him cross the street and knock on the house at the corner.

I closed the door. "Ah gwigh gwigh deh." (How odd.)

I returned to the kitchen and placed the pen with the pencils in the Ferrero Rocher box.

And I realized I forgot to ask for that man's name.

34

Everything was in its place on the kitchen table and on the floor.
The bowl of glutinous rice.
The bowl of mung beans.
The bowl of salted duck egg yolks.
The bowl of pork belly, marinated overnight.
The bowl of peanuts.
The plate of lap cheong pieces.
Two pairs of scissors.
Two rolls of kitchen string.
The bamboo leaves had soaked overnight
and were washed again in an old basin meant for babies.
The huge stockpot was ready on the stove.

We woke up at 4 a.m. You made the instant coffee and we each had a mantou before we started. When we were ready, we rolled up our sleeves. Sometimes we'd turn on the radio. You had taken an interest in CBC's *Metro Morning* and, in a way, I also enjoyed it as it helped me with my English. But most of the time, we preferred the silence.

The leaves rustling.
The pouring of the rice.
The jostling of the wrapping.

We put the string in our mouths.
We both grabbed two leaves and cut the tips off.
Side by side, overlapping slightly.

We folded up the bottom so it looked like a deep pocket.

Holding it in one hand, then scooping the ingredients with the other.

A bit of the rice, then the pork belly, the lap cheong, the egg yolk, the peanuts if we were using (you preferred them in yours, I left them out in mine), topped with more rice and mung beans.

Fold.

    Fold.

Loop the string

        around and around

    and around

and around.

Snip.

And tie like you're tying shoelaces.

And then unroll enough string for the next one.

"Swuy hoy gor lang hay ma?" you asked. (Should I turn on the air conditioning?)

"Ha?" (What?)

"Gnoi heng geen lay yook ha yook ha dor maan hack." (I heard you tossing and turning last night.)

"Oh. Dor maan hack da gee ngit wor." (It was really hot last night, wasn't it?)

"High ah. Hoy gor lang hay ma? Geem nget joong ngit dee." (Yes, it was. So should I turn on the AC? It's going to be even hotter today.)

"Ahhh mm swuy nah. Mor sigh ngan. Gnoi yew gor ba foong seen. Hoy gor cheng joong ho dee." (There's no need. Let's not waste money. I have the paper fan. And opening the windows is better.)

"Gnoi day mm yoong wuy lan wor." (If we don't use it, it'll break.)

"Ahhh mm swuy nah. Mor sigh ngan." (There's no need. Let's not waste our money.)

"Lan jor joong saaaaaaaay." (It would be worse if it breaks.)

"High see. Aiii, bay kwuy hang siew siew, geem saang kwuy la." (That's true. Okay, let's run it for a bit, and then we can turn it off.)

"Ho la. Geem gnoi ut joon hoy la." (Okay. I will turn it on later then.)

Side by side, overlapping slightly.
Fold.
Scoop.
　Scoop.
　　Scoop.

"Hay moong gor teen hay wuy hor bay kwuy day pa loung jow." (Let's hope the weather will be good for the dragon boat races.)

"Hay moong la. Hor see gor weather channel gong wuy hor. Dor dee ngin wuy hwuy high." (We can only hope. I think the weather channel said it would be nice. That way there will be more people to watch the races.)

We spent the next few hours making doong and ended up with close to sixty. Normally we'd make them before the dragon boat festival, but we also liked to make them in the fall, or whenever we had a craving for them.

We were always focused making these doong, looking at each other's creations, every now and then, and who tied them best.

I pointed to a few of yours. "Wah, See Hei, lay bigh geem dor soong." (You're always putting too much ingredients in yours.)

"Gnoi joong yee jing kwuy fei ah mah. Joot joot seng." (I like to make them fat.)

"Yeet joon wuy bow sigh, geem mo joot joot seng." (They'll burst when you're boiling them and they won't be so joot joot seng then.)

We laughed for a moment, not missing a beat in our wrapping.

Fold.
　Fold.
Loop the string
　　　around and around
　　and around
and around.

Snip.

And tie like you're tying shoelaces.

And then unroll enough string for the next one.

You began humming before drifting into singing another one of Teresa Teng's songs. I joined in.

We became really animated, tapping our feet, bobbing our heads.

We both looked up at each other and smiled, still singing.

But then it got softer and softer, faint even, until the words became the wind, and I could only hear my voice.

I took a deep breath

and opened my eyes.

The sounds of the blue jays and house sparrows returned.

The chatter of passersby, of joggers passing through,

shoes hitting against the gravelly, sandy pathway that cut through the middle of the park.

The barking of dogs.

The honking of cars.

The sound of the streetcar passing.

    I took a small bite of the doong and chewed slowly, taking in all the flavours of the fat from the pork belly, the bits of lap cheong, salted duck egg yolk, and rice.

    Just then a small silver car stopped near the sign to the park across from the church with the gold-coloured roof, the front lights blinking. A woman, wearing tan strappy sandals and a white suit got out from the passenger side, holding a clear plastic bag of what appeared to be cooked white rice. Without hesitation, she emptied it onto the grass and returned to the car. In a matter of seconds, a flock of pigeons descended on that patch of grass. She caught me looking at her, but she stared straight ahead, and then the car drove away. I turned around in my seat, still chewing, and stared after the car as it merged back into traffic and I wondered how often she came to do that.

The afternoon sun peaked through the clouds; its rays filtered through the trees, dappling the grass.

A slight breeze came through, picking up a few of the leaves that had fallen from the nearby maple trees. The leaves were starting to turn colour, their edges red. I watched them gently catch the current of the wind, dance in the air, then float back to the ground.

I put the doong down on the plastic bag and buttoned the knotted flower buds on my peach, crimson, yellow, and green floral quilted coat. I started singing that tune softly as I tapped my hand on my knee as an accompaniment. I held that last note a bit longer and closed my eyes.

I cleared my throat and took a deep breath. In and out.

I opened my eyes, picked up the doong, and took another bite.

I stared straight ahead, my mouth curled into a smile, the way your mouth does when you are let in on a secret.

35

The smell of chlorine lingered in the air of the women's change room. Along with the smells of dampness and rust that came from the light blue lockers where I stored my belongings.

There were a few people chatting, waiting for the door to be unlocked. Their voices — a mix of English, Cantonese, Mandarin, Portuguese, and Spanish — echoed in the narrow hallway right next to the showers. Others were already under the shower heads, rinsing themselves. The water from the shower seemed to be cold or lukewarm, judging by people's reactions as soon as it hit their skin. I returned to the bench around the corner, hugging the towel around me. The navy one-piece swimsuit had already started to pill and lose its stretch, despite only being worn a handful of times. The head cap fit snugly even with my hair tucked in.

I noticed a petite woman around my age, standing near the hairdryers. She had one of those tofu plastic buckets, similar to the one I had at home, by her feet. In the bucket, it looked like there were a few items of clothing and a bar of soap. She wore similar slippers to mine — the ones with the light grey foam bottoms and plastic bands criss-crossed on top. Mine were blue and hers were green. These were the type of slippers you'd find in the cardboard boxes along the dark brown tiled staircase at Tai Tai for $1.49, or the ones you'd find in the white wooden bins sometimes on sale at Chaan Lau for ninety-nine cents. I couldn't tell if she was here for the class or not.

I stared at the yellow tiled floor, looking up slightly whenever the door to the change room opened. It made a slight click each time. A few more people rushed in, changing hastily, exchanging pleasantries with others in the room. It amused me to see so many people were not shy to change in front of strangers.

I patted my legs and stared at them. The skin looked leathery, dry, and pale, dotted with liver spots, stretch marks, and visible blue veins. The skin under my arm drooped and shook like the waves of the pool. I chuckled inside.

"It's open," one of the women in line announced.

The voices in the hallway receded. Except for a few drops of water trickling from the showers and the drains gurgling, it was quiet.

I got up and peered around the corner; the hallway was indeed empty. I glanced back at the woman standing by the hairdryers who had not moved from her position. We both looked at each other, and there was a silent acknowledgement about why she was there. But I asked anyway. "Ah Moo, lay hwuy ma?" (Will you be going in?)

She shook her head. "Digh ngay chee." (Another time.)

"Geem lay mang mang ah." (Then you take your time then.)

She nodded but remained where she was.

I hung my towel on the metal bar next to the showers and did what the others did. I pushed the button. "Ai ya!" The water was cold. It took a minute or two before it warmed slightly. I stood there for a few more seconds, then grabbed the towel and wrapped it around me.

I opened the door and stepped through. The music was blaring and the smell of chlorine was even more pungent.

The water in the pool looked turquoise. It shimmered from the overhead fluorescent lights and moved in tandem with the people slowly getting in.

The sound of water lapping and splashing.

The shades on all the windows were pulled down just enough to see the feet of passersby.

A lifeguard sat at the stand in front of me; another stood near the huge wall clock to the right.

A voice in the distance called out, "You can leave your towel on the bench."

I looked in the direction of the voice. It came from a hongngin nwuy. She wore grey-and-white running shoes that had tiny holes at the top. They reminded me of the court shoes that Chaan Lau used to sell, back when the shoe department was where the towel and rug section are now. She wore glasses, and her hair was tied back in a ponytail, topped with a light pink baseball cap.

I nodded, then asked, "Do you speak Chinese?"

She replied, "Siew siew." (A little.)

"Ah siew jeh, gnoi mm hiew yow swuy." (Miss, I don't know how to swim.)

"Mo mun tigh." (No problem.) "You don't need to know. Just make sure you stay here, on this side."

I nodded.

I kicked off my slippers and nervously removed the towel and placed it gently on the bench. I hugged myself, trying to replicate the warmth the towel had given me.

I shuffled my feet across the surprisingly warm blue tiled floors and sat myself down at the edge of the pool.

I dipped my feet in. "Ai ya, gee doong!" (It's so cold!)

"The water is a little cold today, but don't worry you won't notice it once we get started."

I sat there a moment longer and it dawned on me: I had never been in a pool before.

I slowly lowered myself into the shallow end. I started shaking to keep myself warm.

I steadied myself as I walked along the side of the pool, my left hand touching the wall with each step. I didn't realize there was such resistance walking in water.

I looked around: I counted twenty people. They ranged in age, but it seemed to be mostly older people just like what Li Seem had said. A few stared straight ahead, running on the spot to keep warm; others dipped their faces in; a couple others were doing a repetitive motion with their arms; and one person was floating on their back. I tried to mimic some of their movements of walking on the spot and moving my arms. I dared not try to float.

The lady next to me with broad shoulders and short auburn hair with streaks of grey at the roots smiled. "First time here?"

I nodded.

She spoke in a singsong manner that reminded me of our neighbours a few doors down. "It's so much fun, especially with this teacher!"

I nodded.

The music suddenly got even louder. She began jogging enthusiastically on the spot. "It's about to start! Have a good class!"

"OOOOOOKAY, IT'S TIME TO GET STARTED! HI EVERYONE!! It's SO nice to see all of you and see some new faces today. For those of you who don't know, I'm Tracy and I teach the Aquafit class here on Mondays and Wednesdays. It's a fifty-minute class, but it doesn't feel like fifty minutes, right? If this is your first time here, it's okay if you don't do everything. Just take your time and do as much as you can, okay? Alright, how is everyone doing tonight?"

"Okay."

"Fine."

"Woooooohoooooo."

"I said **HOW'S EVERYONE DOING TONIGHT?**" She cupped her right ear and leaned forward.

"GREAT!"

"WONDERFUL!"

"FINE!"

"WOOOOOO!"

"That's better! I know the water is a little cold today, but we'll warm up in no time. Make sure you've got enough space around you. And try not to stand too close to the wall." The teacher motioned to me to move away from the wall.

I looked around. She then came closer.

"Poh Poh, it's okay, you can go further in. You don't want to be too close to here. It's okay."

I hesitated slightly and inched myself away from the wall.

She continued, "Let's lift our knees up like this and swing your arms up, down, and back.

We'll do this ten times.

Now let's bring our legs forward one at a time. Almost like you've had a long day and you're kicking your shoes off, and push the water with the opposite arm.

Excellent!

Now let's bring them back.
Remember opposite arms and legs.
I know, it's tricky, right?!

Now side to side, pushing our arms this way.
Right arm, right leg.
Left arm, left leg.

Now let's go back to kicking our feet in front, and you're gonna walk towards me.

You're all doing an amazing job!!

One more.

Okay, now we're going to kick our legs back, one at a time, while walking backwards. Make sure to look behind you."

The movements came so easily to everyone. I could not keep up.

Struggling.
Left arm, left leg.
No left arm, right leg.
Right arm, left leg.
Left arm, left — right leg.
Looking back.
Everyone was getting closer.

Splash!
    Splash!
Splash!

Maybe this isn't for me.
I moved closer to the edge of the pool.

"Ah Poh Poh!"
I looked up. "Ho lan siew jeh" was all I could say. (It's very difficult, Miss.)
"It's okay. We can try it more slowly. Follow me." And she proceeded to mime the actions again until I got it right.
"You got it. Now try going backwards."

My eyebrows furrowed, the lines on my forehead creased. I was focused like you, See Hei.

Left arm, right leg.
Right arm, left leg.
Left arm, right leg.

"Good job, Poh Poh," she said and then returned to the front of the pool. "We're going to move our arms, like we're buttering a sandwich. First, lightly. And now, harder. Like this. I wanna see waves coming!"

Splash!
   Splash!
      Splash!

"That's it!"

Okay, I am buttering a sandwich.
I am buttering a sandwich.

I looked around, the water circling around me,
moving,
foaming,
thrashing,
letting it unfurl,
like riding the crest of a wave as we bobbled in the pool.

A playful smile rose to my lips and I started hitting the water with all the strength I could muster.

36

The television illuminated my face and the living room with a bluish tint.

I sat in the La-Z-Boy chair, reclined, my legs raised.

The recognizable jingle of *OMNI News* came on.

I patted my legs up and down from the calves to my thighs.

"Hiiigh. Mm yook ha joong toong, yook ha joong toong." (If I don't move, it still hurts; if I move, it still hurts.) Even the dabs of Man Geem Yiew haven't been helping lately.

On the coffee table, I placed a bowl of boiled peanuts and beside it an empty bowl, and a plate of two sliced oranges and three slices of a gala apple.

When the news broadcaster gave an update about Mayor Ford, I sputtered, "Haaa? Joon high yew ngin look jor? Chee seen. Kwuy geem yeng jor. Hiiiiigh!" (Someone actually recorded it? This is ridiculous. He behaved like *that*.)

You would've said, "How can someone do that and still be mayor? Geem da mm fire kwuy. Digh gor ngin geem yeng do, kwuy wuy mo faan gong!" (And he's still not fired! If anybody else did that, they would be out of a job.)

You always reminded me that sometimes there are different rules for different kinds of people.

"Hiiiiigh. Mo lay wor?" I grumbled again at the television screen. (How can that be?)

I had enough of the news for tonight. I patted the side of the chair, searching for the remote control, and turned the television off.

Suddenly it was dark, except for the light from the street lamps filtering in through the curtains.

The sound of the kitchen clock.

The howling wind.

I hugged my cardigan closer.
I switched on the floor lamp beside me.
I looked around the living room.

The plants — the Christmas cactus, the jade plant, the spider plant,
the bromeliad, the money tree — next to the window.
All in their pots — plastic and ceramic, some on aluminium trays.
The small brush painting of mountains, framed, above the fireplace.
Around it, the couplets for good luck and health, the character for fortune.
Stuck to the wall with the clear tape from the 1980s that still held.

My eyes returned to the television. Beside it, on the floor, was a pile of old
VHS tapes. More tapes were also on the dark brown laminate wood bookshelf,
next to the television.

The bottom shelf held books of English pronunciation, a Chinese-
American English dictionary, the Canadian Scene — the citizenship guide
with the illustrations of western red cedar, eastern white pine, and sugar maple
trees on the cover — the *Might's Official Arrow Street Guide 1962*, Consumers
Distributing catalogues from 1985 and 1986.

The top two shelves were the VHS tapes, mainly of Cantonese opera (*Cup
of Butterfly*, *Pavilion of Peony*), some Hong Kong films — *It's a Mad, Mad,
Mad World* was our favourite with Fei Fei, along with *Mr. Vampire*, some old
Jackie Chan films. Bruce Lee too. These were mixed in with James Bond,
Superman, and *Get Smart*.

Next to the films were a couple of your own recordings. You always taped
those David Copperfield specials whenever they were on. Your favourite one
was when he walked through the Great Wall of China. You wrote "Magic 1"
and "Magic 2" on the label stickers that came with the tapes.

You said these shows were your way of escaping.

Escaping from what, I'd always wonder, but never pressed.

There were other VHS tapes, some in black plastic hardcover cases
with ivory labels, others in white, blue, or red cases. BASF, Polaroid,
Memorex.

You also recorded the New Year's specials from Hong Kong and those
variety shows. We'd rent the VHS tapes from that place on the second floor

on Huron that stocked them from floor to ceiling, then you'd set up the two VCRs to record our own copy.

The shelf below had music cassette tapes stacked (mainly music from the '70s and '80s, music in English, Cantonese, Mandarin, Japanese, quite a few from Teresa Teng and George Lam), along with unopened VHS tapes, still in their plastic wrapping. Beside it, Danish butter cookie tins held sewing supplies, buttons, and postcards.

Your record collection lived in that wooden crate by the window. You brought most of them with you, but you also bought many at Wong Wun You on Dundas. They were mainly 33⅓ and came in various colours: the standard black, green, and red. Most of the records were classical Cantonese opera or classical music from Lucky Records. There was an Elvis Presley one in there, and that one from that Coca-Cola commercial. You sent a coupon in, and in return you got the record for free, mailed from the bottling plant on Turnberry. There were three versions, but you couldn't stop playing the original. Something about the world singing, perfect harmonies, and apple trees.

I got up and opened the lid of the crate. I flipped through the records one by one. I picked a random one from the collection, "Raindrops Falling on Banana Leaves," and pulled it out of its sleeve and placed it in the record player. I dropped the needle gently on it and turned up the volume slightly.

The silence was soon replaced by static and then the sounds of the flute, the ewu, violin, and the guzheng.

On the middle shelf were six large photo albums stacked on top of one another.
My eyes rested on the one with the meadow on its cover
with pink flowers and a mountain in the distance. It was my favourite one.
I brought it down from the shelf and returned to the chair.
I let my hand rest on the cover before opening it.
The sticky backing on some of the pages had begun to turn a caramel colour; the plastic protectors torn on some pages.
The photos were in no particular order. If there was space, we'd simply add a photo.

Your own portrait.

The one you sent me.

Standing tall, wearing a black suit.

In your hands, you're holding a rolled-up newspaper or scroll.

Behind you, a background of billowy clouds and mountains.

Beside it: my own portrait.

The one I sent you.

My head tilted.

A soft bob. Rolled curls around. It was very popular back then.

A plain background.

Another photo of you.

You in a pair of black half-rimmed glasses

that reached your cheekbones, wearing a white collared short-sleeved shirt,

suspenders holding your pants, hands in your pockets, standing in front of the

old Wong See headquarters.

Quite similar to the one I saw on the wall that time, except it was just you.

The cigarette hanging at the corner of your mouth.

You always held it there like that, even while talking, walking, and riding the

bike.

I'd shake my head, reminding you that you said you'd quit.

The photo of us on Walton Street next to the house.

I remember its floral wallpaper, peeling, revealing salmon-pink paint underneath.

The step down to get to the kitchen.

Its mint-green and beige checkerboard linoleum floors.

Another one of us standing on the sidewalk side by side with the Mahs and

one with the Lees.

The photo of a dragon dance on Elizabeth Street.

The photo of you in front of Hong Fatt.

The photo of us standing under the pagoda at China Court.

A group photo of the Wongs in front of the white tent, the Wong See banner

behind, at the dragon boat races on Toronto Island.

The photo of us sitting on the grass at Ontario Place.

The photo you took of me at the citizenship ceremony.

A photo of Grange Park, the CN Tower in the background.

In front of the art gallery, our hands clasped behind our backs.

The photo of us in front of this house, standing on the porch.

A photo of you holding the gate open.

I pulled back the plastic and carefully removed the photo.

I closed the album and took another peanut from the bowl and pressed it against my gritted teeth. I dropped the shell in the bowl. I closed my eyes and let the music drift into my ears.

37

When he sang, he crooned like Frank Sinatra.

Not Henry (oh, how he wished he could sing like that), but the hongngin dwuy with his slick and spiky hair, who was usually the emcee at the annual banquets that the Wong See held: one in July to celebrate summer and one in December to celebrate Christmas and New Year's Eve. He'd usually come to these events, smartly dressed in a black suit and shiny black shoes. All of the seems, the baks, and poh pohs would say to him, "Waaah kwuy leck wor!" (He's so talented!) We were amazed that someone who was born here could speak Chinese so well.

The bamboo flute came in first. Then the guzheng.

Suddenly everyone started cheering and clapping as we all recognized the theme song from *The Legend of Master So* that starred Chow Yun-Fat. When the song reached the end, he gestured his hands in a way that made him sing even louder and more powerfully. We all applauded enthusiastically, some of us clanging the glasses with our chopsticks.

Ting!

      Ting!   "Ho yeh, ho yeh!" (That was wonderful!)

        Ting!

          Ting!

            Ting!

              Ting!

He took a slight bow and announced into the microphone, "Dai ga, heck fahn la!" (Okay everyone, it's time to eat!)

The annual Wong See's Christmas and New Year's Eve banquets were held at Chwuy Hor Ting. The summer banquet used to be here as well, but the past few years, they were moved to Hung Bor Sek in Scarborough. It was bigger, and more people had moved there and no longer lived downtown. The Wong See rented school buses to shuttle those who still lived downtown to Scarborough. We only went twice and I remember the ride there was bumpy and the bluish-grey seats were not too comfortable. The driver took one of the highways there and it was probably one of the few times I'd travelled on one. The city blocks in Scarborough seemed long and filled with plazas on almost every other corner, the sidewalks smaller, and the streets wider.

The round tables at Chwuy Hor Ting were covered with white cotton tablecloths with a lazy Susan in the middle, along with two teapots, a bottle of Crown Royal, cans of Sprite, Coca-Cola, ginger ale, and Orange Crush, and toothpicks. The meal was always ten courses: a cold plate with various meats, jellyfish, and lettuce; stuffed crab claws; imitation shark fin soup; scallops with snow peas and mushrooms; lobster with ginger scallion sauce; roasted chicken with chips; steamed grouper with ginger and spring onion; fried rice; braised e-fu noodles; and dessert.

A raffle was usually held at the end of the night. Prizes included Pot of Gold, Almond Roca, or Lindt chocolate truffles; packages of dried premium shiitake mushrooms; packages of ginseng; packages of mui; a twenty-pound bag of jasmine rice; bottles of Crown Royal or Johnnie Walker; and tins of Danish butter cookies. There was also another draw for the centrepiece. Some years it was a jar full of White Rabbit candy or chocolate-covered almonds.

"The winning number is . . . luk hou. Lay yew luk hou, lay yeng jor ah!! Ho yeh! Ho yeh!" (Six. If you have the number six, you have won!! Yay! Congratulations!)

We looked at our numbers and shook our heads. You said, "High. Har gor nen la!" (Maybe next year!)

"Har gor nen," I repeated.

"Ah, gor dee dessert loi la," you pointed out. (The dessert is coming.)

I always looked forward to the dessert at the end of the banquet. You knew the how sa one was my favourite; the teem teem one was yours.

The server came with a large porcelain bowl with a matching plate underneath, steam rising.

"Ahhh, lay juw joong yee," you said. (It's your favourite.)

The server started dividing the soup into the ten bowls. You placed a bowl in front of me and the others at our table before getting one for yourself.

Accompanying the soup were plates of almond cookies, coconut jelly cakes, and orange slices.

At the end of the night, you untied the balloon that was attached to the Crown Royal and handed it to me.

I held the balloon while you put the bottle into the white plastic bag that was already filled with two styrofoam containers of leftover food. Everyone at the table insisted we take the food that remained on the plates at the end of each course as well as the unopened bottle of Crown Royal.

Murmurs of well wishes and greetings echoed throughout the room as we emptied the restaurant.

The servers started clearing the tables as "Auld Lang Syne" rang out from the speakers, then transitioned to "Foon Lok Nen Nen," a duet with Adam Cheng and Liza Wang. You started humming the song on our way out.

There was a light dusting of snow on the ground by the time the banquet ended. As we walked down the caramel-brown tiled staircase, we paused briefly to look out onto the street and see how much it had really snowed. It was the kind of snow that stuck to your eyelashes.

When we got outside, we ran into one of the board of directors, Andy, who asked, "Ah Henry ah, swuy mm swuy giew gor dixi lay ah?" (Do you need us to call you a taxi?)

You quickly hid the cane from view. I wanted to scold you when you did that, but I remained silent. I saw Andy noticed that as well, but he also didn't say anything.

You said, "Mm swuy. Sigh ngan. Gnoi day jee hor kun." (There's no need. It'll just be a waste of money. We live so close.)

"Geem lay day mang mang hang ah." (Then make sure you both take your time walking.)

You nodded. "Gnoi day wuy. Mm swuy deem seem." (We will. Don't worry.)

"Okay, bye-bye. Bye-bye, Wong Tai."

I waved. "Lay mang mang ah. Seen Nen Fai Lok ah!" (You take your time as well. Happy New Year!)

As soon as Andy left, I tied the balloon to the bag and took it from your hand. You did not object.

Three more steps down.

We stood at the bottom of the stairs for a moment.

You then turned right and started to walk in that direction. I pulled you back, guiding you gently to the left. "Ah See Hei, knee been ah." (This way.)

"Oh," you said softly and nodded, then held onto my left arm, the balloon floating between us.

We walked in silence as the snow continued falling, sticking to our coats. The remaining neon signs lit up Dundas on our walk home.

Signs that crowded the street and sky,
overlapping.
Signifying home.

But one by one, they would eventually start to burn out and then disappear.

38

"Lay jee mm jee ah, knee gor sign, kwuy yoong ngay-mahn thlam chin dang ah!" you told me once when we first walked into Chaan Lau. (Did you know that this sign uses 23,000 light bulbs?!) I don't know if it was true, but the lights from the sign certainly brightened the intersection of Bloor and Bathurst, particularly at night, and could be seen from blocks away. I walked past; a few of the window displays on Bathurst showed ladies and misses fashion dresses for $9.99, children's slippers for $4.99, long-sleeved shirts for $3.99, boys and ladies winter boots for $14.99, and fleece blankets for $12.99.

Before going in, I looked at the handwritten sign detailing this week's door crashers and quickly glanced at the flyer affixed to the Bathurst Street entrance to see what was on sale. They were having their 50¢ Daze this week.

Milano Lady Fingers biscuits.
Tea towels.
Sport socks.
I opened the door and pushed through the metal turnstile.
A gentle swoosh.
There were always people crowding around the mirror
that made you look shorter and wider, just inside of the entrance.

On the sound system, music from the 1980s, sometimes earlier, piped through the speakers in the ceiling. Pieces of cardboard lay on the ground to soak up the puddles from the snow that boots tracked in from outside.

I grabbed one of the nylon totes that didn't look too worn or used from the white wooden bin.

When I came to Chaan Lau, there were either certain sections and floors I always browsed, or I walked directly to a section if I had something in particular to buy. But lately I'd been coming just to wander around, not really looking to buy anything. I observed what others were buying, and on other occasions I would run into someone I knew.

Sometimes I came right when they opened for their door crashers, standing in line with the other moos, but more regular trips were made on Wednesday nights. It was on those nights that the employees in the grocery section got out the label gun and affixed reduced price stickers to expired or about-to-expire bread and sometimes canned tomatoes, corn, and ham. Snaking through each aisle, I would look for those neon-orange stickers.

Another time you mentioned there used to be a record section in Chaan Lau, in that small narrow room on Bloor near the old bank-vault door. You were ecstatic when you found an Elvis Presley record and a Jan Garber one there.

The main floor was packed with white wooden display tables filled with an assortment of gadgets, cutlery, and plates. Pots and pans everywhere, as were coffee makers and rice cookers. Housewares that touched upon all cultures.

Grey-and-white terrazzo floors turned to black-speckled green terrazzo floors to grey-and-black terrazzo floors.

I picked up a wooden spoon — an item that was frequently on sale for fifty cents — and dropped it into the tote.

Taking the staircase up to the second floor, you passed old movie and show posters and a strange cuckoo clock on the landing before you reached the men's section. I bought most of your white and grey socks here for ninety-nine cents (sometimes fifty cents). Jogging pants, undershirts too.

Beside the men's section was a walkway that bridged the two buildings where we liked to stand and look out like it was an observation deck.

The "Get Lost" marquee at the top of the building.
The lit-up "Honest Ed Alley" sign.
The string of lights that decorated the laneway, strewn like it was a Christmas tree.
Large posters of shows.
A large version of the weekly flyer.

You'd point to the shop next to the Swiss Chalet on Bloor. "Lay gee duck gor see yew gor Consumer Distributing high neng ma?" (Do you remember the Consumers Distributing over there?)

"Gun high gee duck." (Of course I remember.)

"And on the corner, the Bata shoe," you continued. "Gor McDonald hoong muy gor ice cream por." (The McDonald's and the ice cream shop.)

I laughed inside because you would tell this story almost every time we were here. I was occasionally annoyed, but I knew you liked to tell your stories, especially of how things were, so I just let you. It gave you comfort and that was all that mattered. And even when those stores changed, you always referred to them as what you knew them as.

You'd then turn around and look out on the other side, admiring the CN Tower, not yet obscured by other buildings then.

And finally we'd cross over to the old original side of the building. We'd either walk through the children's section or go straight up to the third floor, to the women's section to find more bargains.

Standing there, on that bridge, I stared out into the alley. A "For Lease" sign was on the old Swiss Chalet building. And I found myself mouthing, "Lay gee duck gor see yew gor Consumer Distributing high neng ma?"

I made my way up to the third floor, one step at a time, holding onto the red lacquered railing. The stairs were starting to get hard on my knees. Lately I'd noticed more plastic buckets with sheets of newspaper underneath at the top of this staircase and in the middle of the third floor. Leaks have become a frequent problem here, after a rainfall or as the snow melts. Sections of the ceiling had turned brown and looked crumbly from water damage, as if they could collapse at any point.

For a time you could smell hot dogs and beef patties when there had been a snack bar in the corner. The smell reminded me of the parties to celebrate Ed Mirvish's birthday in the summer, when we lined up for free hot dogs, popcorn, and Fairlee orange and apple juice cups, joining other moos and baks. Once we got some of these items, we put them in our blue-and-red-striped nylon bags to enjoy for later, or when we got home, and then we'd line up again. And if we stayed right to the end, we were treated to a slice of golden vanilla birthday cake with vanilla frosting and an appearance by Ed himself. There is actually a picture of us and Ed in one of the photo albums!

After lining up for the food we'd sit on the sidewalk on Markham, or on the steps to that comic bookstore with a cartoon figure by the entrance, catching up with the moos and baks and listening to the music. We didn't always understand the words, but the songs sounded joyful.

I scanned the third floor: only a handful of us were scouring for bargains this evening.

One employee was putting some winter coats on hangers. Another was straightening the racks, organizing the sizes from smallest to largest. Their uniform consisted of the salmon-pink light chore jacket with a red patch that said "It's fun to shop at Honest Ed's." Some wore a striped version, while others wore T-shirts with the same red patch.

A row of white short-sleeved shirts with black stripes and green and purple flowers caught my eye. I flipped through to find a small. I took it off the rack and held it up against me in front of the mirror. I looked at the handwritten sign of $9.99 that hung above the shirts and placed it back. "Hiiigh, koi gwuy." (That's too expensive.) I flipped through more of the hangers and at the back was a grey long-sleeved flannel shirt with rose-pink florals. I looked at the price tag and did a double-take. It read $3.99. "Wah, joong peng dee?" (It's cheaper?) Maybe they made a mistake? I brought it to the mirror and gave it some thought, calculating in my head how many more cans and bottles I'd have to collect and the bills this month. I wished it was slightly cheaper, but I knew I would get a lot of wear out of it. I added the shirt to the bag.

As I walked, I peered into the bins seeing what else caught my eye. I touched the fabric of the cardigans, sweaters, T-shirts, and jogging pants, feeling the quality of each piece. It seemed to get thinner and thinner each passing year. To my surprise, I found some shirts with holes in them and some with stitching that was poorly sewn. You really had to comb through the pile to find a good one.

I glimpsed into the sock bin to see what was left. "Bahk moot. Lerng dwuy la." (White socks. Let's get two.) I added them to the bag.

There were winter gloves for fifty cents. I could use them for collecting the bottles and cans. I added a black pair and a blue pair with white snowflakes.

I headed downstairs, the crooked wooden staircase creaked with each step. The blue pegged wall was adorned with fleece blankets with images of wolves, tigers, and polar bears on them. The sign said $12.99, but I'd seen them go down to $9.99.

I quickly browsed through the home section to see the tea towels that were on sale. I felt them briefly before adding two navy-blue and white checkered ones to the bag.

I continued downstairs to the basement, returning to the new section of the building.

I noticed on my last trip that they had started moving things around. The groceries section seemed to be getting smaller; the lights dimmed in certain areas of the vast warehouse-like room. Items were getting squished together; there was no seamless transition. Five- and ten-pound weights and tennis racquets sat next to the cereal and juice boxes.

One of the fridges, where the yogurt was stored, seemed to always have a towel placed at the bottom. I peered into the fridge next to it that contained cheese and packaged meats; the bologna was on sale for $1.99, normally $3.99. I added one package to the bag. You used to make a sandwich with white bread, smeared with Miracle Whip, and a slice of bologna. There was a bit of tanginess to it, but it was surprisingly good. Another time, you made a sandwich using flaked ham from tin cans, also mixed in with Miracle Whip. That was also good.

I walked over to the next aisle where the canned goods were. The luncheon meat was marked down to fifty cents. I picked up a can and looked at the best before date; it was today. "Joong heck da doh." (It's still good to eat.) I took three from the pile.

I made my way to the corner where the yellow package cream crackers were displayed, which were also on sale for fifty cents. I grabbed two packages and a package of those ladyfingers in the next aisle. I rifled through them and grabbed the one at the bottom.

"Aiii, ah Wong Seem, may geen hor noy wor." (I haven't seen you in a while.)

I looked up and grinned. On the other side of the biscuit aisle was Li Seem. "Aiii, ah Li Seem, gnoi da mo geen lay. Gnoi hor moong ah. Lay heck jor fahn may ah?" (Oh, I didn't even see you there. I'm so out of it. Have you eaten already?)

"Heck jor, heck jor. Lay ne?" (Yes, I've eaten. And you?)

"Heck jor. Gnoi ja hang ha, high yew moot yeh migh peng." (Yes, I've eaten. I'm just walking around seeing what's on sale.)

"Gnoi dor high. High ha." (Me too. Just browsing here and there.)

I glanced at what she was carrying in her hand. "Lay migh chipsee mo?" (You're buying chips?)

"Hiiigh. High ah. Knee pigh how hun ah. Yew see seng heck chipsee, yew see seng heck beng gong. Hoong muy goong jigh mien. Ang ah jun, gnoi lor gor doy." (Yes. I've been getting cravings lately. Sometimes it's for chips, sometimes it's for cookies. And some instant noodles. Just a second, let me get a bag.) She grabbed a bag off the hanger. "Knee koi pigh deem yeng ah?" (How are things with you lately?)

"Knee koi pigh . . . Gnoi okay." (These days . . . I'm okay.)

I'm
okay,
I said silently to myself.
I'm okay.

"Lay ne?" (How about you?)

"Gnoi okay. Mo meh yeh. Fwoon gow, heck fahn, jip jun. But gwor . . . hiiigh . . . gor say dew geck. Knee koi pigh gee joong ah." (I'm okay. Not doing much. Sleeping, eating, collecting bottles. But my damn legs. They've been swelling a lot lately.)

"Lay yew mo high yee sang? Kwuy yew mo hoy yiek?" (Did you go see the doctor? Did they prescribe any medication?)

"Hiiigh mo yoong. Ja giew gnoi heck Tylenol." (It's pointless. They just say to take some Tylenol.)

"High. Geem lay yew siew seem. Mang mang ah mah." (Then you have to be careful. You need to take it slow.)

"Gnoi ay tui. But gwor, mm jor mm duck. Yew jaan cheen. High. Lay joong jip ma?" (I know. But I can't just not do anything. I have to make money. Are you still collecting?)

"Joong jip. Gee sin foo." (Yes, I'm still collecting. It's quite back-breaking.)

Li Seem laughed. "Gun high la. High easy, gor gor ngin wuy jip. Lay wuy jup gwaan." (Of course it is. If it was easy, everyone would be doing it. You'll get used to it.)

"But gwor, gnoi seng wan gor faan gong. Gee lan wor." (But I've also been trying to find a job. It's so hard though.)

"High ah. Gnoi dee lor ngin ga, gor gor gwuy gnoi day mo yoong la. Geem lor ngin gum geem siew. Hiiigh. Mor nam knee dee yeh." (It's true. We're old, so everyone thinks we're useless now. And the old age pension is so little. Let's not think about these things.)

"High ah. Ho dee yew geen hong hoong muy hoy seem seem." (Yes. It's better to have good health and be happy.)

We gradually made our way to the metal shelf where they put the reduced bread, next to the ninety-nine-cent flavoured teas. It looked like the bread had been picked over already. What was left were a few bags of Dempster bagels (plain and whole wheat) marked down to fifty cents and a few loaves of Dimpflmeier whole wheat bread marked down to ninety-nine cents. The whole wheat was never popular.

"Lay heck bagel ma?" (Do you eat bagels?)

Li Seem shook her head. "Ho lan heck ah. Heck jor, gor dee gna gee toong ah. Yee ga mor geem dor gna." (They're hard to eat. Once I tried to and my teeth hurt afterwards. I don't have too many of my teeth left.)

"Lay yew jing kwuy. Naam dee." (You have to steam them. They'll be softer and easier to chew that way.)

Li Seem grimaced. "Eee ya, naam bep bep." (Then it becomes too soft.)

We chuckled. And I realized again that it had been awhile since laughter escaped my mouth.

A few shoppers looked at us as we spoke. I did notice our voices carried two aisles over. Li Seem gave them a sideways glance and raised her voice slightly. "Che! Sigh moot gong geem thligh seng?" (Why do we have to whisper?)

I nodded and said aloud, "High ah. Lerng gor pang yiew may geen hor noy! Mm king ah guy mor?" (Yes, that's right. We're just two friends who haven't seen each other in a long time! We can't even catch up?)

We shared another laugh as we each took a loaf of the whole wheat bread.

"Lay joong hang ma?" (Are you still going to walk around?)

"Mm hang la. Gnoi fahn gwuy." (No. I'm going to go home.)

"Ng. Gnoi dor high." (Yes. Me too.)

We went up the stairs, one step at a time, to pay in the old building. Through the doors, there was a prominent display of huge bottles of body lotion for fifty cents that came in aloe, carrot, and vanilla.

"Wah, ng hor doo! Ho mm ho ne? Whoo ma?" (Fifty cents! I wonder if it's any good? Do you want one?)

I thought about it. "Oi yeet gor la." (Alright I'll take one.) We each got one bottle and put it in our bags.

The cashier stations were a worn lacquered brown in the west building, fitted with old registers. The week's flyers were displayed behind the cashier. There was a lineup at each of three checkouts that were open. We joined the shortest line closest to the pharmacy. Most people in front of us carried bags filled to the brim.

"Wah, migh koh oah yeh!" Li Seem exclaimed. (They're buying a lot of stuff!)

I whispered, "Ng hor doo ah ma." (Fifty cents, remember.)

She nodded, then asked, "Lay wuy hwuy lun doy gor for gai ma?" (Will you be lining up for the turkey?)

"Gun high la. Lay ne?" (Of course. How about you?)

"Gun high la. For gai. Daan go. Hiiigh. Mm jee kwuy wuy pigh gee noy. Joong mm jee gee see saang." (Of course. Turkey. Cake. Who knows how much longer they'll keep handing those out. We still don't know when it will close.)

"High ah. Joong may gong. Gnoi day lerng gor hwuy la? Ho mm ho ah?" (Yes. They still haven't said. How about we both go together? Sound good?)

"Ho la." (Sounds good.)

Sometimes the supervisor who had a hairstyle similar to Paula Tsui was there to help bag, but she wasn't there tonight. When we got to the register, the cashier was one of the Chinese ladies who worked there.

"Ah siew jeh, lay jee gee see saang moon ma?" (Miss, do you know when you'll be closing?)

"Ahh, joong mm jee wor. Lor bang da mo chut seng." (We still don't know. The boss hasn't even said anything.)

"Oh."

"Wah, mean bao gum peng wor." (The bread is a good price.)

"Mm chor ne." (It doesn't look bad either.)

"Teng yet doh kay wor." (It expires tomorrow though.)

"Joong heck da doh." (You can still eat it.)

"Sup say mun luk hor ng jee." (That'll be $14.65.)

I opened my wallet and handed her the money. I took my bag from her and waited for Li Seem at one of the closed cashier counters.

We then exited through the doors, down the two red rickety wooden steps, and out onto Markham into the bitter cold air.

39

The howling wind shook the windows. I parted the curtains in the living room and looked out: a thick layer of fresh snow glistened underneath the street lights.

The kind of snow that hadn't been walked on,
not dirtied by car exhaust fumes,
not yet turned to grey slush,
and not the soft snow that gave way with each step.

The news said it would stop around 6 p.m. for an hour or so before it resumed again.

If I went out now, the sidewalks wouldn't be cleared yet. If I waited until the morning, they should be, but the cans and bottles might be gone. "Nam ha, nam ha." (Let me think about this.)

"Hiiigh. Mo lan la. (Don't be lazy.)

Hoong hay. (Fresh air.)

Hang ha. (Exercise.)

Doong migh doong, mor sor wigh." (If it's cold, it's cold, what can you do?)

I thought about the route aloud. "Geem maan hang ah Bata-guy, geem hwuy Lippincott, geem hwuy Borden, geem fahn gwuy. Ho la." (Tonight I'll walk Bathurst, then Lippincott, then Borden, then home. Sounds good to me.) I nodded.

I wore what had now become my winter uniform: a pair of long johns, the waffle-knit kind, under the jogging pants (sometimes the brown or forest-green corduroy pants); an undershirt, also waffle-knit; a long-sleeved flannel button-up shirt; topped with the purple, mauve, and grey rose-patterned mohair cardigan.

I wrapped the charcoal-grey knitted scarf twice around my neck, slipped my arms through the purple and seaweed-green winter coat, put on a velvet black hat with a flower sewn at the front, and slipped on the grey winter boots — the same pair I got for my first winter here. The boots were still stained from the road salt the other day, leaving a dry white residue on them, that even a bit of vinegar and water couldn't remove. When the streets had a similar marking, you knew it was cold outside.

I pulled out the gloves I recently got from Chaan Lau and put them on.

I looked in the mirror and chuckled. "Fei dee dee, gnigh chee chee." (So round and short.) We used to say that to each other in the winter, or whenever we wore bulky clothing. We did not care how much bigger we looked in our layers, or winter attire, as long as we were warm; that was all that mattered.

The shopping cart was back in the hallway closet for the duration of winter. I took it down from the hook and unfolded it. I placed the election signs inside to line the cart and outfitted it with a few reusable bags. I saw another moo do that as a way of separating the bottles and cans while she collected. I added three of the Metro bags and I looped a grey, red, and white plaid shopping bag on the handle. I patted my pocket to make sure I had my inhaler and a few extra plastic bags.

Then I took out the shovel to clear the snow in the front yard and sidewalk before heading out. I pushed the snow aside along the pathway. When I got to the gate, I saw the sidewalk had already been cleared and salted.

I looked to the neighbour's side — their sidewalk was also cleared. I said aloud, "Aiii oow de nay. Lay day joon high hor ngin ah." (Ahhh, thank you, thank you. You really are good people.)

I put the shovel just inside the door on the boot tray and locked the door. I brought the cart down and closed the gate behind me. The sky was already getting dark.

By the time I reached College, the clock tower rang five times.

I walked west along College, then crossed over to the other side of Bathurst.

Although the sidewalks haven't been shovelled yet, small pathways had been created from people walking the same line. But with the snow piled up and most of the bins set out for collection, there was little room to walk on the sidewalks with the cart, particularly between College and Ulster.

The majority of the cans and bottles were set next to their bin, or on top of the lid. Others had left them near their gate or fence. Some were found nestled in the small snowbanks that had started to form.

As I walked up Bathurst, I could feel the stares through the darkness, silently judging me, from the cars and streetcar that were all at a standstill from the stalled traffic. Li Seem once told me a story that she was on the 511 when the streetcar route was replaced temporarily by buses that year, and a man tried to get on with his cart filled with several bags of empty cans. He asked for the ramp to be lowered, but the driver refused. She said she heard the driver curse under his breath but loud enough so the man could hear that he should not be riding the bus with that much stuff. She told me she gave the driver an earful.

"High. Mo lay kwuy," I told myself. (Just ignore them.) I continued to stare straight ahead. I was on a mission. I had to collect enough tonight to earn at least twenty dollars.

Just past Harbord, there were only a few houses that set their cans out. One particular building that was made up of several apartments usually had quite a few. Tonight there was a bag of cans in a grey plastic bag, tied in a loose knot, that sat on top of one of the large blue bins. I took it and dropped it into the cart. I left the cart by their staircase as I poked around the other bins next to it with the stick and found a few more bottles and cans.

I continued north, but then up ahead I saw the man and his bike also looking through the bins. I'd run into him before on Bathurst. "Hiiigh. Gnoi mang. Kwuy figh dee." (I was too slow. He beat me to it.) I decided not to go any further. In certain neighbourhoods, it became a race of who could get there faster.

I turned around and went back to Harbord and decided to go down Lippincott.

When I reached Ulster, the snow was starting to come down even more, blowing fiercely into my face. I stopped for a moment to brush the flakes that had gathered on my coat and hat. It became harder to see and push the cart against the strong winds and blistering snow.

Every few minutes, my nose dripped from the cold, wetting my scarf. I was breathing heavier with my mouth slightly open, which added to the moisture.

As I passed some of the houses, the curtains were left open, and the lights from the living rooms spilled onto their front yards.

Some of the Christmas trees were visible from the sidewalk.

Decorated with tinsel, ornaments, lights strung around them, top to bottom. Greens, yellows, reds, oranges, blues, and whites.

We also had a Christmas tree — a plastic one we got from Chaan Lau in the early 1970s. When put together, it came up to my height.

The box bulged at the seams as we could never fit it back in after we took it apart. Some of the tinsel would also remain stuck on the needles. We stored the tree in the cellar room in the basement, along with the box of decorations, rolls of wrapping paper, next to cases of Coca-Cola and ginger ale, Kleenex boxes, toilet paper, and the stacked bags of rice.

It came out every year, but this Christmas I decided not to bring it up.

Winter, the snow, and the cold kept some people inside.
While their voices kept me company on my walks during warmer months,
I also did not mind the silence.
Something I have gotten used to now.

I looked up.
I was charmed by the way the snow piled up like soft pillows
on top of the telephone lines and poles,
on the branches of the two spruce and pine trees on this street.
Just like the way it does on Christmas cards.

The snow crunched on the ground as I walked.
The dark orange glow from the street lamps brightened the snow even more
and helped me see into the bins
and lit up the side streets as I kept going, trudging along,
passing houses worth more than I would ever make.

The tracks from my boots and the cart were traces
of where I'd been, but they would soon be covered up by the snow.

The wind blew fiercely once more, like a ghost releasing its anger. The snow showed no sign of stopping, despite what the forecast said earlier.

My hands were beginning to numb despite wearing the gloves.

But I kept pushing, breathing in and out the frigid air, thinking about the cans and bottles I still had to collect from the remaining streets. Just a bit more to Lippincott, then Borden, then back home. I'm halfway there.

But each step was more laborious than the last. I felt like a salmon swimming against the current. And like the salmon, you have to push against the current to survive.

It soon became clear that it was easier just to walk on the street where the cars have already made a path. A few cars honked, but I kept walking. Eventually, they just went around me. I could sense their glares, but I thought there was room for the both of us.

Suddenly I have a lot of time to think about things.
I wish we had more of it
back then.
But we never thought about that,
back then.
And I'm reminded of all the things I never said to you.

Winter had come and gone; the streets slicked from the melting snow.
The mounds of garbage, cigarette butts, and debris slowly revealed themselves
in the spring after months of being buried in the snow.
Someone had replaced the flowers attached to the pole at the corner
with both fresh and synthetic ones.
White, pink, yellow, orange, purple, and red hues brightened that intersection
once more.

I still did not know who tended to it.

I read in the *Sing Tao* that forty people were killed by drivers that year.
You were number nine.

Lives reduced to a number.
Lives remembered and marked with bouquets of flowers.

But you were never those things.

To me, you will always be ah Wong See Hei.

41

When I reached for the door to Kim Moon, I almost lost my footing because I wasn't expecting the door to be locked.

"Di gai geh?" (How come?)

I tried the door again. Still locked. I looked at my watch: it was just after 11 a.m. It should've been open by now. I peered inside; it was dark, except for a light in the back. I knocked on the glass door in case, but no one came. I looked down at the floor and a pile of mail and flyers were scattered inside.

"Saang jor moon? Mo lay wor. Gor nget joong hoy moon wor." (They're closed? How can that be? I'm sure they were still open the other day.)

I searched for any handwritten signs that they were closed, or on vacation, but there was nothing.

"Joon high saang jor?" (Can they really be closed?)

Kim Moon made the best ahn tat and we regularly bought them there. They were seventy-five cents per tart, much more than the three for one dollar that the other bakeries in the vicinity were charging, but those were smaller. And there was something about the ones from Kim Moon that made it worth it to spend the extra bit of money.

I held onto the aluminium tart shells afterwards. I cleaned them and reused them when I made my won how doy tee or nen go during the Lunar New Year. You weren't always fond of this, gently suggesting I should just buy them new at Tap Phong. But to me, the reused ones were just as good as the new ones.

We each had our own way of eating the tarts. You would flip the tray upside down and cup the tart with your hand and take big bites, the way I would roll noong into an oval shape and sprinkle it with salt. When I ate an anh tat, I took a teaspoon to eat the egg custard first, then I broke the flaky crust into pieces. It was a peculiar way to enjoy ahn tat, but I liked to taste each part separately.

The exterior of Kim Moon used to be clad in these dark orange rectangular tiles. And before you walked in, there was a window display of cakes to the left, usually two- to three-layered sponge ones with whipped cream frosting and garnished with fresh strawberries, honeydew, grapes, and peaches. The black forest cake was a popular choice for birthdays.

As soon as you opened the door, the smell of coconut buns, egg tarts, and milk bread wafted into your nose. A few ladies in red uniforms would greet you at the counter.

You'd point and tell her your order and she would neatly place the items in their customary red-and-white cardboard box.

Beside the glass display cases was a dining area where you could eat your purchased baked goods or order dim sum dishes. At the back was the dumb waiter, which brought dishes to the upstairs portion of the bakery. The bakery was always busy, but the sounds — the bustle — got quieter and quieter as the years went by. Especially after the shop changed hands.

I went across the street to Dai Loong Phong Beng Ga to buy the ahn tat there instead. They were smaller and came in paper liners rather than aluminium trays. They were also two, and not three, for one dollar, like the two bakeries on Spadina. I grabbed a pair of tongs and put six on the red plastic tray.

When it was my turn to pay, I inquired at the counter, "Ah siew jeh, Kim Moon saang jor mo?" (Miss, did Kim Moon close?)

"Oh, gnoi mm jee wor. Gnoi mor yow ee cee." (I'm not sure. I haven't been paying attention.)

"Gor moon lock jor. Geem ngip bin haak sigh." (The door was locked. And it was dark inside.)

"Mm ay tui wor. Yew mor foong ga?" (I don't know. Did they go on vacation?)

"Hay moong wor. Kwuy high gor doh gee dor nen. Deem wuy saang ne?" (I hope so. It's just they've been there for so many years. They wouldn't have closed, right?)

A deep voice piped up from behind. "Hiiigh . . . high geem yeng la. Mor saang ngee, migh jeep jor lop. Gee dor poo how high geem yeng." (It's like that now. If you don't have enough business, you close. We have lost so many shops this way.)

I turned around to see a man around my age wearing a grey

newspaper-boy cap and a beige polo jacket sitting at one of the tables with a coffee in an orange and white paper cup and a pineapple bun.

"Chaam wor," I said, shaking my head. (It's such a shame.)

"Mor faat jee." (That's how it is.)

I nodded, then left with the bag of ahn tat. I was so distracted by Kim Moon being closed that I forgot to ask the lady to put them in a box.

I stopped on the stoop just outside of Hong Fatt to reorganize all the bags of food.

I hadn't gotten used to how quiet this corner had become. There used to be fruit and vegetable vendors where I was standing as well as across the street. In the summer, they also sold flowers and plants. Now only the grocery store on Huron sold small seedlings.

Huron itself was looking more rundown than usual. I remember reading that the City wanted to transform the street into a square or a park with tables for playing mah jong. That would be nice to have some place to sit.

I picked up the bags and continued along Dundas, catching glimpses of my reflection every now and then in the shop windows and imagining you there beside me.

But I know the time will come when I will no longer see you.
When you will become a shadow,
only seen when the light hits at the right moment.

42

It was just before 8 a.m. when I left the house. I decided to stay in the area, rather than go up to Harbord. It would be a variation of the Wednesday and Friday routes; I'd walk up to College, then over to Spadina, then make my way down and go through St. Andrew, Kensington, Baldwin, Augusta, and finally back home.

While walking up Bellevue, I ran into the older Italian woman who always dressed in black. No matter the weather, it would either be black shoes with a slight heel or black boots. A black dress or a black skirt. A black cardigan or a black coat. And in the crook of her right elbow, she carried a structured black leather handbag that had a gold clasp in the middle. We only knew each other by face as we would find ourselves walking on Bellevue at the same time — around 8:15 a.m. on a Sunday.

Once when we happened to both be waiting at the intersection at College and Borden, she told me she was on her way to church. St. Peter's for the 9 a.m. service. When she spoke, her words sounded round and full. I wondered if she ever felt insecure about the way she spoke, the way I sometimes did. If she did, she never let on about her accent, nor mine.

That morning, she had asked if I liked what I was doing, and I found myself nodding and saying yes.

There was some silence between us as we stood there. The light seemed to take a very long time to change at that intersection, especially early in the mornings. She then blurted out that she missed the procession that used to happen down Bathurst on Good Friday. She would always go to the corner of Bathurst and College and wait at the side of the bar with the colourful sign and mural for them to come. One year, she waited and waited but the chorus of low baritone voices dressed all in black never came walking down. She thought maybe there was a last-minute cancellation. But then the following year, it didn't happen again. And the year after that, the same thing. She came to the conclusion that maybe people got older and grew tired of such traditions. Or maybe people stopped believing, or their beliefs strayed to other things. She found it hard to accept that something she had been doing for over twenty years could suddenly stop.

She had spoken so fast that I did not understand everything she said. But I didn't want her to feel embarrassed for what she had told me so I just nodded. And we stood there until the light changed.

Sometimes the memory of something can be enough,
and sometimes it is never enough.
So we hold on to whatever we can.

"Good morning!" she said as soon as she saw me.

"Good morning," I replied.

"I go to the church now. You go walking?"

"Yes. Here, College-ee, Spadina."

"Good for you. Good to walk."

I nodded.

We matched in our pace until I spotted two wine bottles on their side at the foot of the bench at the corner of Bellevue and Nassau. I stopped to pick them up.

She shouted over her shoulder, "I have to keep going! Have a nice day!"

"You too!"

She continued walking at a brisk pace; the shape of her got smaller and smaller as I took my time.

As I rolled the cart along College, I could hear the sound from my shopping cart wheels and a few bottles clinking against one another. When I got closer to Spadina, I noticed three young people swaying and moving about. They looked like they were dressed for summer, wearing sneakers without socks, T-shirts, jeans and jackets unzipped. One person even wore a yellow tutu! And all of them wore necklaces that looked like they glowed.

"Wah, kwuy day mm doong meh?" (Are they not cold?) I was dressed as if a last-minute winter blizzard would come: the purple and seaweed-green winter coat, a fluorescent-orange toque on top, the charcoal-grey scarf wrapped twice around the neck, brown corduroy pants, and the grey winter boots.

I'm not sure where they were going or where they were coming from so early in the morning. Although I do remember Lem Seem mentioning a place just north of here, by the shelter, where people go to dance. She said that if you were waiting in line for the shelter's light breakfast, there would often be people coming out of a black door that had flyers taped to it, their eyes readjusting to the light.

As soon as I turned the corner and passed them, the one with the tutu shouted, "Hey Grandma, love your hat! Come dance with us!"

I looked back and they were wiggling their hips, tapping their feet, and flailing their arms. I chuckled at their movements and gave them two thumbs-up. They moved better than I did at the Wong See's line dancing classes. I closed my eyes for a moment, remembering the time we danced in the middle of Elizabeth Street, along with others, just outside Nanking Tavern, during a street festival and fundraiser. Curious onlookers watched us as we twirled, spun, and moved to the music. It was the summer of 1972. The last year we lived on Walton.

I opened my eyes, politely smiled, and shook my head. They resumed dancing to some imaginary music in their heads as I continued south along Spadina.

The construction boarding at Baldwin was still up, plastered with graffiti and flyers advertising upcoming concerts and films; the corner was still vacant from a fire many years ago and now taken over by overgrown weeds and littered with garbage and toppled bricks. We were surprised nothing had been built here yet.

I turned right on St. Andrew; you could smell the coffee from Moonbean here as well. On our way home from Kim Moon and the corner vendors at Huron and Dundas, we would end our shopping at St. Andrew Poultry, before heading home. The smell of raw chicken hit you as soon as you opened the door. Its reddish-brown tile floors littered with soft wood shavings that stuck to the soles of your shoes as you approached the glass-fronted refrigerated case displaying the various cuts of meat and chicken.

We'd buy chicken legs, sometimes a whole chicken, and occasionally our eggs, but we went to Chaan Lau most of the time because they sold a dozen for $1.99.

Part of the chicken mural on the side of the poultry shop had been neglected and defaced with big black block letters covering some of the drawn chickens.

I saw two cans in one of the concrete planters just outside the big parking garage. I picked them up and shook any leftover liquid before adding them to the cart.

I turned right on Kensington. Up ahead was a butcher shop that moved in a couple of years ago; it was originally located a few doors down. The red and white sign was replaced with a cursive red one with wooden backing.

I peered inside. We never went in after the previous butcher and deli closed down. It looked like there was still a numbering system, but the place seemed different to me. Words like o-r-g-a-n-i-c, m-i-l-k-f-e-d, and a-r-t-i-s-a-n were printed on signs. They were too small to read the prices from here, but I imagined that they were more than the shop before or the one on St. Andrew. Down the middle, there were two displays of red sauces and maybe pickled eggs.

"Hiiigh, gun high gwuy. Mm swuy high." (It's probably expensive. I don't need to look.) I turned, and beside the wooden fence were two beer cans.

"Wah, gum ngam!" (What a coincidence!) There was also a styrofoam box in front and I took that as well. I could use the box for the garden.

I continued walking along Baldwin and turned left on Augusta, passing another whiff of coffee at the corner and the smells of fresh fish, coconut bread, and dried fruit in-between.

While on Augusta, I heard music coming from the brown weathered upright piano that sat outside the store that sold greeting cards and posters. There was a young woman playing; a small crowd had gathered around her. A few people had their phones out, filming her playing. Most of the people watching were blocking the sidewalk and did not move when I tried to pass.

"Mo kwigh gwuy," I muttered under my breath. (No respect at all.)

Was it always this way?

Lately, this area was where people flocked to on weekends, crowding the streets, the sidewalks, lining up for bread or cheese, taking a number to buy meat and fish, buying clothing unlike anything in my closet, taking photos in front of graffitied walls.

I waited until a car drove by before walking on the road. I crossed over to the park and cut through. The sounds of a guitar and hand drums eventually drowned out the piano.

I brought up the red wooden square table from the basement.

I steadied it against the wall as I unfolded its legs, one by one.

First the top,

then the right,

then the bottom,

and finally the left.

I lifted it up, holding it by its sides, and turned it upright.

I noticed a bit of red candle wax was still stuck on the surface of the table.

I scratched it until it came off.

I wiped the table; my jade bracelet clacked against it as I moved the cloth side to side.

I then brought up the metal garbage can that contained a smaller tin can — filled with previous years' ashes and joss sticks and the pry bar — and stuck them under the table.

I added three small red plastic cups and three pairs of red chopsticks to the table.

I poured from the old bottle of Johnnie Walker, its red label peeling, into the cups, almost to the rim.

I took out two blue-rimmed enamel shallow bowls and stacked three oranges in one and three apples in the other.

I positioned the styrofoam containers of roasted pork and steamed chicken I got from Hong Fatt.

"Aiii, joon high ho may ah." (It really smells good.)

I pulled out one of the chairs from the kitchen table and sat down.

The clock ticking.

The refrigerator humming.

I fiddled with my bracelet. "Jor lay duck la." (It's almost ready.)

I stared at the kitchen table.

The pile of newspapers and flyers has both grown and yellowed.

The stack of receipts has gotten smaller, but the number of pencils stayed the same.

I wiped a thin layer of dust that had collected on the Kleenex box.

The light from the rice cooker went off and the button sprung back up.

A wisp of white steam rose from the lid.

The rice was ready.

I scooped the rice into three blue-and-white porcelain rice bowls and placed them on the table, along with the chicken, pork, apples, oranges.

Almost done.

I lit the three thick red candles.

I pulled out three joss sticks from the drawer and lit them as well.

I waved them in the air, letting the flames go out, leaving an orange glow on each of them.

I held them in my hands and bowed three times.

Eyes closed.

Mouth moving.
        Whispering.

I opened my eyes and lit the paper money and dropped it into the metal bin.

Then I put the joss sticks into the small can and waited.

I poured the liquor down the sink.

I brought the food over to the kitchen table, leaving it in the containers. I put the rice back into the cooker and mixed it in with the remaining rice, then ladled the grains into one bowl.

I brought the bowl to the table and sat down.

I took a deep breath. In and out.

The sound of the clock.

The sound of embers.

The smell of incense.

I picked up the chopsticks, selected a few pieces of pork, and put them on the plate, then a couple pieces of chicken. I poured a bit of the ginger scallion sauce on top and mixed it in.

"Lay figh dee heck ah. Lay joon high hor tor gnor." (You better start eating. You must be so hungry.)

I brought the bowl to my mouth and began to eat.

And I imagined you smiling, the way you did in the photographs.

And then saying, "Heng tien high, ah Cho Sum, heng tien high." (Look ahead.)

The window was wide open. The white linen curtains swayed gently as the thick summer air entered and lingered in the room.

The calls of blue jays, cardinals, and robins.

The humming of air-conditioning units and their fans.

The sound of laughter and guitars strumming from Bellevue Park.

The ambulance sirens from a distance.

The traffic noise on Dundas.

The sound of an airplane overhead.

The air, smells, and sounds filling the room, the space, the house, the home you have left behind.

I sat on your side of the bed and looked out. My eyes rested on the leaves of the dogwood tree across the street. The leaves were a dark forest green similar to your old winter coat.

I took hold of your jacket — the grey houndstooth one — and brought it to my nose. I breathed in deeply. The musty smell of mothballs, the faint smell of aftershave, and of you.

I put my hand in the right pocket and felt a familiar texture. I brought it out and chuckled.

Peanut shells.

And an empty mui wrapper.

I put my hand in the other pocket and found an unopened roll of haw flakes, and suddenly I had a craving for the flakes, mui, and peanuts.

"Gnoi how hun." (I have cravings.) I'd say that to you whenever I brought home snacks like the Garden coconut wafers, the Khong Guan lemon puffs, Ruffles sour cream and onion chips, or those cream crackers in the yellow package from Chaan Lau.

A ray of afternoon sunlight entered the room, hitting the foot of the bed, me, and the hardwood floor.

You could see bits of lint and dust float within that beam.

The black and taupe steamer trunk with WONG engraved on the top.
Once filled with dreams and belongings, now empty and lined with pages
from the *Toronto Star* from 1953 and holding a musty smell that would not
go away.
The closet was full of things we'd saved over the years.
Things we'd refused to throw out because they could be mended.
And things we simply just kept.
The left side of the wooden dresser was yours; the right side, mine.
Your ties still hung on the rope you strung on the door.
Jackets in the clear plastic dry-cleaning bags now coated with a layer of dust.
Your cotton polyester vests and sweaters still folded neatly in the drawers.
Pants from Woolworths, tags still intact.
Your charcoal-grey suit.
Your shoes.
The oxford ones, your running shoes, your black winter boots.
Your black fedora.
The crisp white cotton shirts.
The shirts and the polos all had pockets on the left-hand side, so you could
always carry that notebook, pen, and comb of yours.
The white paint-splattered navy-blue chore coat.
And the ivory one.
The white cook's jackets from Mei Hong, Hong Fatt, and Hat Moon Low.

Unwrapped boxes of things still left in their packages. Pristine condition.
Blankets, bedding from Simpson's (a luxury), from Chaan Lau.
Towels, also from Chaan Lau, with the price tags attached with small sewing pins.
In the basement, unopened boxes and packages remain stored
next to the bags and cardboard boxes filled with bottles and cans I've collected,
waiting to be brought to the be jow por.
Glassware, the meat grinder, Fruit of the Loom and Stanfield's undershirts
and long johns,
those floral fitted sheets with matching pillowcases — gifts we'd received
over the years, saved, waiting to be used.

Bottles of Crown Royal and Johnnie Walker
brought home from the Wong See's banquets.
Only opened and used during the bigh seen and Ching Ming rituals.
Christmas wrapping paper on sale from Chaan Lau, BiWay, and Woolworths,
left intact.
Unopened boxes of Christmas cards that were 75 percent off, purchased on
Boxing Day.

Decades of saving.
A life spent saving,
waiting for the right time, for the right moment.
A moment that never arrived, continually delayed, postponed.
Because we assume there will always be another time,
another moment.

Why do we wait?

I started putting items into a large waxed cardboard box that I got from the side
of Hua Long.
The Foodland Ontario symbol on the bottom right corner,
and in the middle it read bok choy and napa cabbage.
It hadn't travelled very far.

3 x pairs of thick polyester pants: black, grey, and chocolate brown
3 x striped polo shirts: light blue, yellow, and red
2 x white long-sleeved dress shirts
1 x white short-sleeved dress shirt
1 x grey houndstooth wool jacket
1 x light grey tie
1 x striped yellow, teal, and grey tie
1 x dark blue baseball cap

In a plastic bag,
1 x pair of black winter boots
1 x pair of white, silver, and grey running shoes

I knew these pieces as what you wore to work, on walks around the neighbourhood,
what you painted with, what you wore to the supermarket, what you wore for exercising,
what you wore to my citizenship ceremony, what you wore to meet me at the airport.

And whoever takes them will never know these details, these stories, the life behind them.
They will see them just as they are: men's pants, shirts, jackets, boots, shoes, ties, and a hat.
But the neighbourhood seemed to like old and used clothes.

I brought the box down and put it outside on one of the chairs on the porch. I got a sheet of paper and wrote "FREE" and taped it to the box.

Then I placed it gently on the sidewalk just outside the gate.

Chloe was sitting on her porch and came over, standing over the box. "Hey, Poh Poh, what are you doing? Are those your clothes?"

"Koh-lee. How are you? No. They are Gong Gong's."

"You're going to give them all away?"

"Not all."

"Oh . . . It's good to keep some things, right?"

I nodded.

"But it's also okay to let some things go?"

I nodded again and closed my eyes. I could hear the birds chirping above.

"Poh Poh, can I use your marker?"

I handed it to her and watched what she added underneath my "FREE."

She gave me back the marker. "Now people will know."

I smiled. "You stay here?"

"Yeah, I'll be outside for a while."

"Okay." I went back inside to retrieve some items I had forgotten on the bed.

V-neck navy and tan pullovers.

A crimson-red and a dark grey vest.

I draped them over my arm and held them.

I glanced out from the bedroom window and saw two people rifle through the clothes.

A sense of anxiety filled my chest.

My heart raced and an unsettling feeling festered.

What was I doing?

I hurried down the stairs, rushing to get outside, my hand on the doorknob.

I closed my eyes.

Deep breaths. In and out. In and out. In and out.

I opened the door slightly and stood there.

I left my hand on the doorknob for a moment, but I did not step outside.

I waited until they were gone before I went back out to where Chloe was standing.

"They took one of the polo shirts," she said. "The light blue one. And the cap."

I held onto the sweaters and vests for a moment before adding them to the pile, then quickly picked them up and decided to lay them across the fence, like they were laundry waiting to be dried.

My eyes started to well. I could sense Chloe watching me. I turned away from her slightly; I did not want her to see me cry.

I looked up and down the street still thinking you might reappear around the corner.

I stared up at the sky and quickly wiped my eyes.

The tops of the trees that lined our street were starting to get full again.

I felt something brush my right hand, and I thought maybe it was a bee so I tried to brush it away, but it was not.

I looked down and saw Chloe's hand curled up in mine. I had forgotten what it was like to feel someone else's warmth and love, and I almost flinched.

I looked at her and smiled. I cupped my hand over hers and patted it.

That year, fall and winter came and went.
Spring and summer too.

Days became months.

Months became years.

46

I brought out the shopping cart from the closet and rolled it onto the porch.

One of the wheels had started to squeak and I had been putting off trying to fix it.

I took an old can of WD-40 from the closet and pressed the nozzle and sprayed it onto the back right wheel.

I rolled it back and forth; the sound was smooth as can be.

The cart is still lined with election signs, and once in a while I line it with garbage bags. I've put in a few reusable bags to separate the different kinds of cans and bottles. I even tied a small stick in the front so I could hang two more reusable bags.

And after walking the same streets these past several years on a daily basis, I could walk them with my eyes closed. Li Seem was right: I got used to it.

Which streets to pass.

Which houses knew how to recycle.

Which houses mixed their recycling with their garbage.

Which houses placed concrete blocks on the lids of their bins that silently implied: you are not welcome here.

Which houses were expecting, moving, leaving.

The comings and goings.

Families.

Students.

Older people.

Who took care of their gardens.

What they grew.

Who shovelled their sidewalks after a heavy snowfall.

Which park people liked to drink in.

Which people were nice.
Which people looked down on you.
Watching their lives from the streets, from afar, at a distance.

There were now many more of us on the streets, after hearing from others that collecting could be profitable or at the very least it would help with groceries and bills. Many gave up, but those who continued found some solace in each other's company. We created our own community, built on glass and tin.

A hello when we passed each other.
Catching up on our lives and gossiping at the be jow por.
Commenting on our carts if someone managed to get a new one.
Informing each other which streets to go on, or avoid.
Which be jow por had closed (the Queen and Markham location).
Trading bottles and cans.

But there were also a few who refused to acknowledge you: the couple who brought their beagle with them, the middle-aged woman who wore a corduroy newspaper-boy hat collecting with a tote bag that said lulu and lemon, and the older woman who hobbled with a wheelchair she used as a walker and made a huge mess after each bin she looked through.

I didn't let them bother me.

I walked now, a rhythmic pace in sync with the sounds of the neighbourhood, of the city itself.

I became a part of it, the way nondescript buildings blend into the city, largely ignored, and only visible if you really cared to notice.

All of Toronto was wearing T-shirts. Sweat stains under the armpits and on the backs of shirts seemed unavoidable. It was the third straight day the city was under an extreme heat alert.

I was outside tending to the garden in the front, picking weeds, when a hongngin dwuy called out from the gate. I looked up and saw someone wearing pointy brown shoes with chambray long shorts, a dress shirt, and a white linen jacket. "Wah, jeck geen lauw? Kwuy mm ngit?" I muttered to myself. (He's wearing a jacket? Doesn't he feel hot?)

"Hello, sorry to bother you. Do you live here?" I nodded. "I thought I'd tell you I'm a real estate agent. I help people sell their houses. And Poh Poh, you should sell," he insisted.

"Sell?"

"Yes. If you sell the house, then you can get lots of money! Ho dor cheen ah."

His words tumbled so quickly, one sentence after another.

"Don't you want to travel with your husband?
You work so hard all your life. It's time to enjoy it.
Are all the children gone?
It's good to downsize. Small is good, especially for you and your husband.
You don't need something like this.
You don't want to be a burden to your children, right?
Do you know what you could do with a million dollars? Lots!"

"You speak Chinese?" I asked.

"Ahh, gnoi gong siew siew Gwongdong wa toong migh siew siew Gwokyee." (I speak a bit of Cantonese and a bit of Mandarin.)

"High knee doh choot sigh?" (Were you born here?)

"High ah." (Yes.)

"Migh ho la." (That's good.)

"Here's my business card. Now is the perfect time to sell. The market is good! I can help you like I'm helping your neighbour down the street." He pointed to a few houses down. I didn't realize Manny's family was moving.

I looked down at his business card: Vince Leung. "Oh, sing Leung."

"Yes. What's your name?"

"Sing Wong."

"Well, what do you think, Poh Poh?"

"Think?"

"Yes. Of moving."

"Moving? Gnoi day joong yee knee doh wor. Honggnin guy hor kun! Migh sloong da hor kun. Gor Wong See high neng. Yee ga gnoi da hok gun gor ewu." (We like it here. Chinatown is so close! Buying our groceries is also convenient. The Wong Association is right there. I'm even learning to play the erhu now.)

"Ah Poh Poh, yee ga downtown mm ho. Gor gor move hwuy Scarborough, Richmond Hill, Markham." (Downtown isn't that great right now. Everyone has moved up to Scarborough, Richmond Hill, Markham.)

We have made this our home. How could I leave?

He continued, "Gum digh gaan. Mm oi sigh gaan dee?" (It's so big. Don't you want to live somewhere smaller?) "So many places in Chinatown and Kensington go for a lot of money . . ."

I closed my eyes for a moment. His words started drifting in and out for me.

"Don't you want to live somewhere new? You know this corner, Denison and Dundas, is going to change. Bigger and newer buildings and units."

I quickly opened my eyes. "Gor corner? Denison hoong muy Dunda?" (That corner? Denison and Dundas?)

"Yes. The southeast side. That whole block is going to be gone."

I stayed silent while he continued talking. "Maybe you'd want to live there if you didn't want to move far. It'll be so close. You know Honest Ed's, they're building over there too. Or maybe a lor yun ga is better for you. Some of these seniors homes are like apartments now!"

I looked up and down the street, and I saw what drew you here. What drew us here.

"What do you think, Poh Poh?"

He spoke these words as if these houses, this neighbourhood, Chinatown, Kensington, and I were nearing our end, even though we were all still firmly planted here.

I smiled. "Gnoi day wuy nam ha." (We'll think about it.)

"Okay, but don't wait too long. You have my business card. Give me a call when you change your mind."

I nodded.

"Thank you for your time, Poh Poh. And you have a very nice garden. It reminds me of my nai nai."

I watched him turn and walk down Denison in the direction of Manny's house. I had taken his card out of politeness, but I knew I would throw it in the garbage later. For now I put it in my pocket. I went back to pulling the weeds.

I had learned to walk these streets like I belonged, head held high.
These memories — a whole life here, on this concrete, on these corners — will not last. I will hold on to them as tightly as I can because I know they are already fading.

We seem to be all fighting for something to call home.

48

We used to go up to the third floor of Tai Cheong, at 310 Spadina, for a quick breakfast, or lunch even. Because it was fairly cheap, we went every few weeks. On occasion we'd ride the rickety old elevator, but we liked to get our exercise by taking the stairs.

We'd arrive on the third floor and catch our breath before opening the doors. Once through the doors, you couldn't miss the natural light that shone through the large windows that fronted Spadina.

The smells of each stall were both strong and flavourful, but we always came back for the lo bak go. The texture of the turnip mixed in with the lap cheong and green onions was firm and had the right amount of crispness and burntness when fried. We filled our styrofoam cups with bo lay cha from the huge carafes stationed at the end of each food stall and then we looked for a table.

The tables and chairs were spread out in the vast room, but they were small themselves, so our knees would graze when we sat across from one another.

After our lunch, we would head downstairs and occasionally browse the stationery store; I still have one of the paper fans I got from there. It had a black metal handle and the fan itself had a blue and green hummingbird. I brought it with me on hot days when I was out selling my vegetables.

Further back on that floor, there was a pet store that sold fish and birds; their chirping echoed down the hallway.

Once we were outside, I would glance at our grocery list on the back of the receipt, figuring out where we should go next.

I stood in front of the building now. The yellow awnings were gone. Most of the windows of Hua Foong were now boarded up. One spot remained uncovered. Hands cupped up against the dust-covered windows, I peered inside.

The fluorescent lights that lined the middle of the supermarket were left on, spotlighting the now bare wooden table that used to display the cucumbers, green onions, gai lan, and napa cabbage and the "Cashier 2" sign. I could see other handwritten signs as well: "5 for $1.00" and "3 for $2.00."

An empty hanger where the roll of plastic bags used to be was still nailed to the top of the wooden display bin.

This side of the street seemed so much quieter now that Hua Foong was gone.

The cries of "Luk gor chaang leng mun ahhhhhh. Ho teem, ho teem ahhhhhh!!" (Six oranges for two dollars. They are very sweet and juicy!!) were replaced with hammering and drilling. On the floor, items were left behind from the tenants on the top floors who were given little notice to leave. A 2018 calendar left open on December, a pamphlet of services offered from the Cross-Cultural Community Services Association, a broken magnifying glass, business cards, wooden hangers, and a blue Maxwell House ground coffee tin.

To make room for plans that did not include them.

Industrial sewing machines, desks, drafting tables, books, mannequins, dress forms — all thrown into rented garbage bins that made a loud rumbling noise, reverberating through the parking lot at the back.

I stopped in front of the development plan, stapled to a triangle made of two-by-fours. There were already "For Lease" signs stuck to the windows, advertising huge office spaces that boasted hardwood floors, exposed beams, and restored brick. The beige building would eventually be painted over in a dark grey stucco, a colour that I imagined would loom over Chinatown like a dark cloud, one that could take over the city. The same kind of plan was also in the works for Seen Kong. The yellow and orange building and its green tiled roof would disappear, replaced with that same grey.

Buildings devoid of warmth,
      emptied of a life we once knew.

I made my way to Dai Loong Phong Beng Ga and bought a coffee, two mantou, and three ahn tat. Over the years, Gwokyee quietly replaced the sounds of Toisan wa and Gwongdong wa in the bakeries and throughout some of the restaurants, shops, and supermarkets. Traces of home were slowly disappearing.

I sat in front of the window.

I looked around. There were a couple of us on our own, sitting at the few tables, each with a coffee, a pineapple bun, an egg tart, or a bao. The man behind me was reading the *Sing Tao* and I suddenly wondered where in Chinatown the bak who sold the *Sing Tao* outside Hat Moon Low, before it closed and was boarded up, moved to. Every morning he meticulously rolled the newspapers in half, wrapped them with an elastic band, and sold them throughout the day. He usually sold out by two or three in the afternoon. And at his feet sat his coffee in a black-and-dark-brown paper cup from Fu La Wa, sometimes from Ding Dong, or Tim Hortons. Occasionally, he'd bring his portable radio with him, listening to the news.

I took a sip of the coffee from the orange paper cup
and stared out through the window, watching people go by.
At the beginning, the days felt longer.
But now it seems time has caught up and was moving quicker and quicker.
And I have fallen behind.

I continued staring out at the window.
Long gone was the recognizable yellow sign of Kim Moon.
So many restaurants and shops have closed.
So many changes happening now.
It was hard to keep up.

I took a deep breath.

49

It was just after 6:30 a.m.

I could smell coffee being roasted at Moonbean from blocks away, blowing
through the metal chimney just above the roaster.
Deliveries were being packed and hoisted into the back of the truck
just outside of Augusta Fruit Market.
Trays of patties and coco bread were baking in the back kitchen of Golden Patty.
Fresh tofu was being pressed at Fong On Foods.
The bakeries —
Maheng Mean Bao Phong, Ding Dong, Hong Dou, Dai Loong Phong Beng
Ga, Fu La Wa Beng Deem —
filled the air with the sweet smell
of baos, egg tarts, coconut buns, pineapple buns, milk bread.
A few workers were having a smoke outside
Hua Long Supermarket before starting the day's work.
The sounds of the 510 and 505 streetcars came swooshing through.

The way the sun hit the sides of the buildings and the houses.
That warm early morning orange glow.

The melody of house sparrows and robins in their morning chorus,
greeting one another from up above the trees, or from the telephone wires.

The wheels of a shopping cart filled
with bottles and cans moving along at a steady pace.

The city was awake.

50

One foot shuffled after the other, softly.
Where the sidewalk ended and the
street began.
Step after step.
Now with a cart in tow.
Clink, *clink*.

       Clink, *clink*.

              Clink, *clink*.   *One by one*
I stood there,   *the houses that were old and needed*
staring up at the house.   *work were sold over asking.*

This two-and-a-half-storey old brick
house
that held memories and stories.
That still felt like home.   *Bought by those who would fix and*
                                resell them at an even higher price.

The reddish-orange-hued bricks, now
painted purple.
The attic with its pointed roof.
The bay windows.
The bedroom's curtains drawn open.   *New coats of paint,*
The sky-blue diamond pattern along   *covering up imperfections,*
the porch, repainted.   *hoping its past life doesn't seep through.*
A fresh coat on the railing.

The two white plastic chairs remained
on the porch all year round, now
weathered.
                                People forced to leave.

When it was warm out, I sat and
watched people walk by.
Many of our neighbours have moved   *Neighbours replaced by people who*
on.   *stayed for a night, or a week.*
Gardens replaced with stones and
rocks.

I opened the gate and let my hand rest *The signs were everywhere again.*
there.

I took a deep breath,   *"Closing."*
holding on.   *"For Sale."*
                                        "Sold."
                                        "For Lease."
                                        "Newly renovated."
                                        "Looking for long-term tenants."
                                        "Going out of business."

Everything about the house suggested
two people still lived there.
And I always held on to this thought.

I looked at things more carefully,
because they might not be there
tomorrow.   *Shop windows covered with yesterday's*
                                        news.

I took another deep breath.
                                        The area was changing.

Here we were again.   *Development*
                                        after
                                        development
                                        made us feel unwelcome.

Blue and white signs
grew like perennials,
multiplying with each passing year,
sharing glimpses of what was to come.

False hopes.
Broken dreams.
Another lost battle.
Once more.

Selling futures, tomorrows, and newer
dreams that were never your dreams to
begin with.

Never look to the past, for fear you will
be stuck there.

Rumble!

Boom!

Smash!

The smells of Chinatown and
Kensington Market still linger,
and I wonder for how much longer.

Sounds and smells of progress took over
sounds and smells of familiarity and
comfort.

A life lived within a series of city
blocks
was all that I have known.

Chinatown colours began to turn grey.
Replaced by those who saw a different
kind of Chinatown.

As the shops and restaurants
that resonated home
slowly disappeared,
one by one.

Expensive cars now parked and rode
the streets of Kensington, revving their
engines through neighbouring streets
like it was theirs for the taking.

Shops replaced by shops that sold items
and food that cost more than what we
made in a day.

The languages of our villages,   *The shadows of people and their stories,*
of our mother tongues,   *replaced by murals*
the sounds and smells of a home we   *painted on buildings*
once knew that still existed in our head *that cast shadows*
and wandered these streets   *onto the streets*

was all that was left.   *are all that is left.*

I looked down Denison.

I heard a car speed through Dundas and I shook my head.

I walked, rolling the cart, up the steps.

I took another deep breath.

I opened the storm door, turned the key, and opened the main door.

I know now that this city and its people have a way of forgetting about you.

But I keep holding on.

And I keep going,

because that is what I have learned to do.

51

Clink, *clink*.

        Clink, *clink*.

The sound of bottles hitting against each other woke me up. I went to the window and saw a petite figure in the shadows pushing a cart with various reusable bags inside and hanging from the handle.

It was Poh Poh!

Her back was slightly hunched. It wasn't always like that. But she pushed the cart with such determination despite her small frame.

I closed the curtain. I didn't want her to see me staring, in case she looked up. I always wondered where she went with all those bottles and cans. I imagined them piled up somewhere in the shed, the backyard, or the basement. I asked Mommy once and she told me to stop being so nosy.

I pulled the curtain away very slightly to see if I could still see her, but she was already gone.

        Clink, *clink*.

                Clink, *clink*.

                        Clink, *clink*.

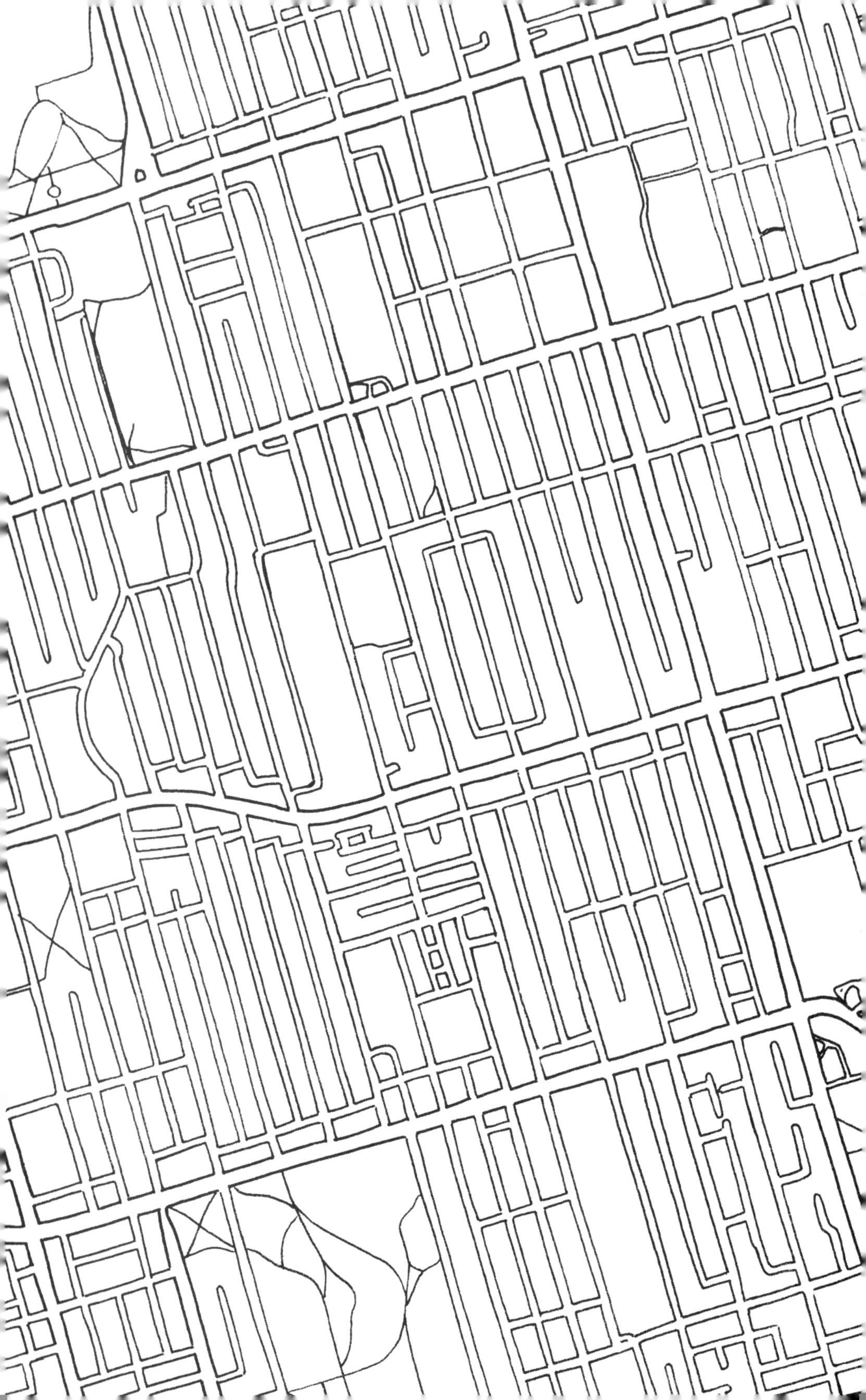

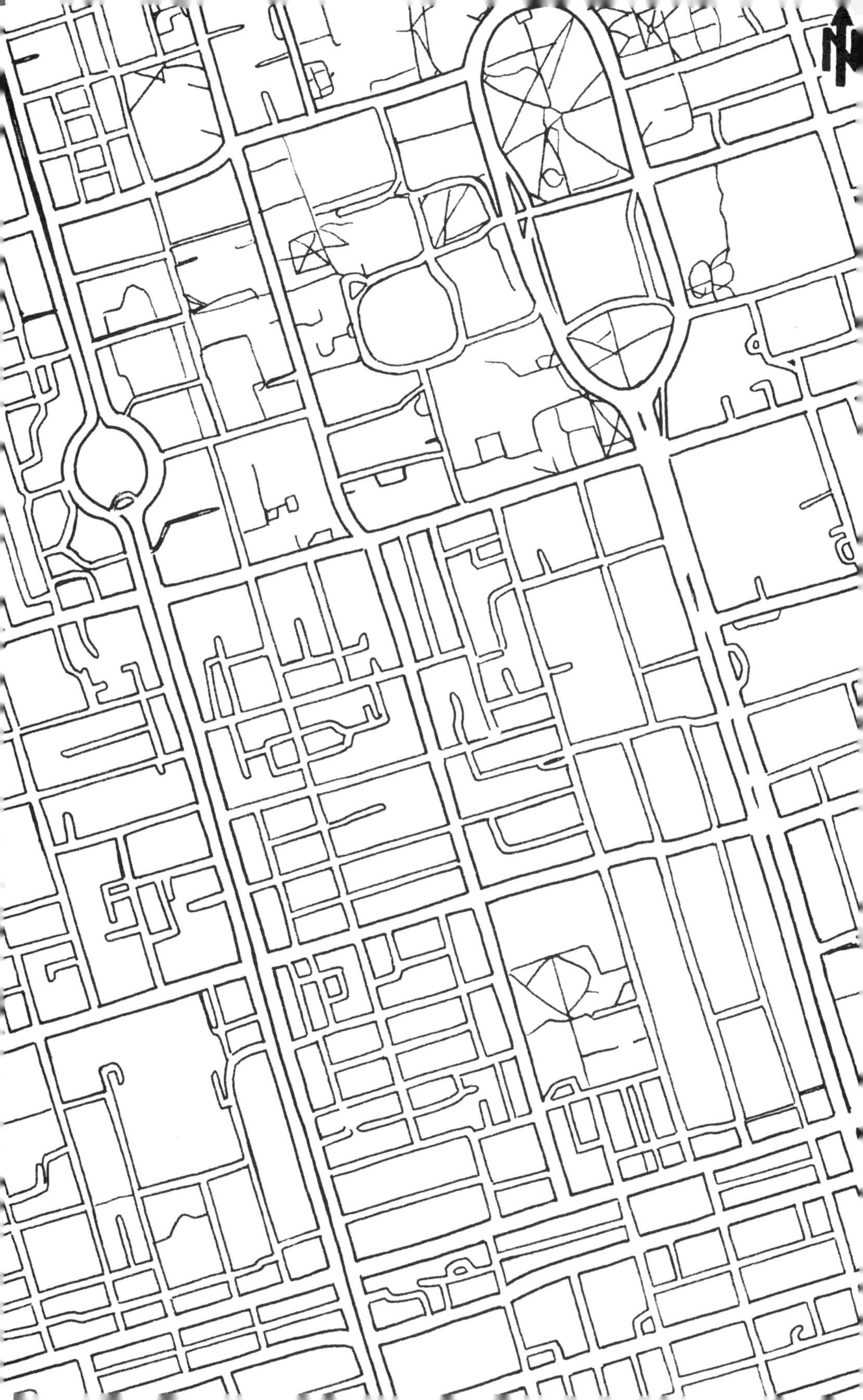
N

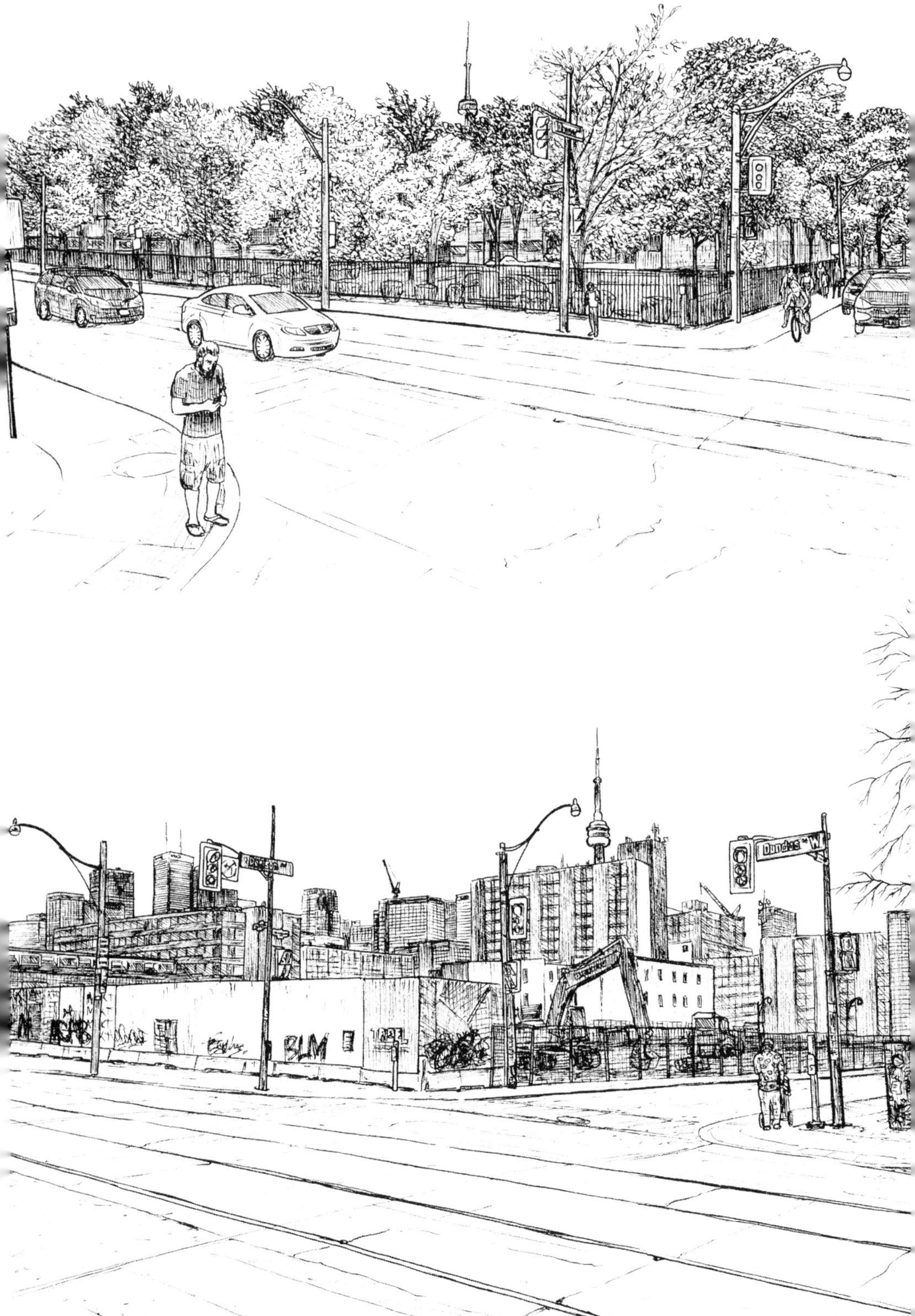
BLM
Dundas W

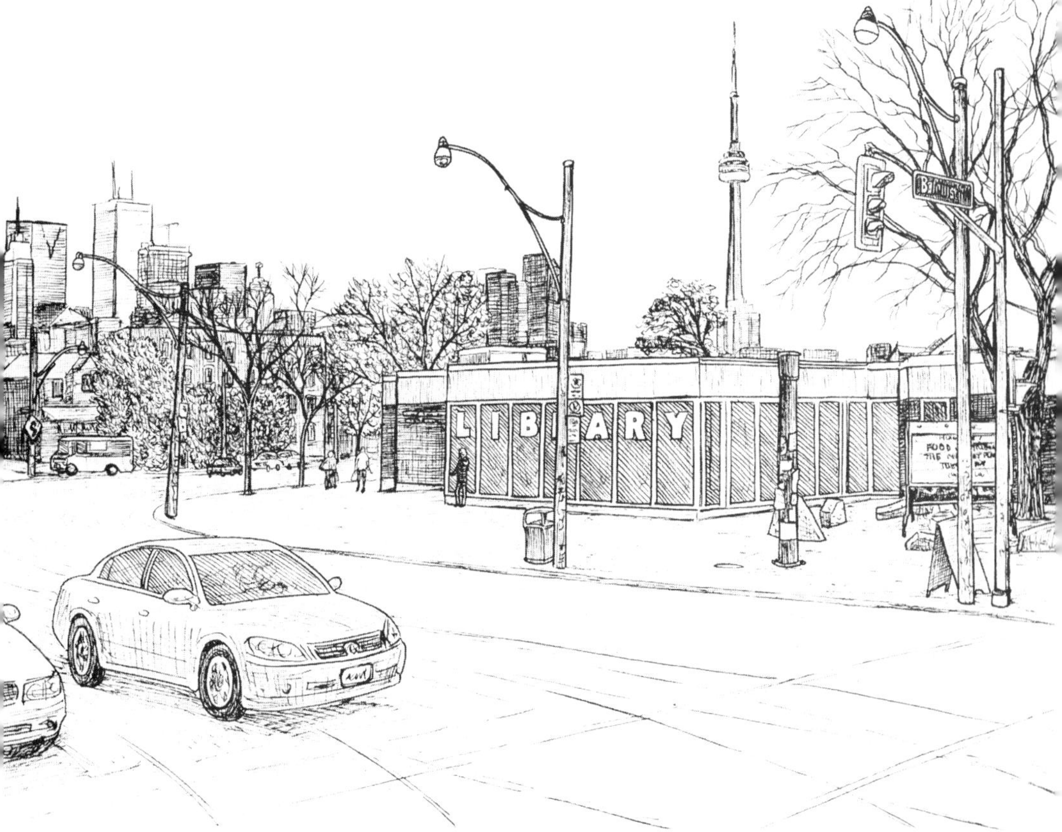
LIBRARY

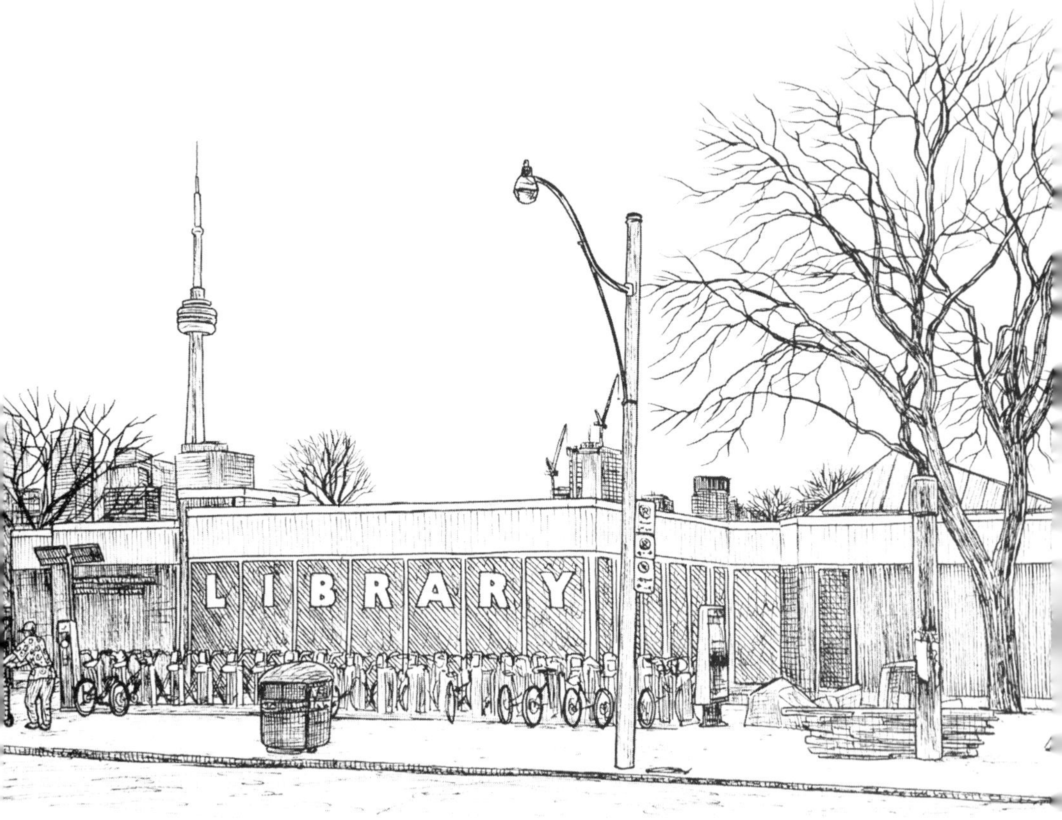
LIBRARY

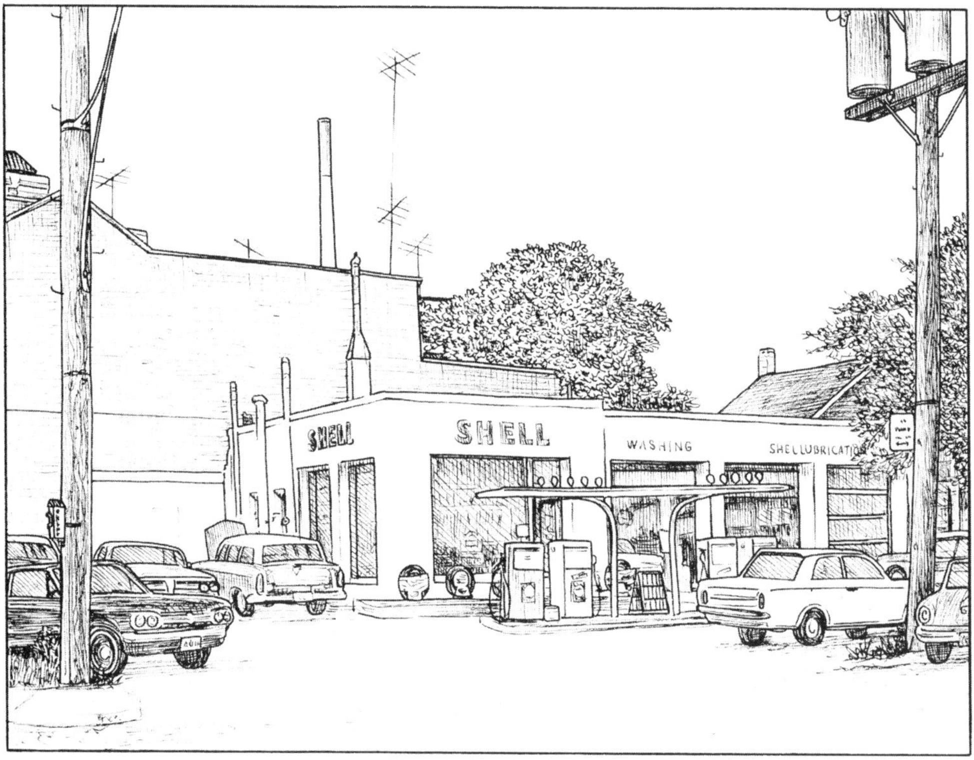
SHELL
SHELL
WASHING
SHELLUBRICATION

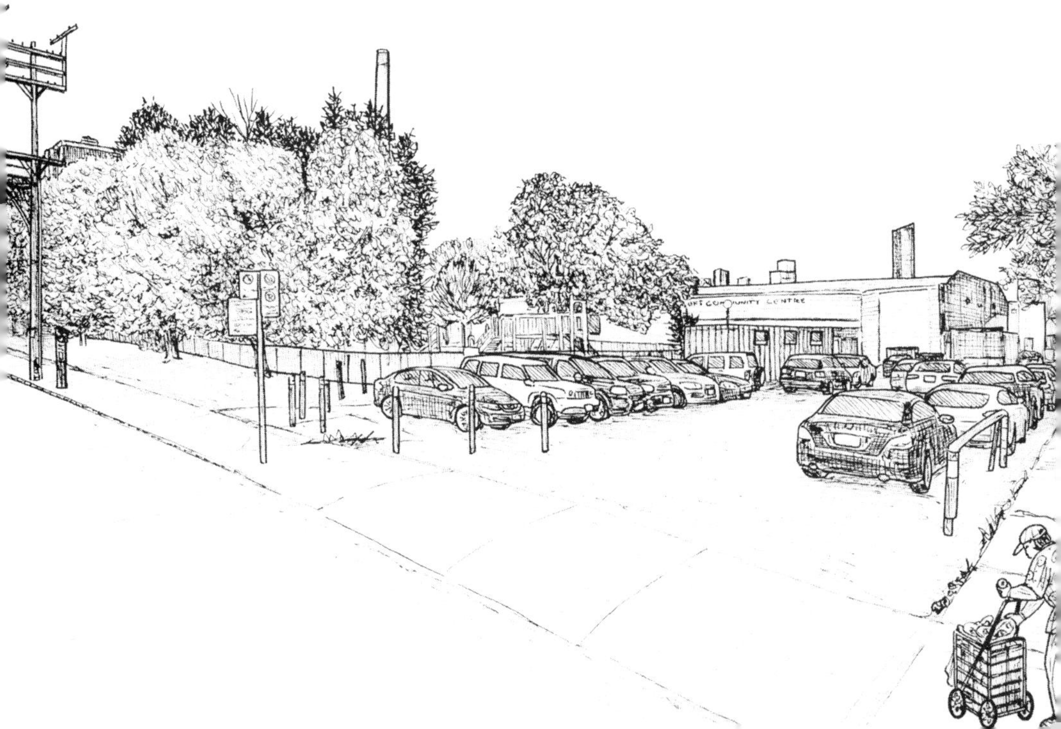
COMMUNITY CENTRE

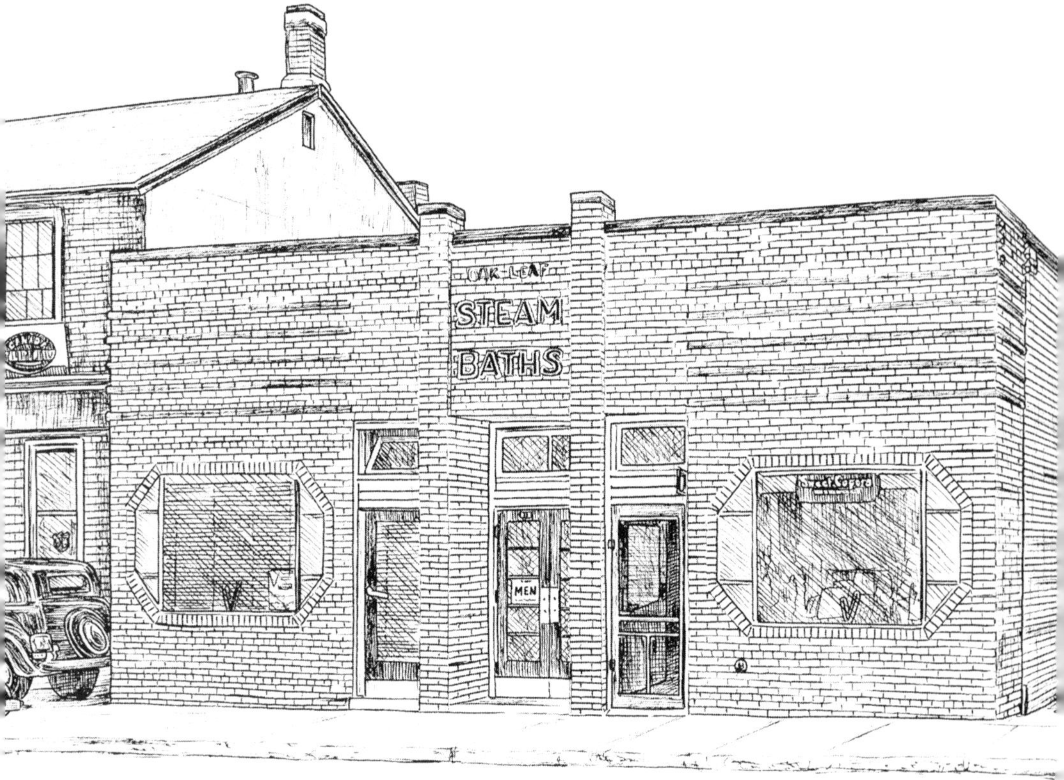
OAK-LEAF
STEAM
BATHS
MEN

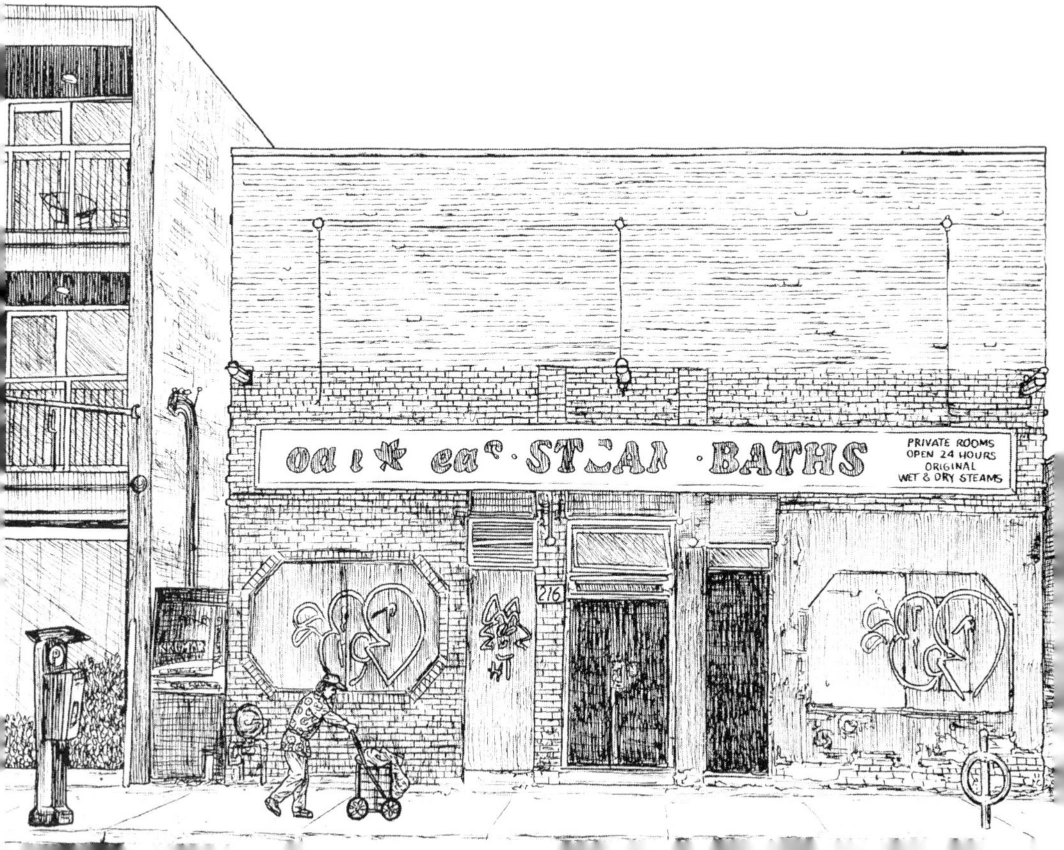
oa ✱ ea · STEAM · BATHS
PRIVATE ROOMS
OPEN 24 HOURS
ORIGINAL
WET & DRY STEAMS
216

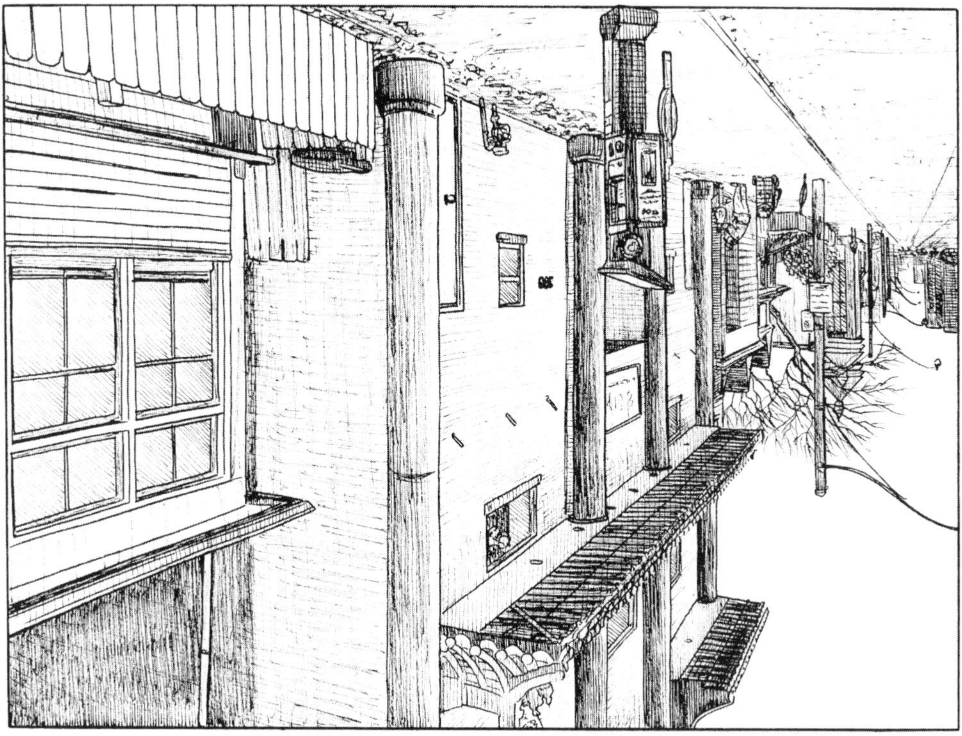

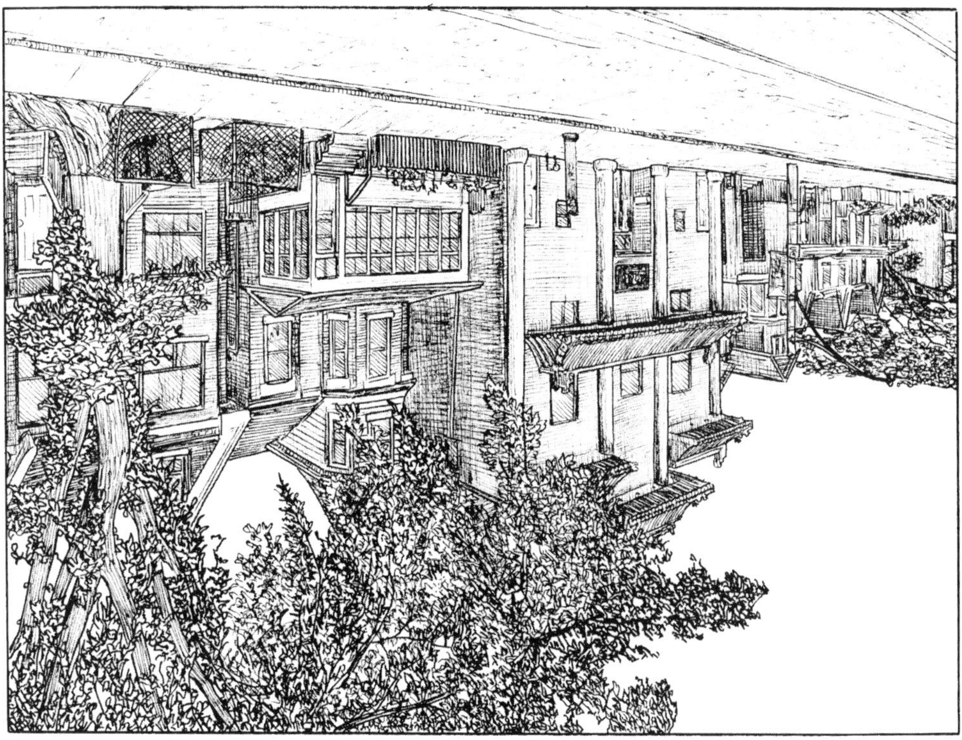

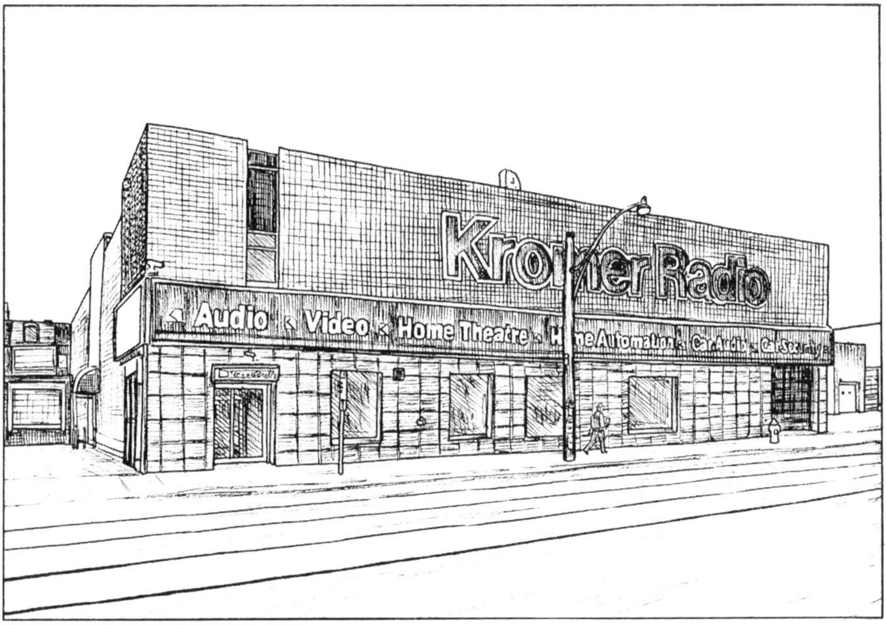
Kromer Radio
Audio
Video
Home Theatre
Home Automation
Car Audio

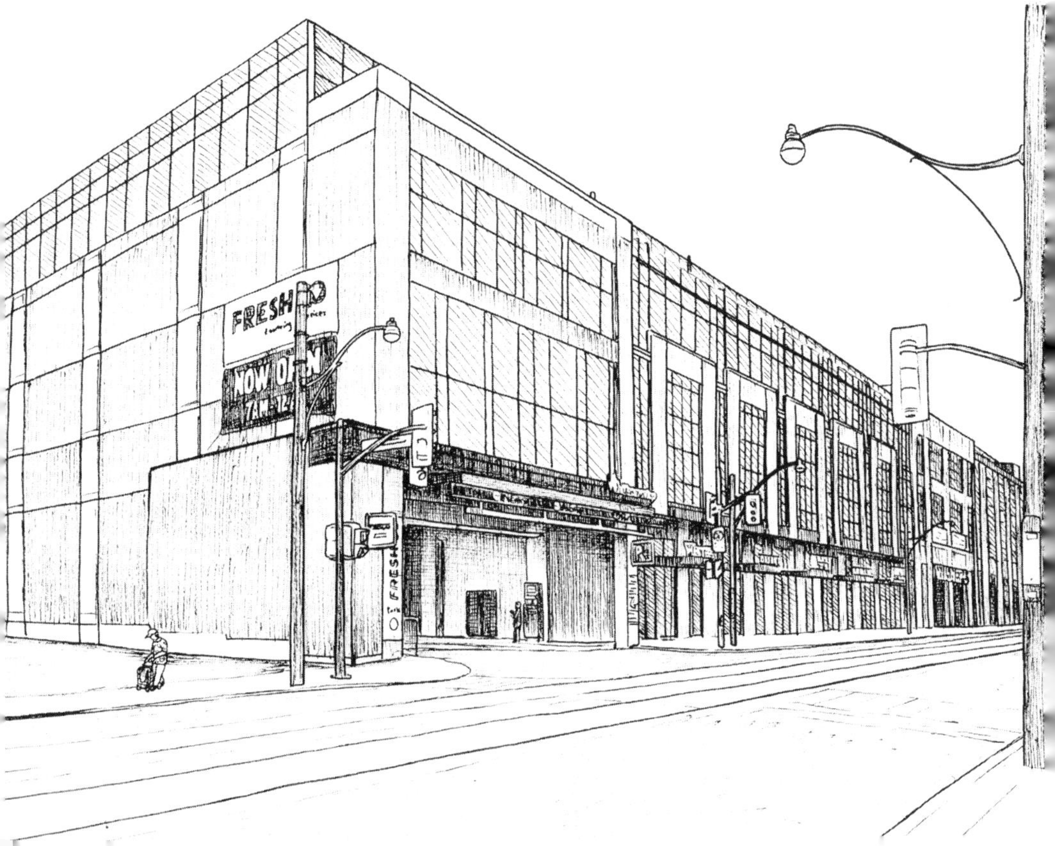
FRESH
NOW OPEN

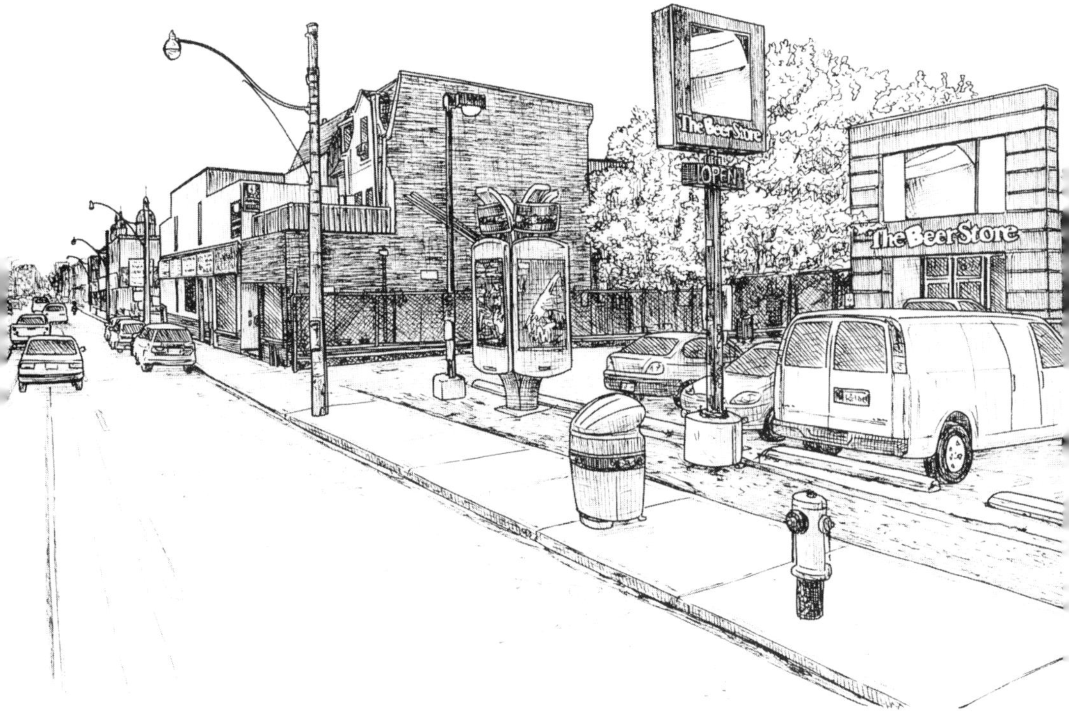
The Beer Store
OPEN
The Beer Store

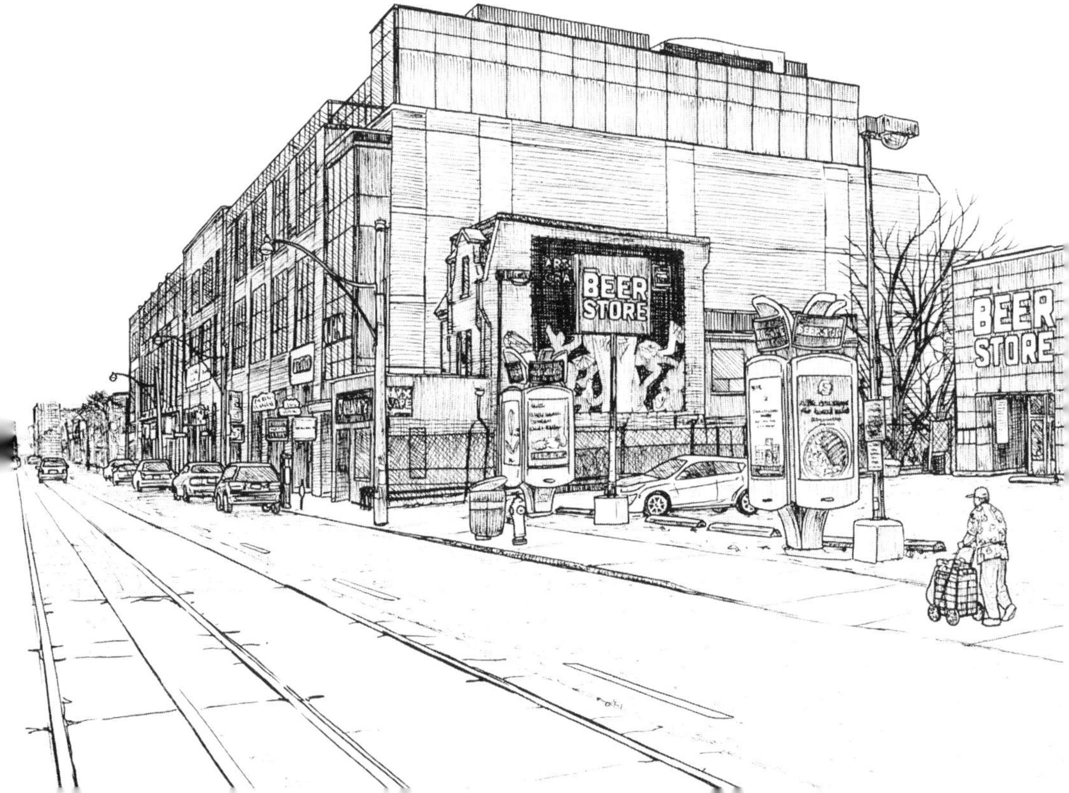
BEER
STORE
BEER
STORE

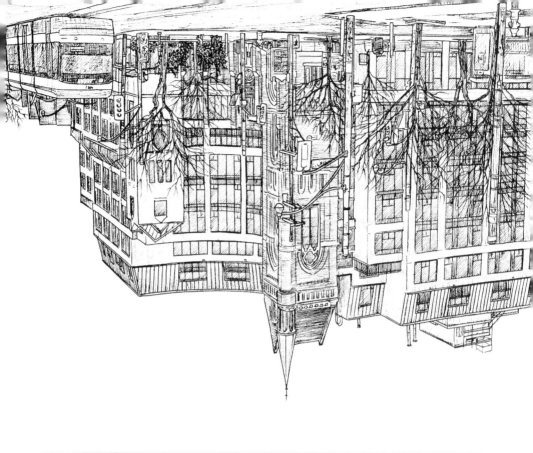

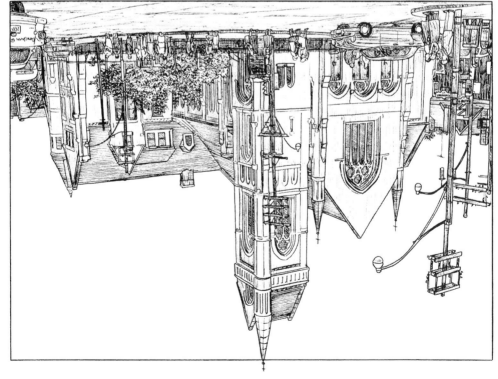

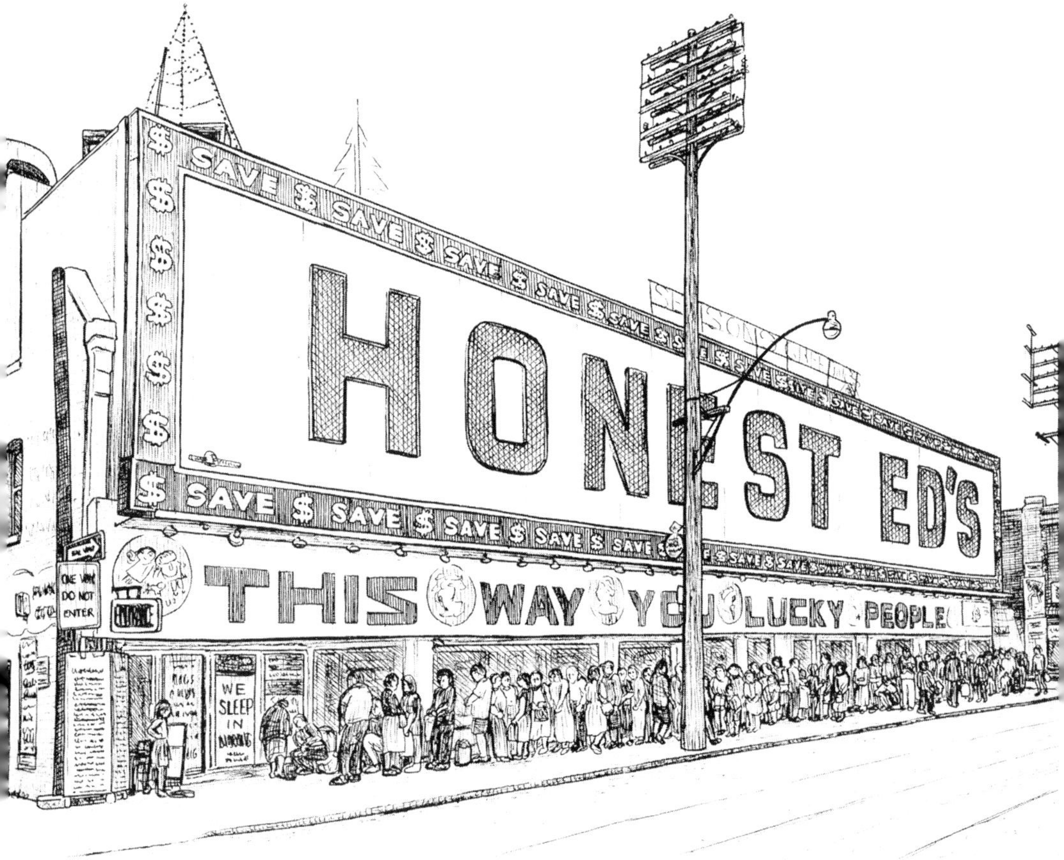

SAVE $ SAVE $ SAVE $ SAVE $ SAVE
HONEST ED'S
THIS WAY YOU LUCKY PEOPLE
ONE WAY
DO NOT ENTER
ENTRANCE
WE SLEEP IN

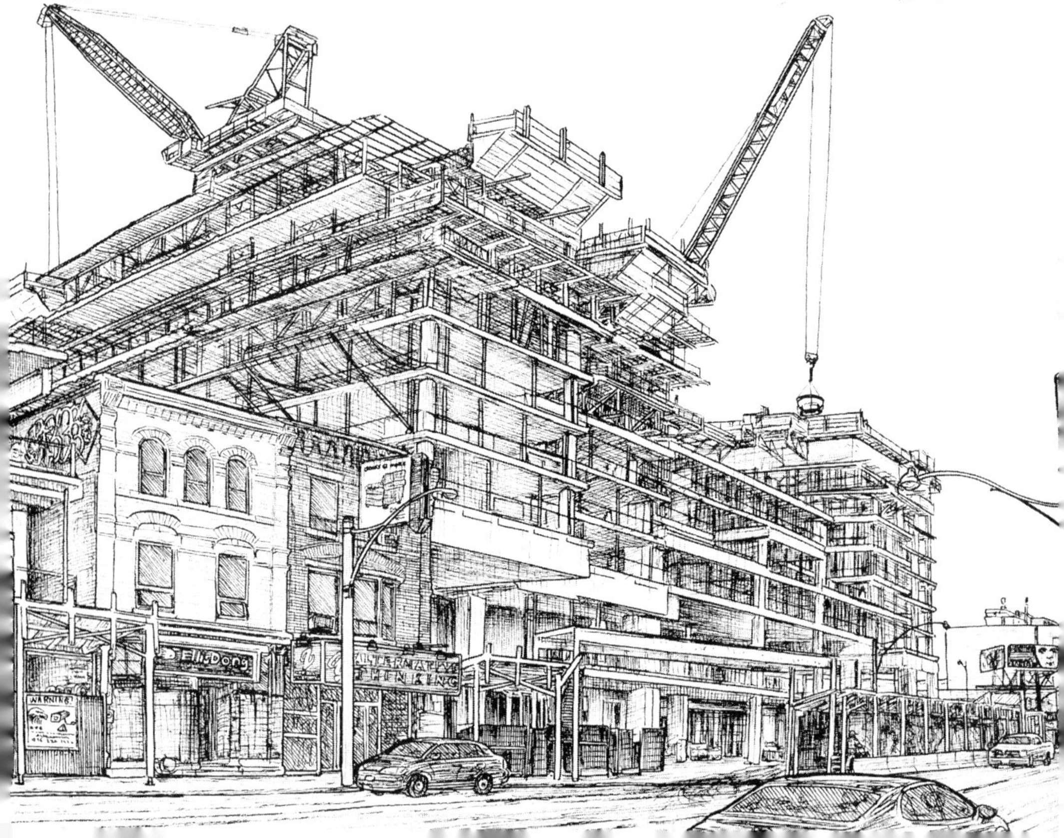

Ellis Dong
ALTERNATIVE THINKING
WARNING!

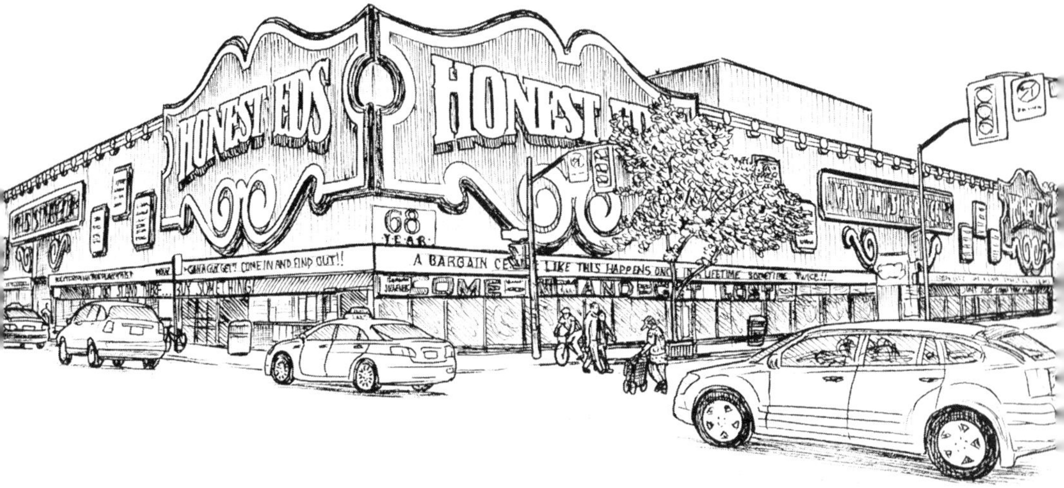
HONEST EDS
HONEST ED
68
YEAR
A BARGAIN CE
LIKE THIS HAPPENS ONC
LIFETIME SOMETIME TWICE!!
COME
AND
LOST
COME IN AND FIND OUT!!
BUY SOMETHING!

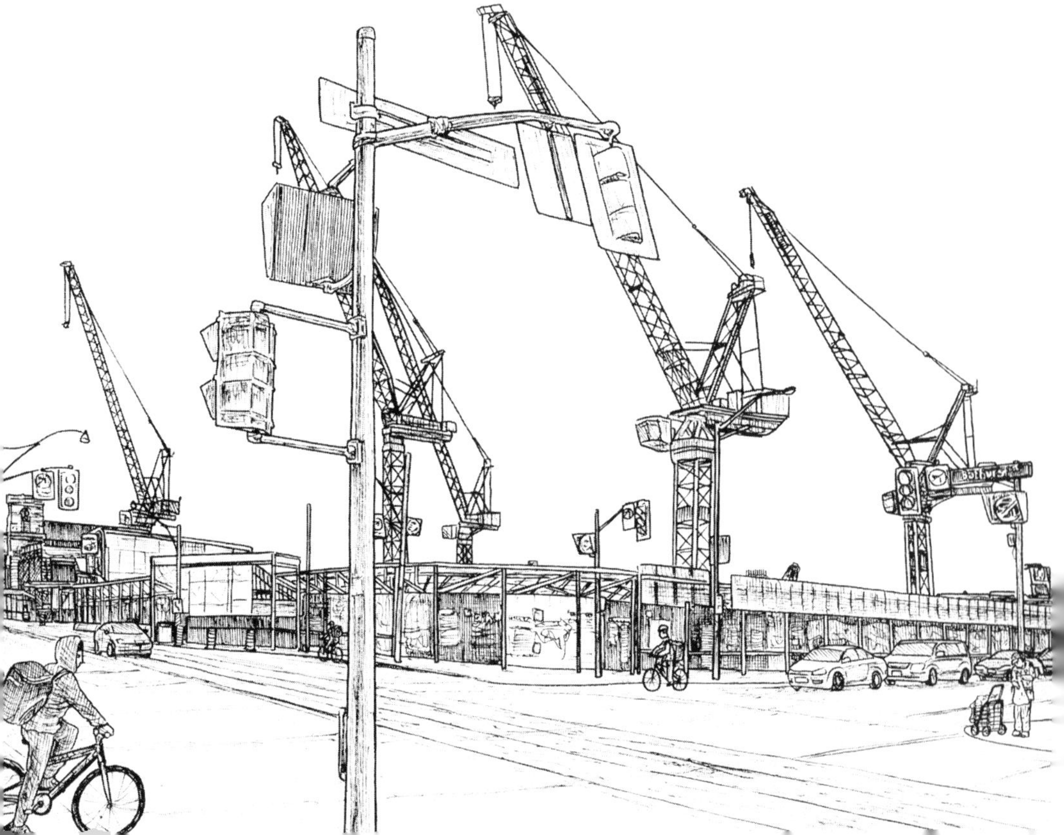

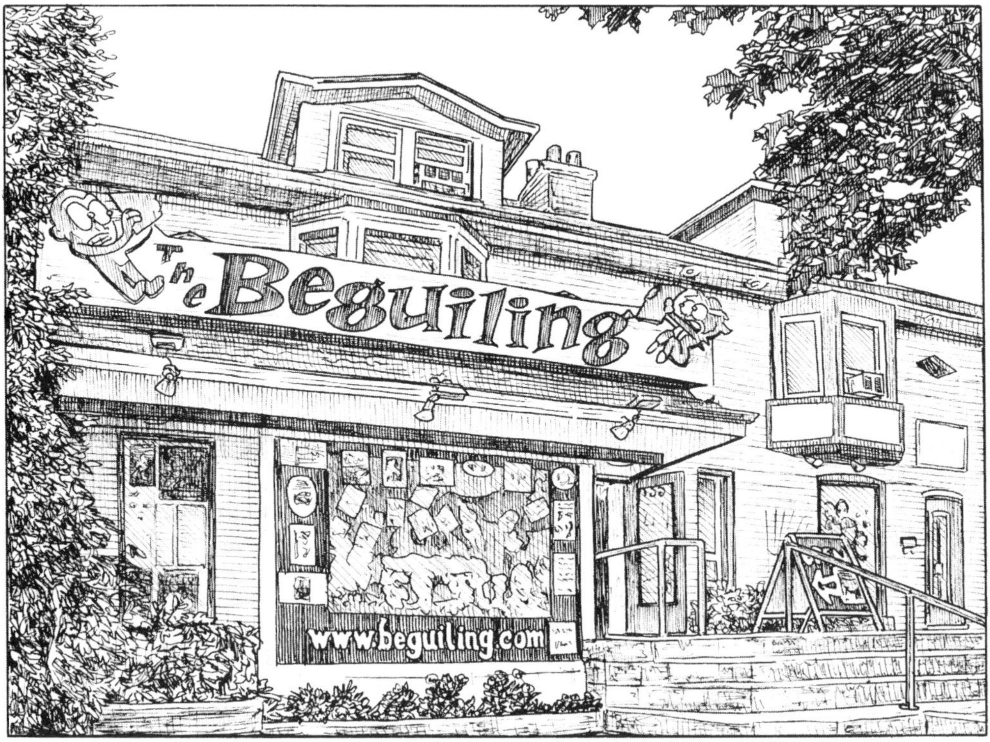
The Beguiling
www.beguiling.com

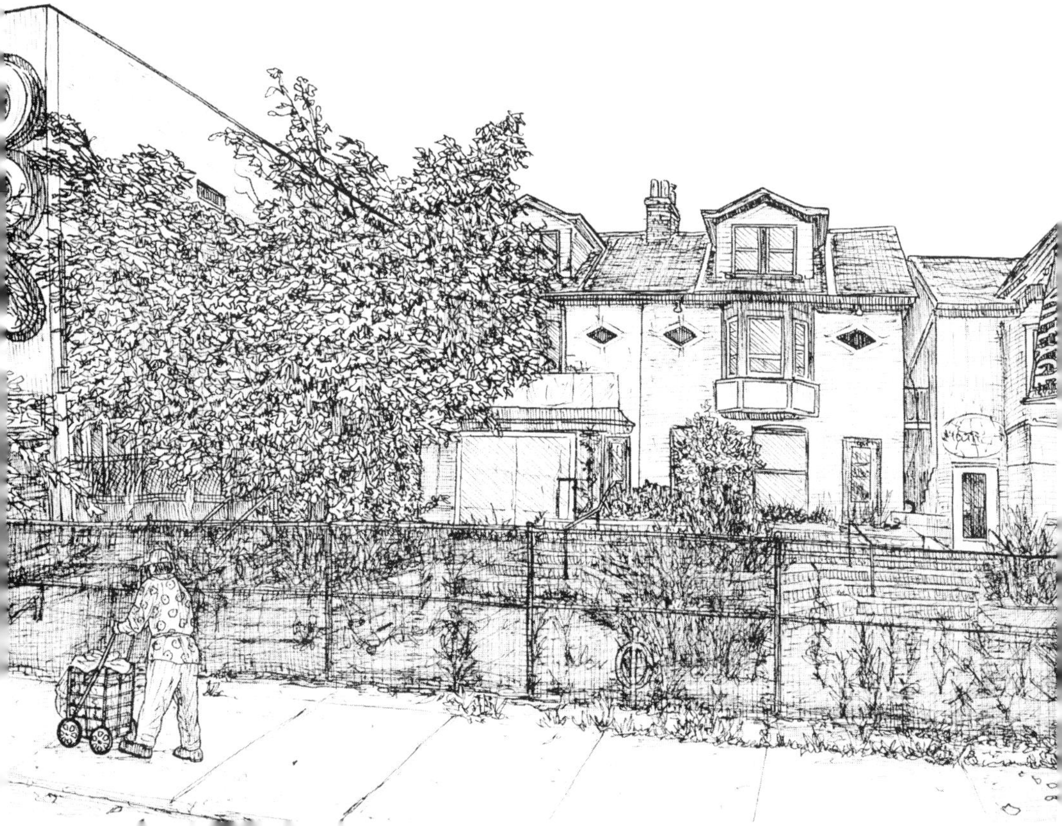

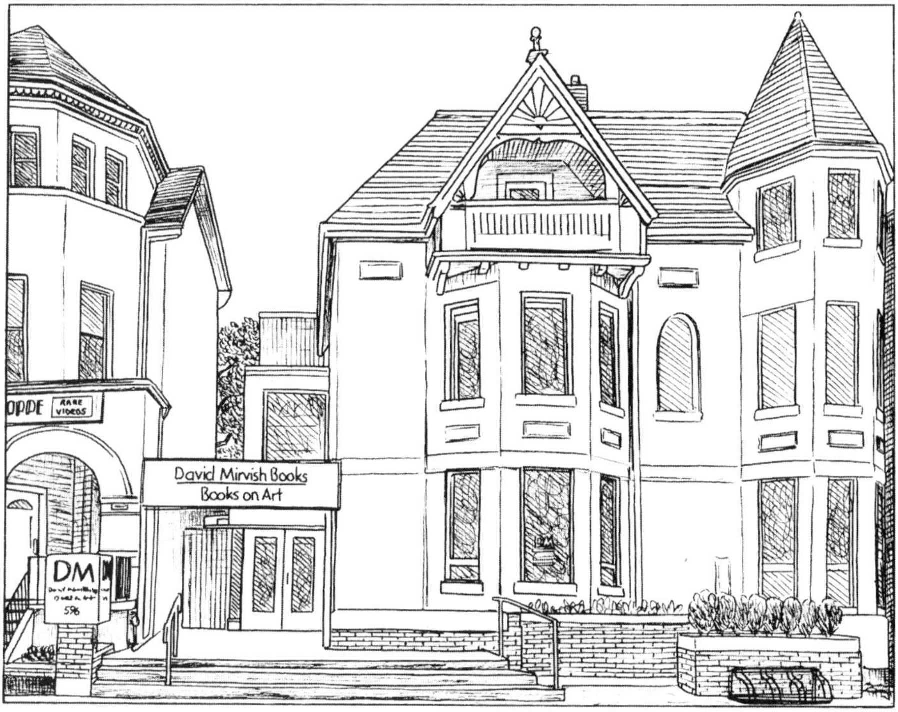
David Mirvish Books
Books on Art
RARE VIDEOS
DM
596

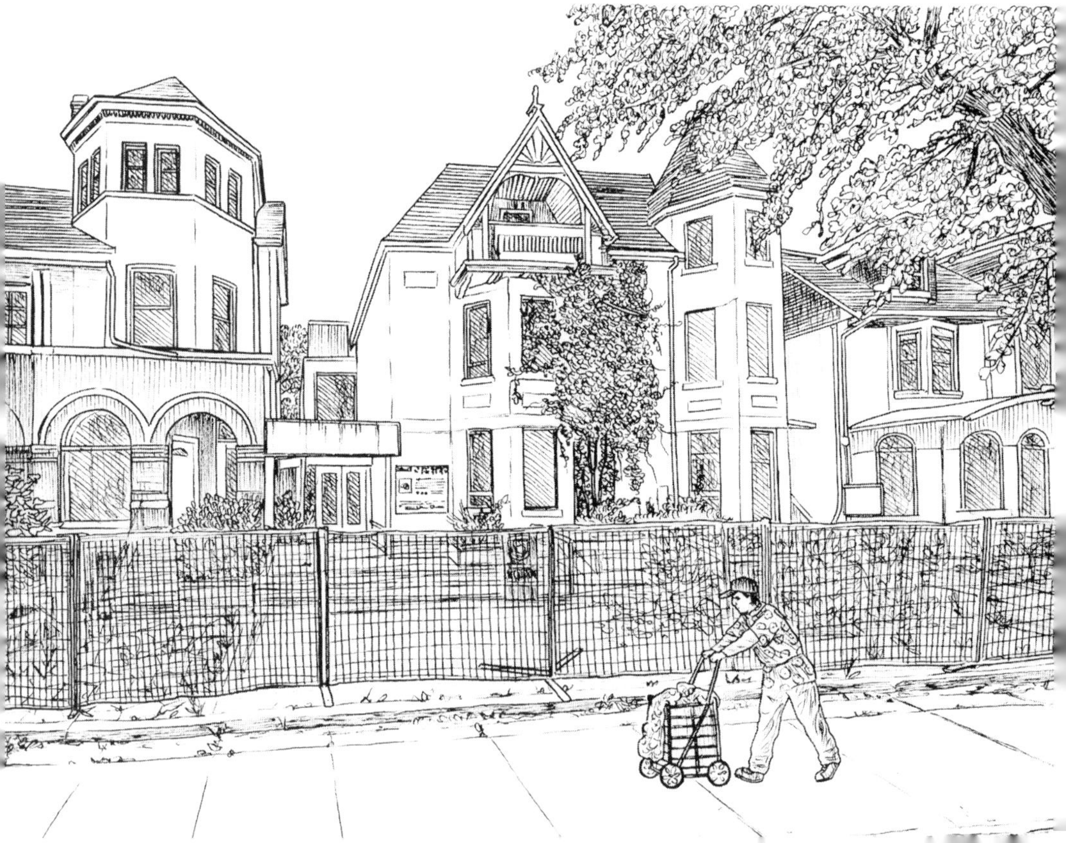

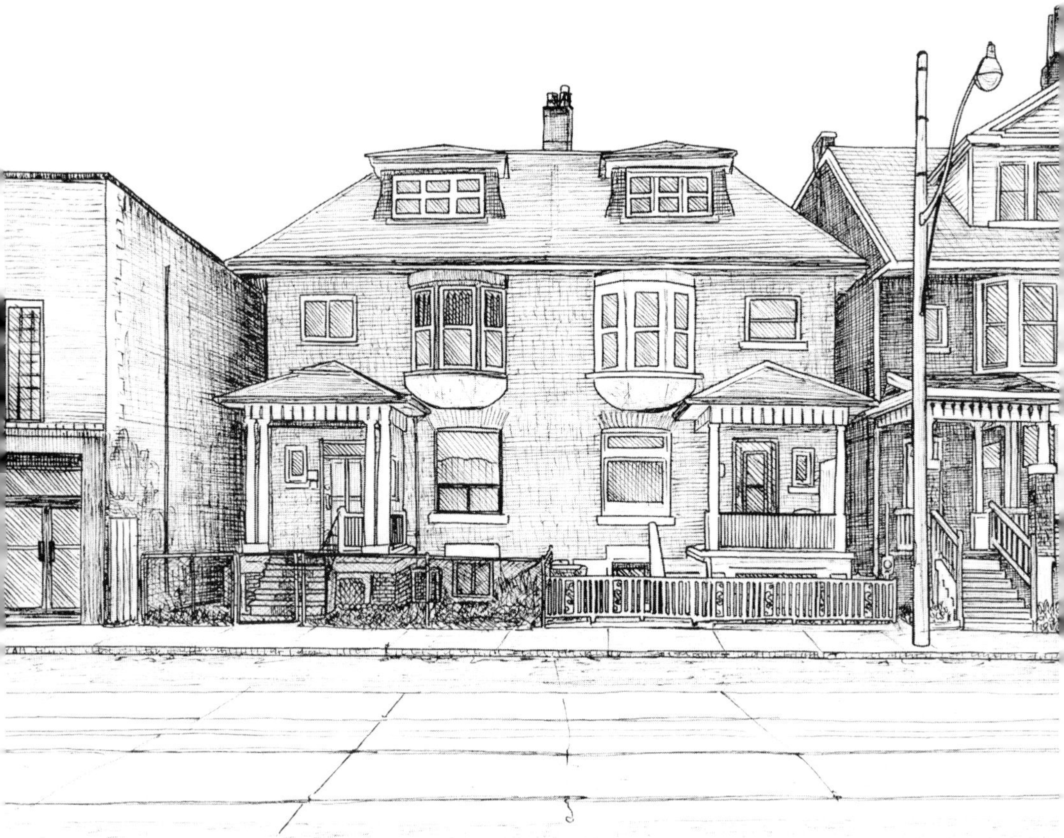

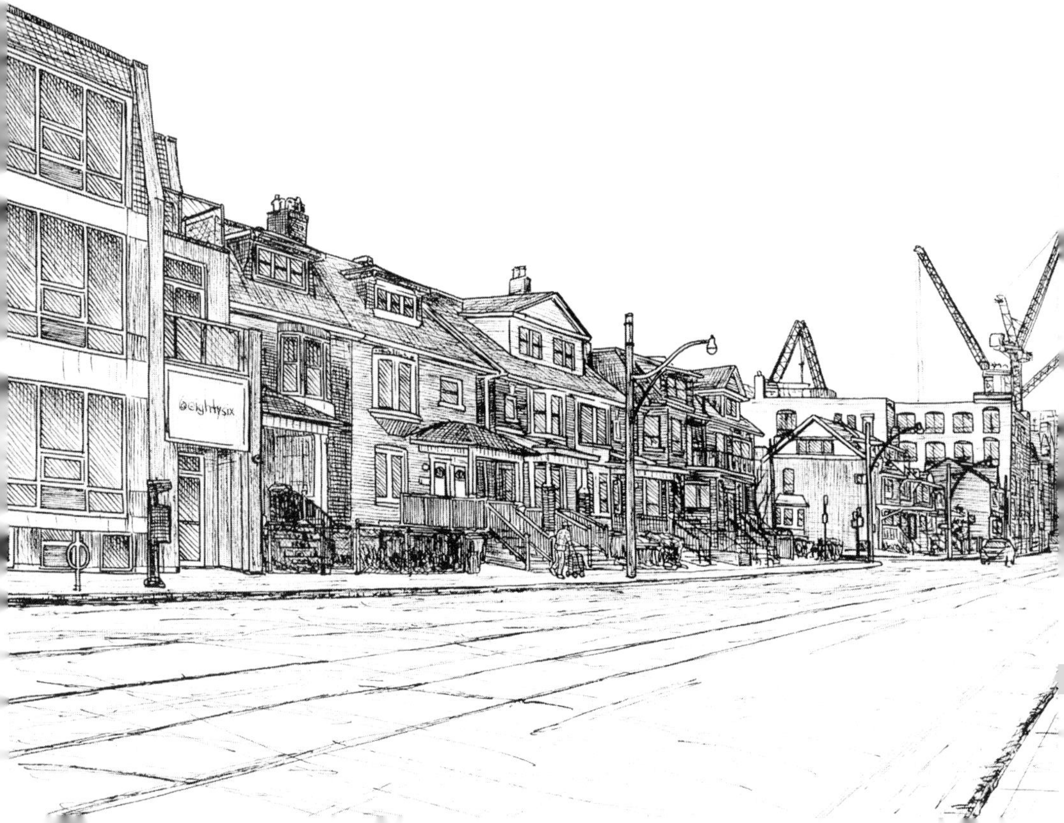
@eightysix

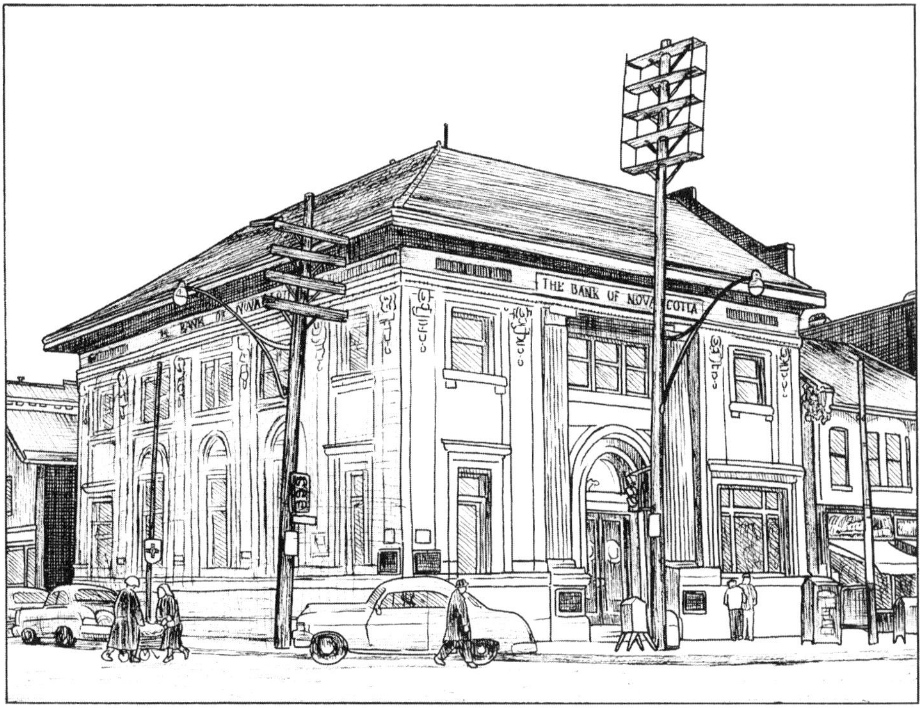
THE BANK OF NOVA SCOTIA

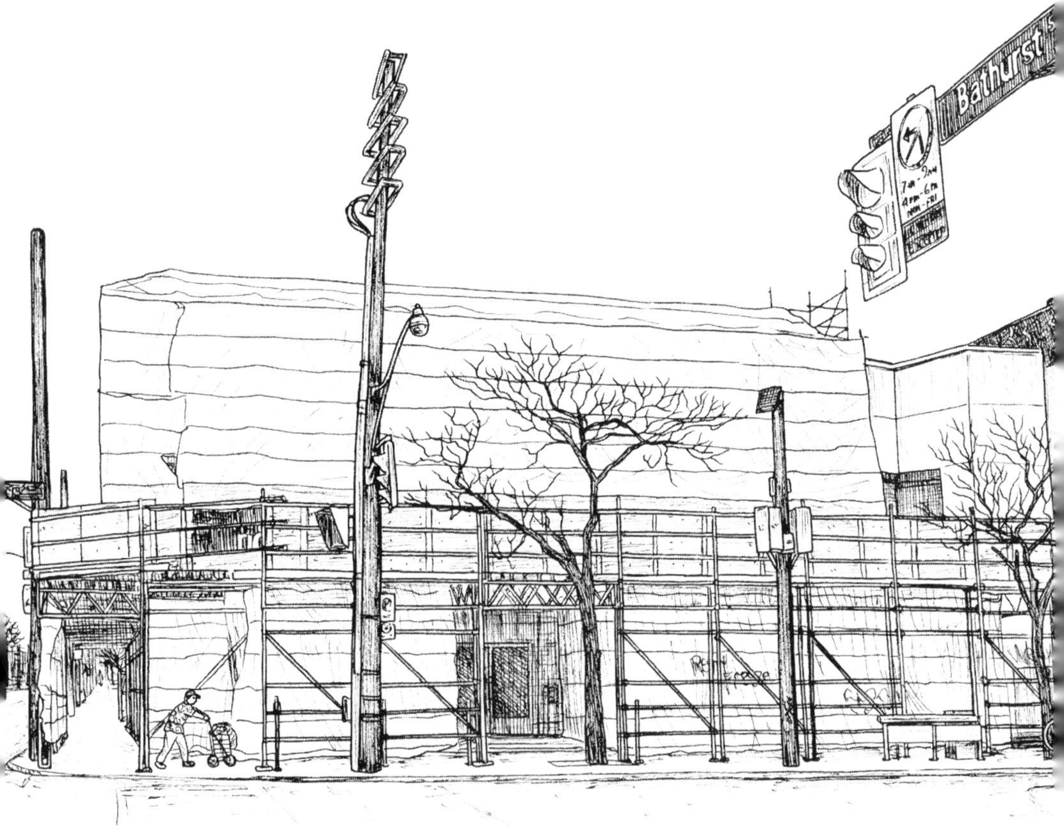
Bathurst
7am - 9am
4pm - 6pm
MON - FRI

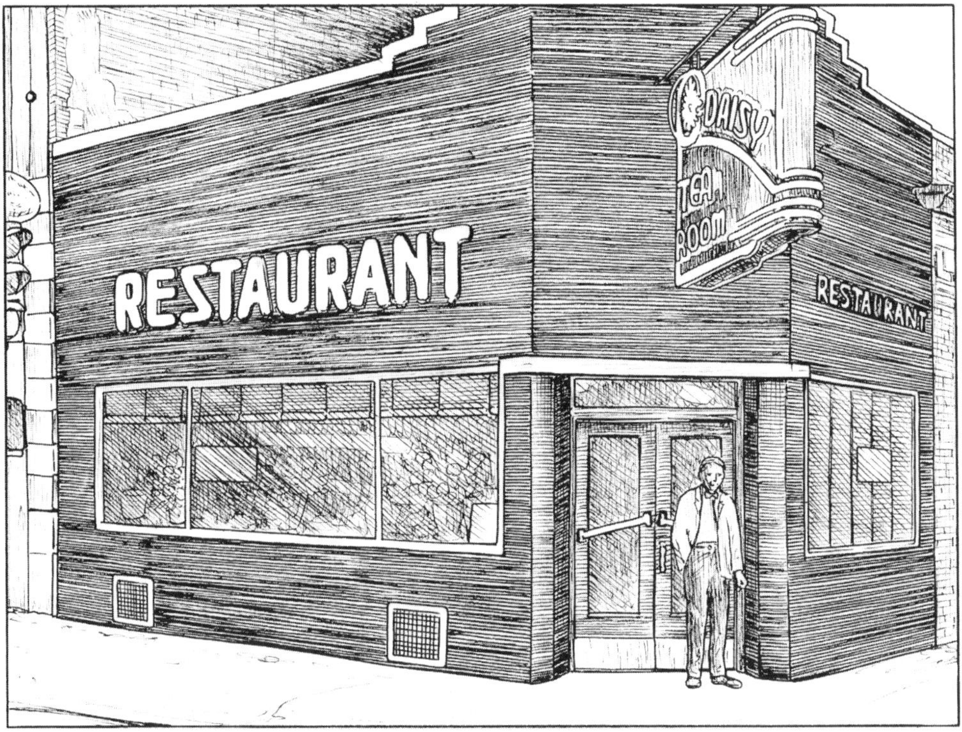

DAISY
TEA ROOM
RESTAURANT
RESTAURANT

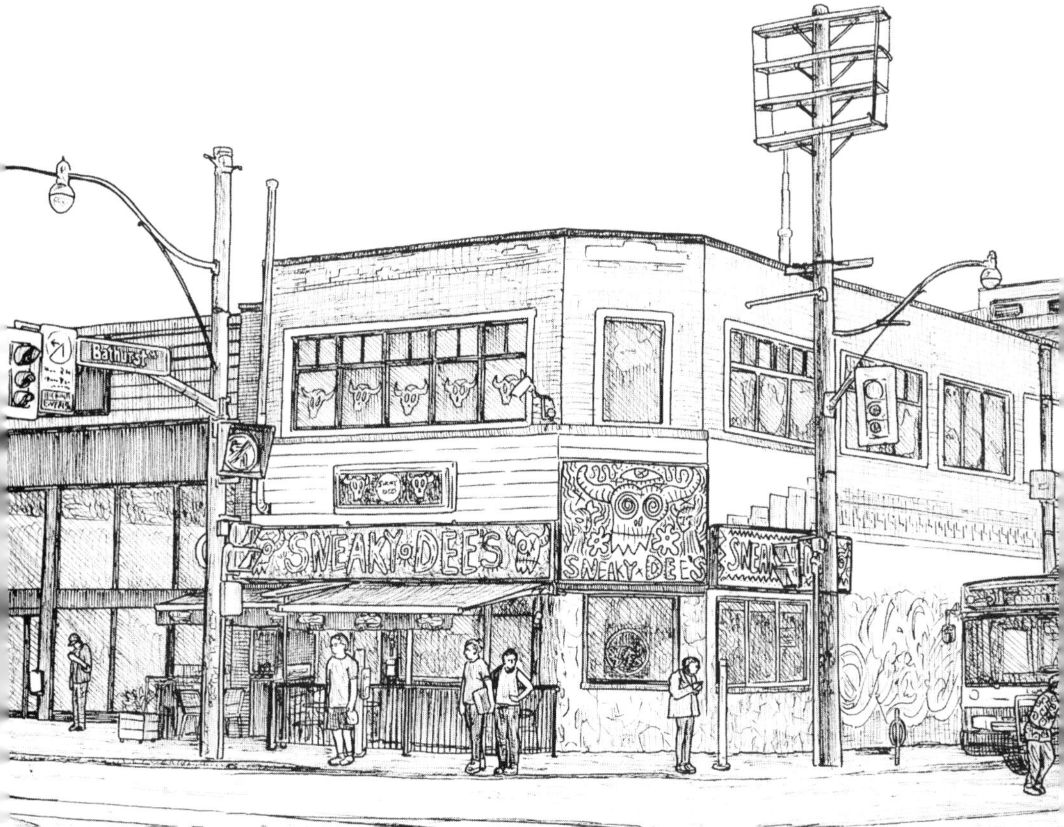

Bathurst St
SNEAKY DEE'S
SNEAKY DEE'S

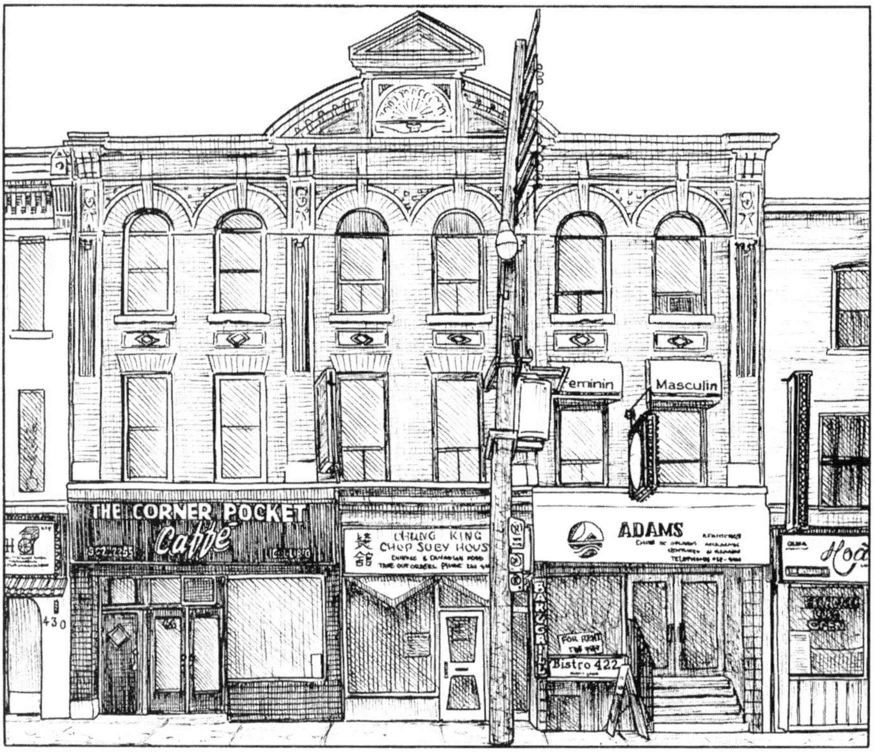
THE CORNER POCKET
Caffé
CHUNG KING
CHOP SUEY HOUS
CHINESE & CANADIAN FOOD
ADAMS
Feminin
Masculin
BAR&GRILL
FOR RENT
Bistro 422
430

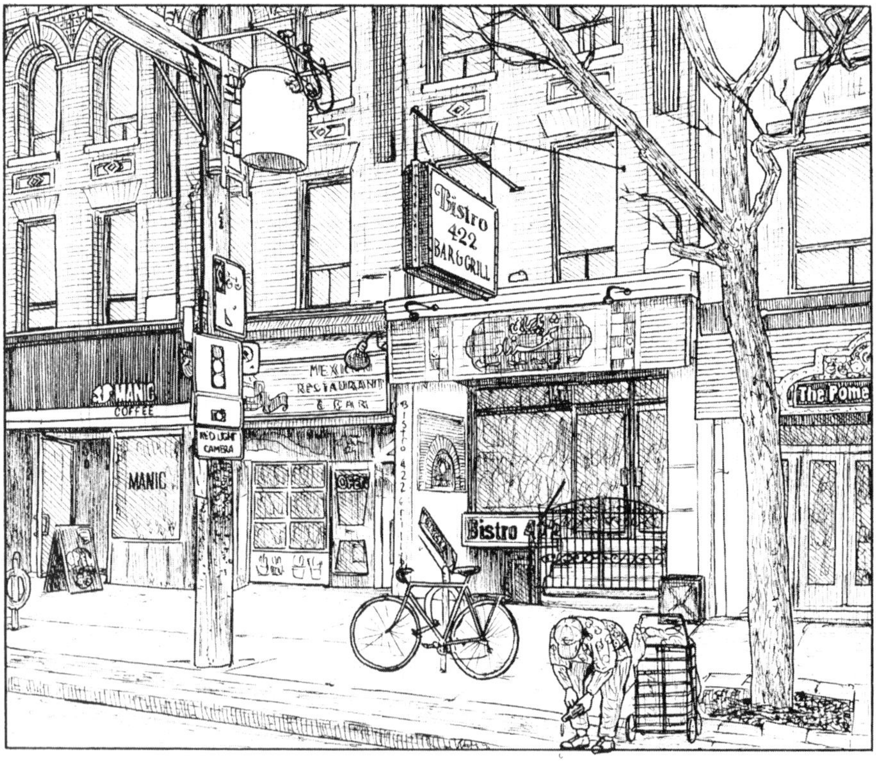
Bistro
422
BAR&GRILL
MEXICAN
RESTAURANT
& CAFE
MANIC
COFFEE
MANIC
RED LIGHT
CAMERA
OPEN
Bistro 422
The Pome

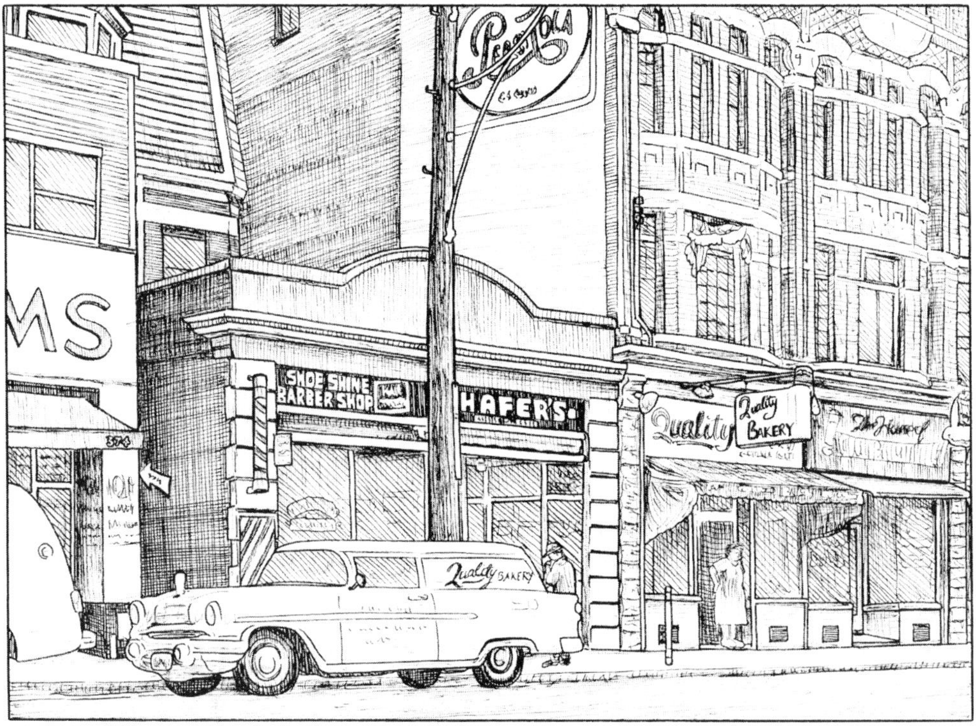
SHOE SHINE
BARBER SHOP
HAFERS
Quality
Quality BAKERY
Quality BAKERY

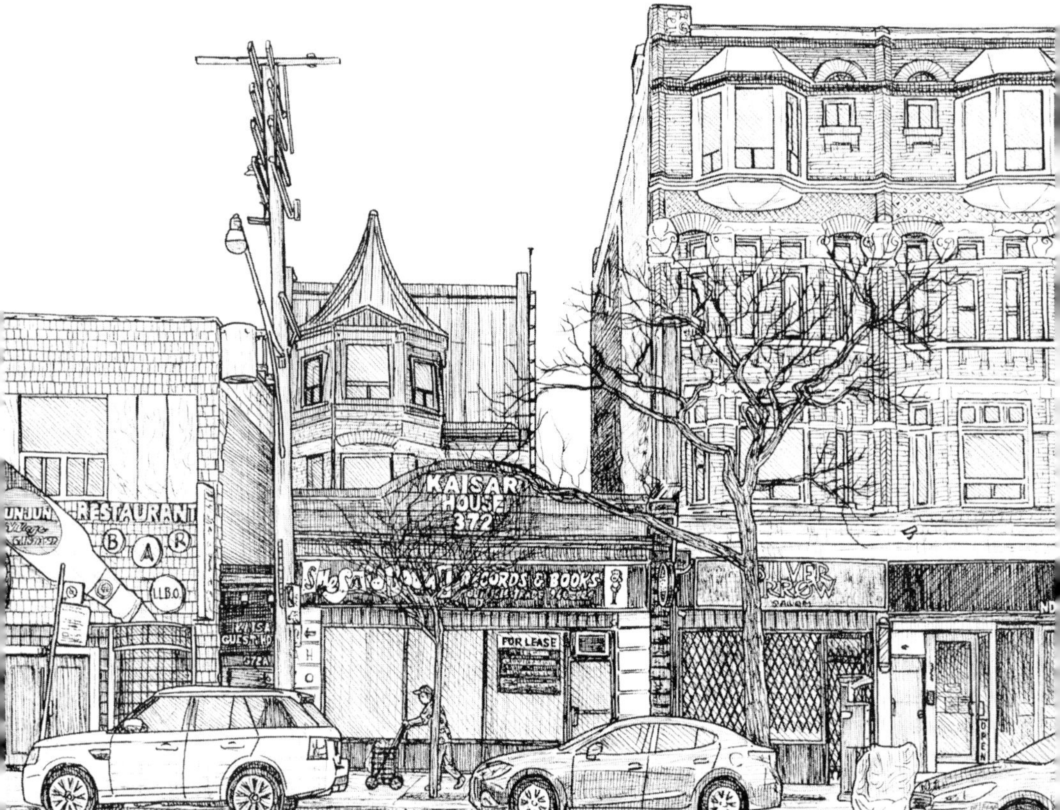
KAISAR HOUSE 372
RECORDS & BOOKS
FOR LEASE
RESTAURANT
B A R
L.L.B.O.
OPEN

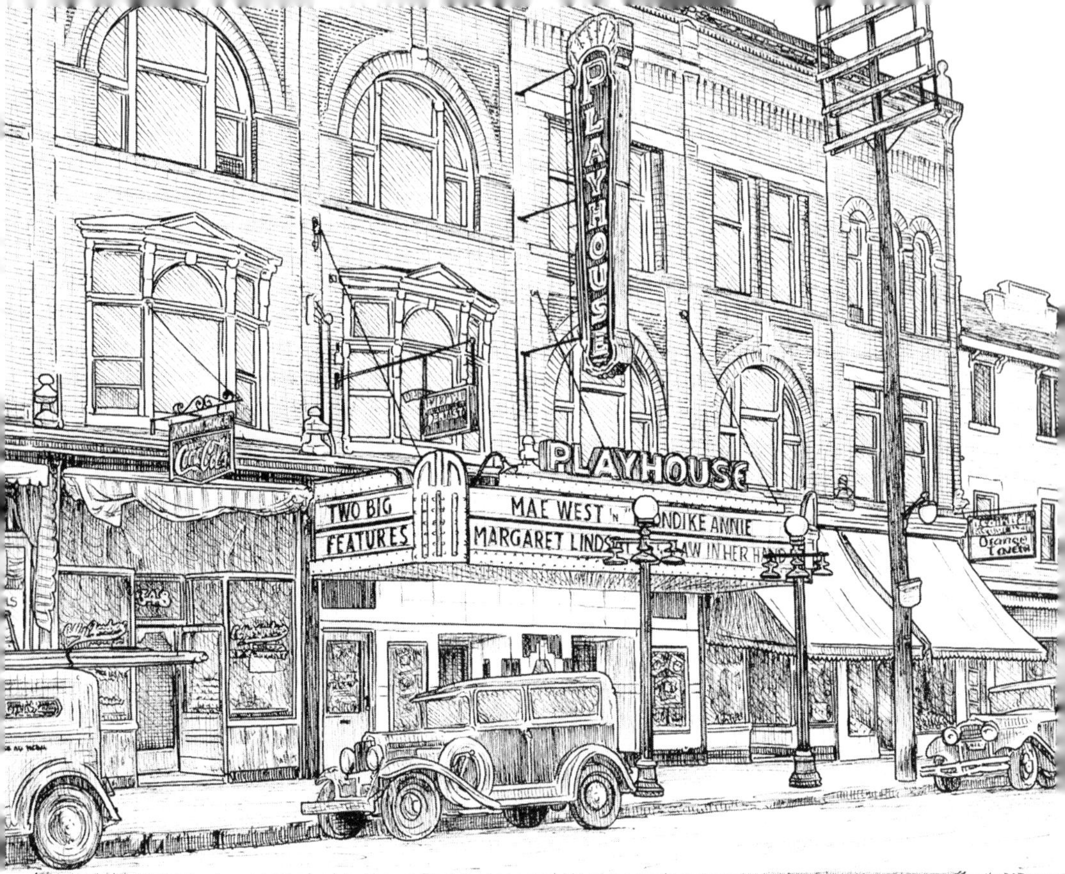
PLAYHOUSE
PLAYHOUSE
TWO BIG FEATURES
MAE WEST 'N' ...NDIKE ANNIE
MARGARET LINDS... ...AW IN HER HAND
Coca-Cola
Orange Crush

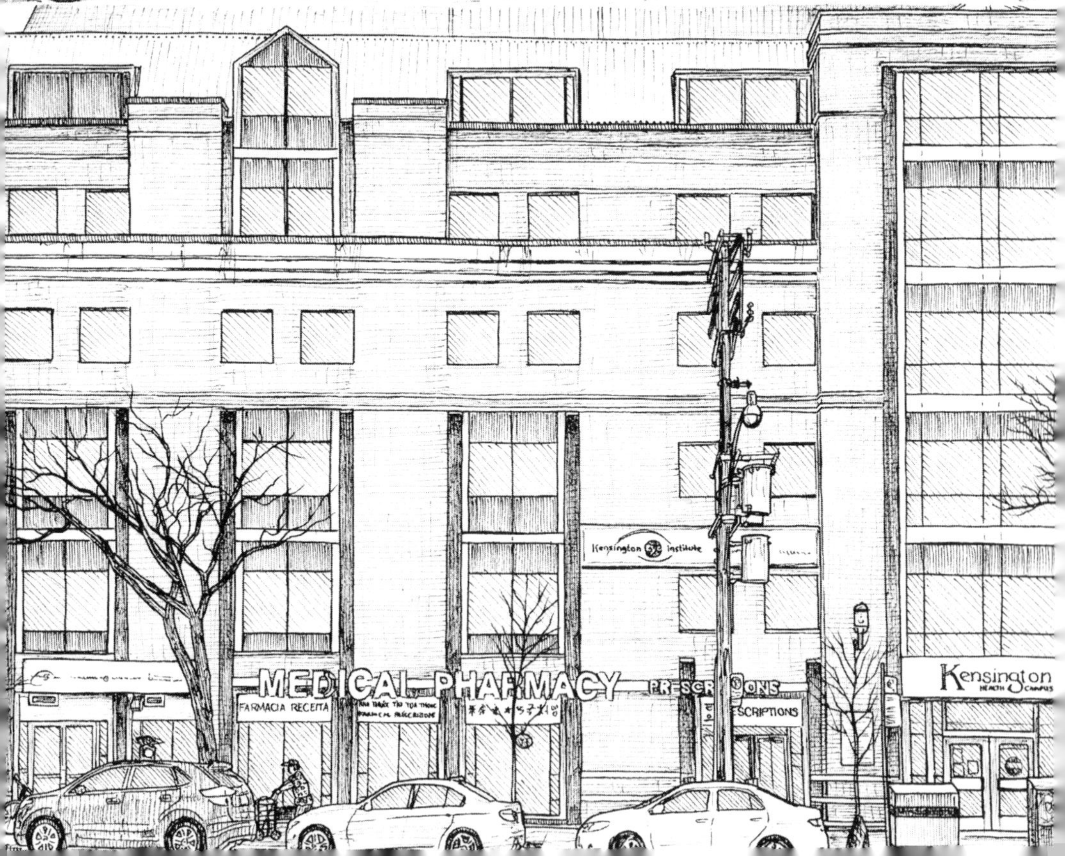
MEDICAL PHARMACY
PRESCRIPTIONS
FARMACIA RECEITA
PRESCRIPTIONS
Kensington institute
Kensington HEALTH CAMPUS

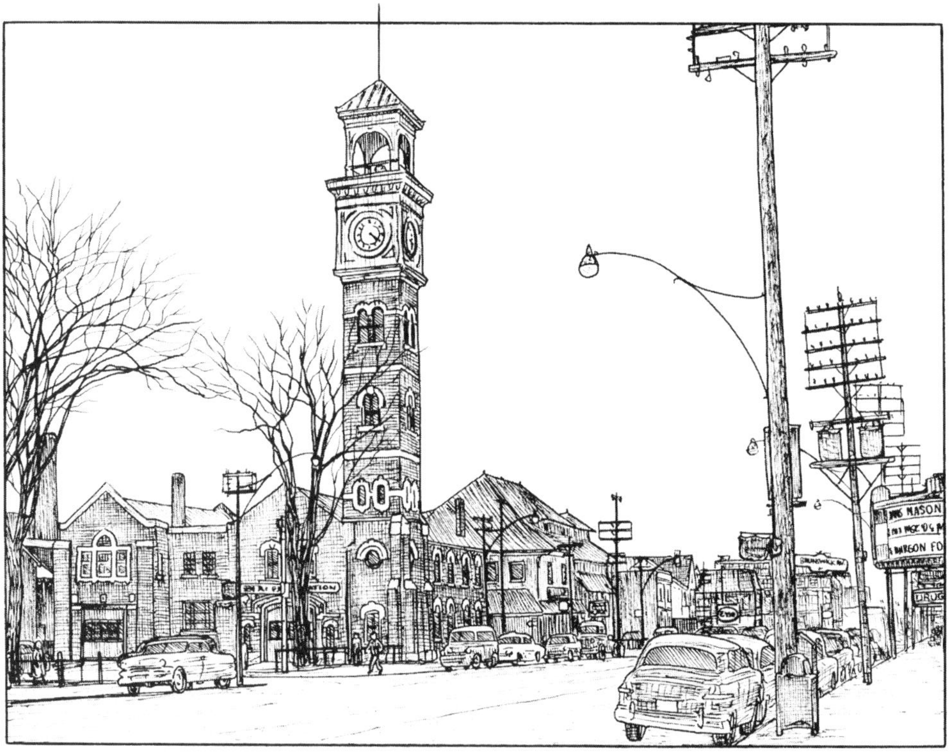
MASON
DRUG

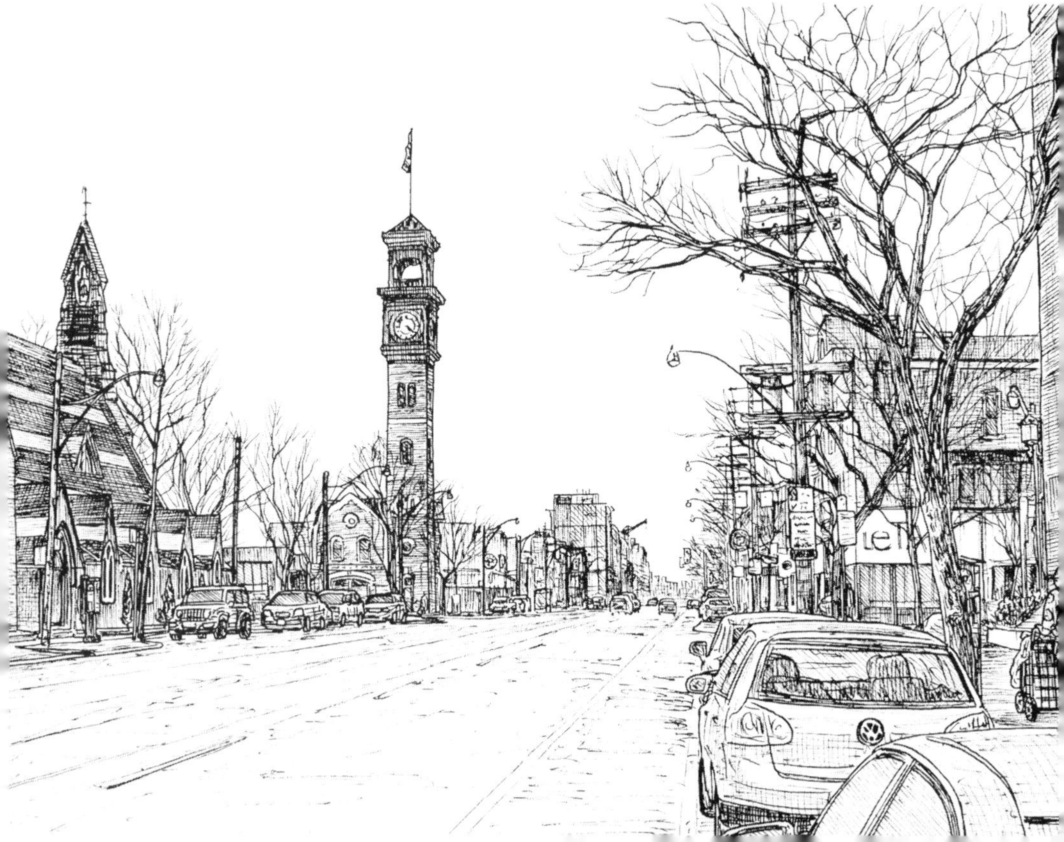

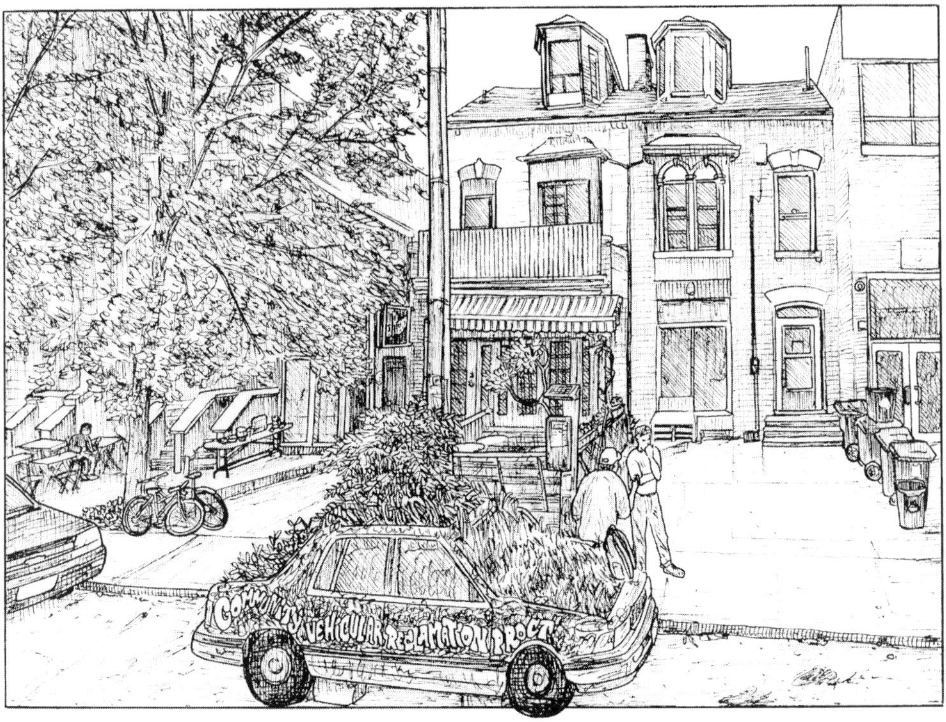
COMMUNITY VEHICULAR RECLAMATION PROJECT

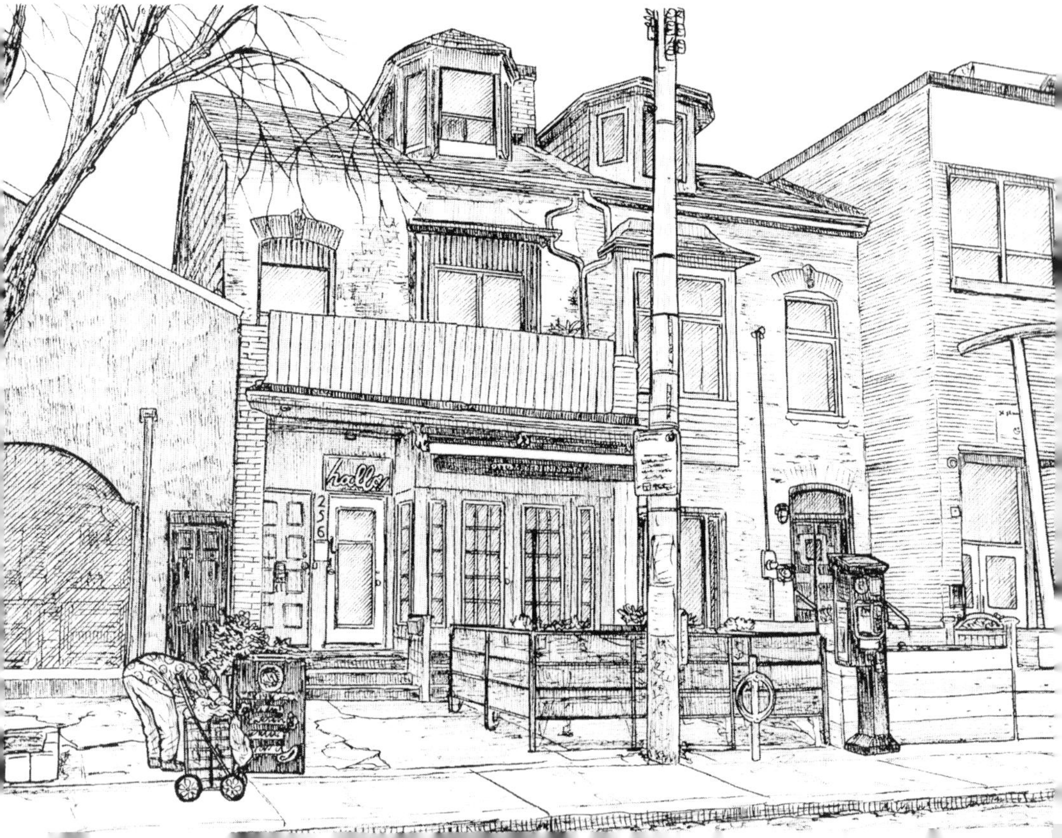
hallo
256

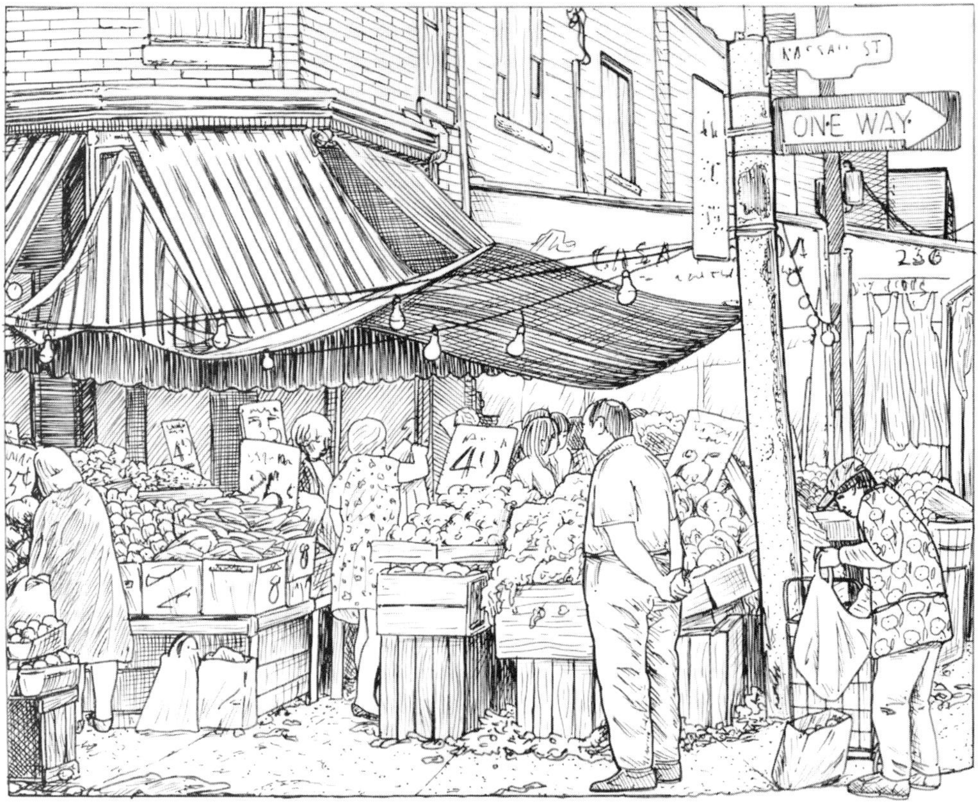
NASSAU ST
ONE WAY
236

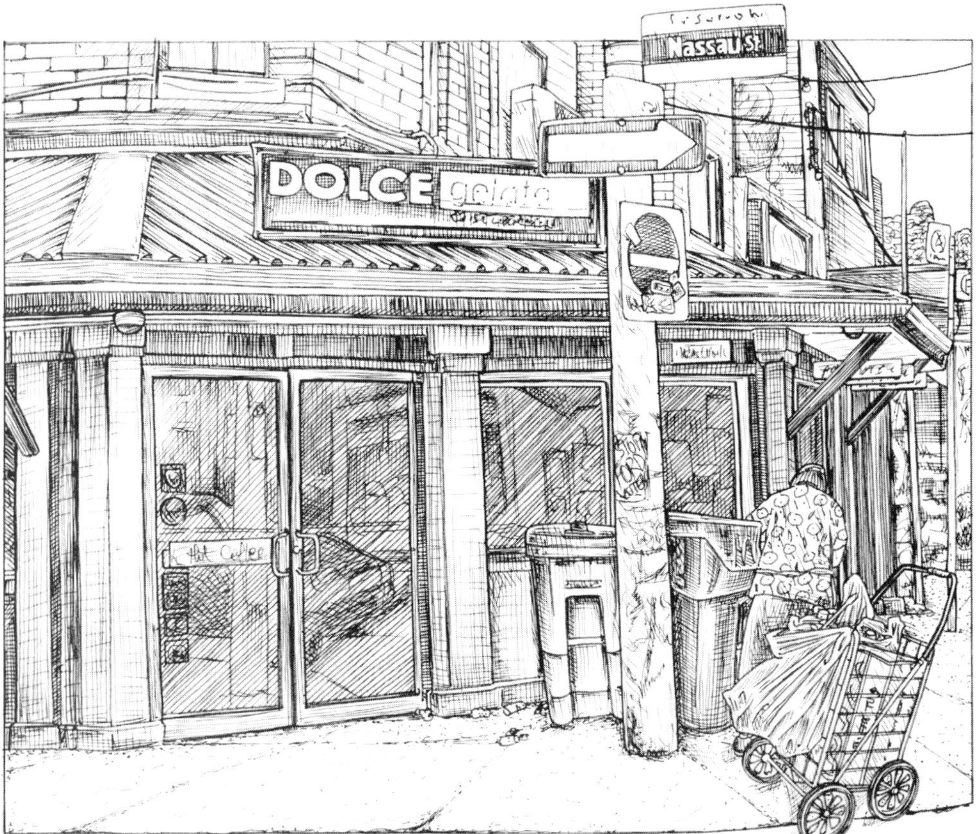
Nassau St
DOLCE gelato

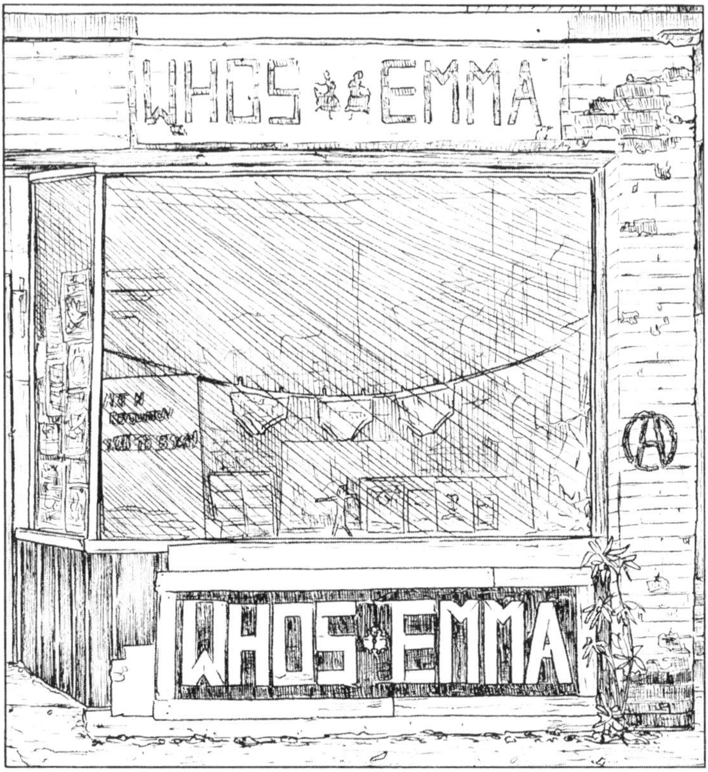
WHOS EMMA
WHOS EMMA

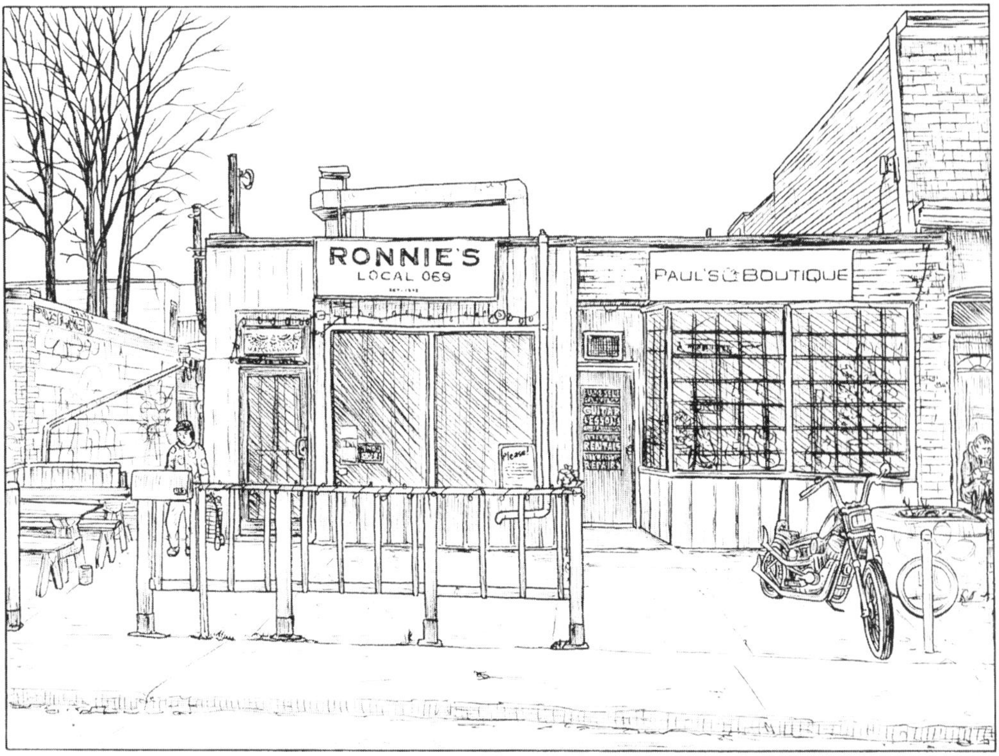
RONNIE'S
LOCAL 069
PAUL'S BOUTIQUE

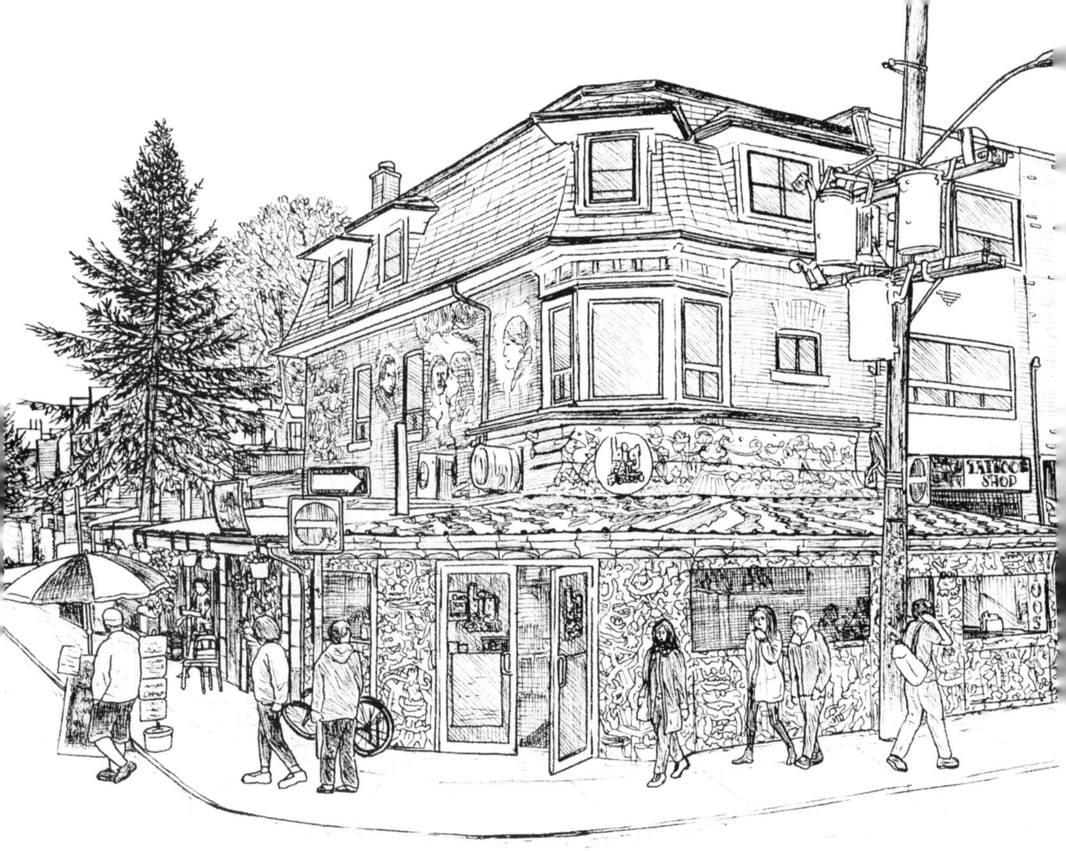
TATTOO SHOP

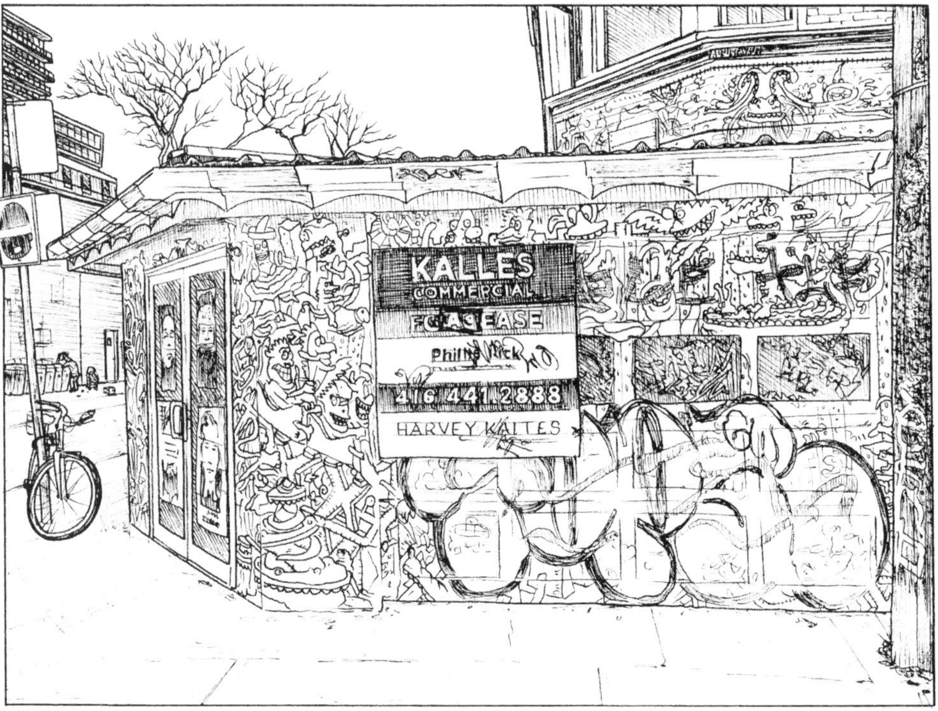
KALLES
COMMERCIAL
FOR LEASE
416 441 2888
HARVEY KALLES

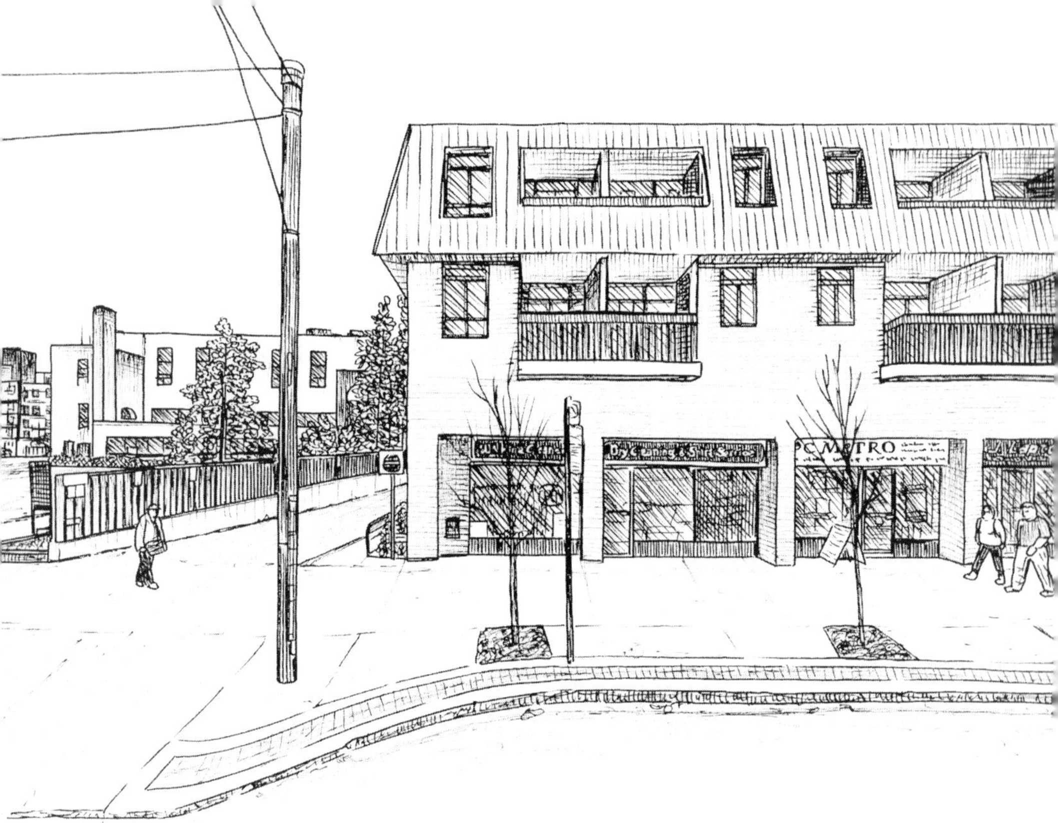
PC METRO

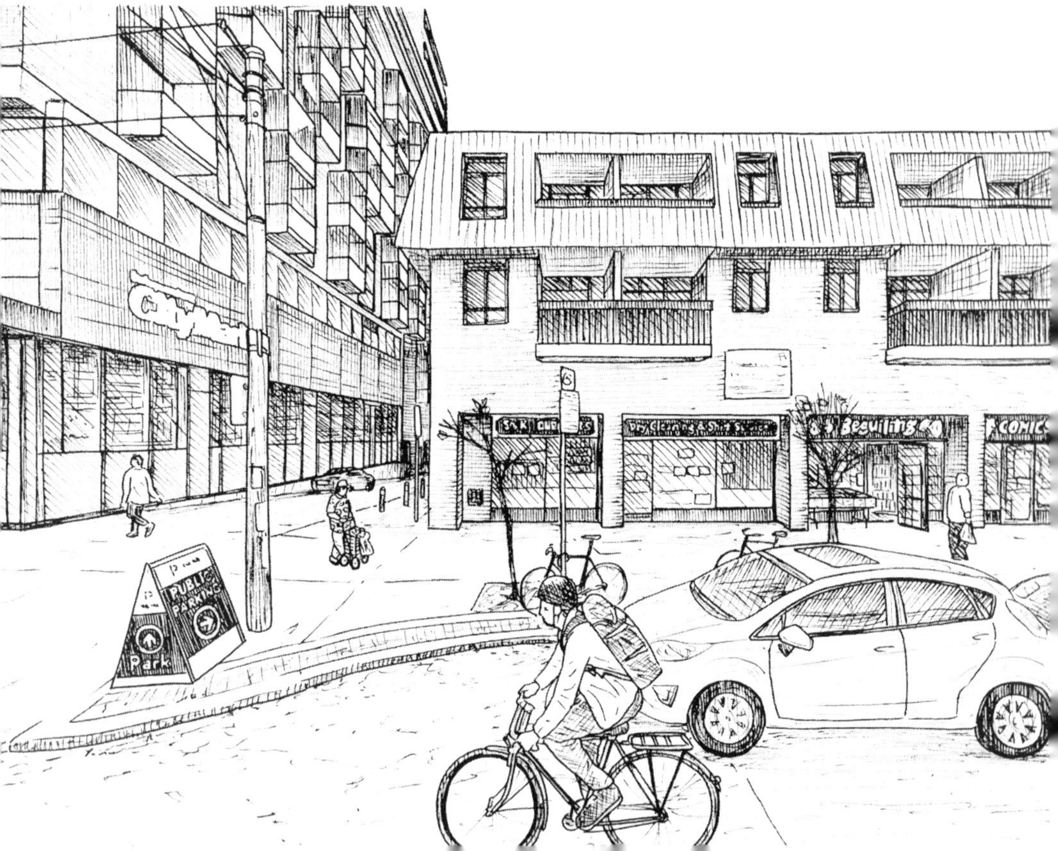
PUBLIC PARKING
Park
COMICS

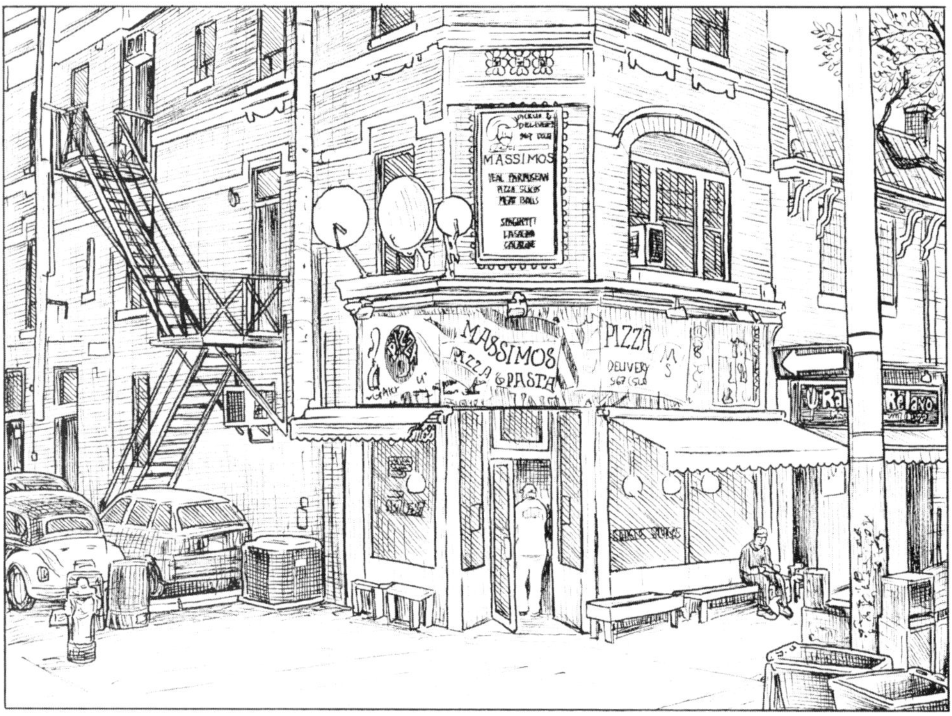
MASSIMOS
VEAL PARMESAN
PIZZA SLICES
MEAT BALLS
MASSIMOS
PIZZA & PASTA
PIZZA
DELIVERY

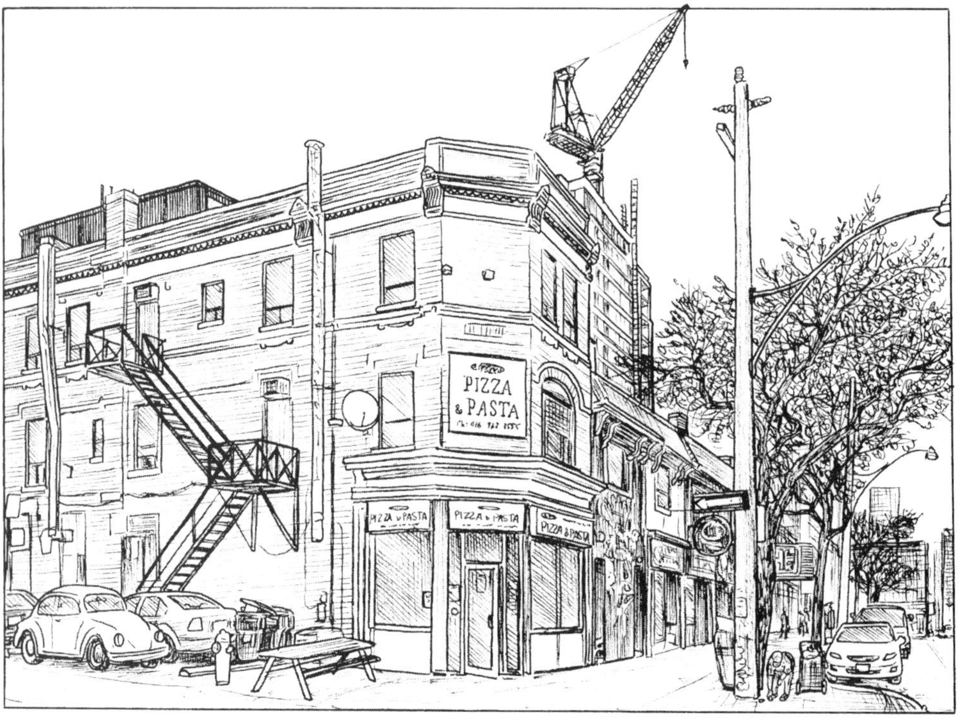
PIZZA & PASTA
PIZZA & PASTA
PIZZA & PASTA
PIZZA & PASTA

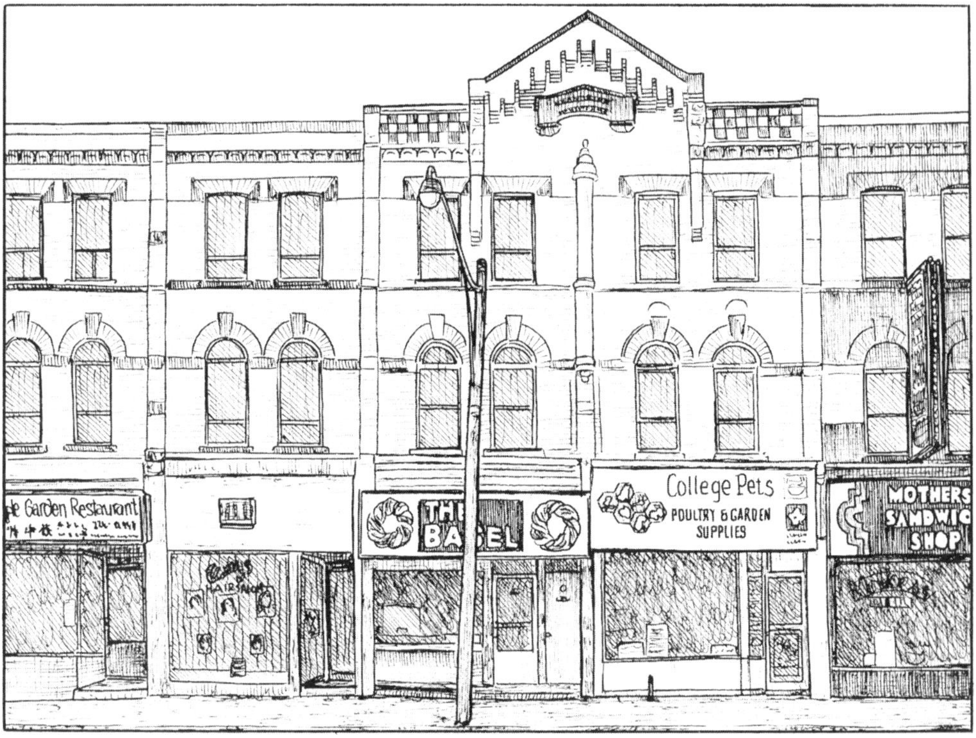

le Garden Restaurant
THE BAGEL
College Pets
POULTRY & GARDEN SUPPLIES
MOTHERS SANDWIC SHOP

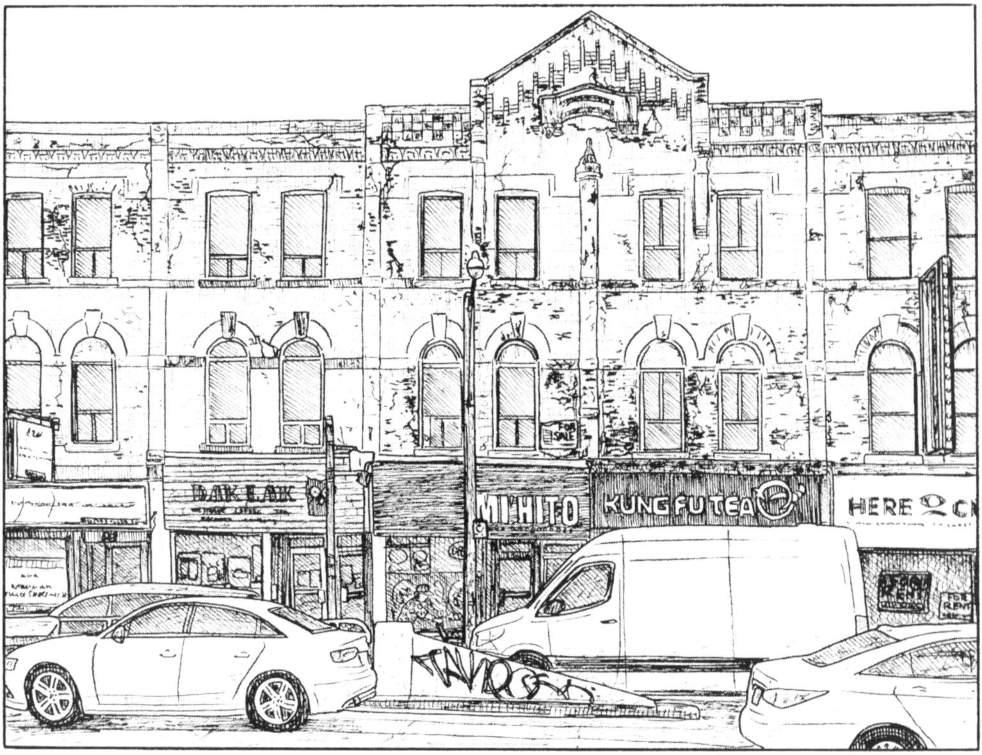

DAK LAK
FOR SALE
MIHITO
KUNG FU TEA
HERE C

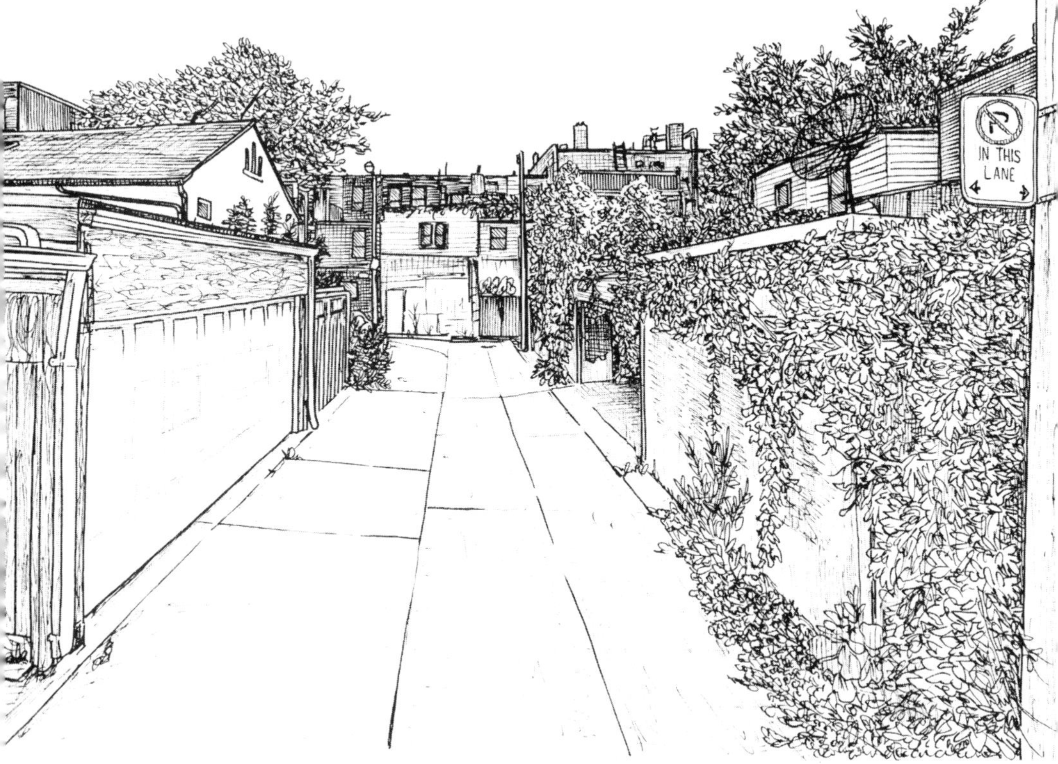
IN THIS
LANE

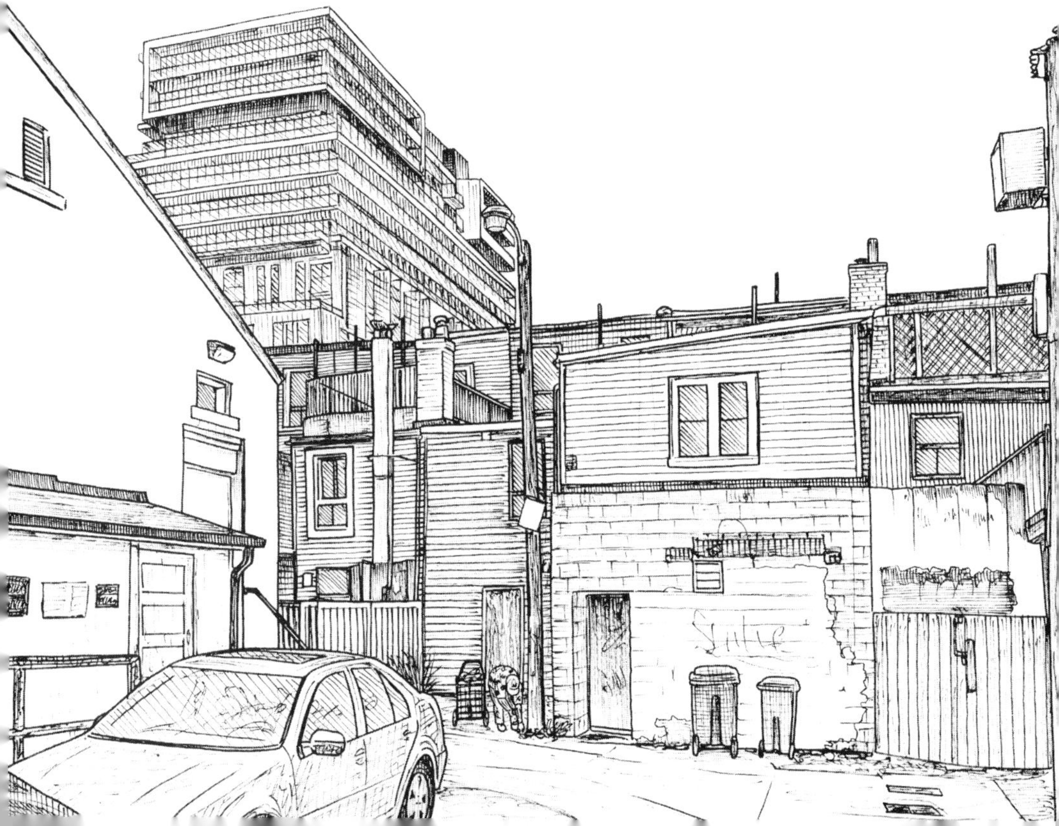

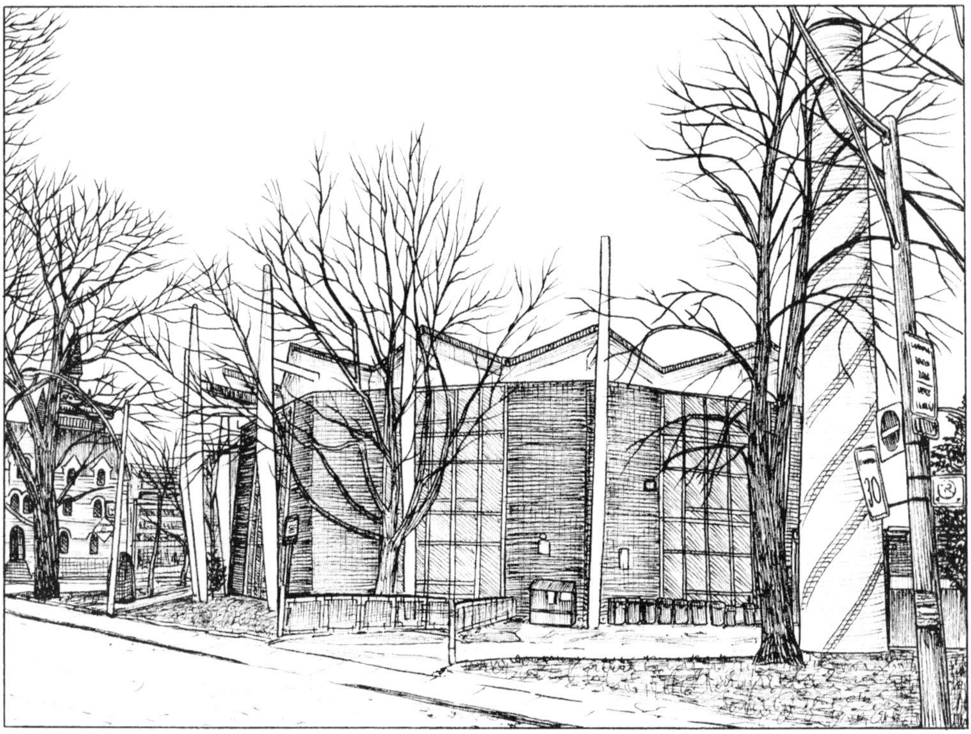
30

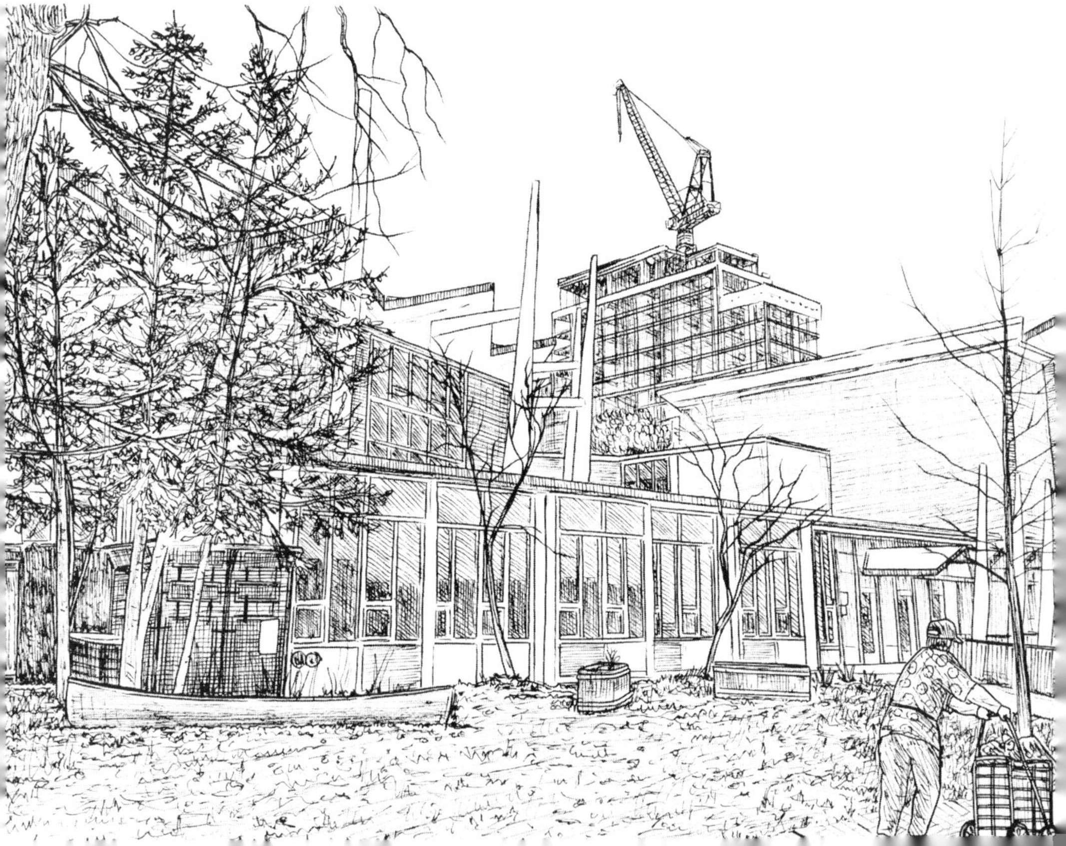

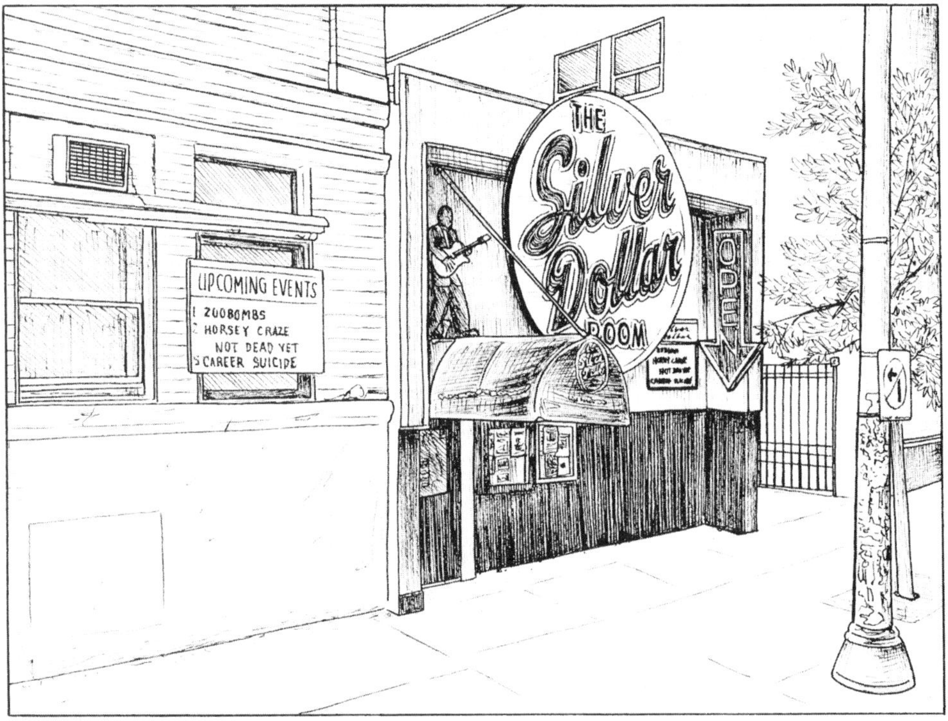
THE
Silver Dollar
ROOM
OPEN
UPCOMING EVENTS
1 ZOOBOMBS
2 HORSEY CRAZE
NOT DEAD YET
3 CAREER SUICIDE

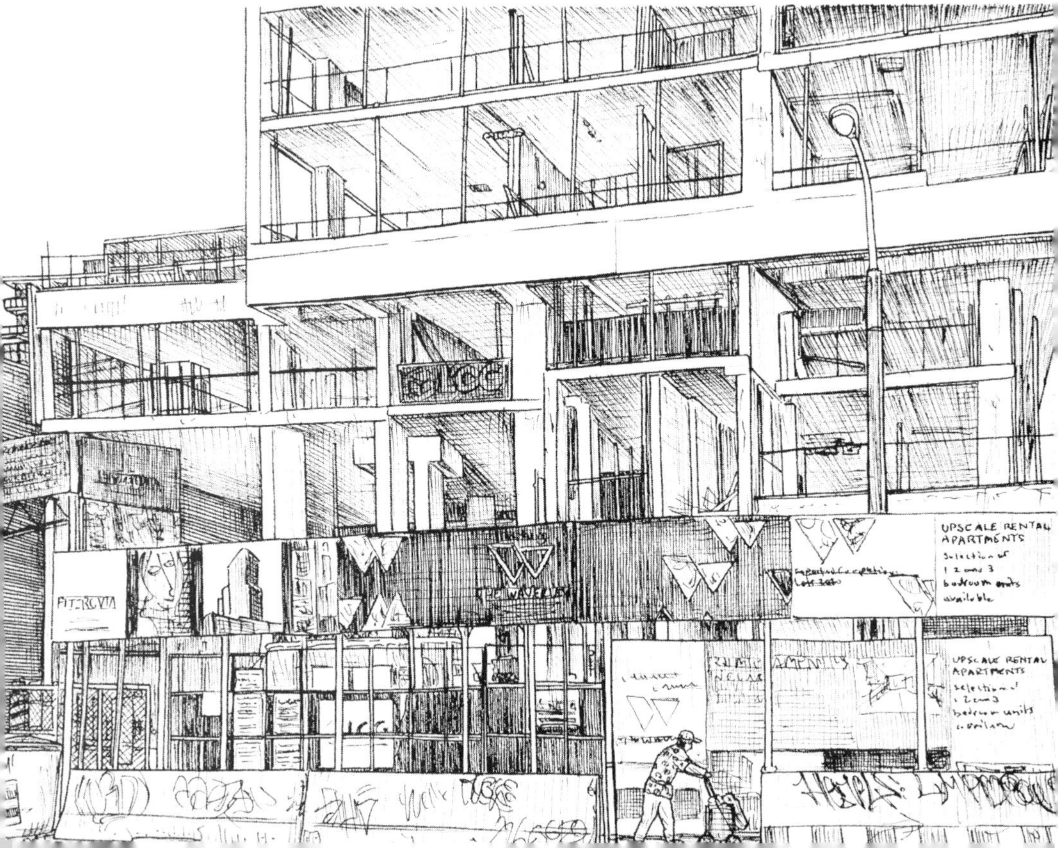
FITZROVIA
THE WAVERLEY
UPSCALE RENTAL APARTMENTS
Selection of
1 2 and 3
bedroom units
available
UPSCALE RENTAL APARTMENTS
selection of
1 2 and 3
bedroom units
available

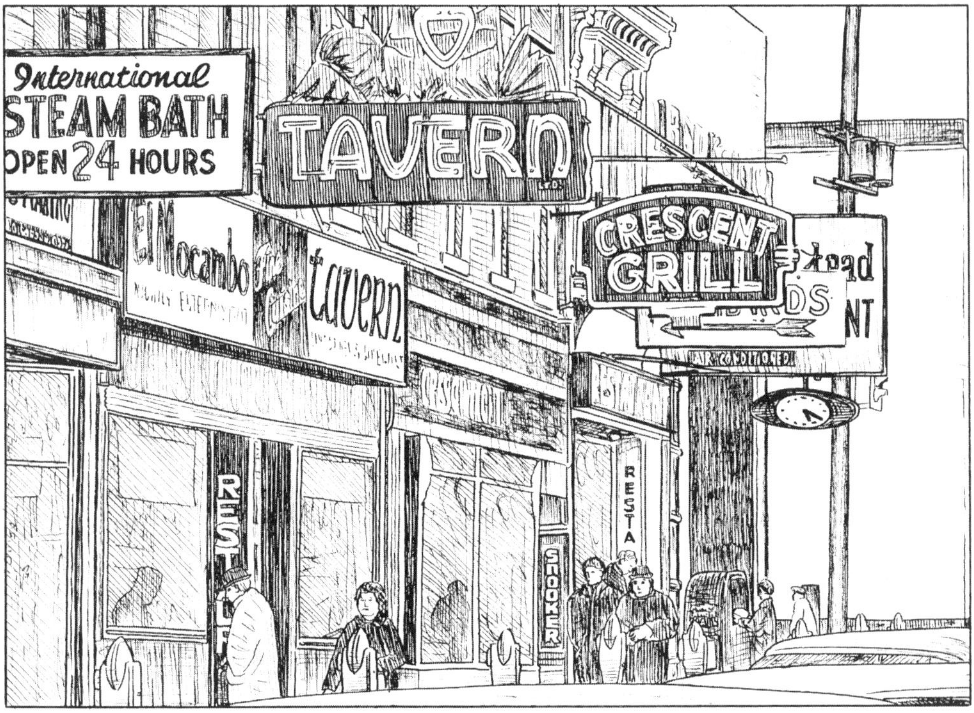
International
STEAM BATH
OPEN 24 HOURS
TAVERN
El Mocambo
TAVERN
CRESCENT
GRILL
AIR CONDITIONED
SNOOKER
RESTA

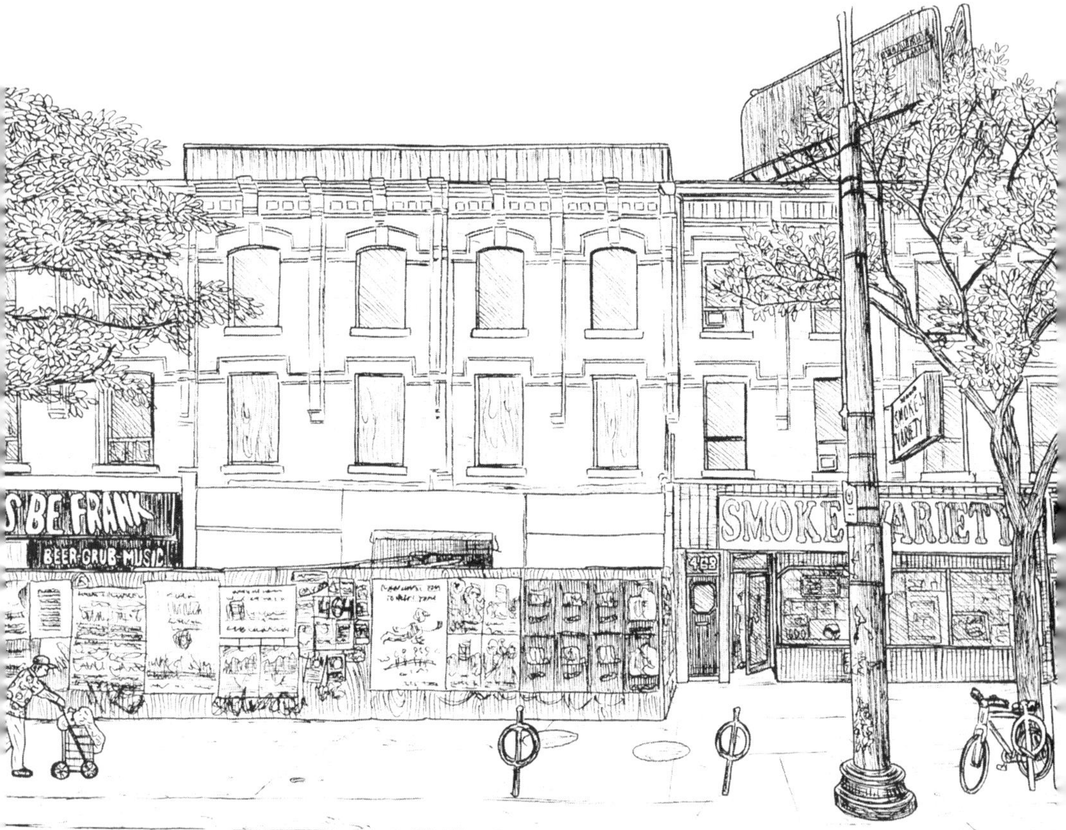
BE FRANK
BEER-GRUB-MUSIC
SMOKE VARIETY
468
SMOKE VARIETY

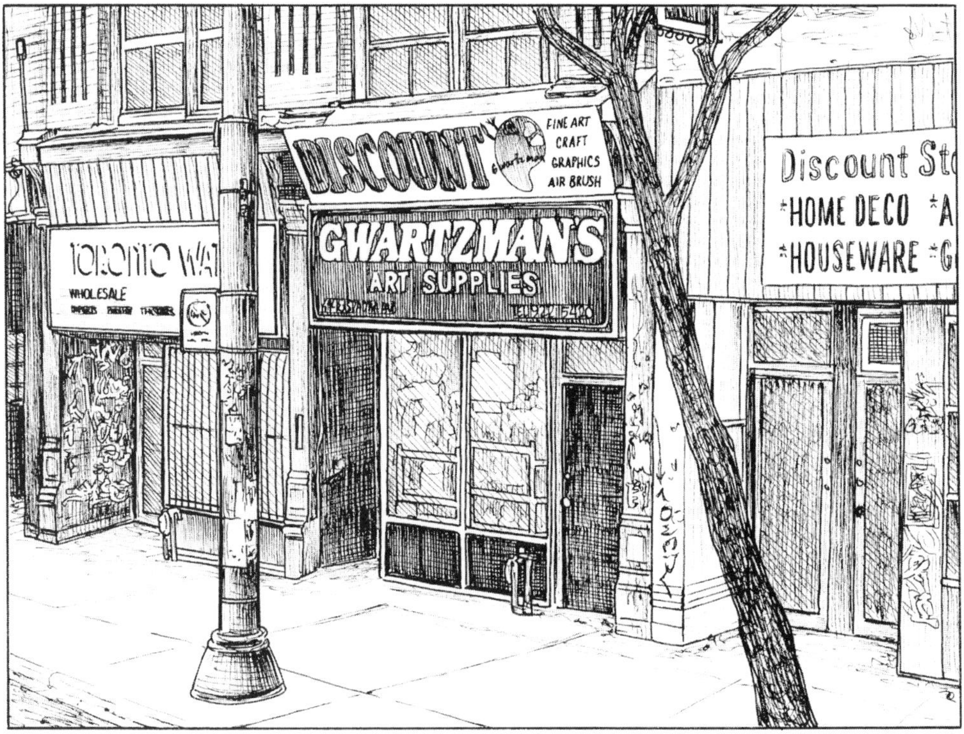
DISCOUNT
FINE ART
CRAFT
GRAPHICS
AIR BRUSH
GWARTZMAN'S
ART SUPPLIES
TORONTO WA
WHOLESALE
Discount St
*HOME DECO *A
*HOUSEWARE *G

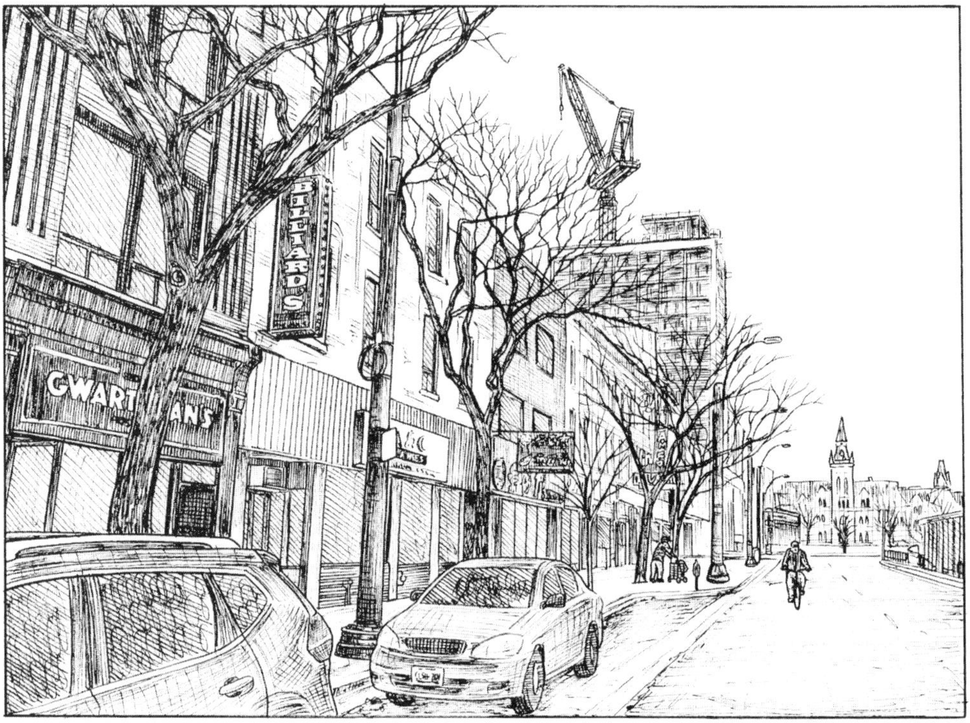
BILLIARDS
GWARTZMANS

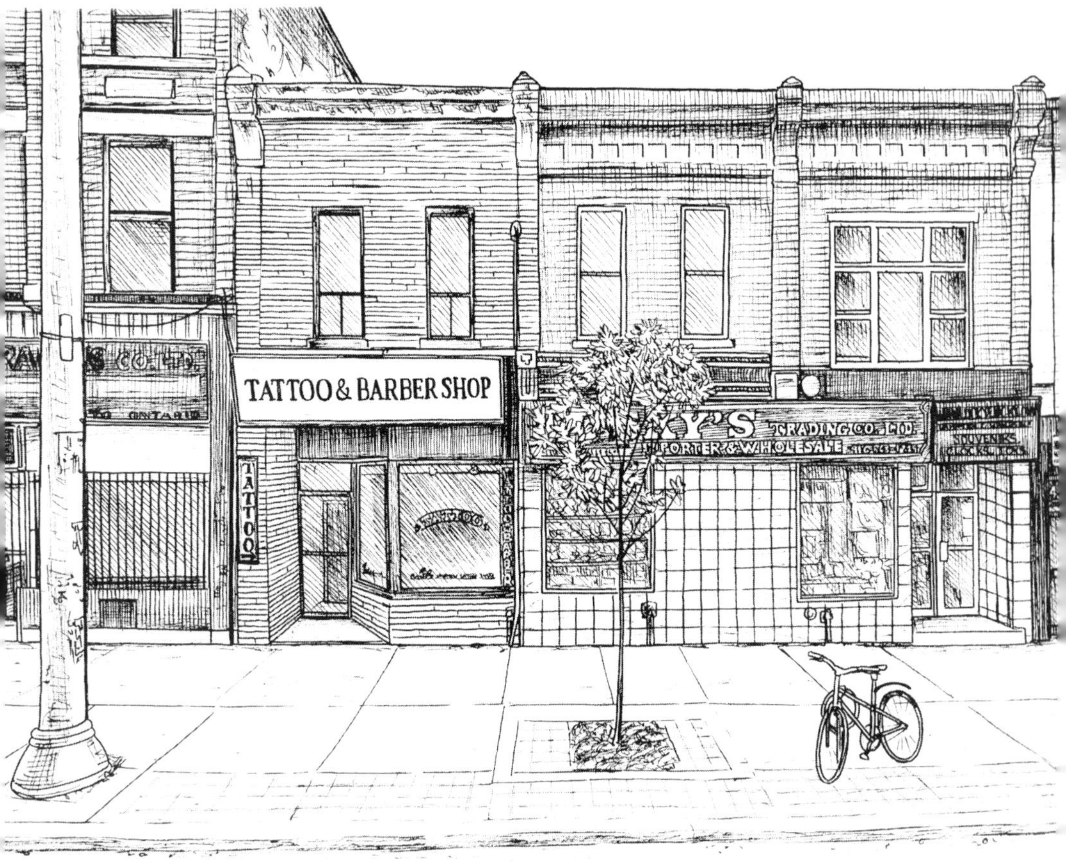
TATTOO & BARBER SHOP
TATTOO
Y'S TRADING CO. LTD
PORTER & WHOLESALE
SOUVENIRS
CLOCKS, TOYS

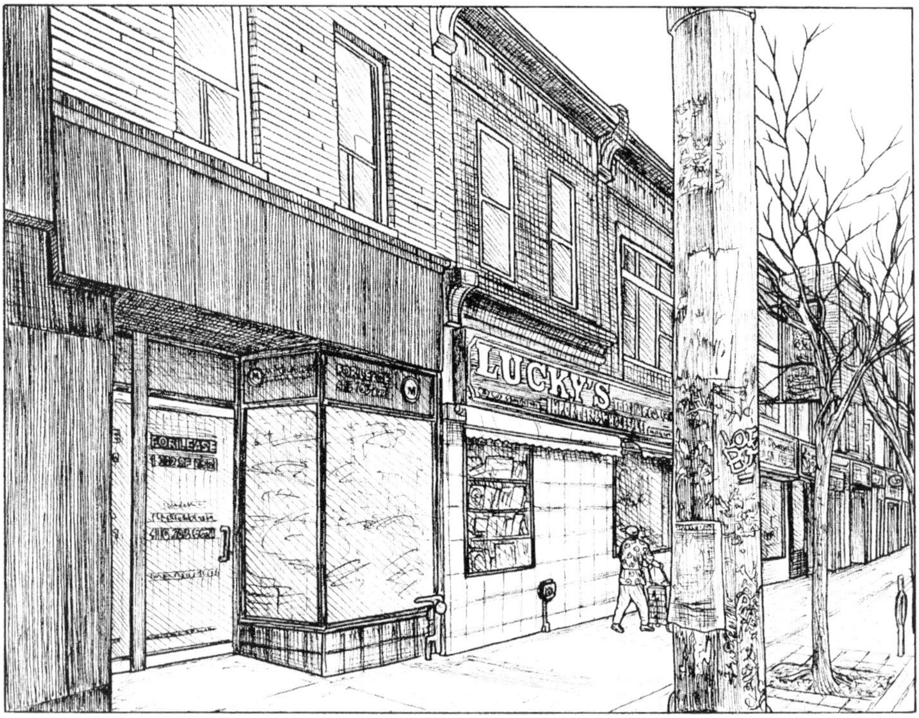
FOR LEASE
LUCKY'S

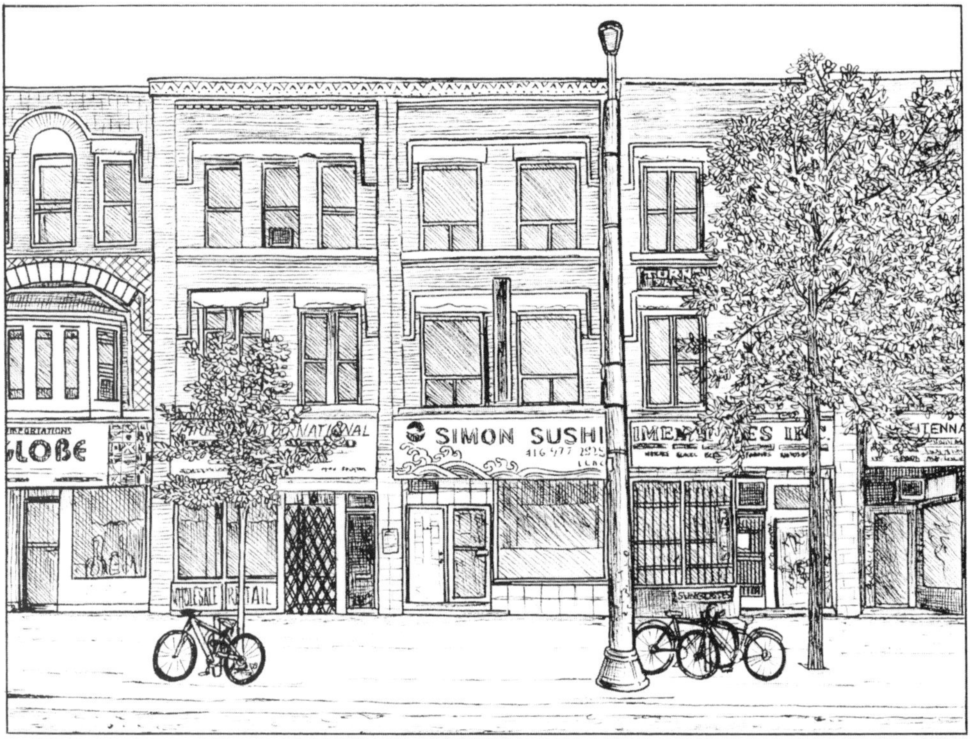
GLOBE
SIMON SUSHI
416 977 2925
WHOLESALE RETAIL

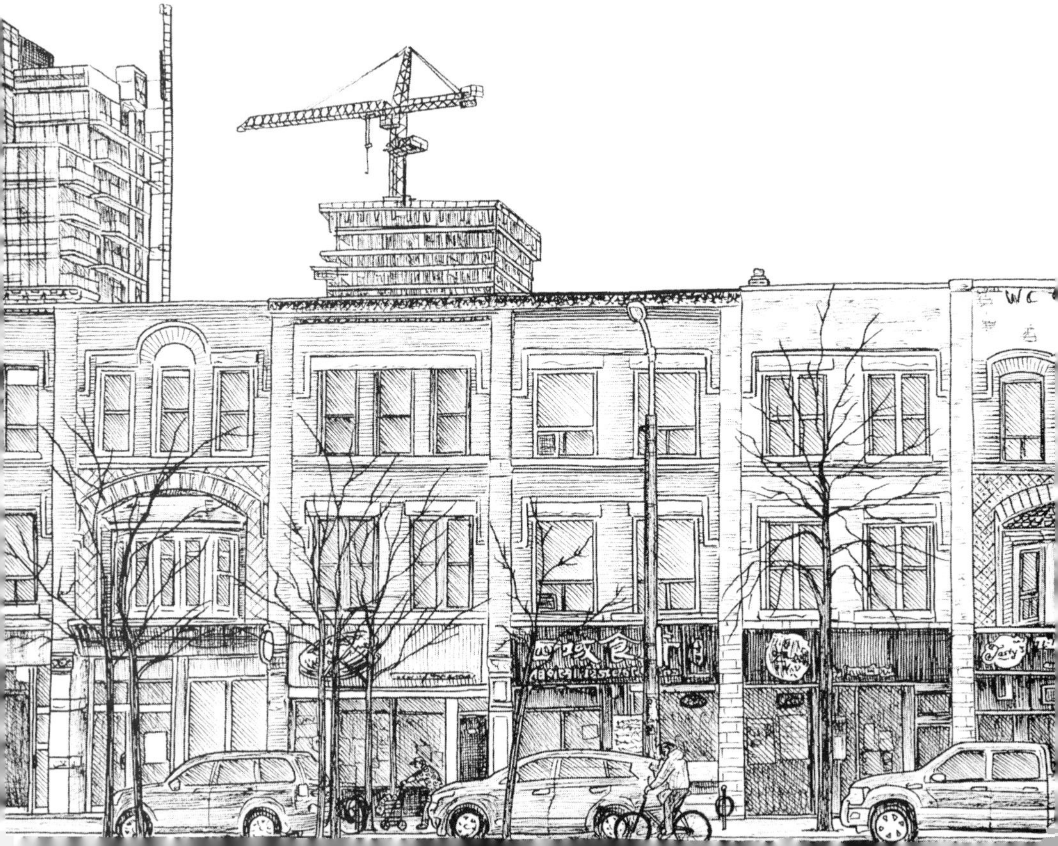

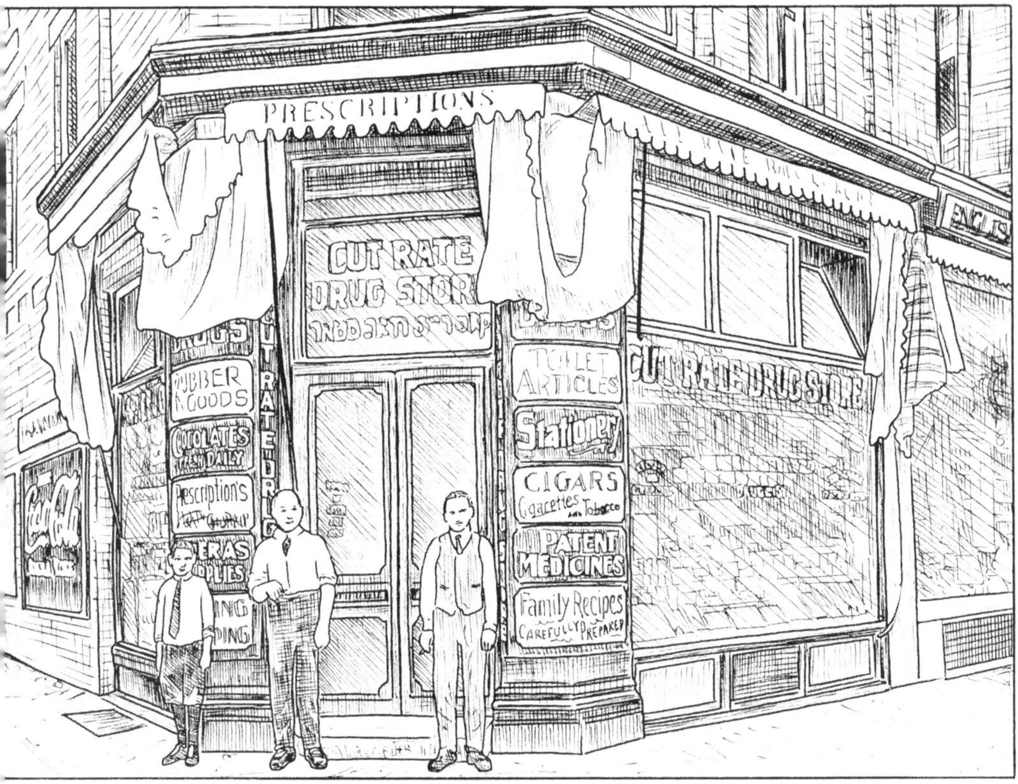
PRESCRIPTIONS
CUT RATE
DRUG STORE
RUBBER GOODS
CHOCOLATES FRESH DAILY
Prescriptions
TOILET ARTICLES
Stationery
CIGARS
Cigarettes and Tobacco
PATENT MEDICINES
Family Recipes
CAREFULLY PREPARED
CUT RATE DRUG STORE
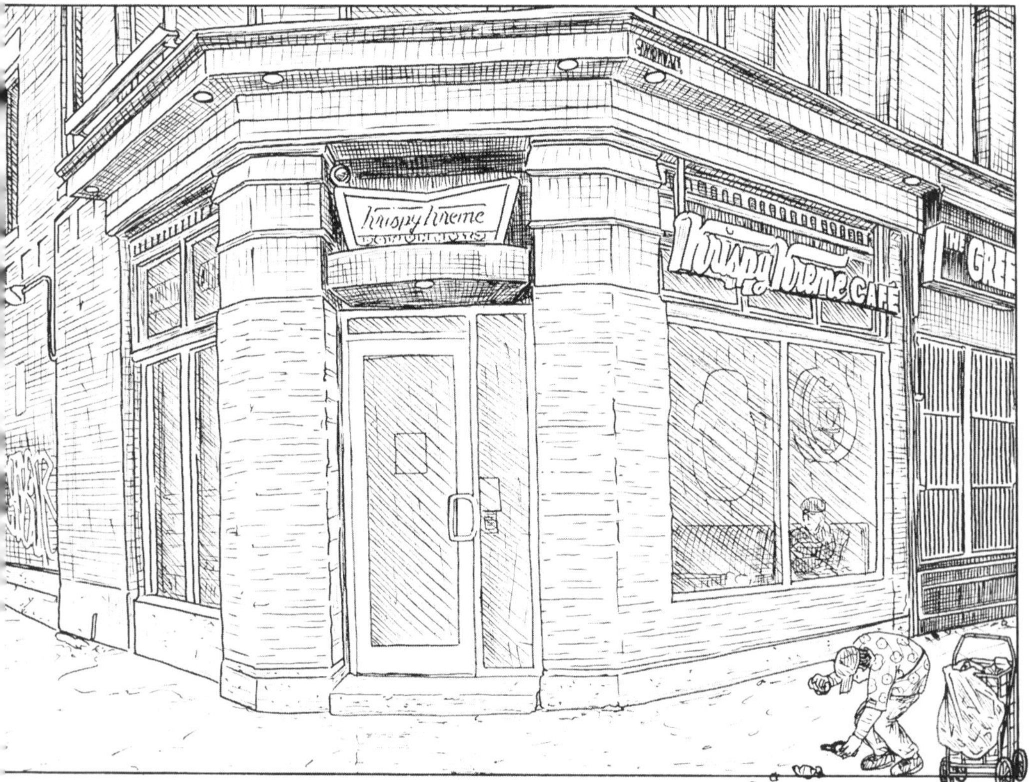
Krispy Kreme
Krispy Kreme CAFÉ

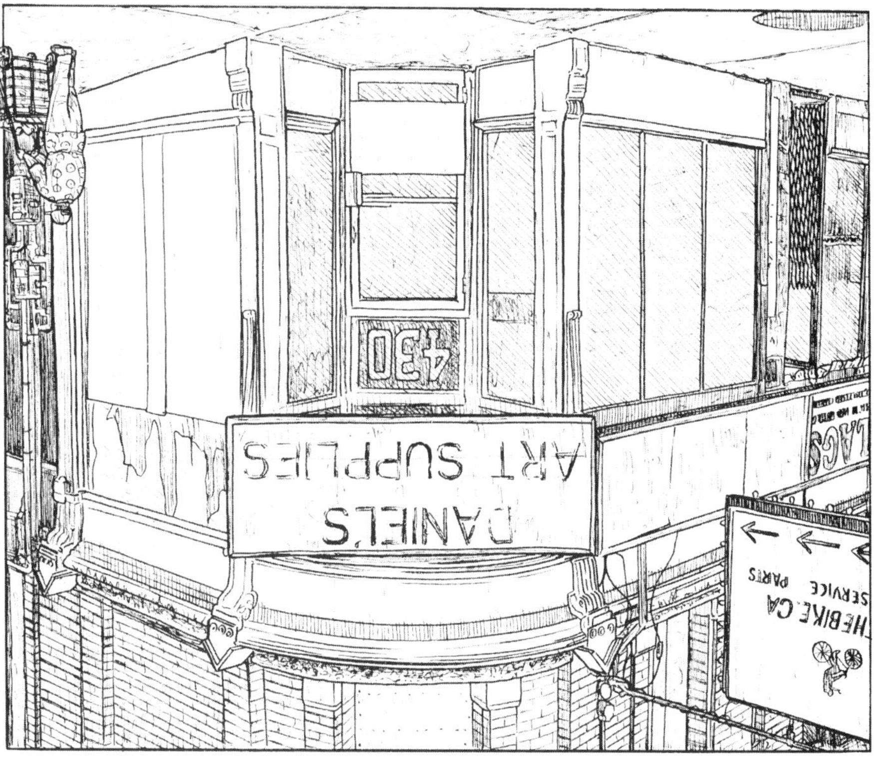
DANIEL'S
ART SUPPLIES
430
THEBIKE.CA
SERVICE PARTS

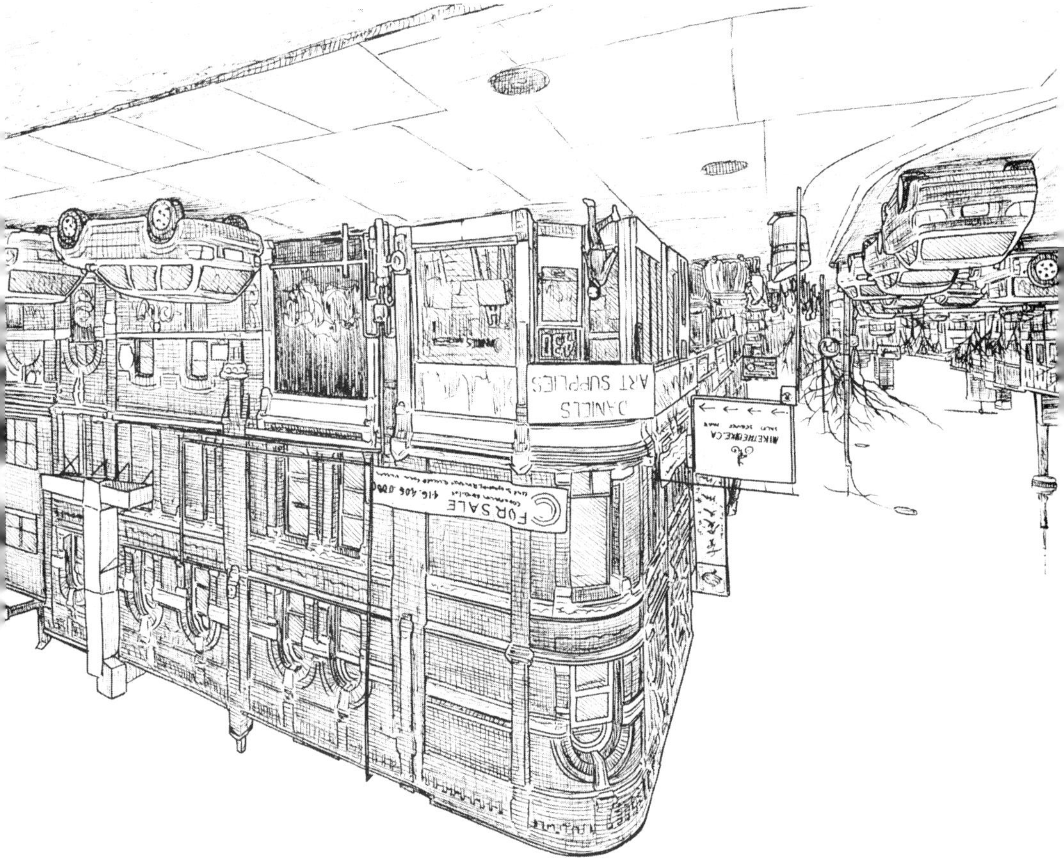
DANIELS
ART SUPPLIES
430
MIKETHEBIKE.CA
FOR SALE

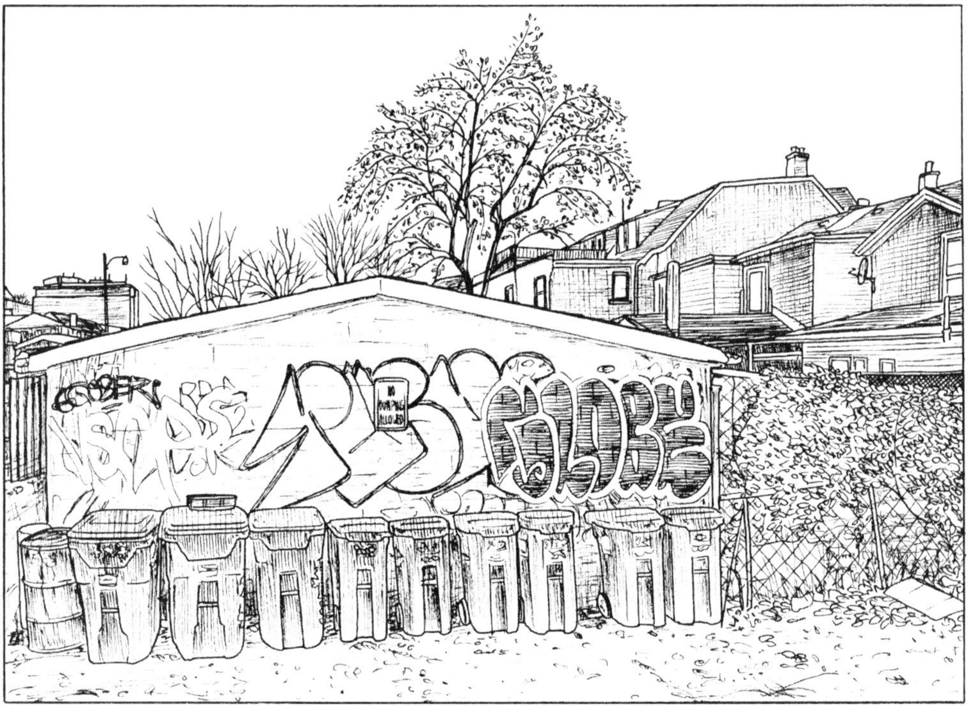
NO DUMPING ALLOWED

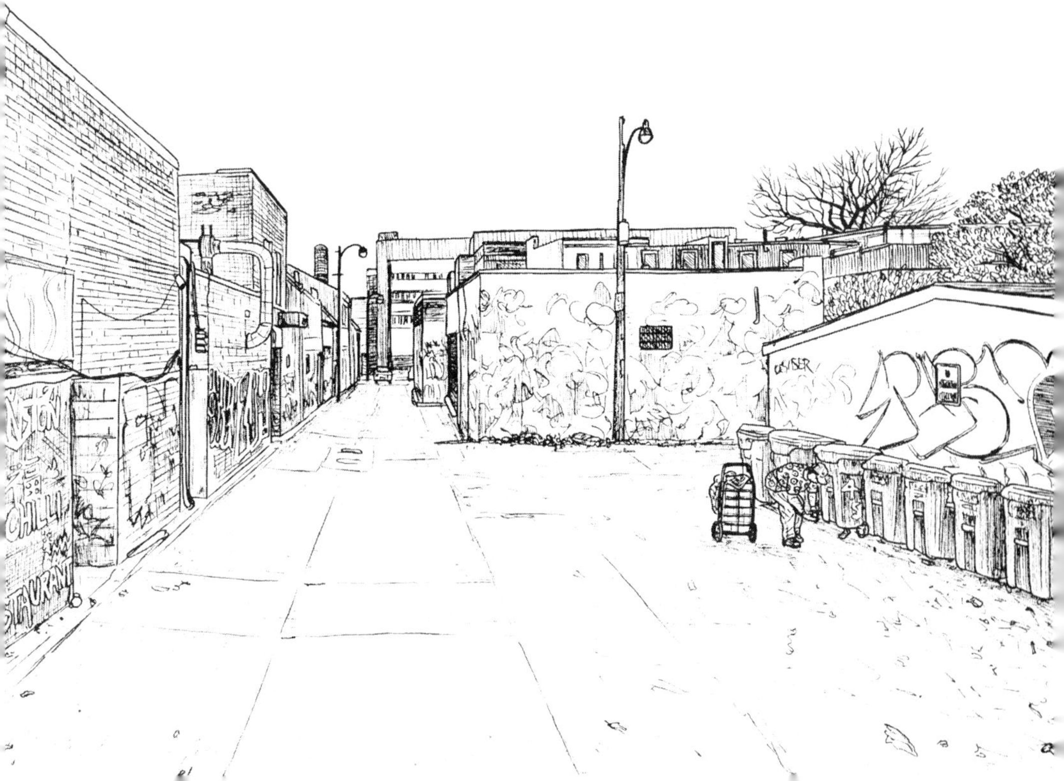

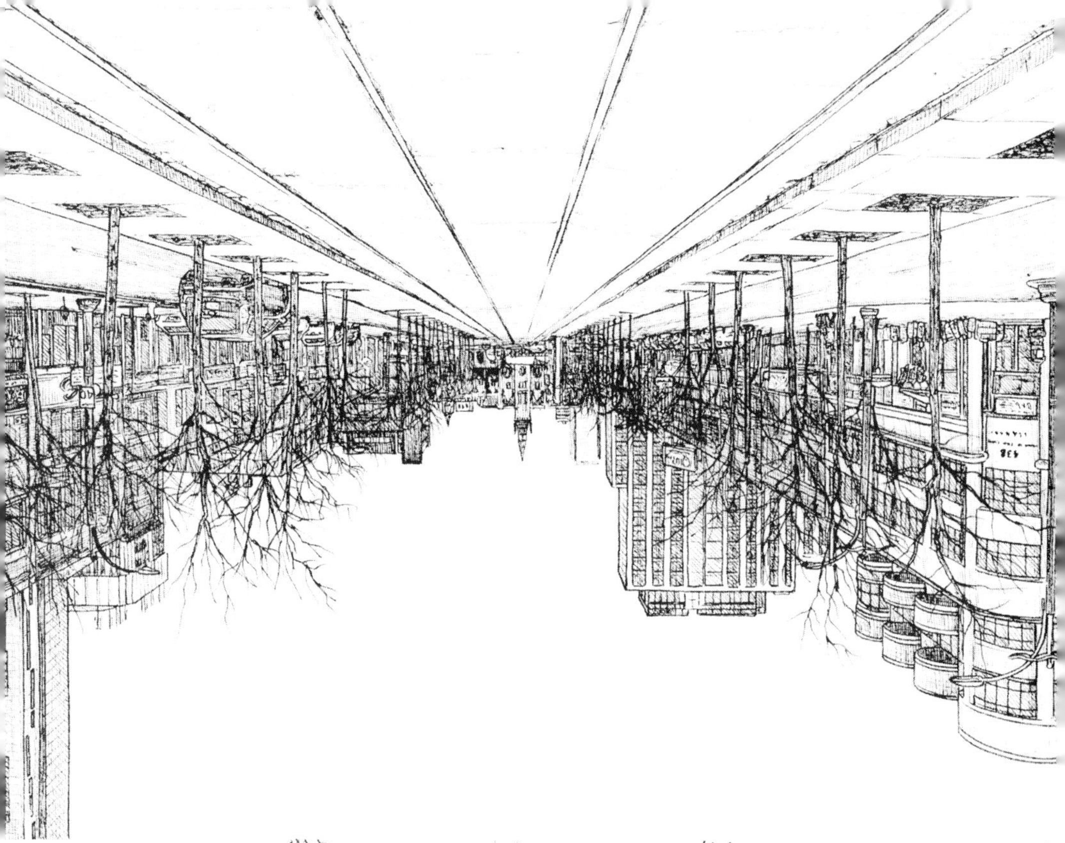

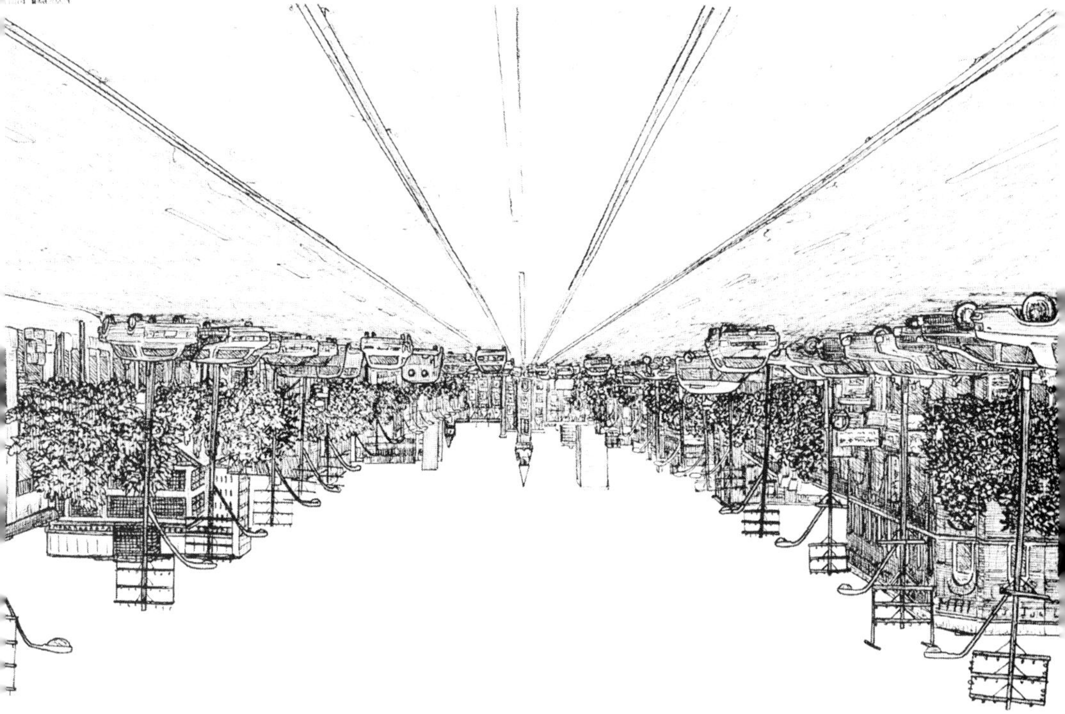

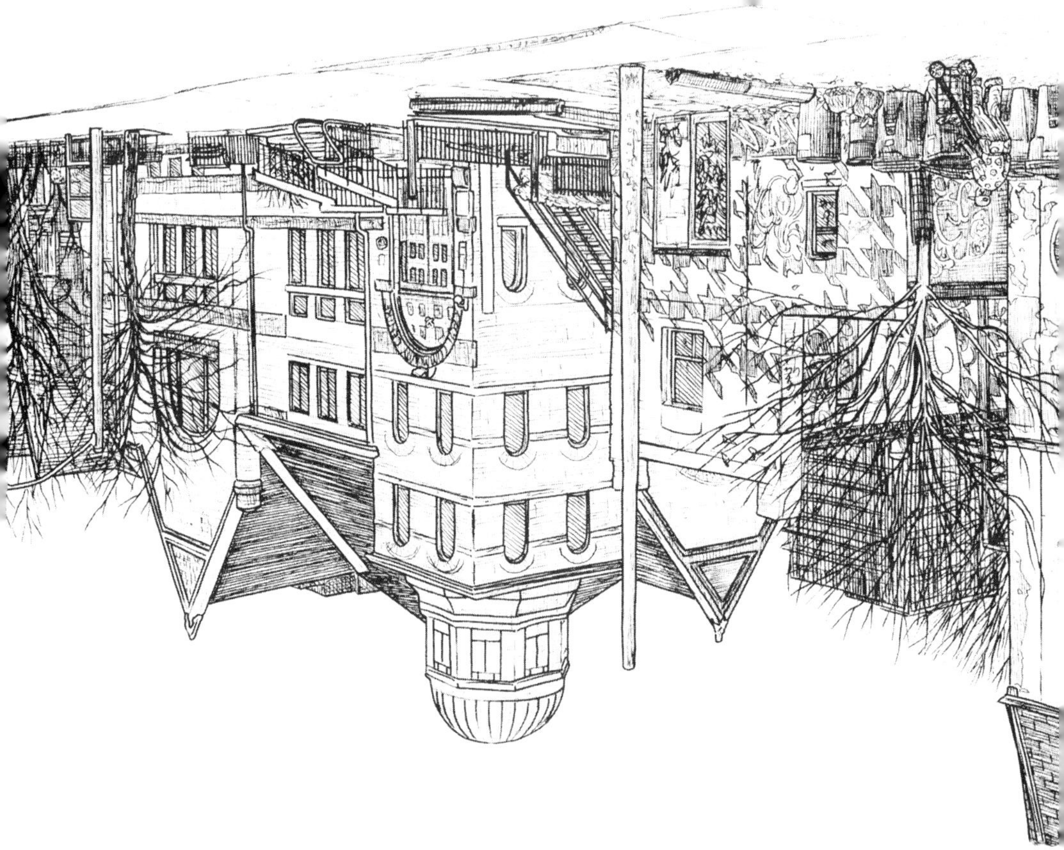

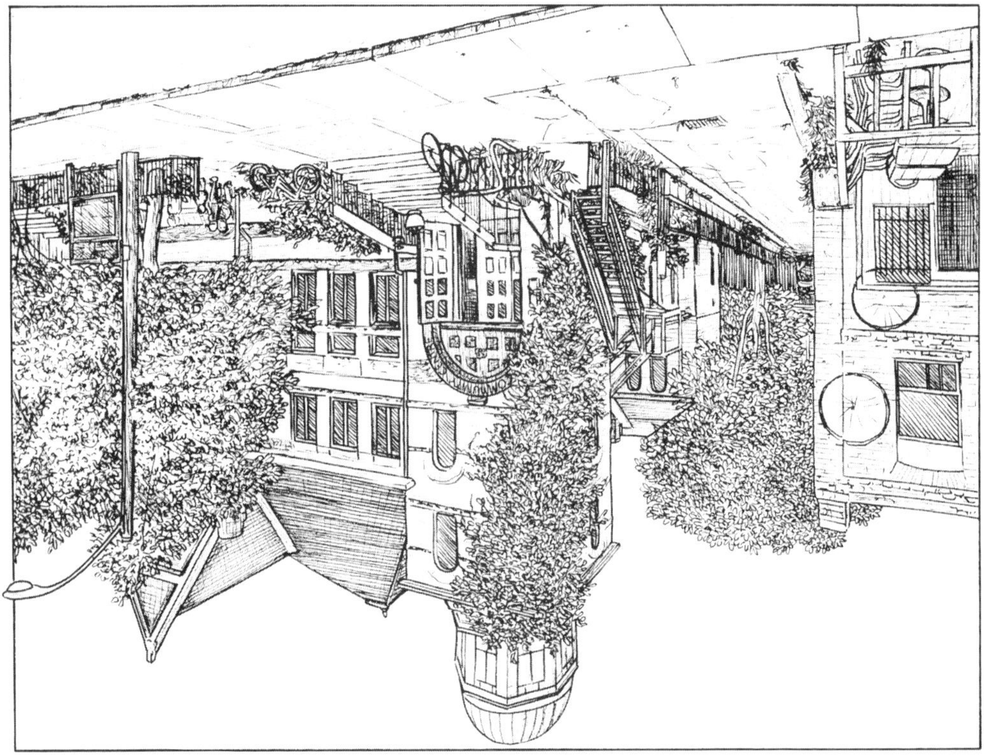

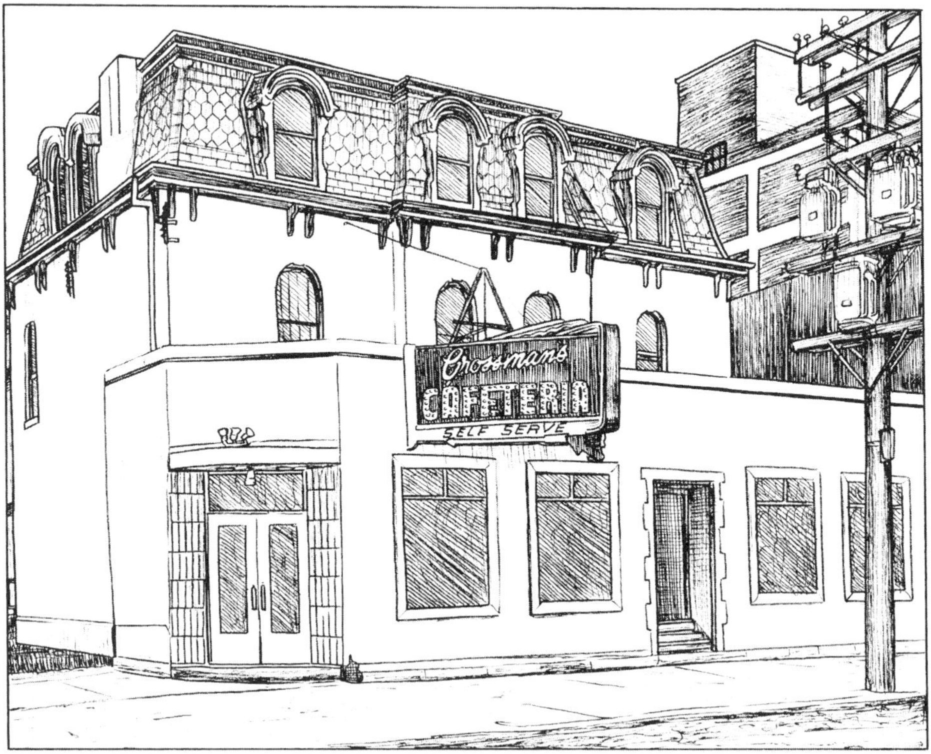
Crossman's
CAFETERIA
SELF SERVE

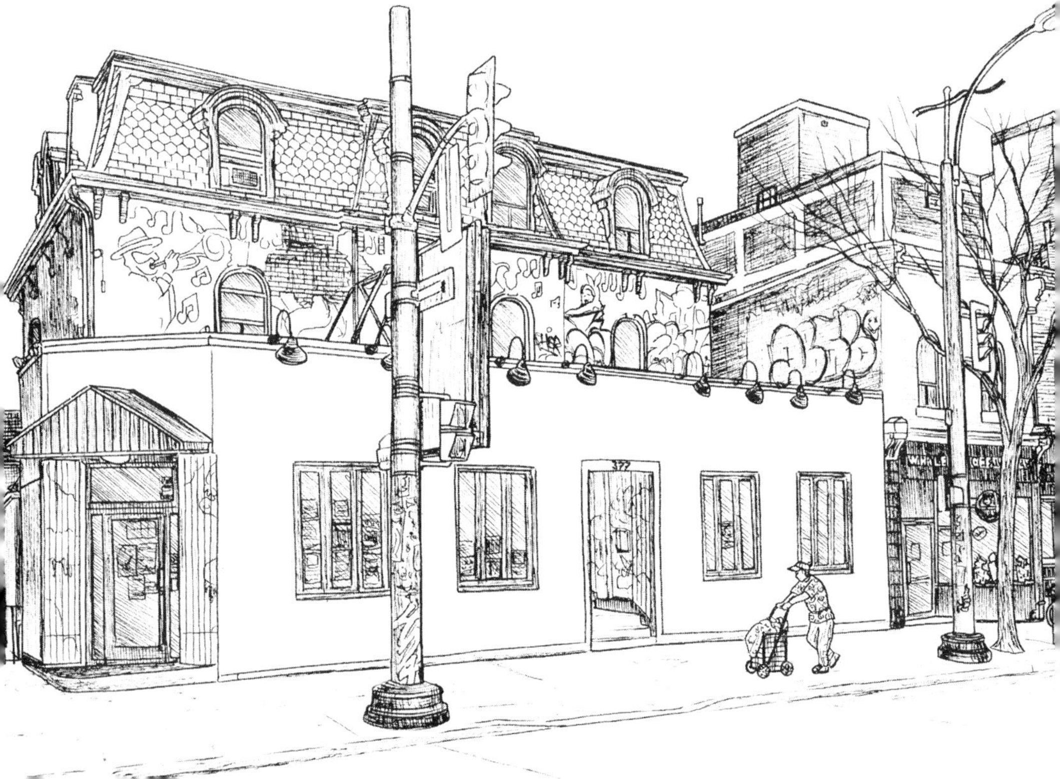
377

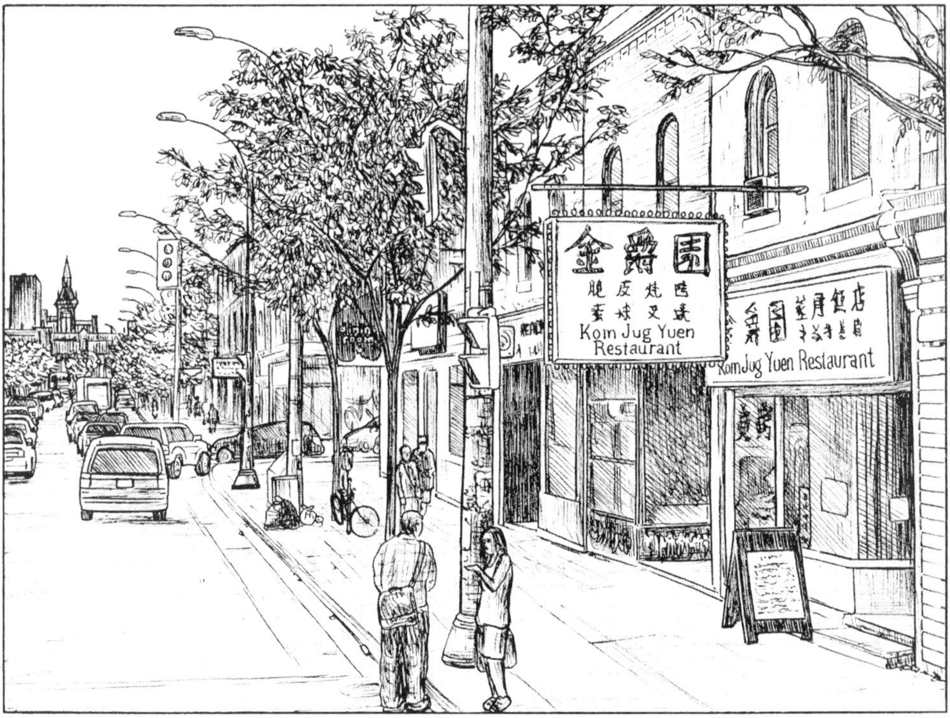
Kom Jug Yuen Restaurant
Kom Jug Yuen Restaurant

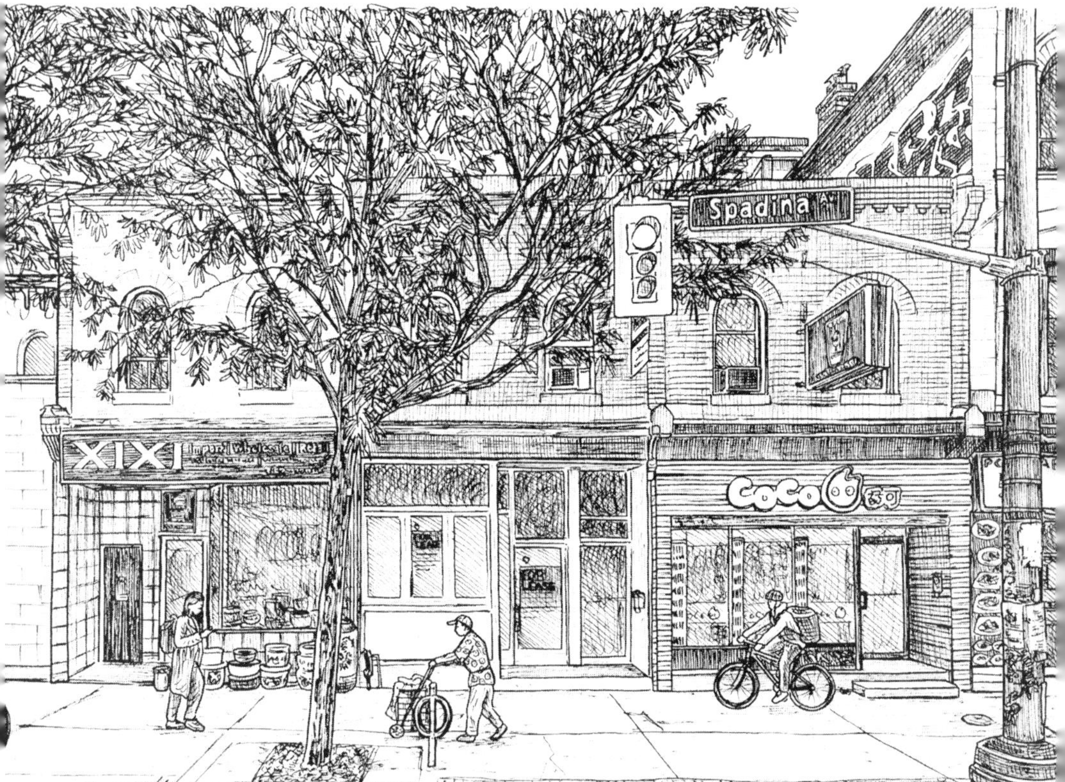
Spadina
XIXI
CoCo
FOR LEASE

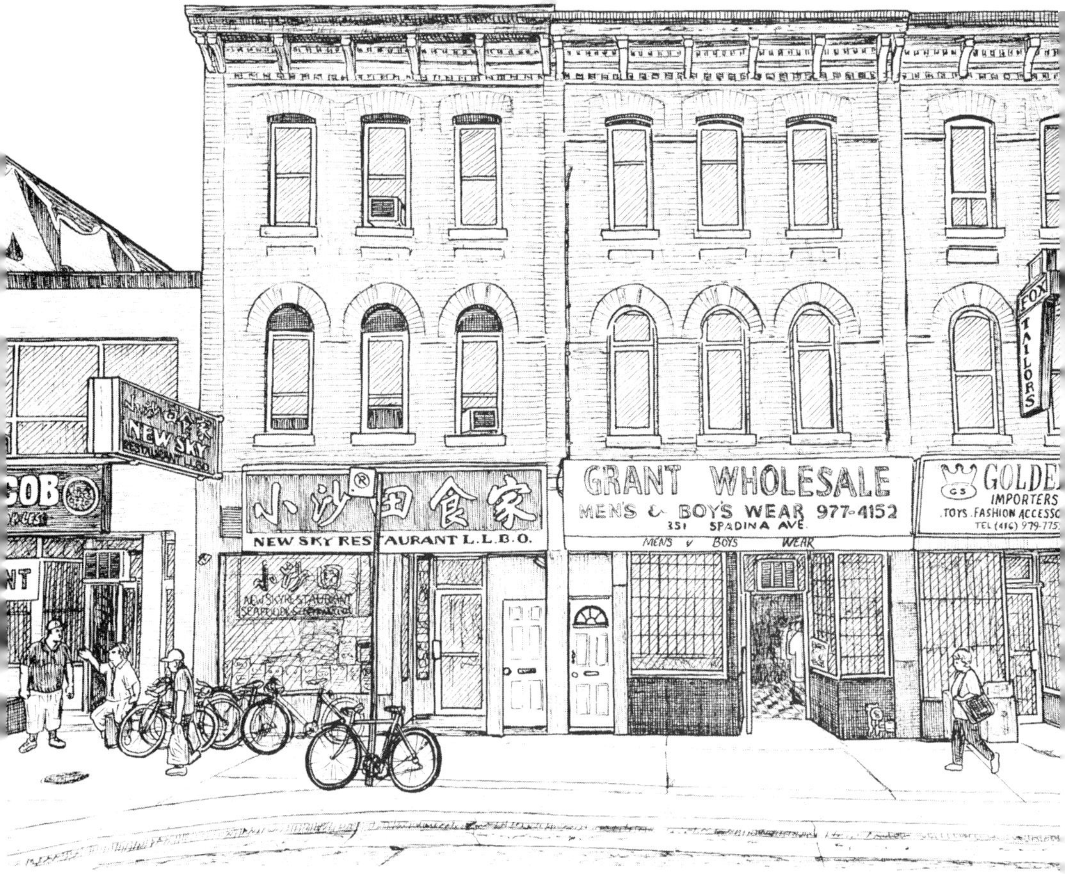

FOX
TAILORS
NEW SKY
小沙田食家
NEW SKY RESTAURANT L.L.B.O.
GRANT WHOLESALE
MEN'S & BOY'S WEAR 977-4152
351 SPADINA AVE.
MENS & BOYS WEAR
GOLDE
IMPORTERS
TOYS. FASHION ACCESSO
TEL (416) 979-775

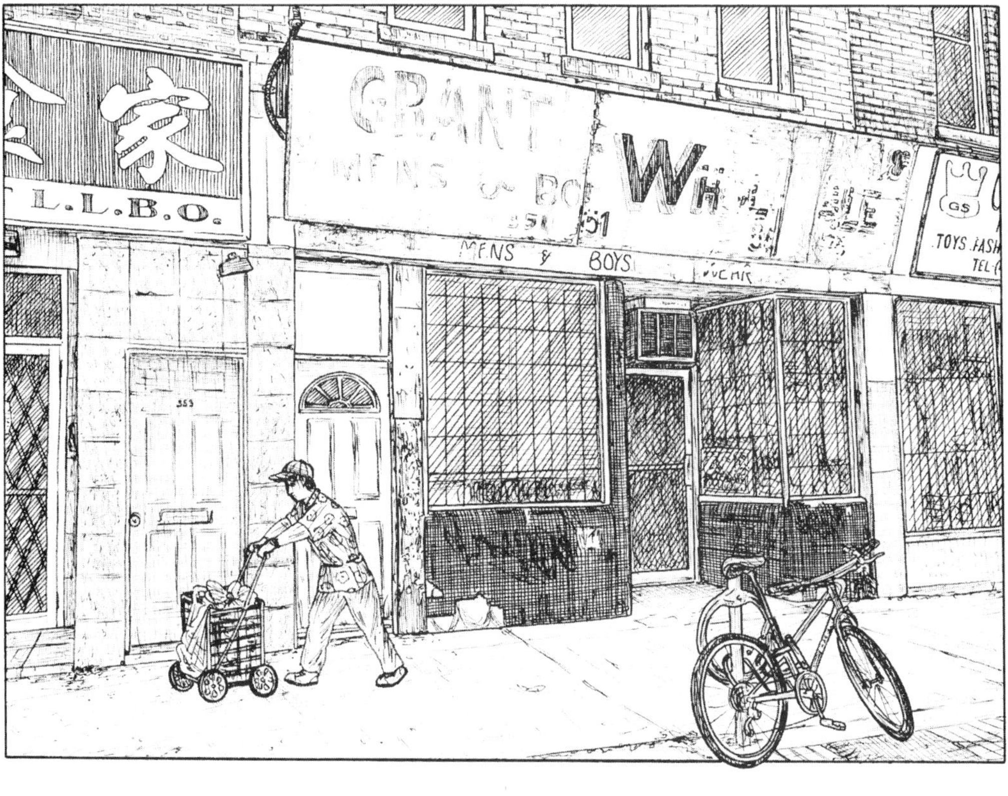

家
L.L.B.O.
MENS & BOYS
TOYS. FASH

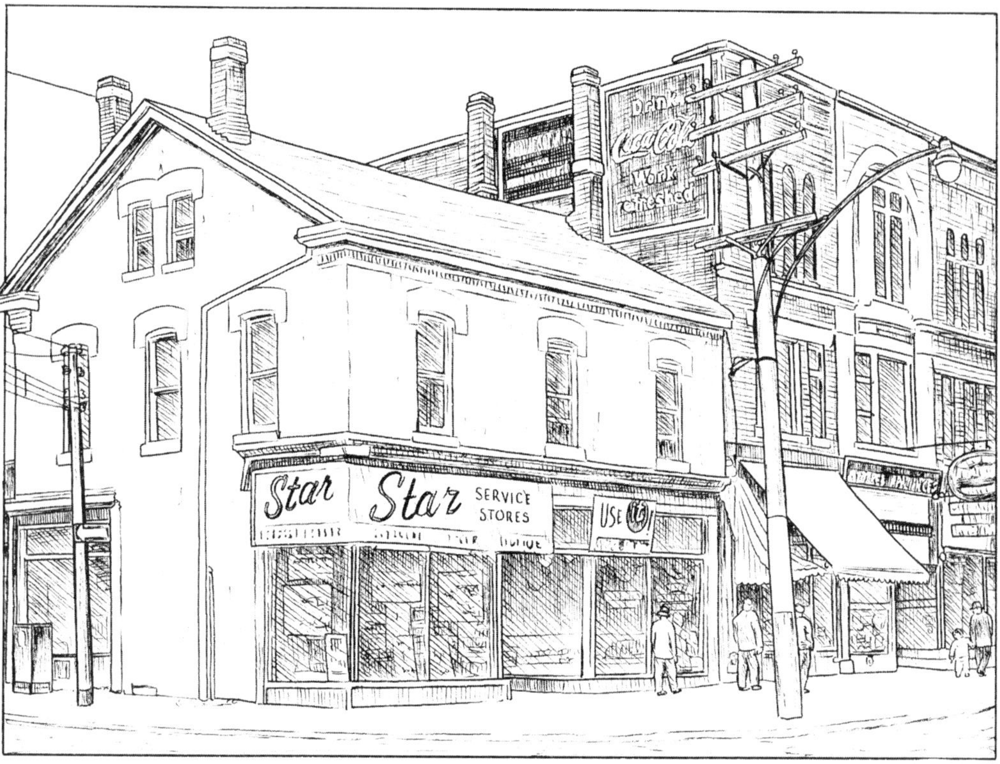
Drink
Coca-Cola
Work
refreshed
Star
Star
SERVICE
STORES
USE it!

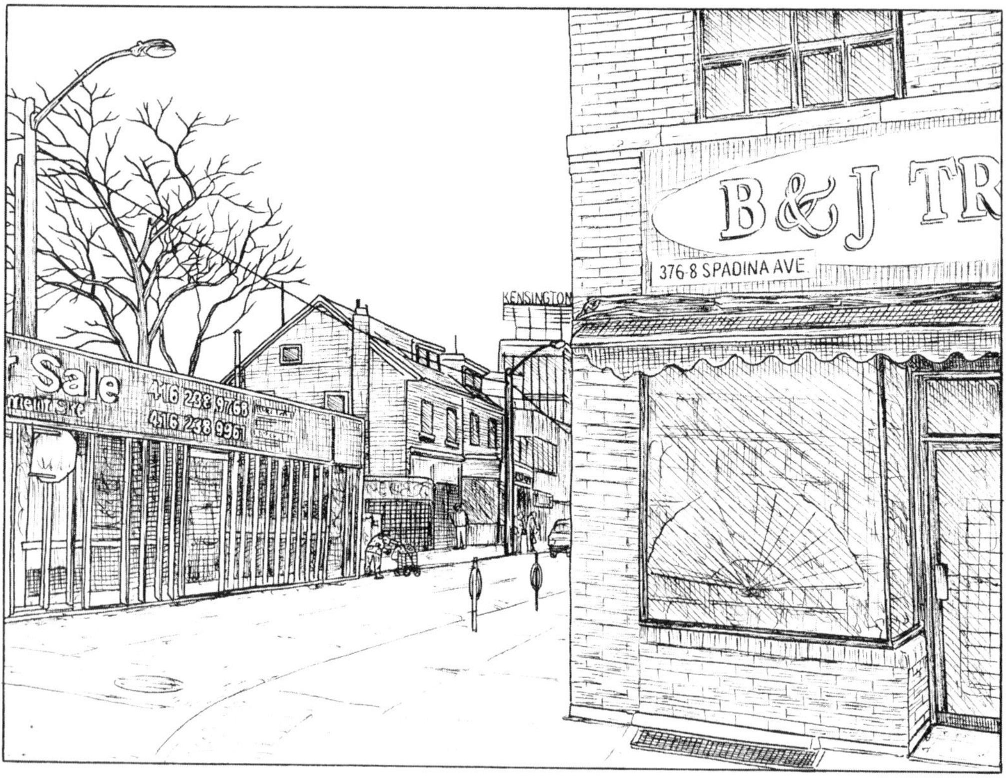
Sale
416 238 9768
416 238 9961
KENSINGTON
B&J TR
376-8 SPADINA AVE

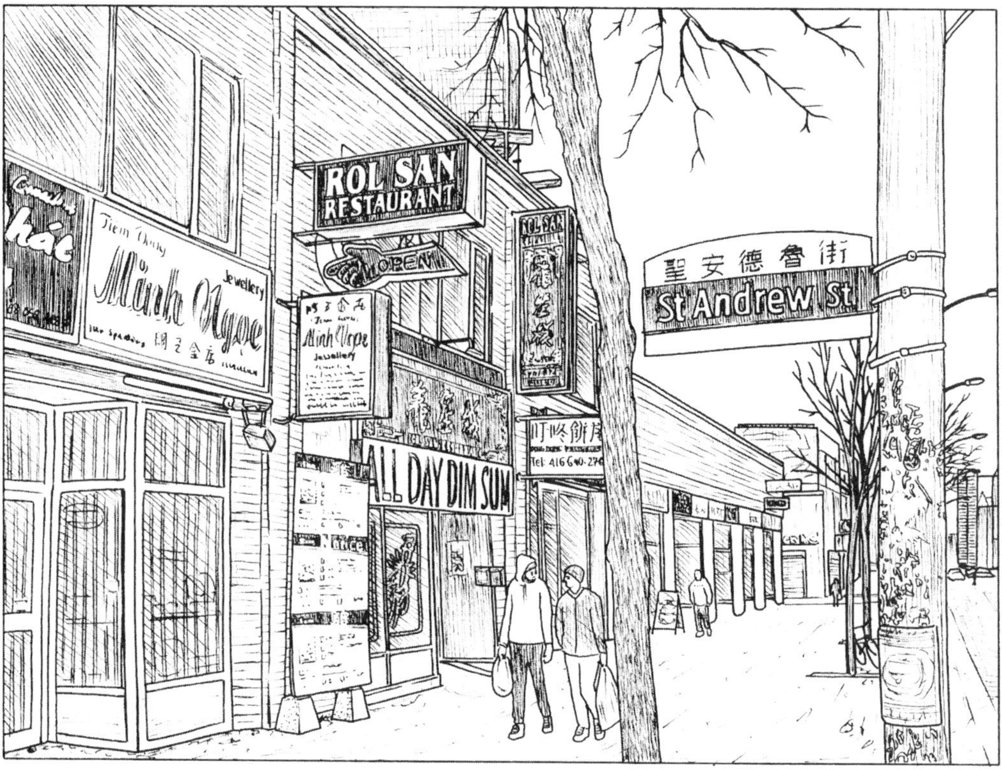
ROL SAN RESTAURANT
OPEN
Minh Ngoc Jewellery
聖安德魯街
St Andrew St
ALL DAY DIM SUM
Tel: 416 640-27

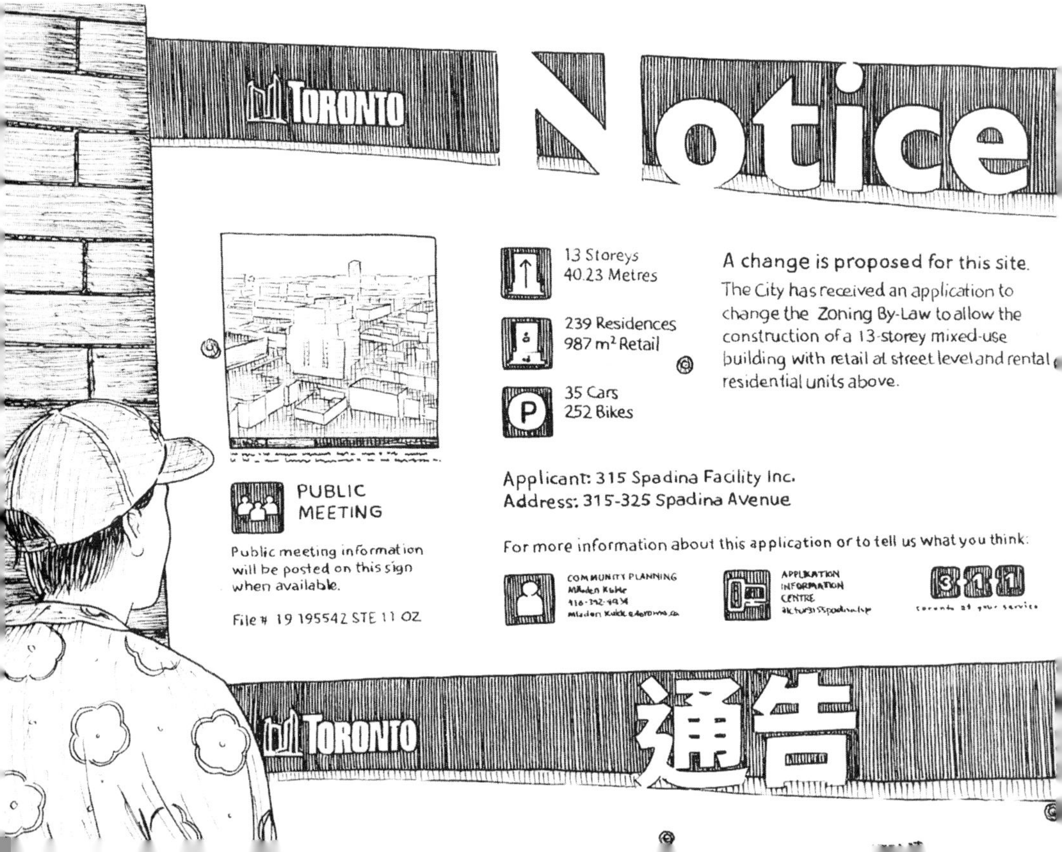
TORONTO
Notice
A change is proposed for this site.
The City has received an application to change the Zoning By-Law to allow the construction of a 13-storey mixed-use building with retail at street level and rental residential units above.
13 Storeys
40.23 Metres
239 Residences
987 m² Retail
35 Cars
252 Bikes
Applicant: 315 Spadina Facility Inc.
Address: 315-325 Spadina Avenue
PUBLIC MEETING
Public meeting information will be posted on this sign when available.
File # 19 195542 STE 11 OZ
For more information about this application or to tell us what you think:
COMMUNITY PLANNING
APPLICATION INFORMATION CENTRE
311
TORONTO
通告

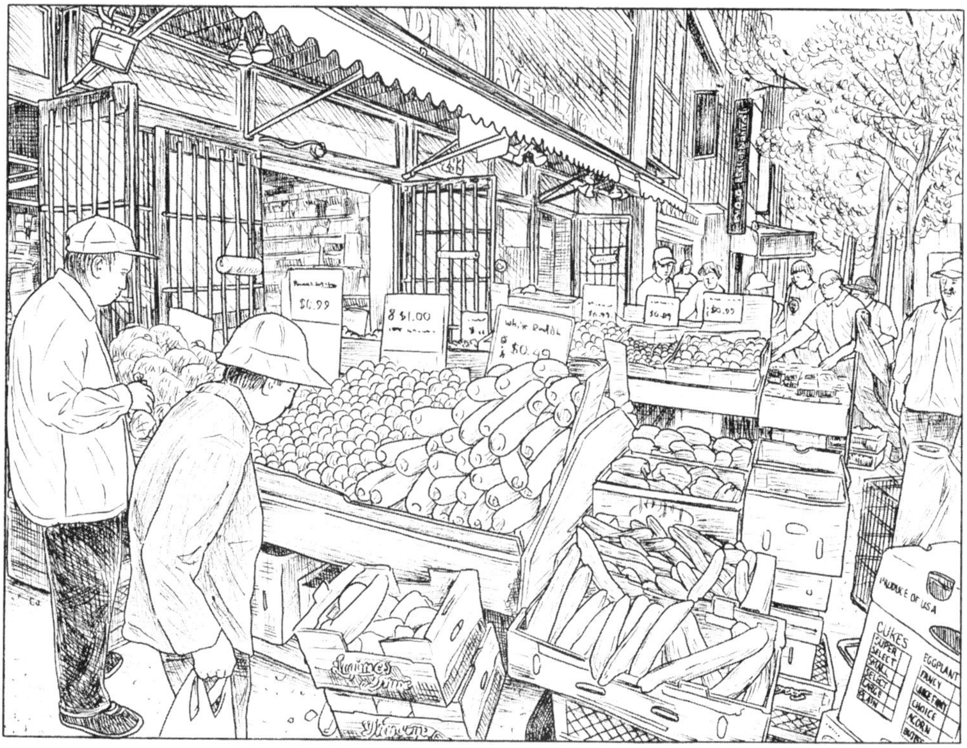
$0.99
8 $1.00
White Radish
$0.49
$0.99
$0.89
$0.99
PRODUCE OF USA
CUKES
SUPER
SELECT
SMALL
SELECT
LARGE
PLAIN
EGGPLANT
FANCY
LARGE FANCY
CHOICE
ACORN

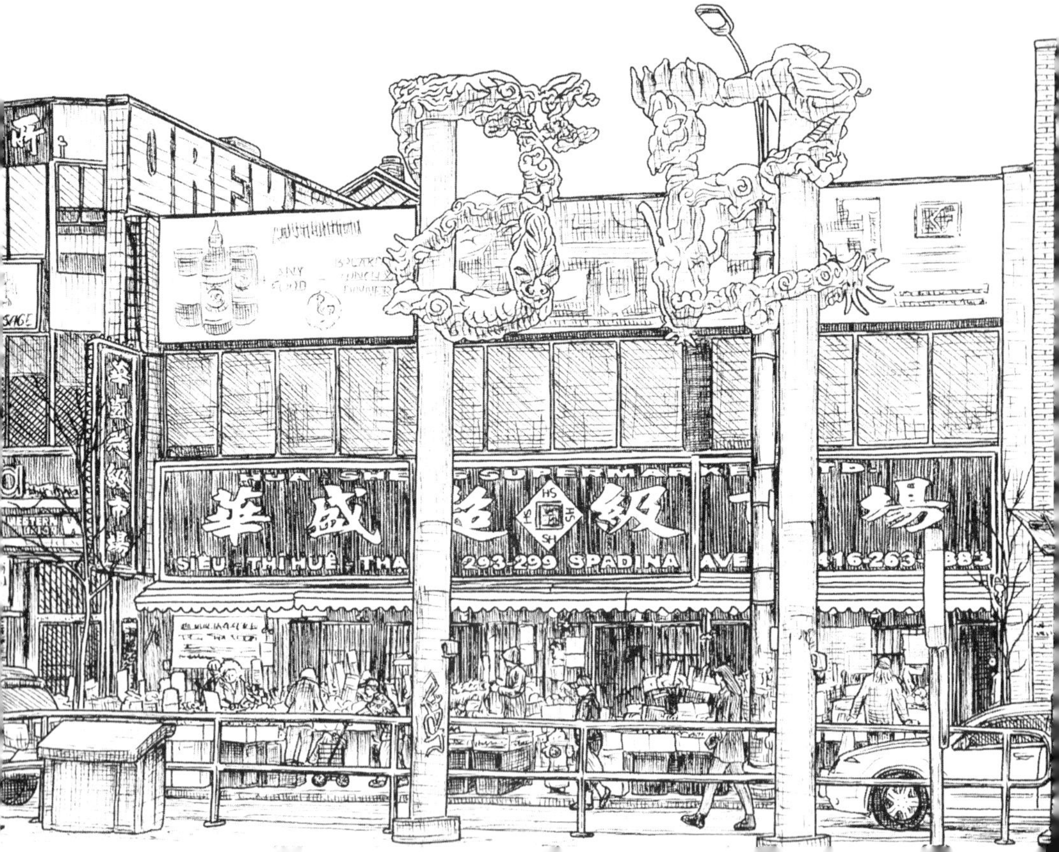
華盛超級市場
SIEU THI HUE THA
293-299 SPADINA AVE
416-263-1883
ANY
FOOD

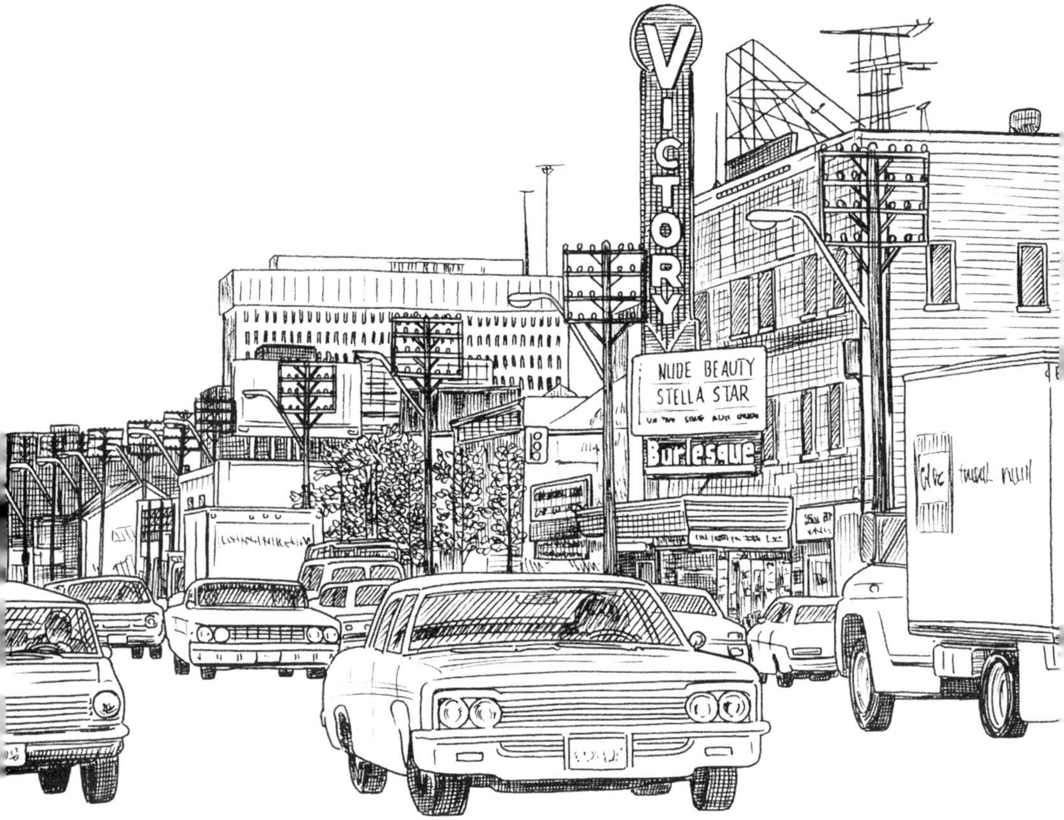
VICTORY
NUDE BEAUTY
STELLA STAR
Burlesque

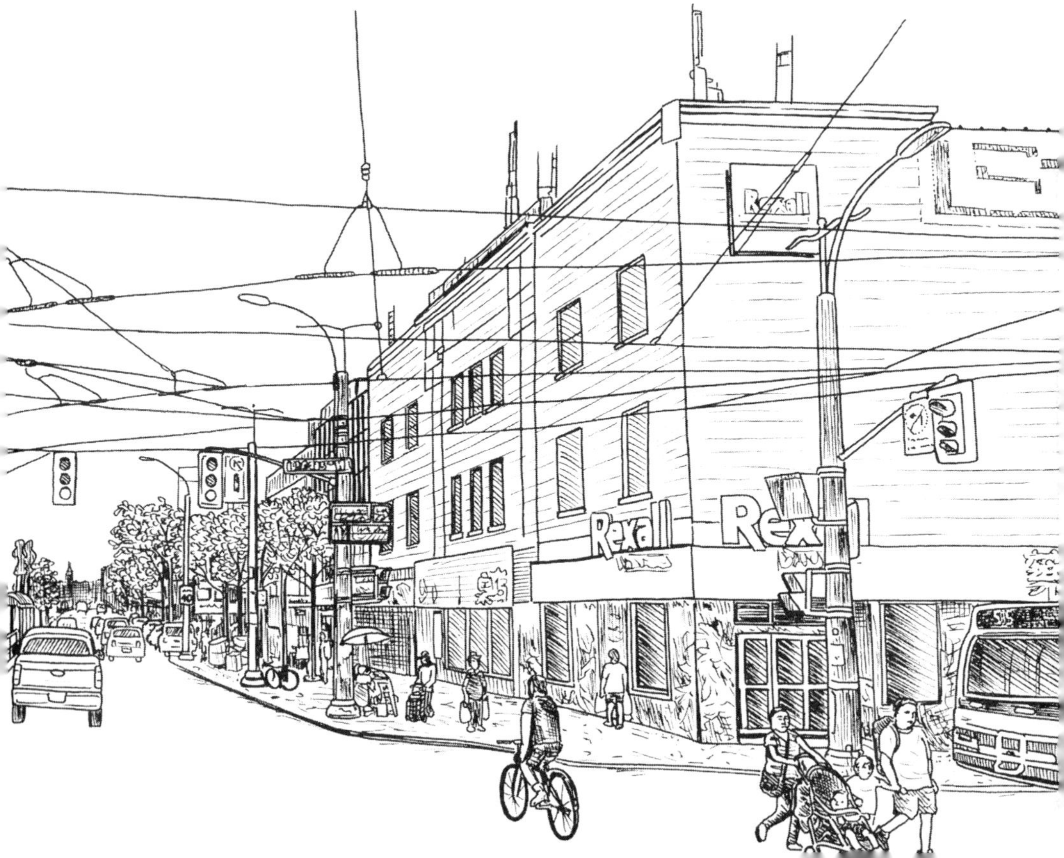
Rexall
Rexall
Rex

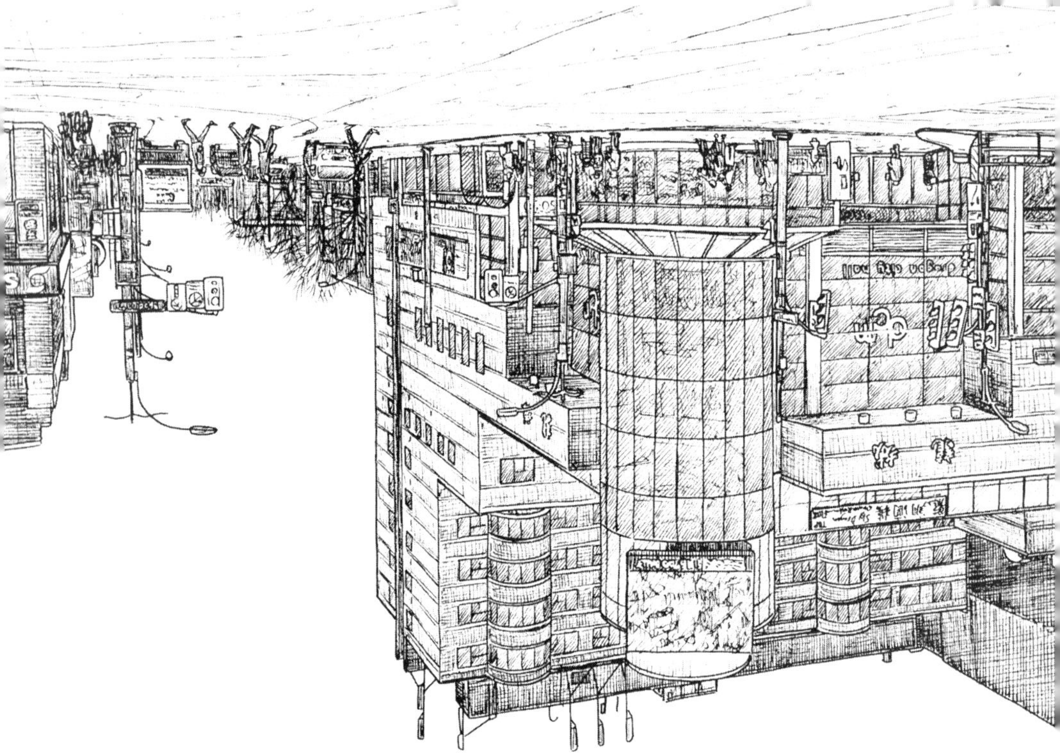

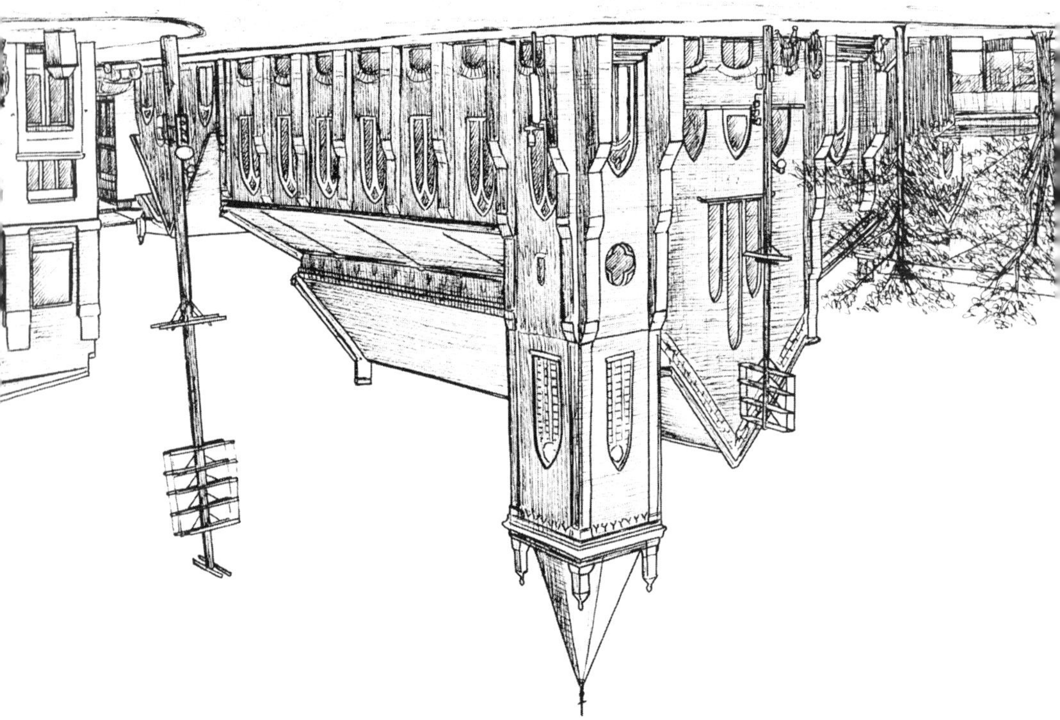

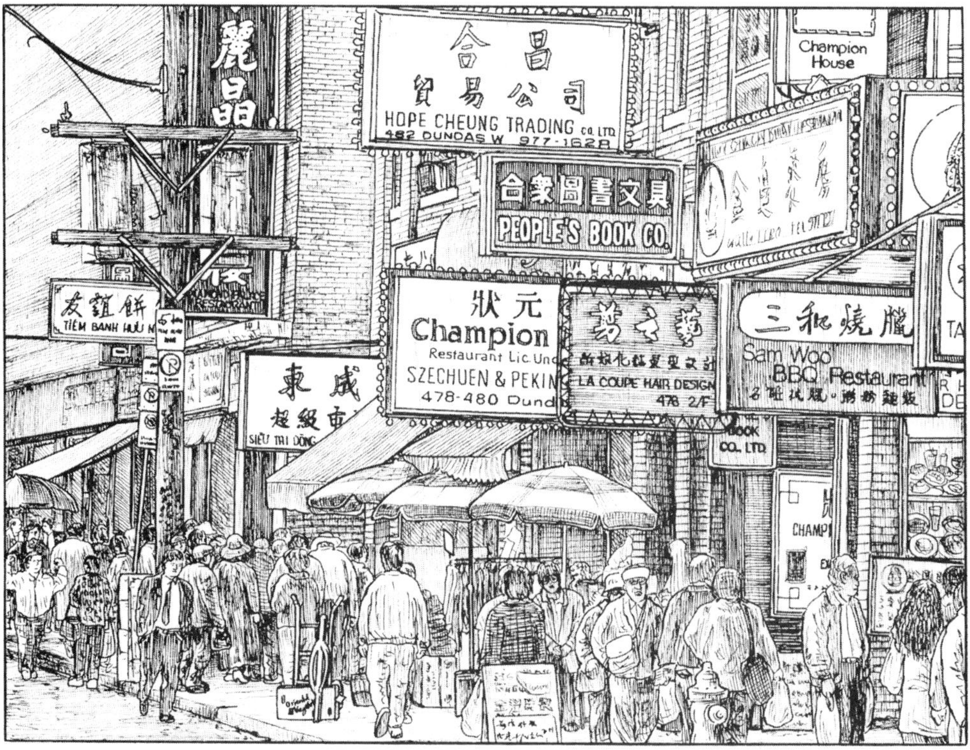
麗晶
合昌
貿易公司
HOPE CHEUNG TRADING co. LTD.
482 DUNDAS W 977-1628
Champion
House
合眾圖書文具
PEOPLE'S BOOK CO.
狀元
Champion
Restaurant Lic. Und
SZECHUEN & PEKIN
478-480 Dund
LA COUPE HAIR DESIGN
478 2/F
三和燒臘
Sam Woo
BBQ Restaurant
TIỆM BANH HỮU N
東威
超級市
SIÊU THỊ ĐÔNG
CO. LTD.
CHAMPI

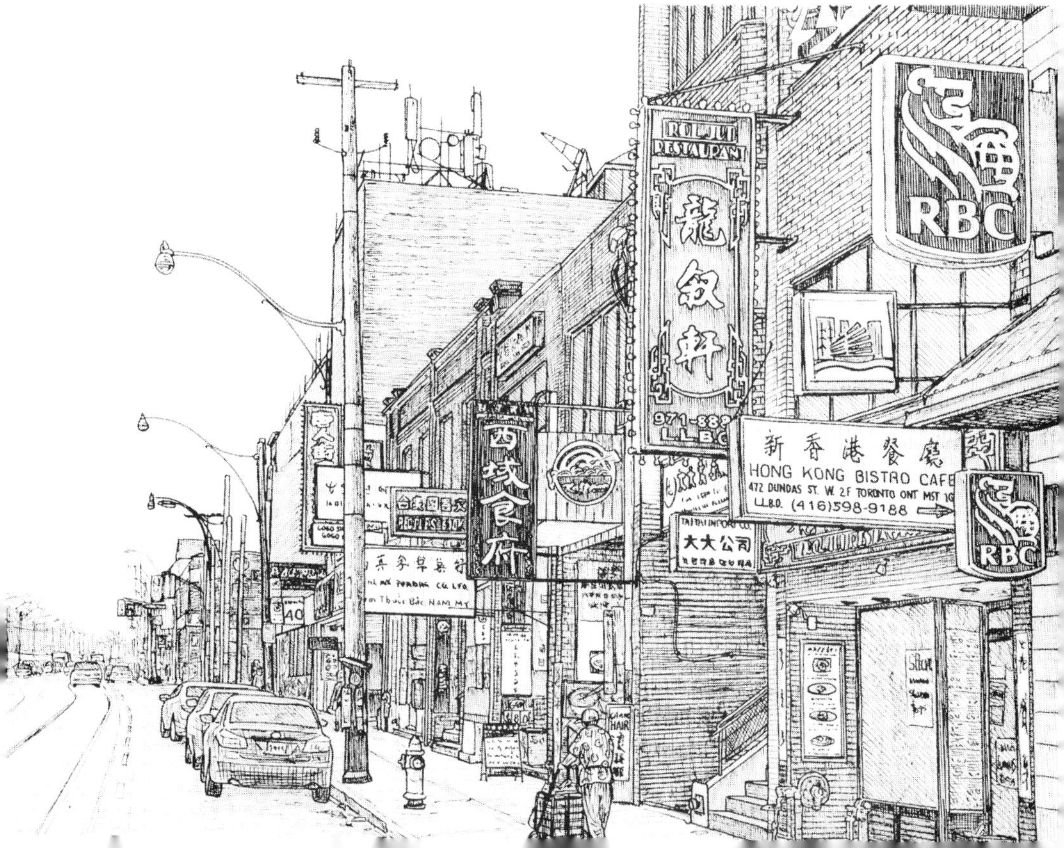
RBC
龍敘軒
971-889
L.L.B.O.
新香港餐廳
HONG KONG BISTRO CAFE
472 DUNDAS ST. W. 2F TORONTO ONT M5T 1G
L.L.B.O. (416)598-9188
RBC
大大公司
西域食府
40

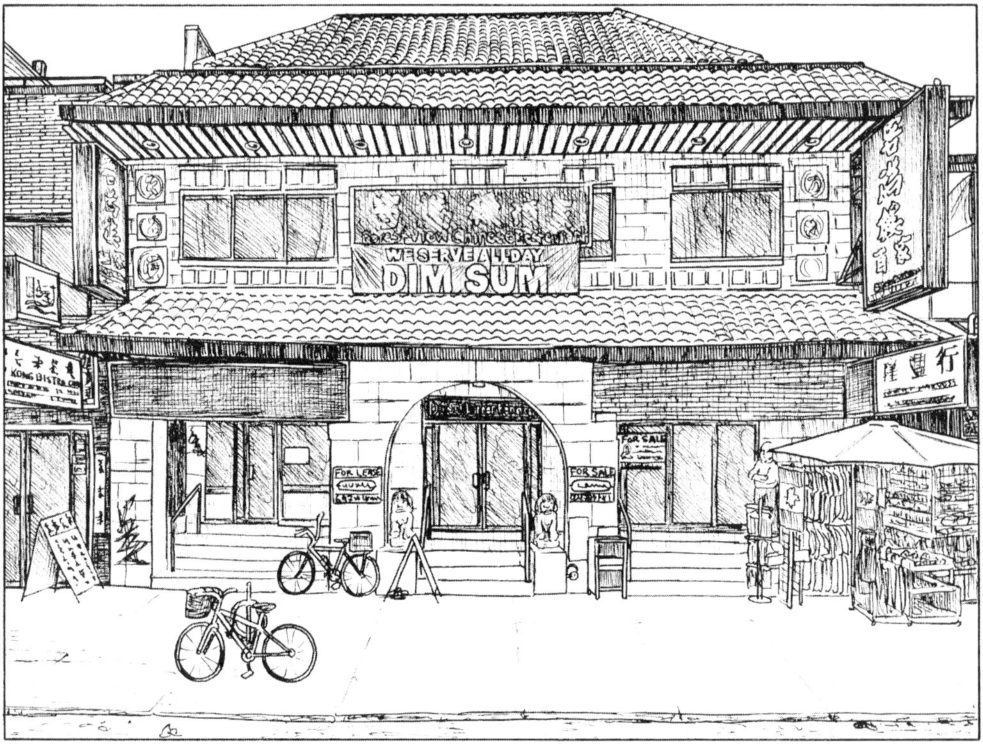
WE SERVE ALL DAY
DIM SUM
FOR LEASE
FOR SALE
FOR SALE

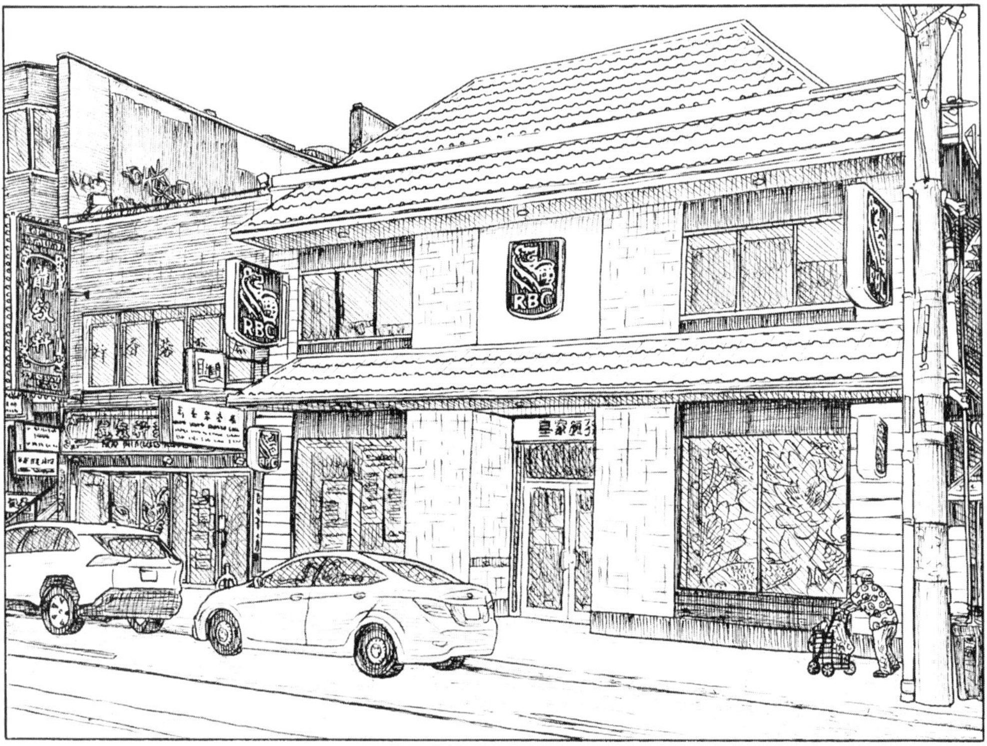
RBC
RBC
RBC

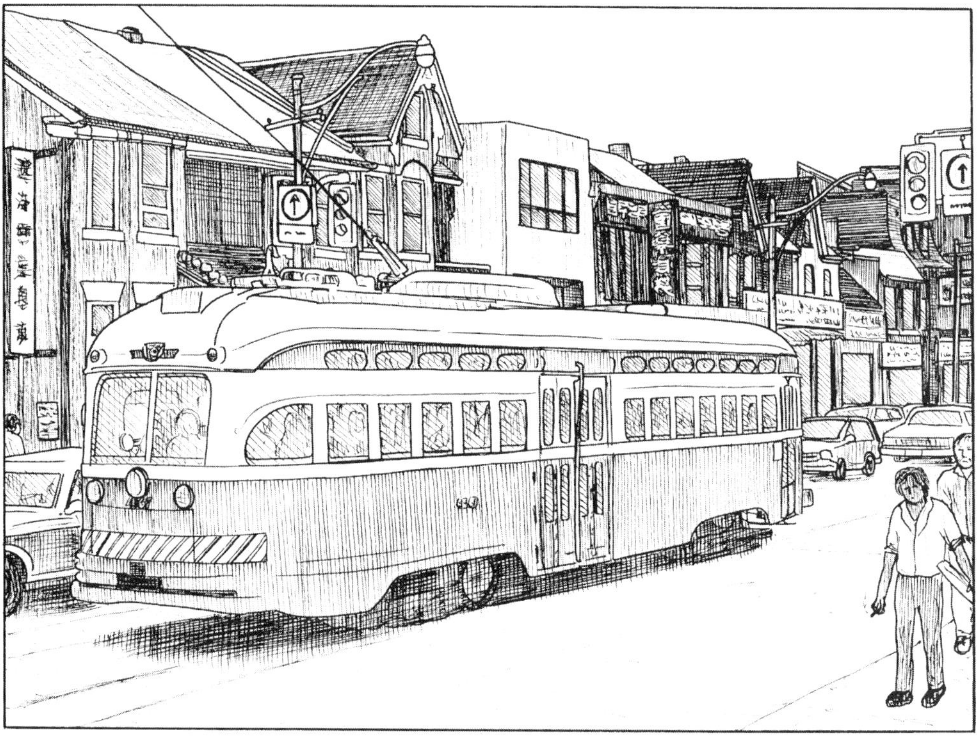

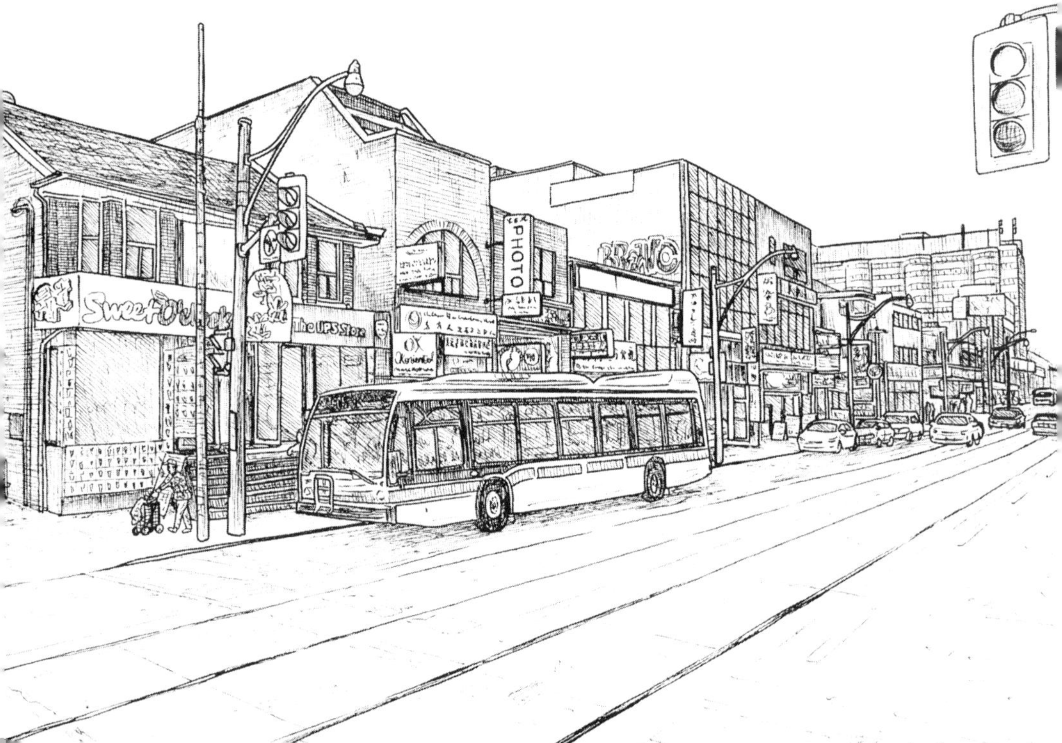
PHOTO
The UPS Store
BRAVO

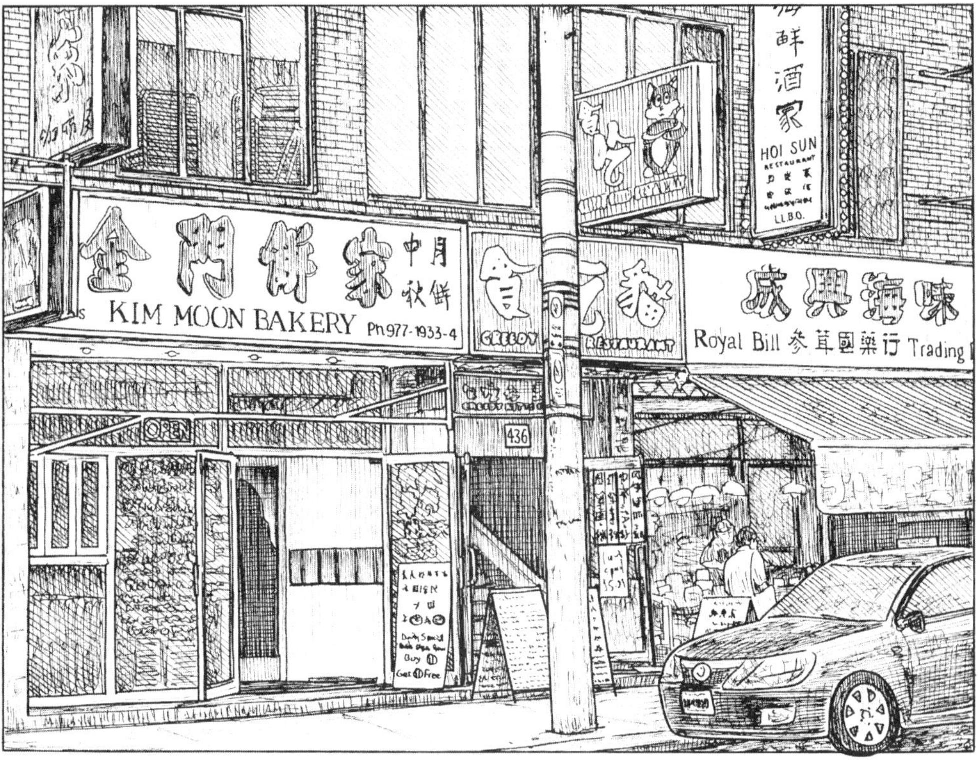
金門餅家
中月
秋餅
KIM MOON BAKERY
Ph 977-1933-4
GREEDY
RESTAURANT
海鮮酒家
HOI SUN
RESTAURANT
LLBO.
成興海味
Royal Bill 参茸國藥行 Trading
OPEN
436
Buy 1
Get 1 Free

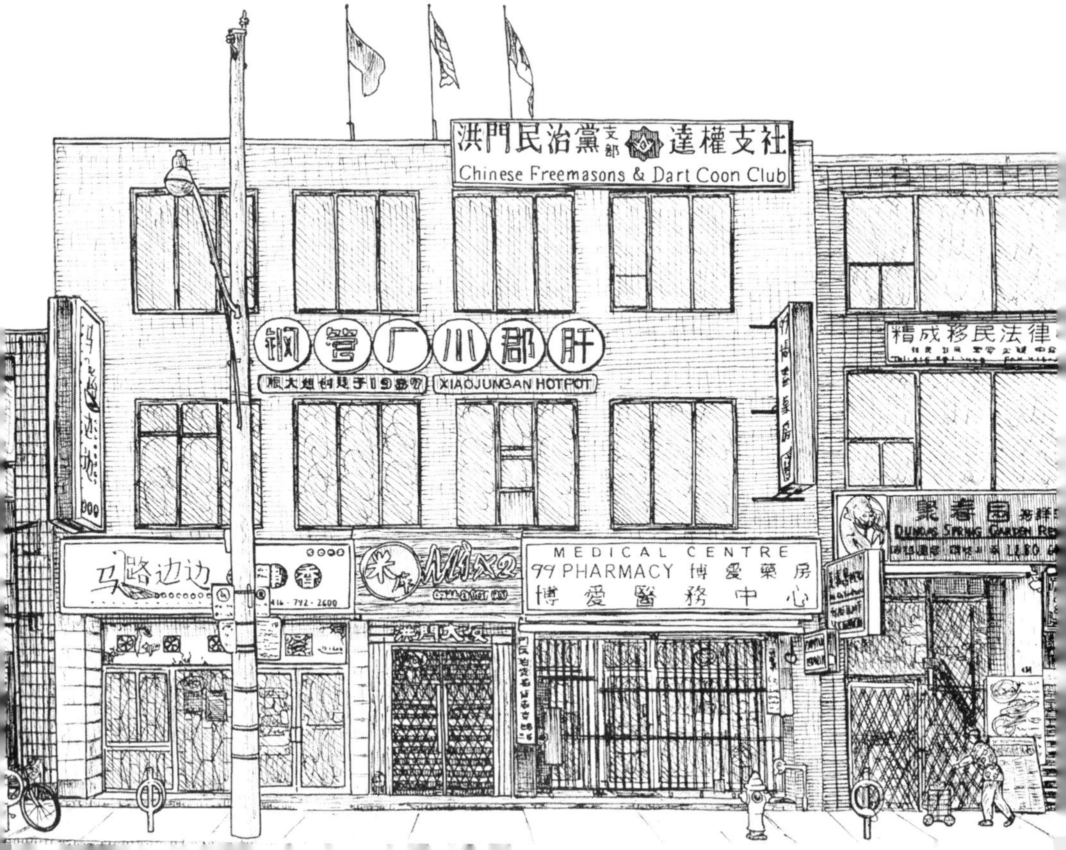
洪門民治黨支部 達權支社
Chinese Freemasons & Dart Coon Club
XIAOJUNGAN HOTPOT
MEDICAL CENTRE
99 PHARMACY 博愛藥房
博愛醫務中心
精成移民法律
马路边边
416-792-2600
LLBO

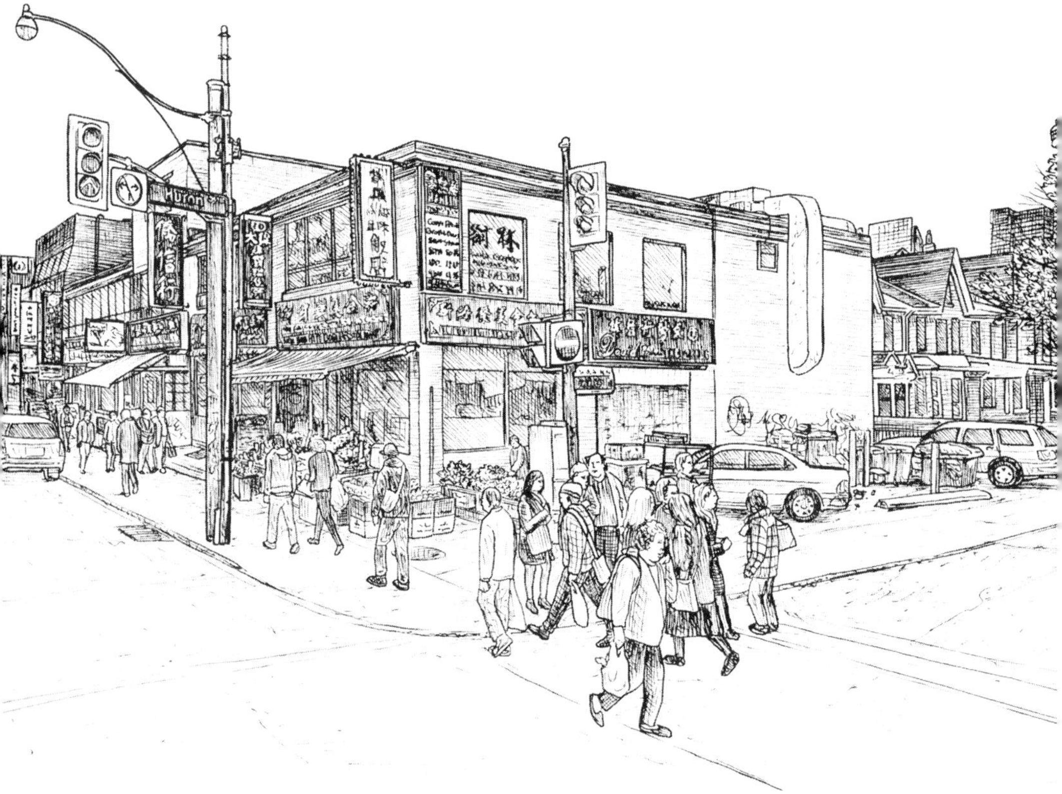
Huron

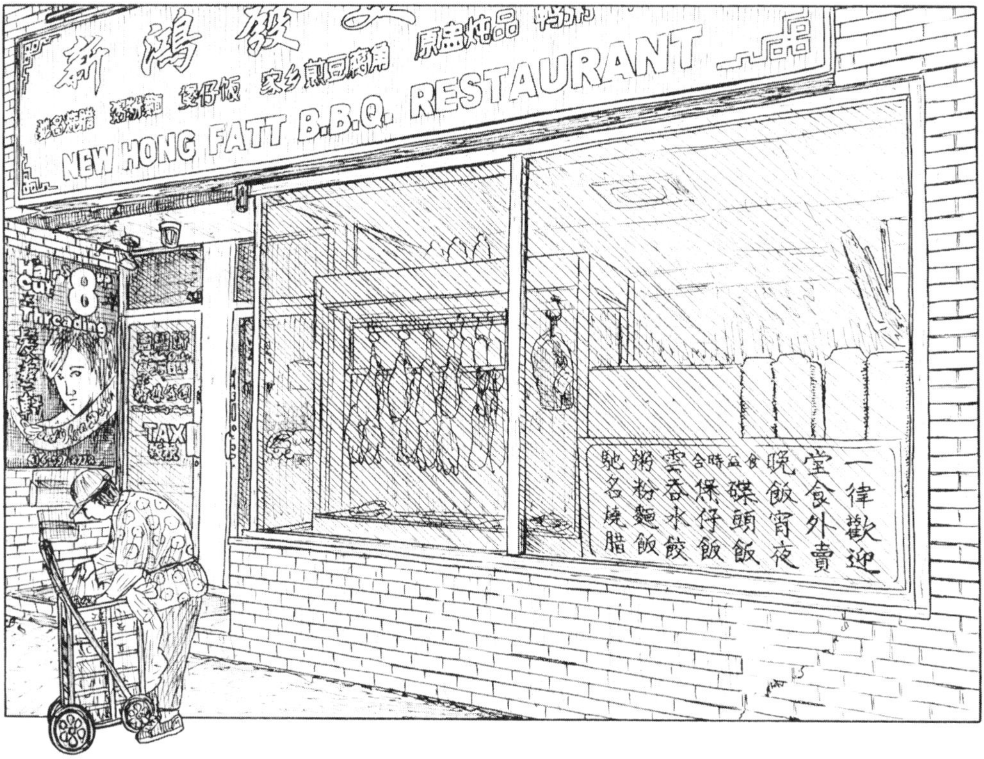
新鴻發
NEW HONG FATT B.B.Q. RESTAURANT
一律歡迎
堂食外賣
晚飯宵夜
碟頭飯
煲仔飯
雲吞水餃
粥粉麵飯
馳名燒臘
Hair Cut 8 Threading
TAX

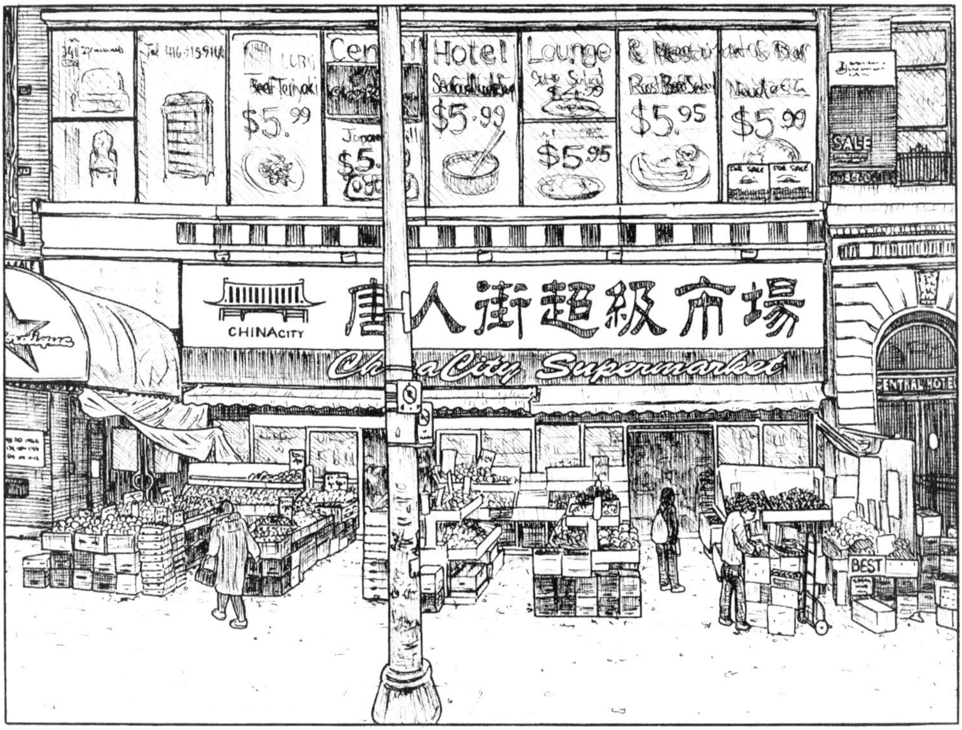
Hotel
Lounge
$5.99
$5.99
$5.95
$5.95
$5.99
唐人街超級市場
CHINACITY
ChinaCity Supermarket
CENTRAL HOTEL
SALE
BEST

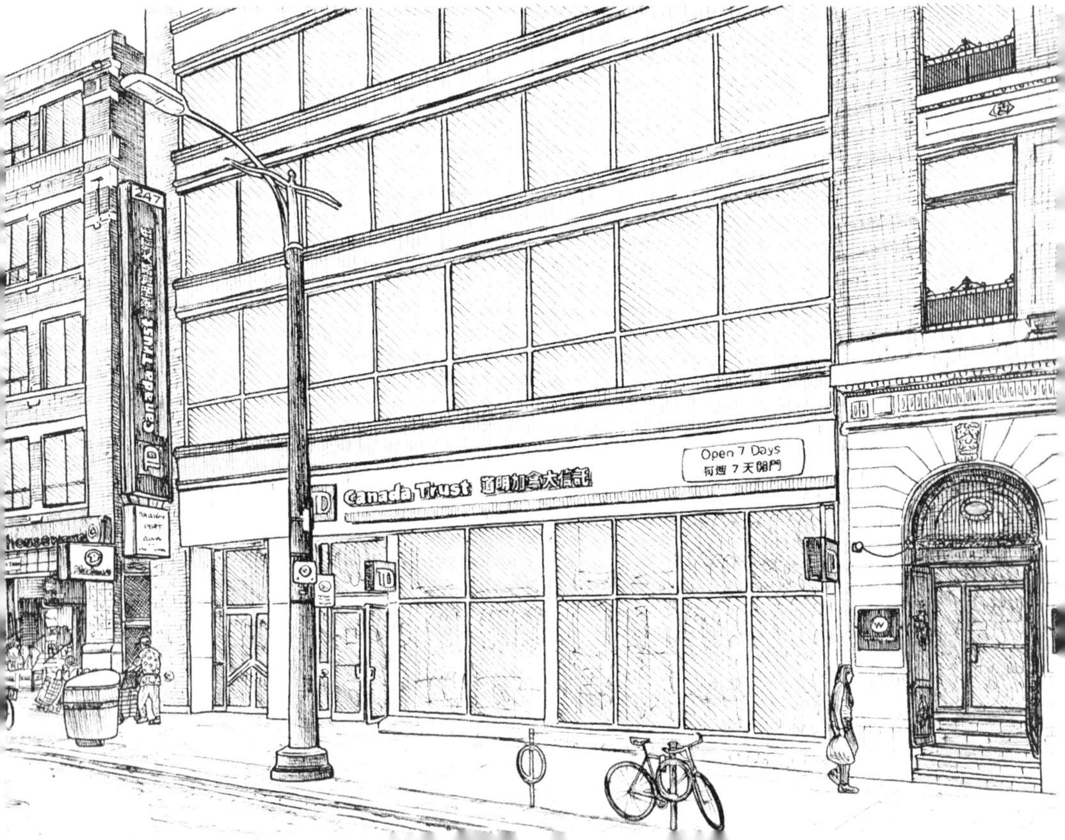
Canada Trust 道明加拿大信託
Open 7 Days
每週 7 天開門
247
Canada Trust

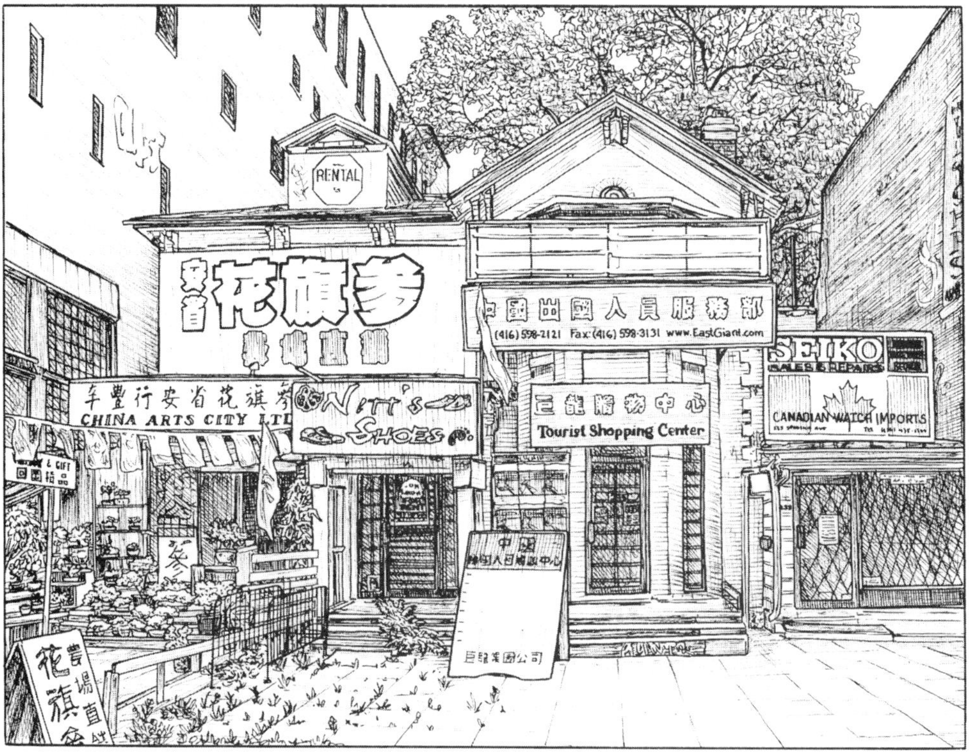
RENTAL
花旗參
CHINA ARTS CITY LTD
NITT'S SHOES
中國出國人員服務部
(416) 598-2121 Fax: (416) 598-3131 www.EastGiant.com
SEIKO
SALES & REPAIRS
CANADIAN WATCH IMPORTS
Tourist Shopping Center

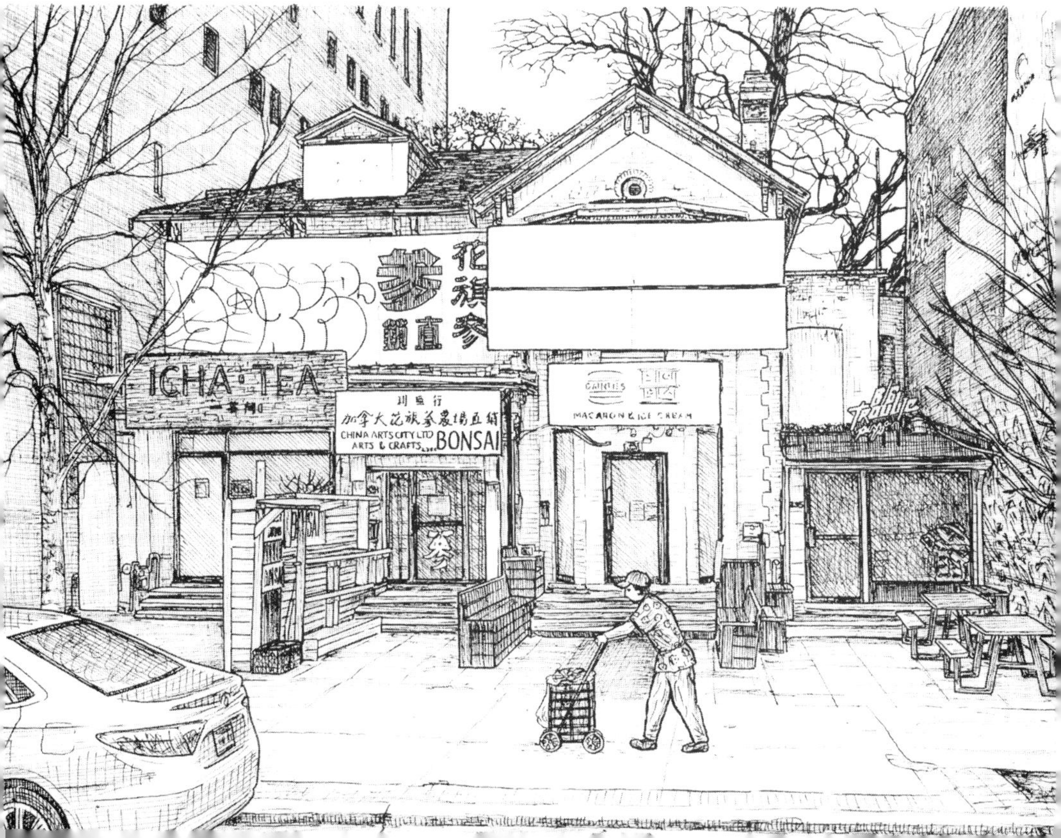
花旗參
ICHA TEA
CHINA ARTS CITY LTD
ARTS & CRAFTS
BONSAI
MACARON & ICE CREAM

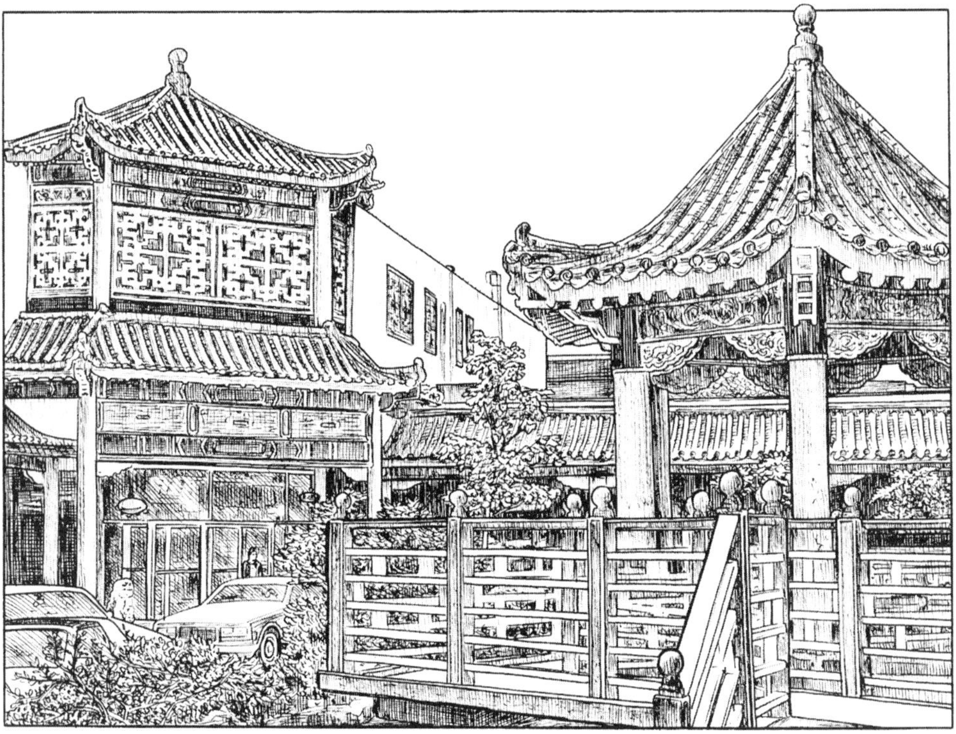

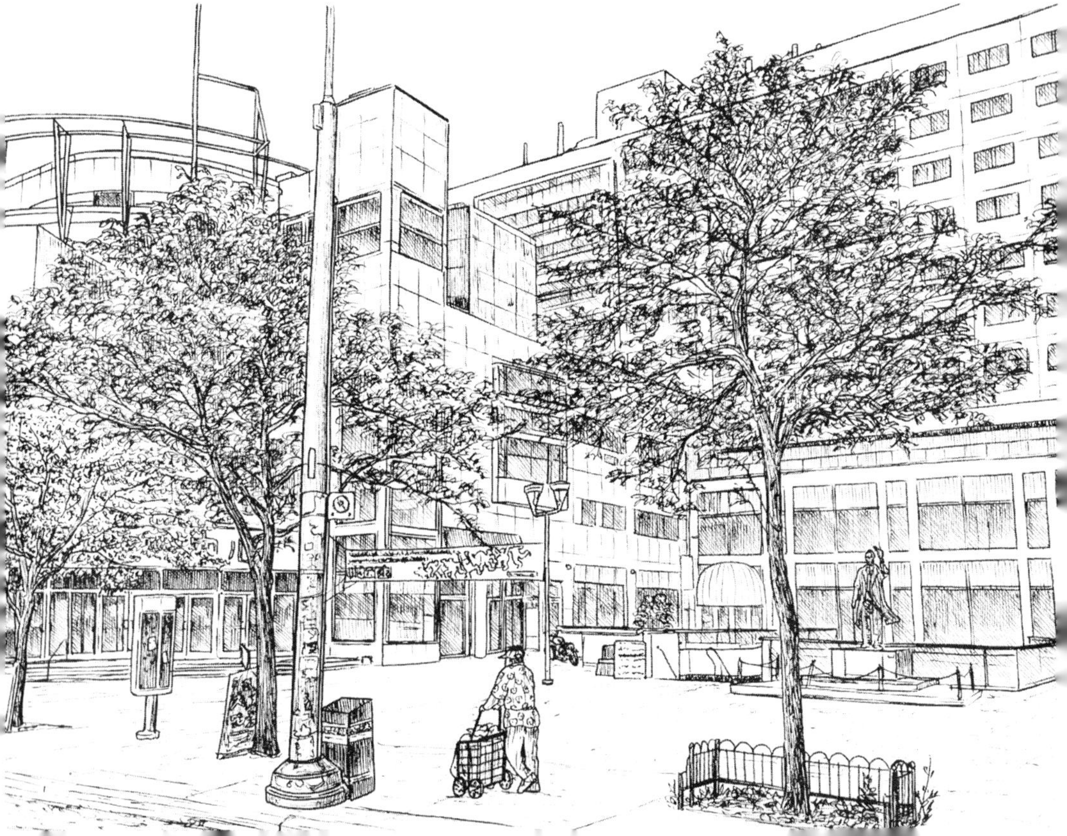

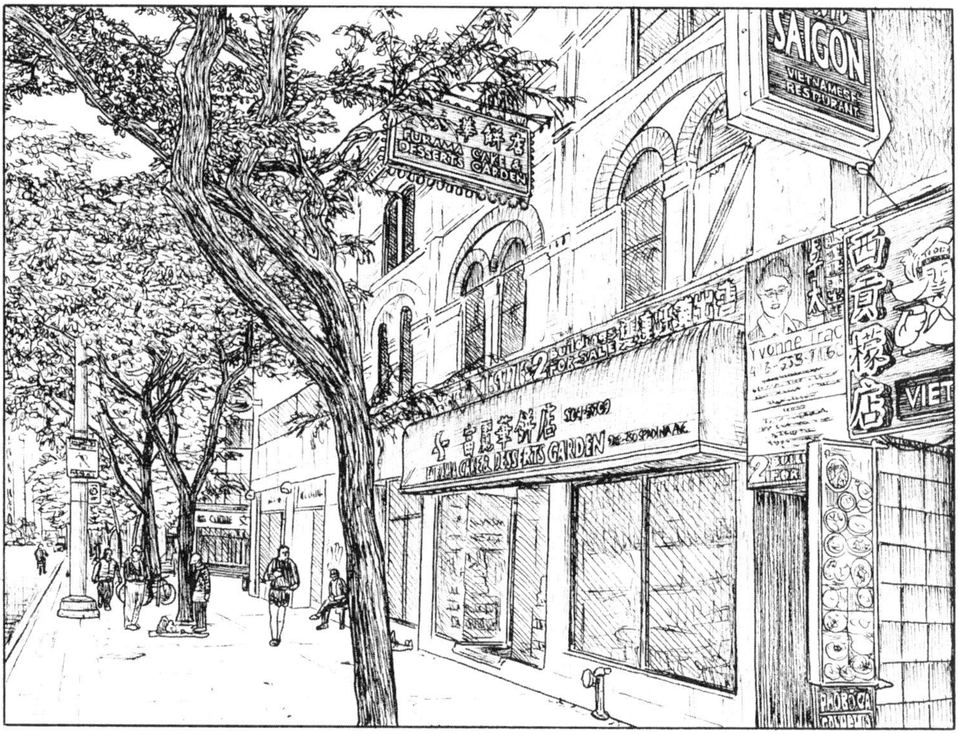
SAIGON
VIETNAMESE RESTAURANT
富麗華餅店
FURAMA CAKE & DESSERTS GARDEN
富麗華餅店
DESSERTS GARDEN
2 buildings FOR SALE
Yvonne Trac

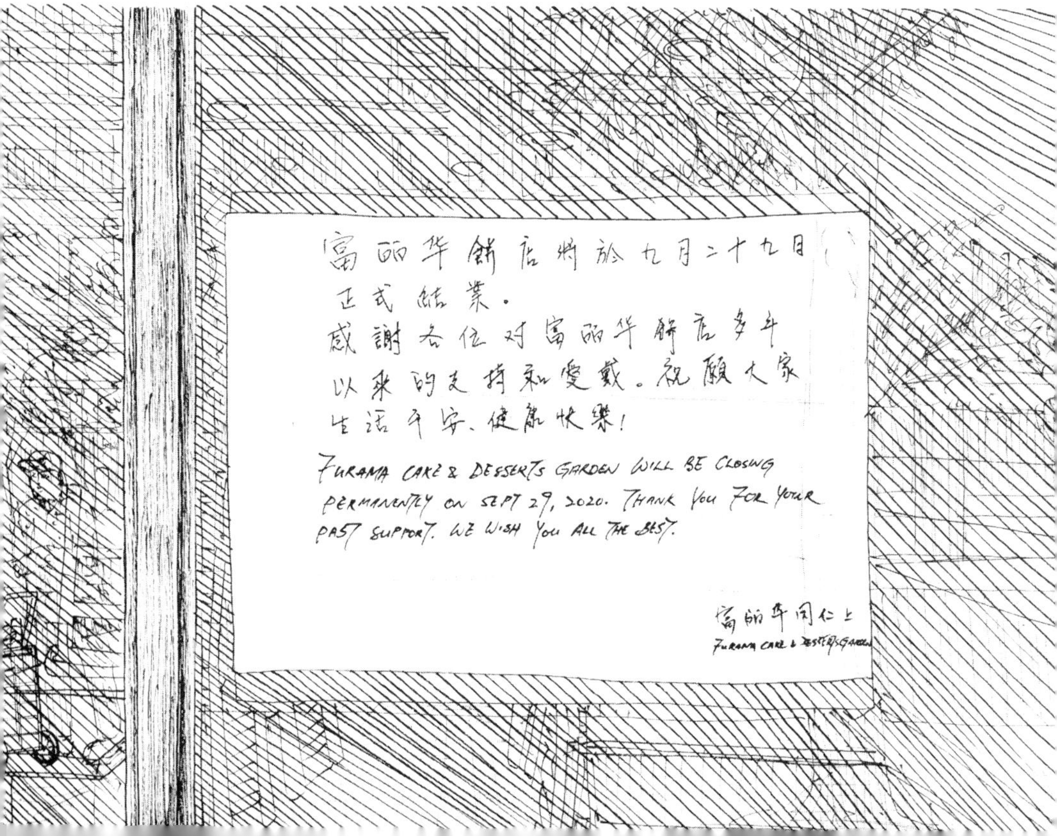
富丽华餅店將於九月二十九日
正式結業。
感謝各位对富丽华餅店多年
以來的支持和愛戴。祝願大家
生活平安、健康快樂！
FURAMA CAKE & DESSERTS GARDEN WILL BE CLOSING PERMANENTLY ON SEPT 29, 2020. THANK YOU FOR YOUR PAST SUPPORT. WE WISH YOU ALL THE BEST.
富丽华同仁上
FURAMA CAKE & DESSERTS GARDEN

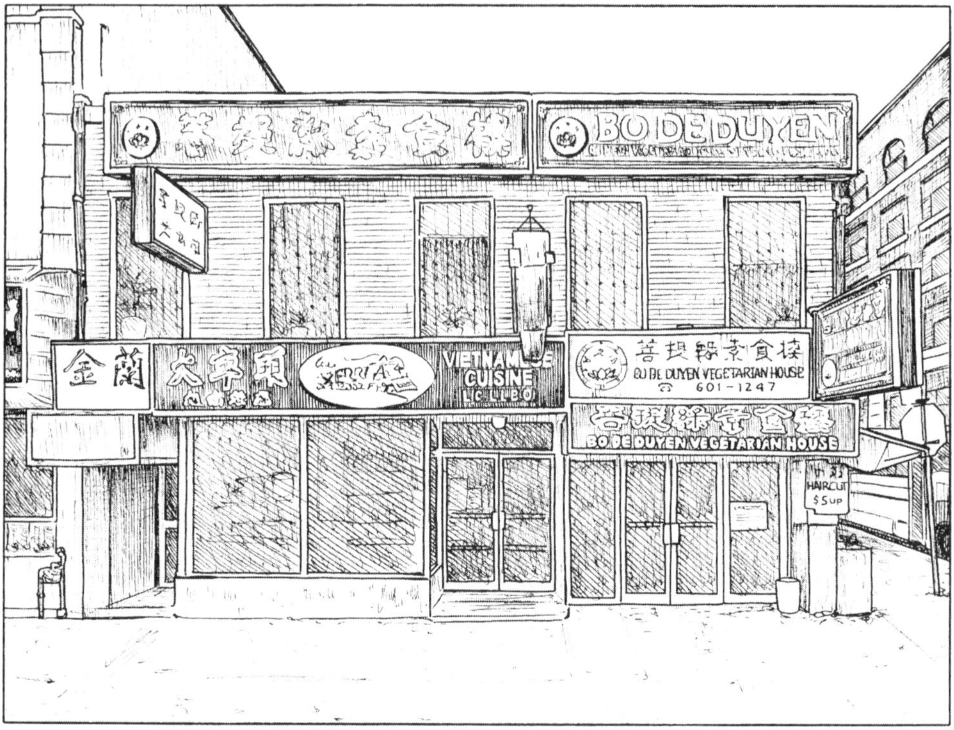
菩提緣素食樓
BO DE DUYEN
金蘭
VIETNAMESE CUISINE
菩提緣素食棧
BO DE DUYEN VEGETARIAN HOUSE
601-1247
BO DE DUYEN VEGETARIAN HOUSE
HAIRCUT $5 UP

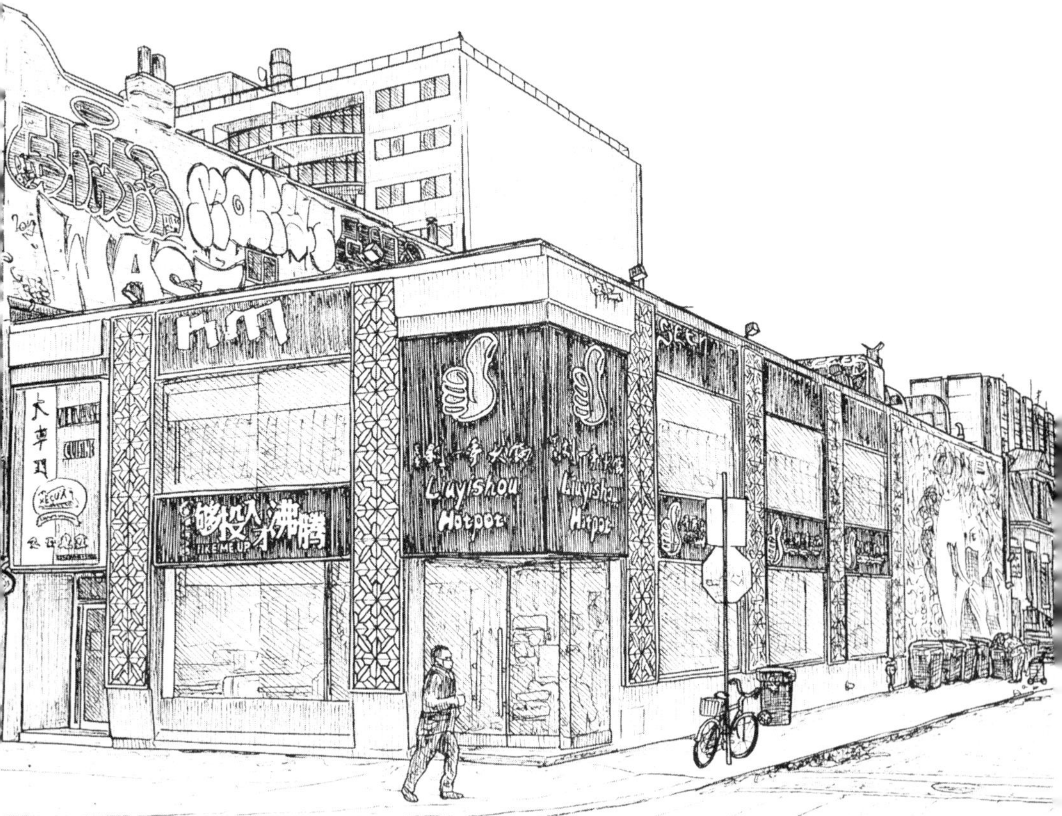
TAKE ME UP
Liuyishou Hotpot
Liuyishou Hotpot

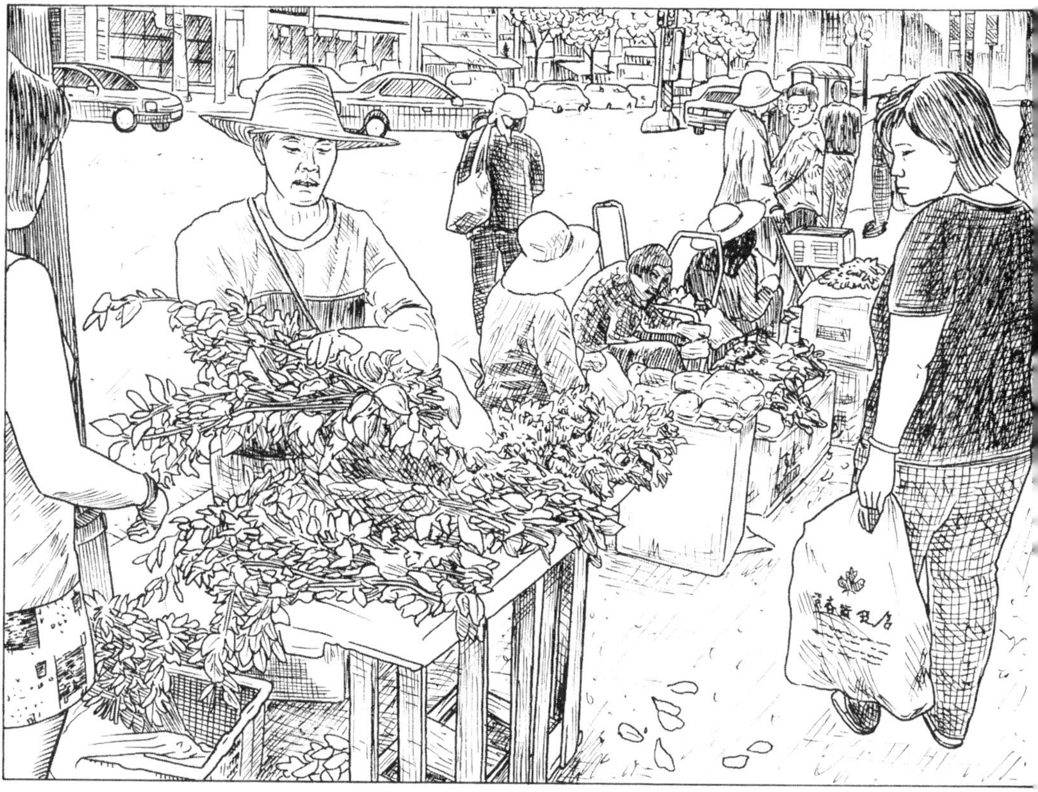

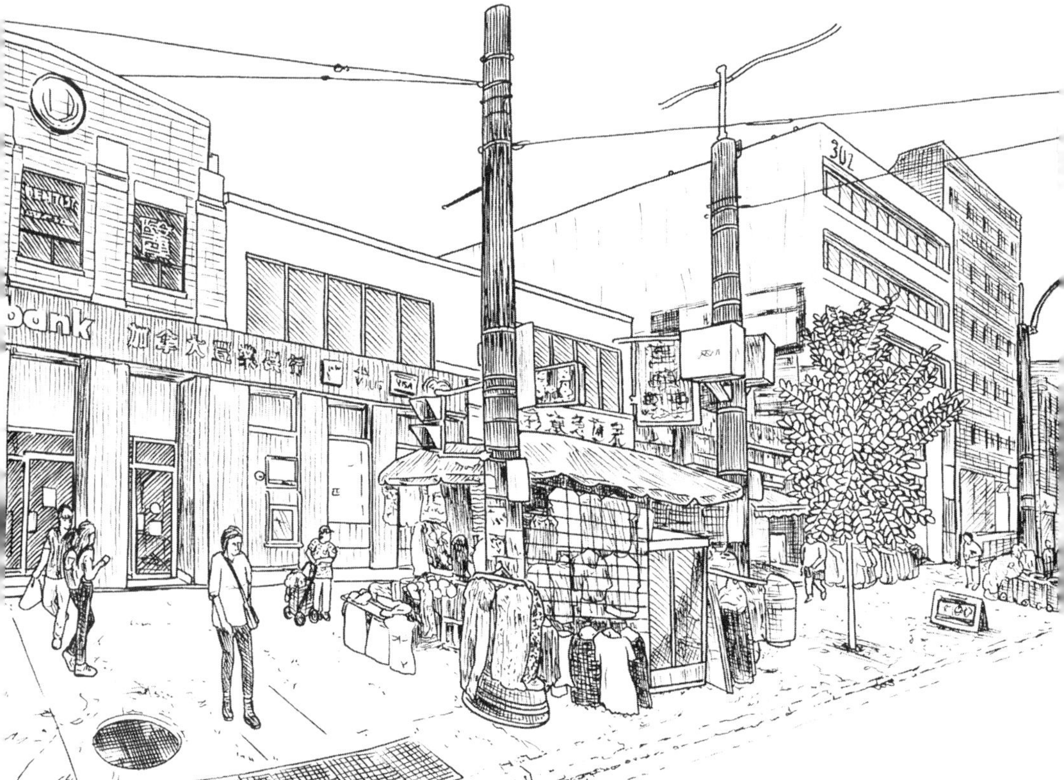
bank
加拿大豐業銀行
VISA
302

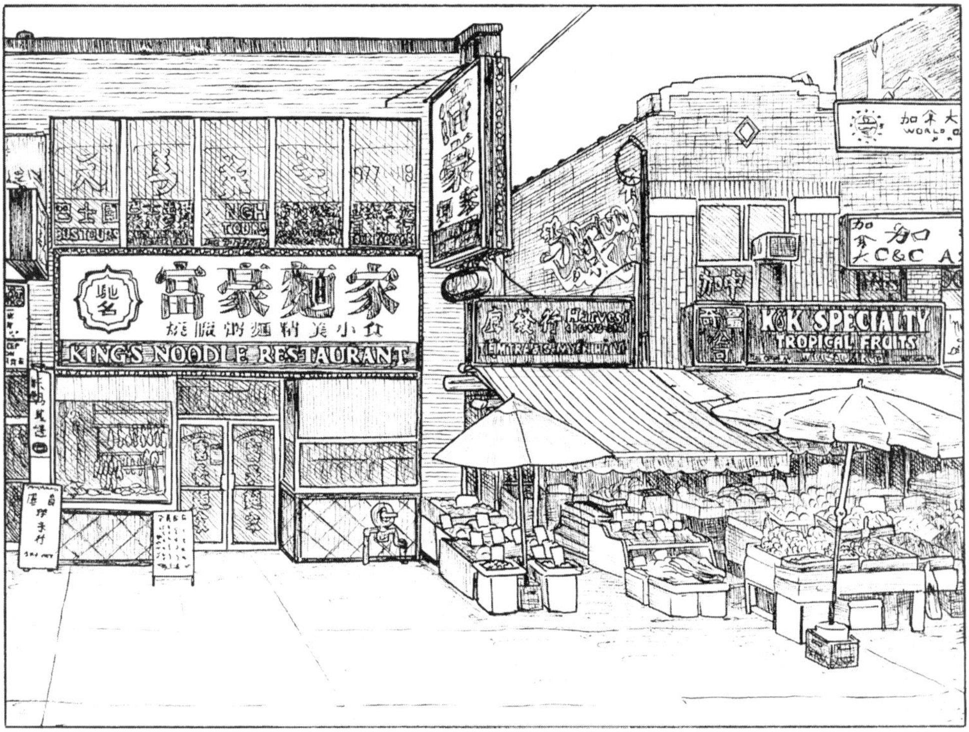
高豪麵家
燒臘粥麵精美小食
KING'S NOODLE RESTAURANT
BUS TOURS
K&K SPECIALTY
TROPICAL FRUITS
Harvest
C&C
WORLD

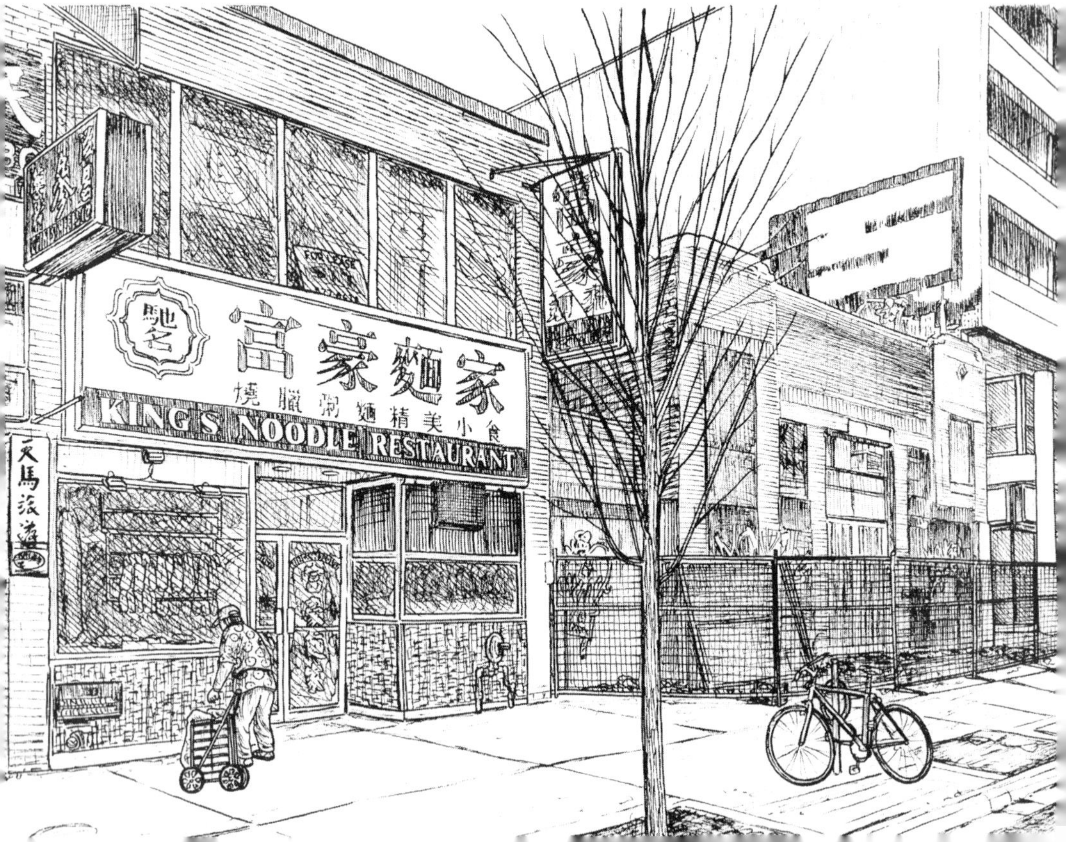
高豪麵家
燒臘粥麵精美小食
KING'S NOODLE RESTAURANT
FOR LEASE

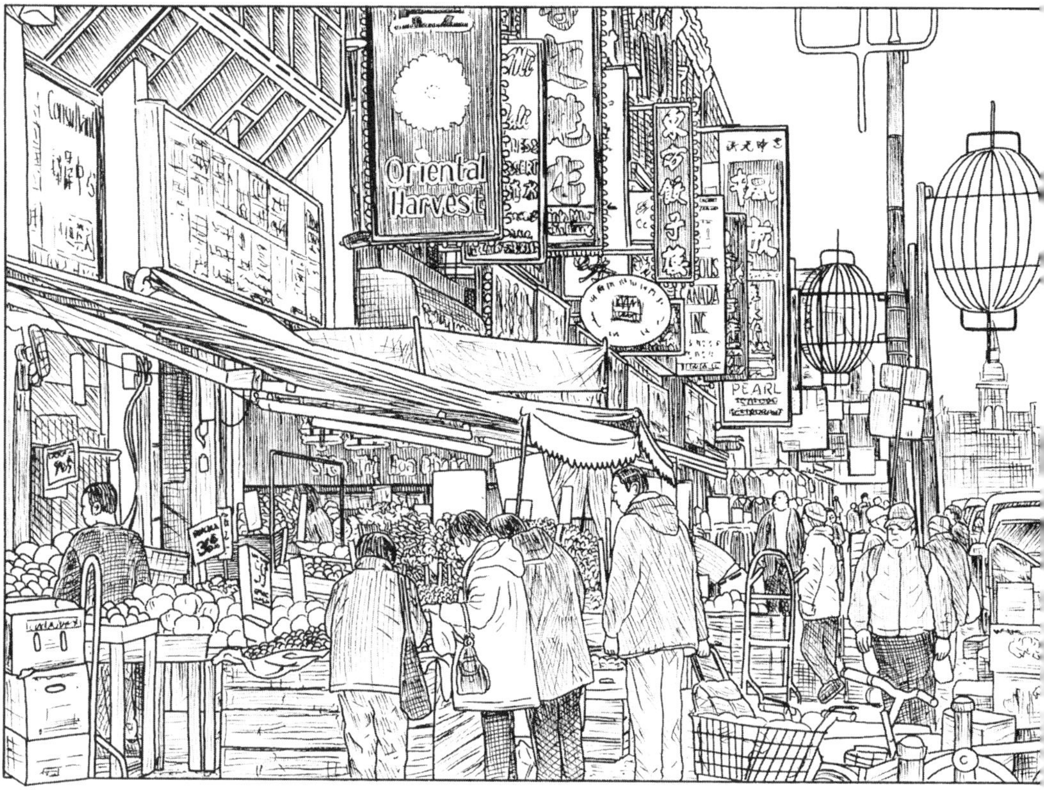
Oriental Harvest
PEARL
CANADA
INC
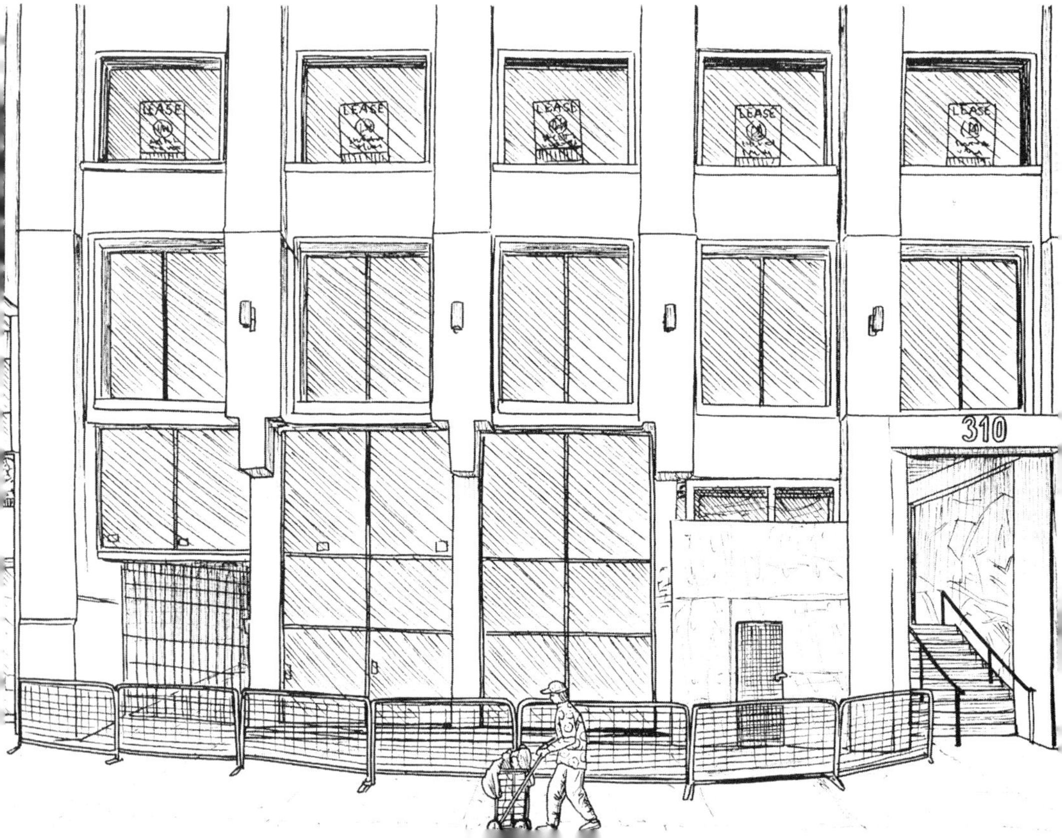
LEASE
LEASE
LEASE
LEASE
LEASE
310

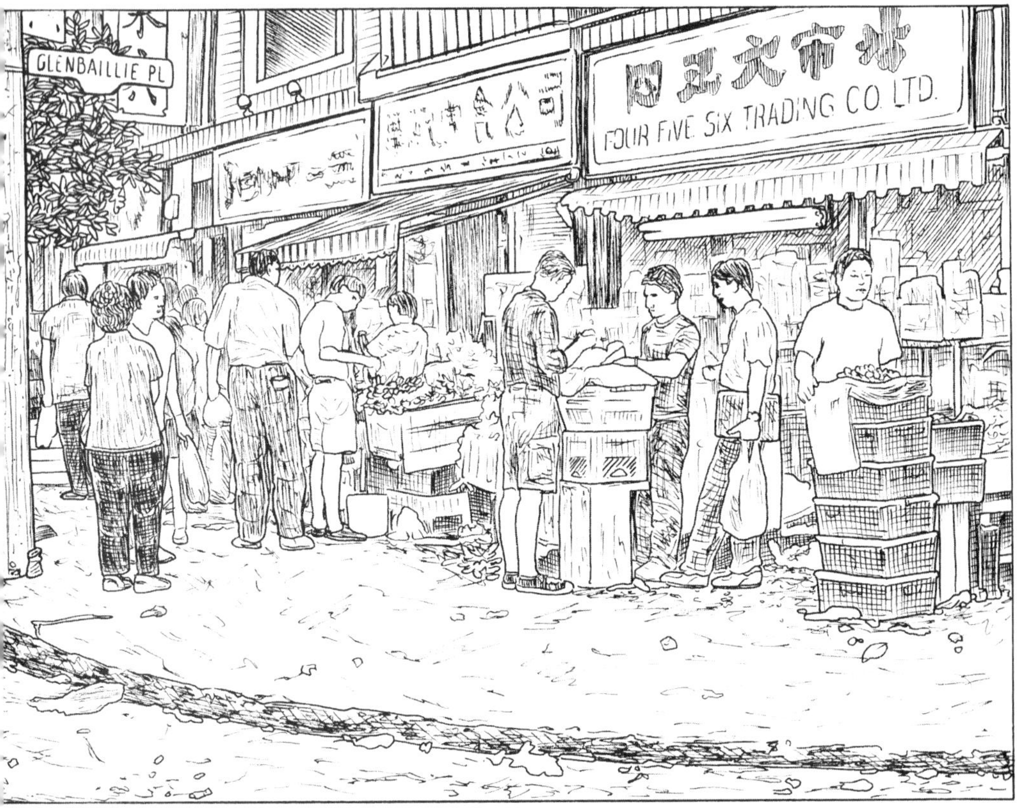
GLENBAILLIE PL
FOUR FIVE SIX TRADING CO. LTD.

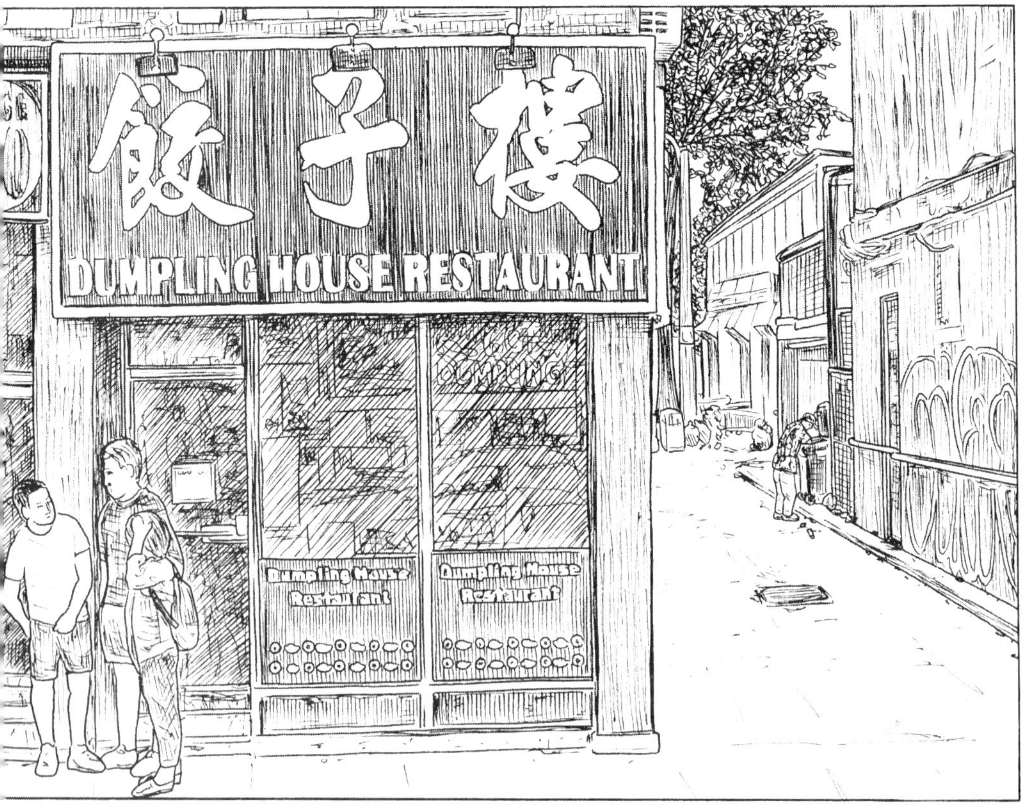
餃子樓
DUMPLING HOUSE RESTAURANT
DUMPLING
Dumpling House Restaurant
Dumpling House Restaurant

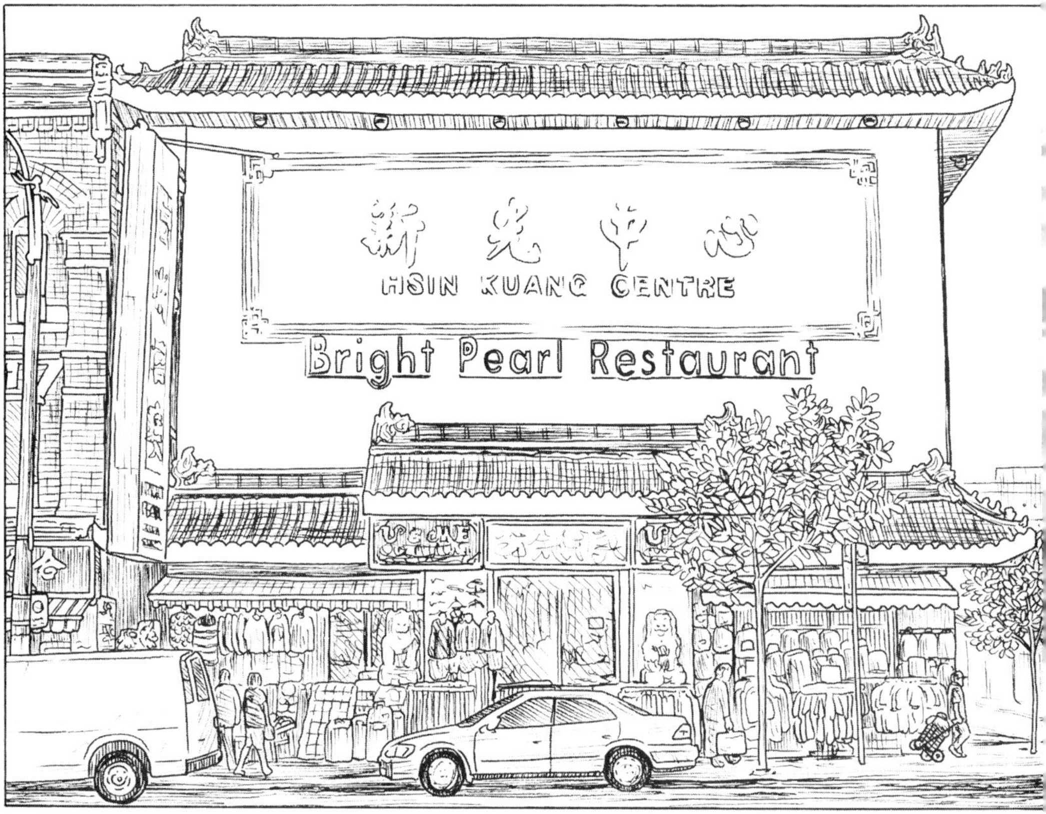
新光中心
HSIN KUANG CENTRE
Bright Pearl Restaurant

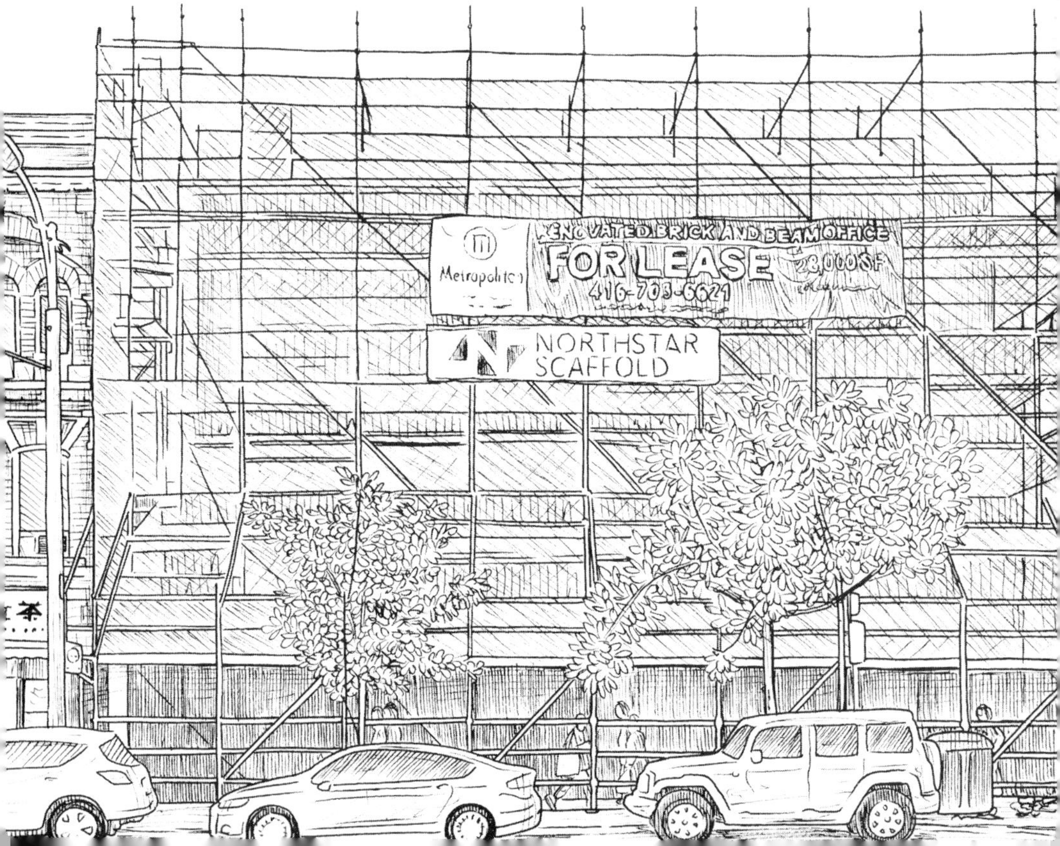
RENOVATED BRICK AND BEAM OFFICE
FOR LEASE
28,000SF
Metropolitan
416-703-6621
NORTHSTAR
SCAFFOLD

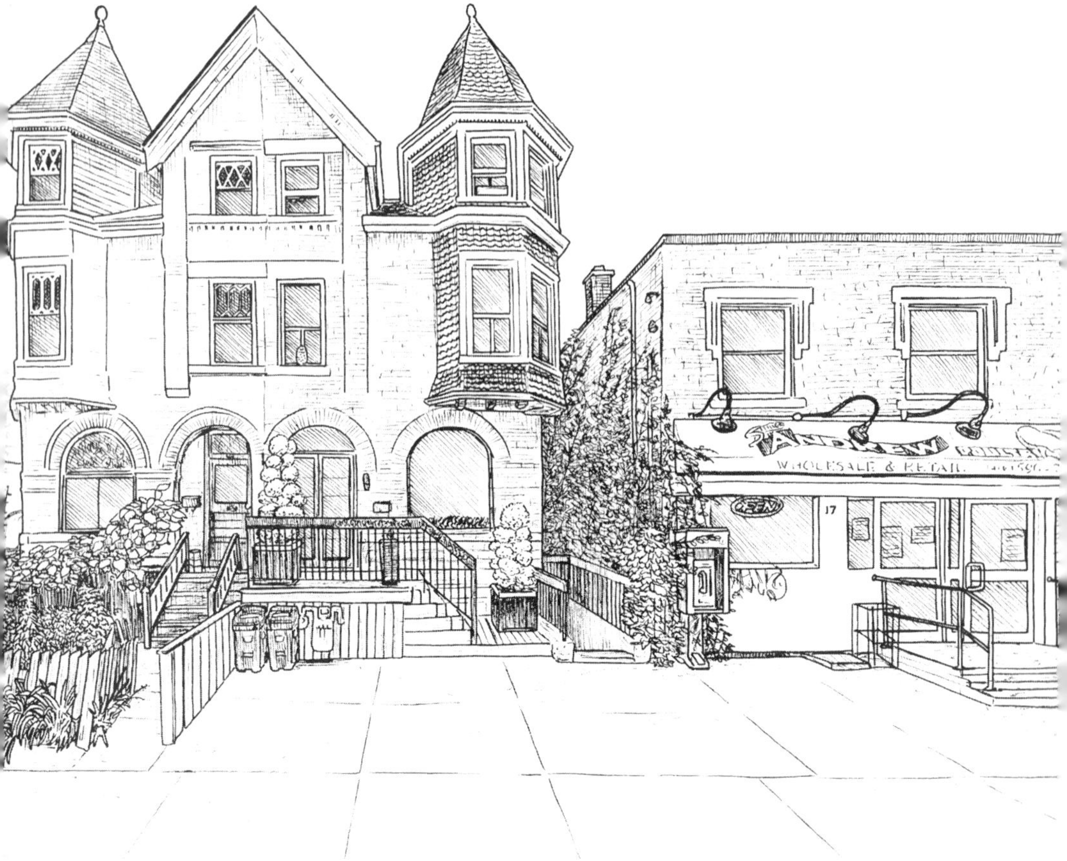
ANDREW
WHOLESALE & RETAIL
17

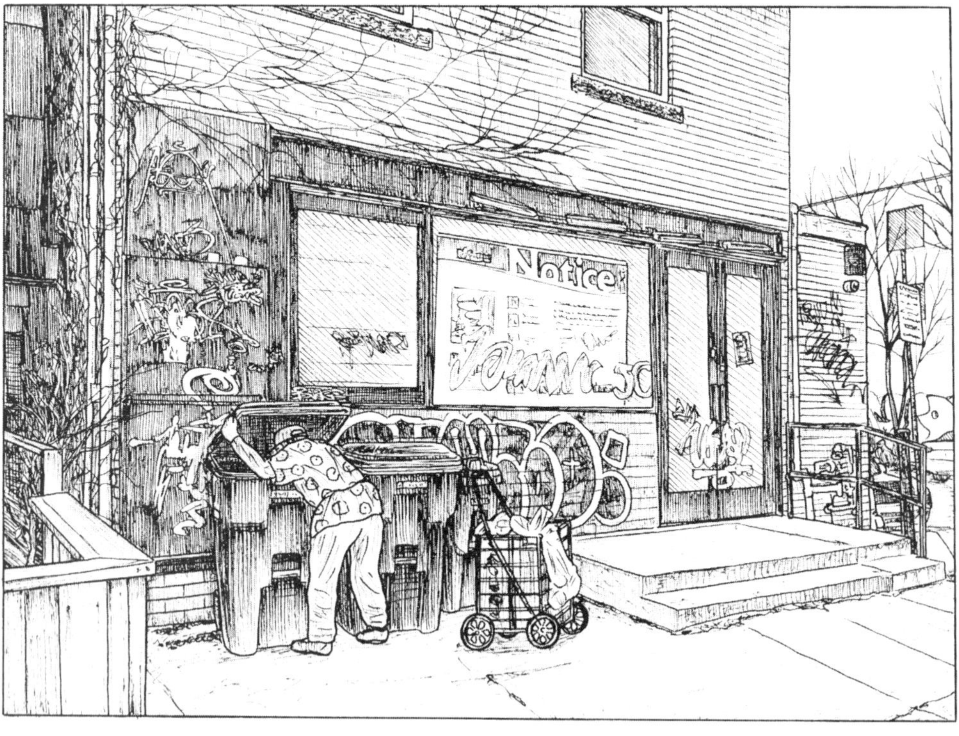
Notice

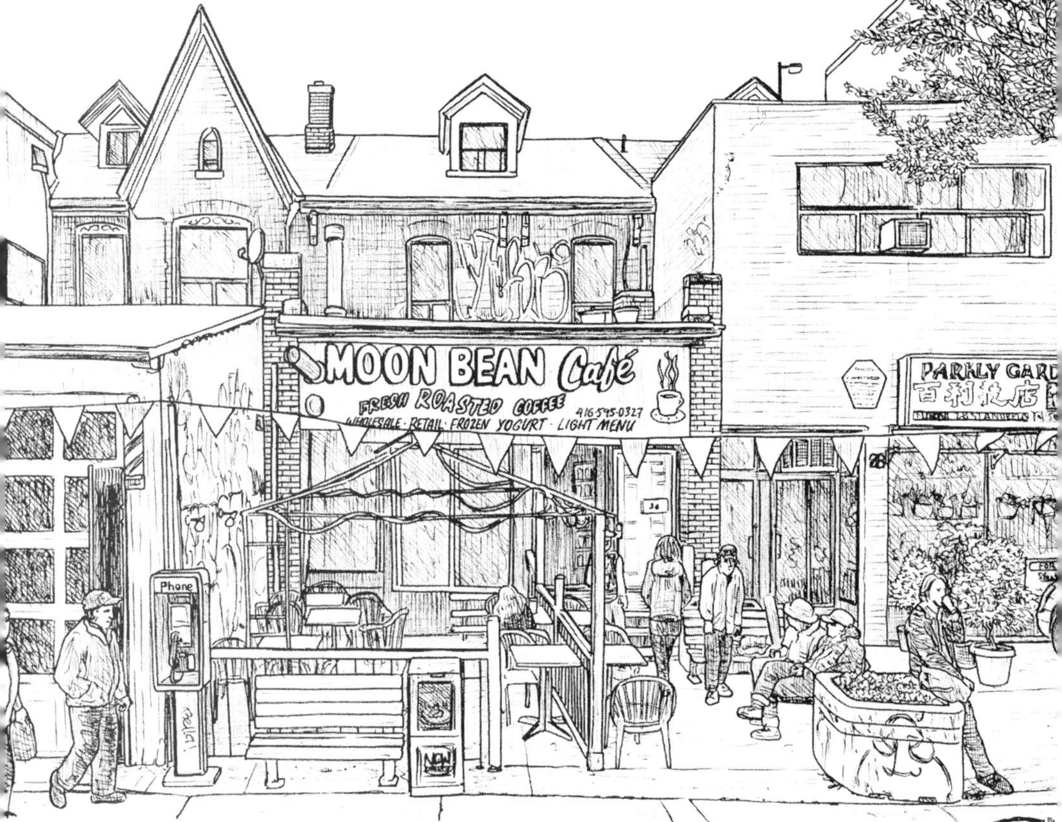
MOON BEAN Café
FRESH ROASTED COFFEE
416-595-0327
WHOLESALE · RETAIL · FROZEN YOGURT · LIGHT MENU
Phone
NOW

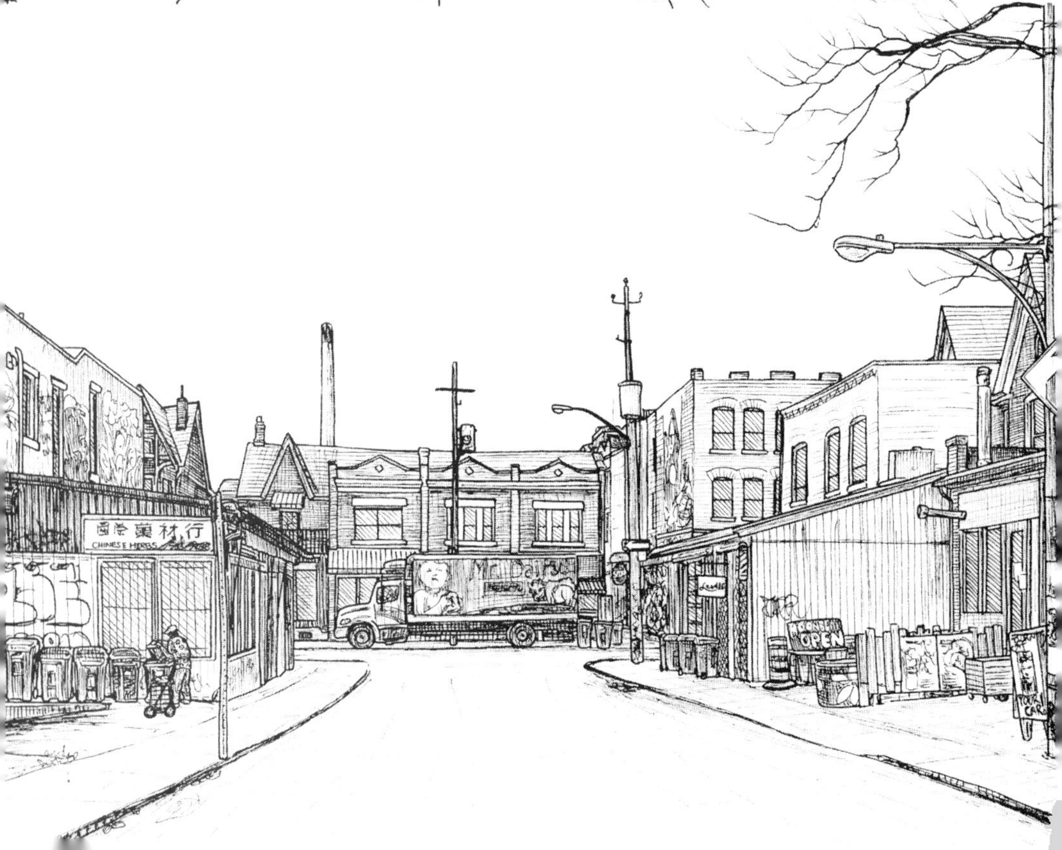
CHINESE HERBS
OPEN

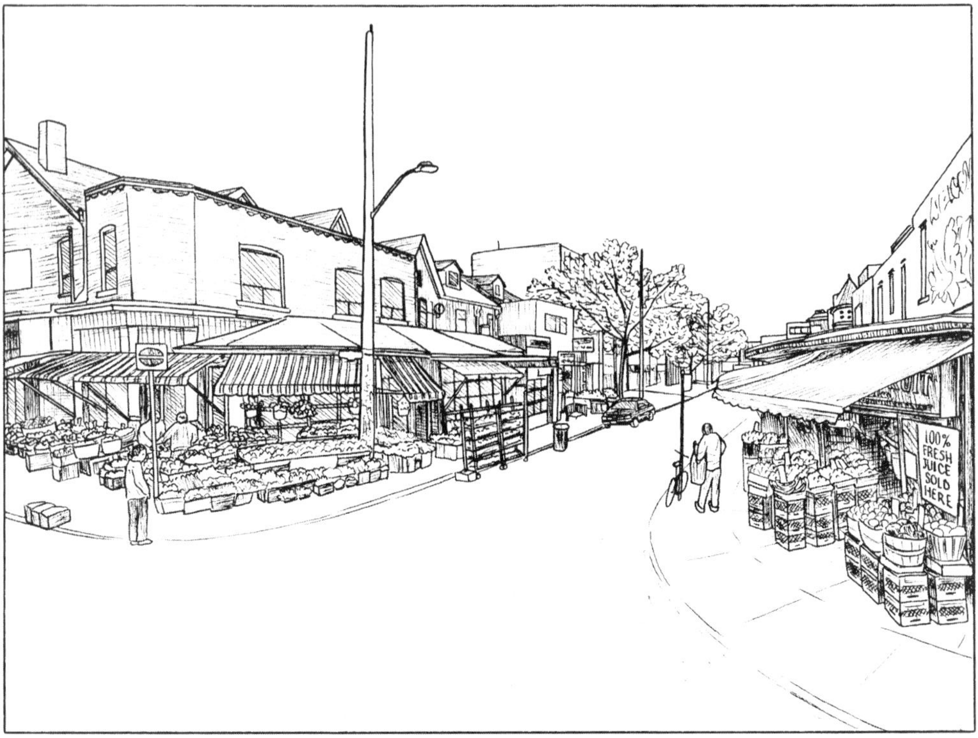

100% FRESH JUICE SOLD HERE

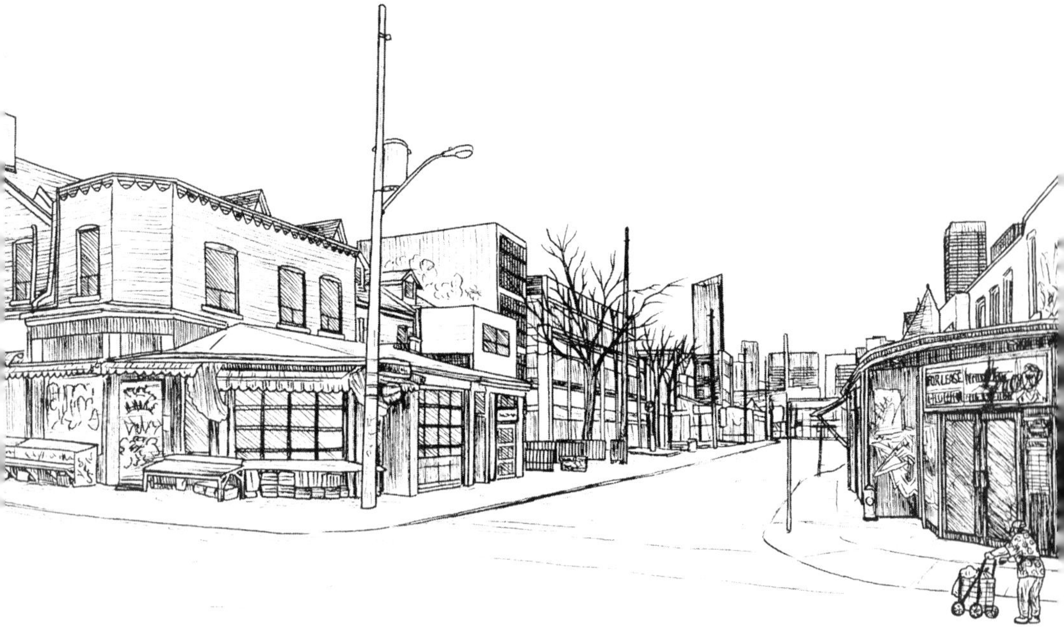

FOR LEASE

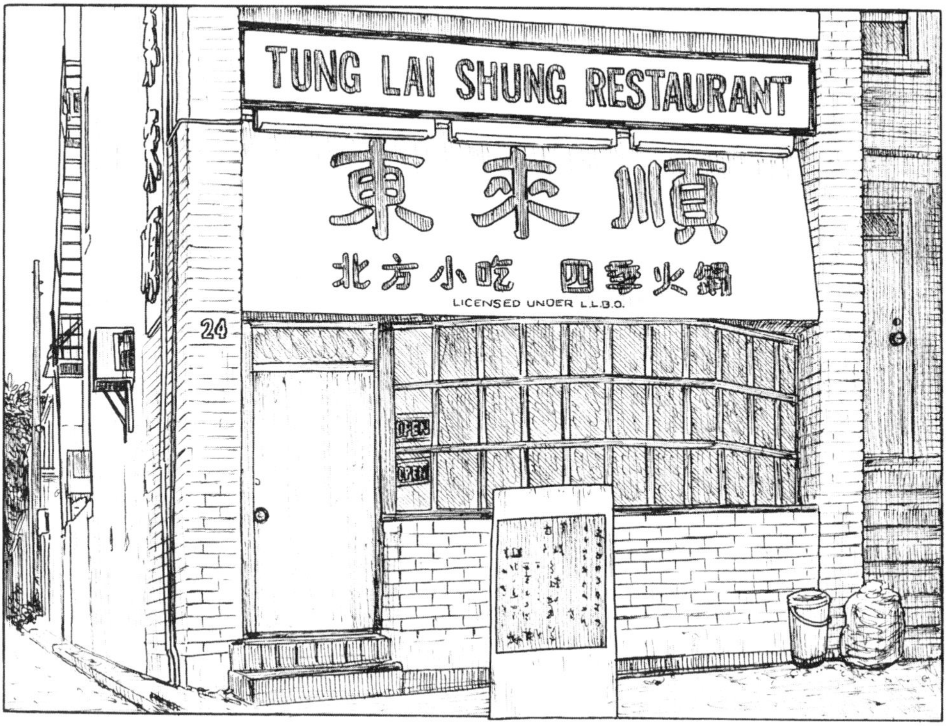
TUNG LAI SHUNG RESTAURANT
東來順
北方小吃 四季火鍋
LICENSED UNDER L.L.B.O.
24
OPEN
OPEN

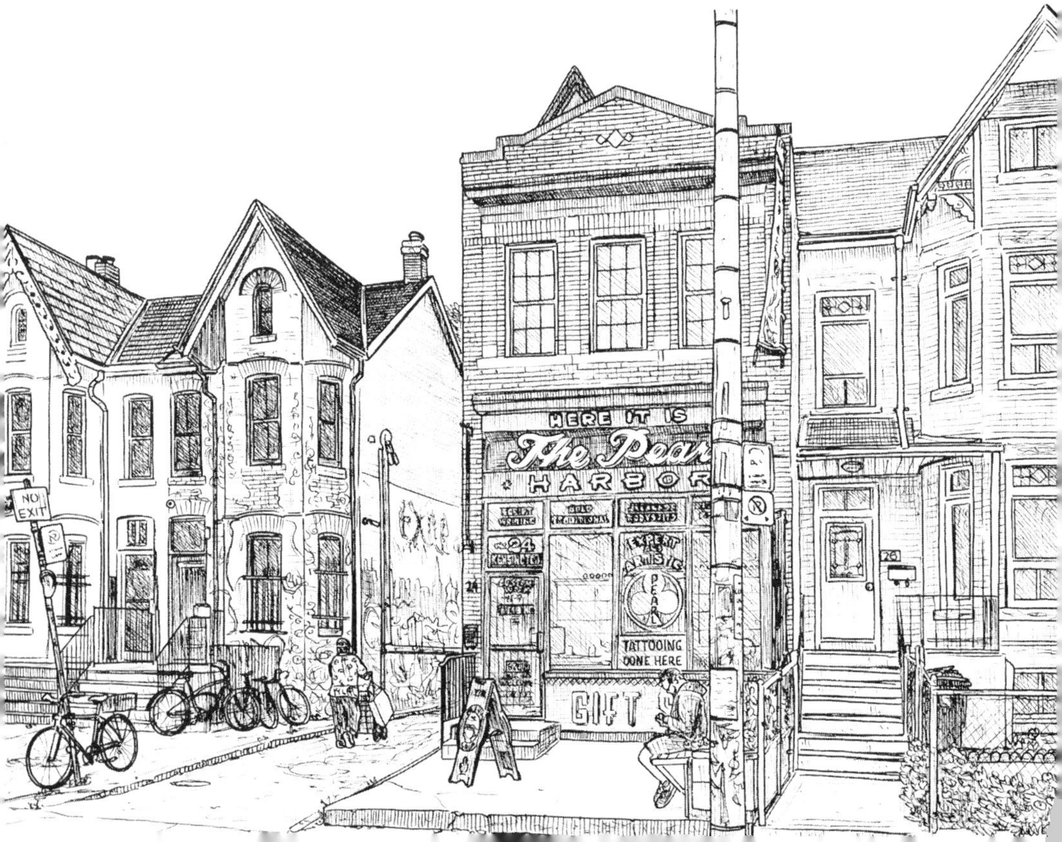
HERE IT IS
The Pearl
HARBOR
TATTOOING DONE HERE
GIFT
NO EXIT
24
26

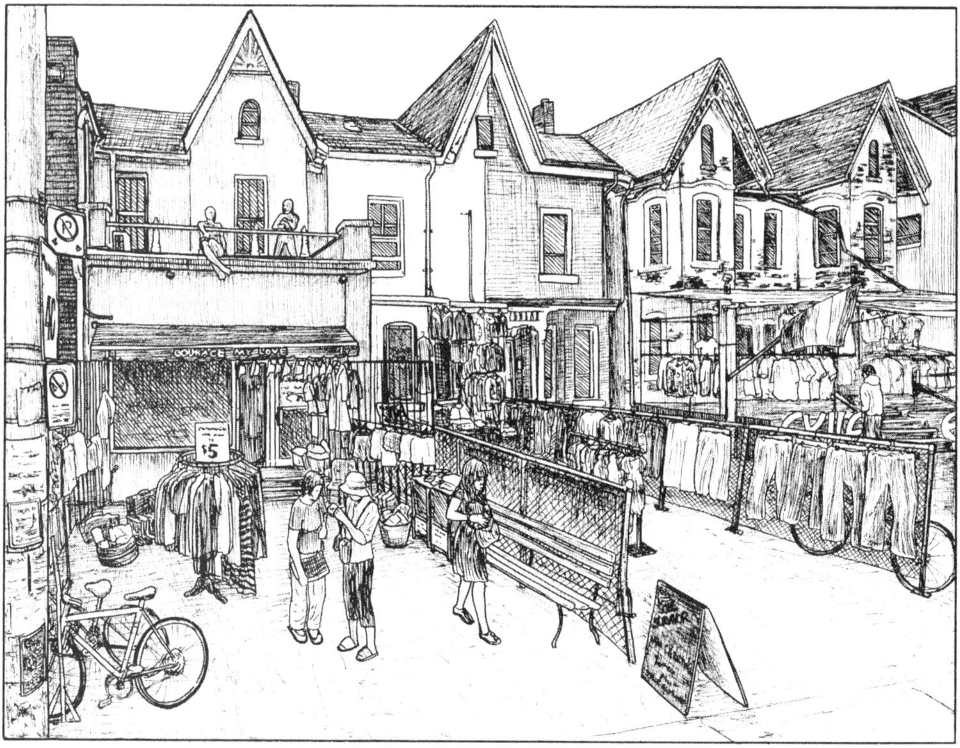
COURAGE MY LOVE
$5

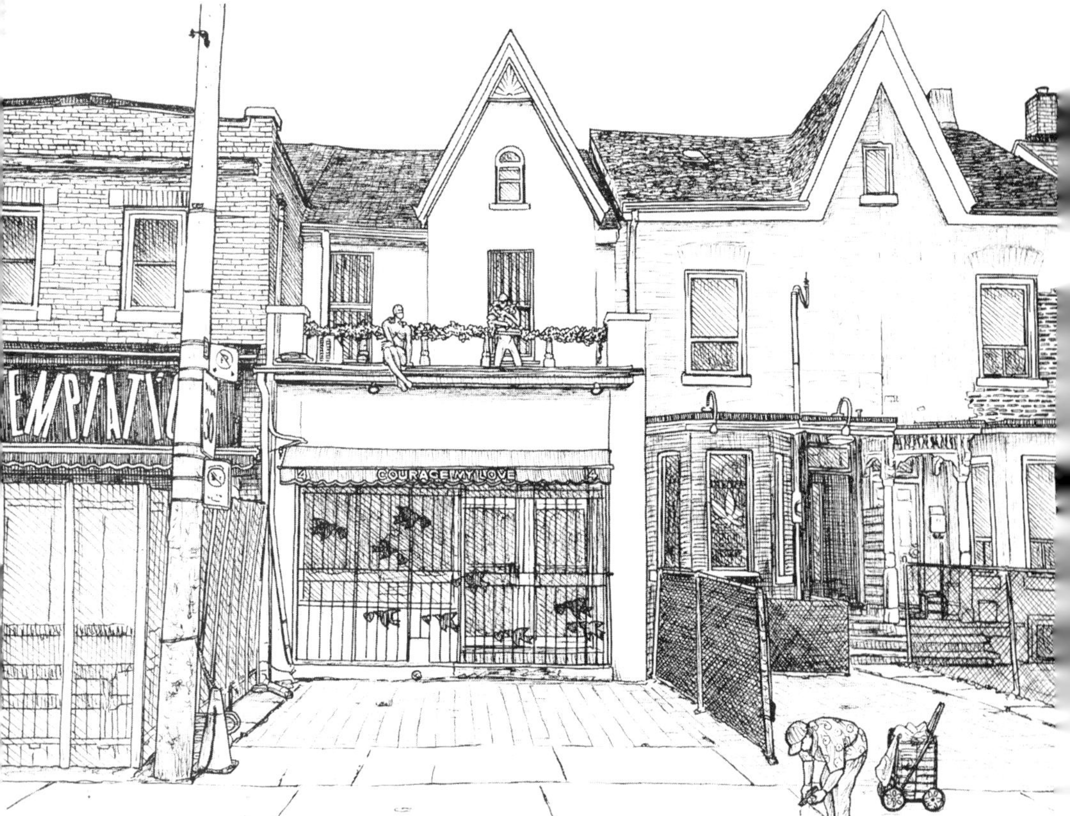
EMPTATI
COURAGE MY LOVE
30

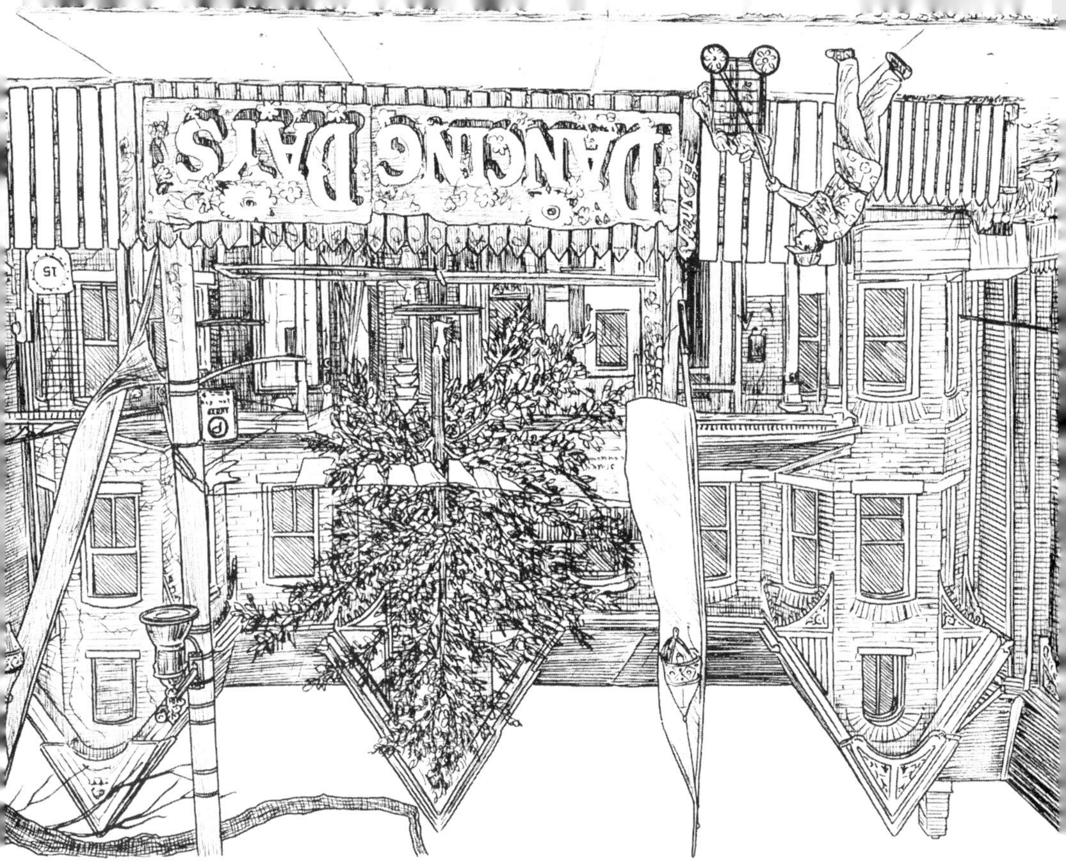
DANCING DAYS

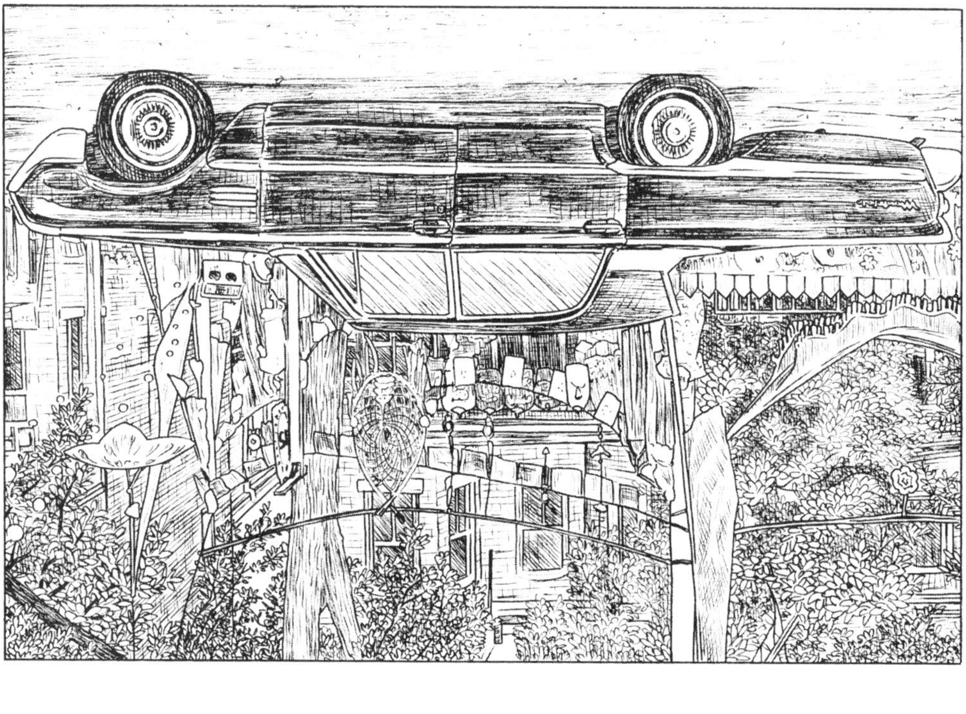

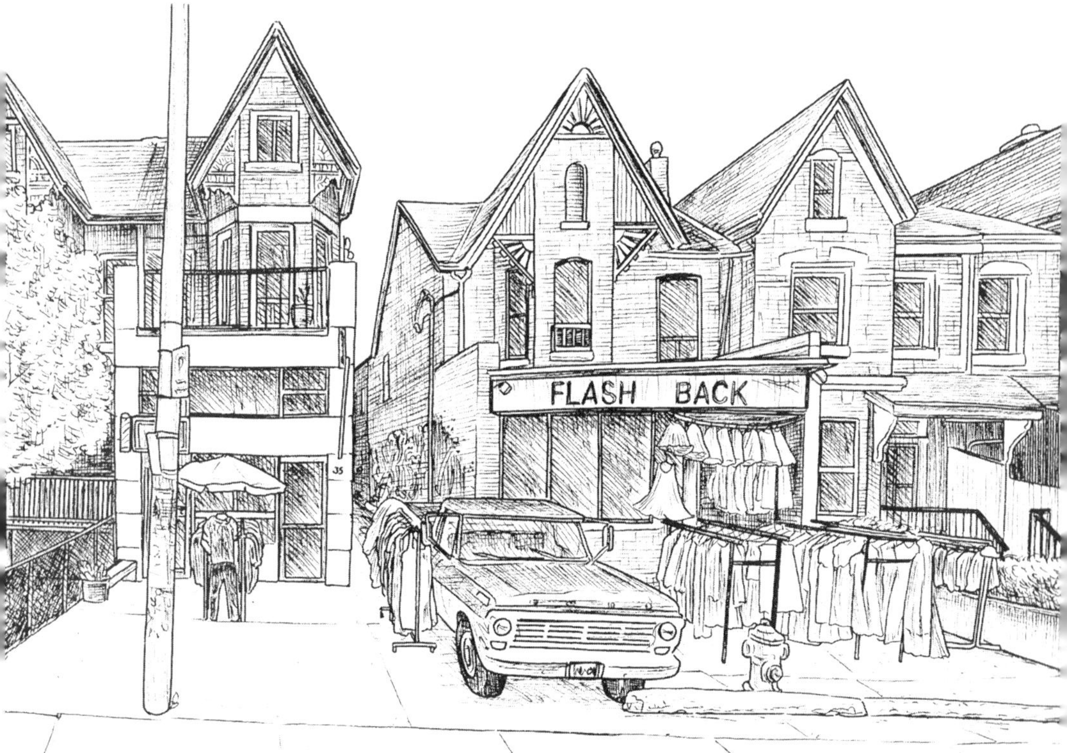
FLASH BACK
35

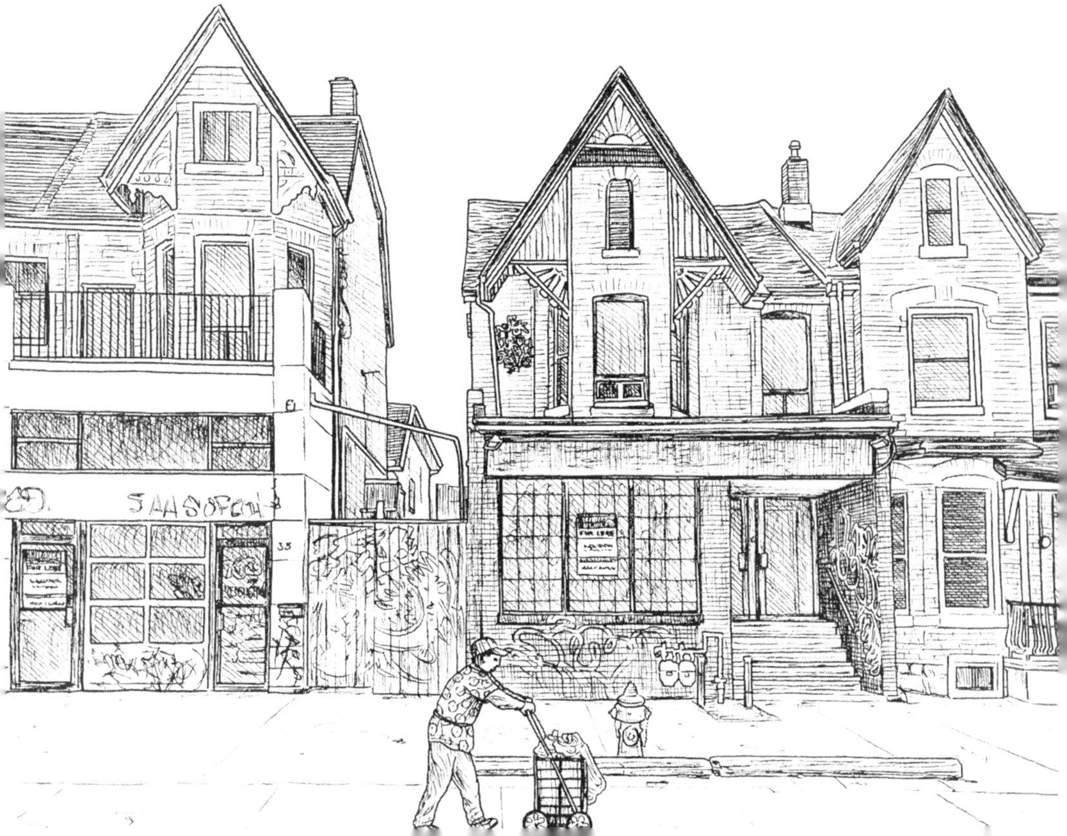
35

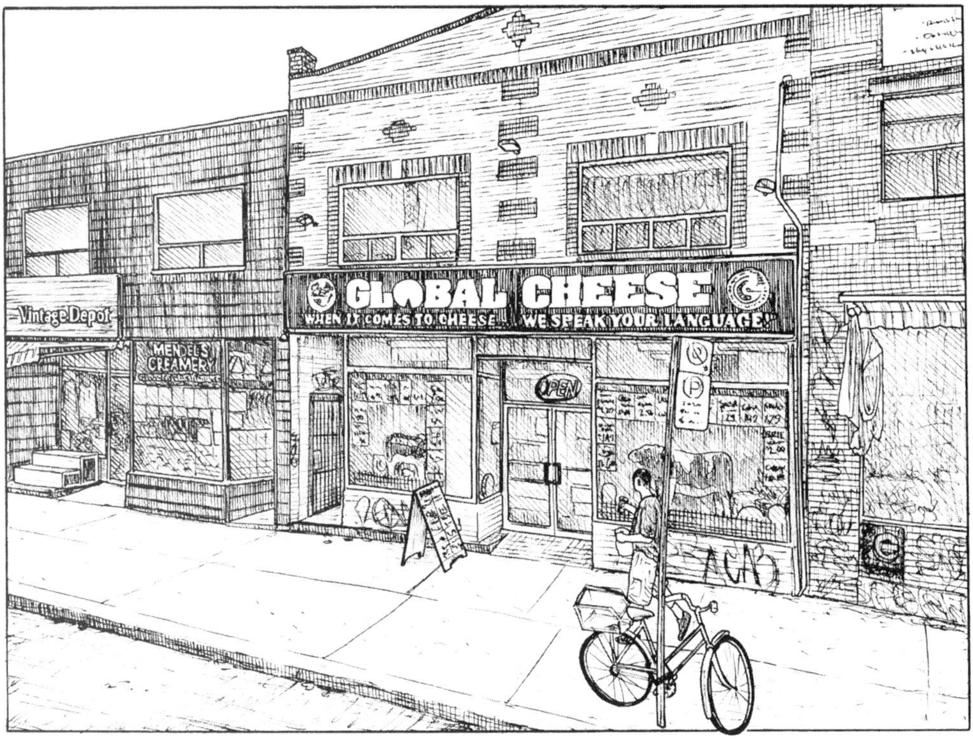
Vintage Depot
MENDEL'S CREAMERY
GLOBAL CHEESE
WHEN IT COMES TO CHEESE... WE SPEAK YOUR LANGUAGE!
OPEN

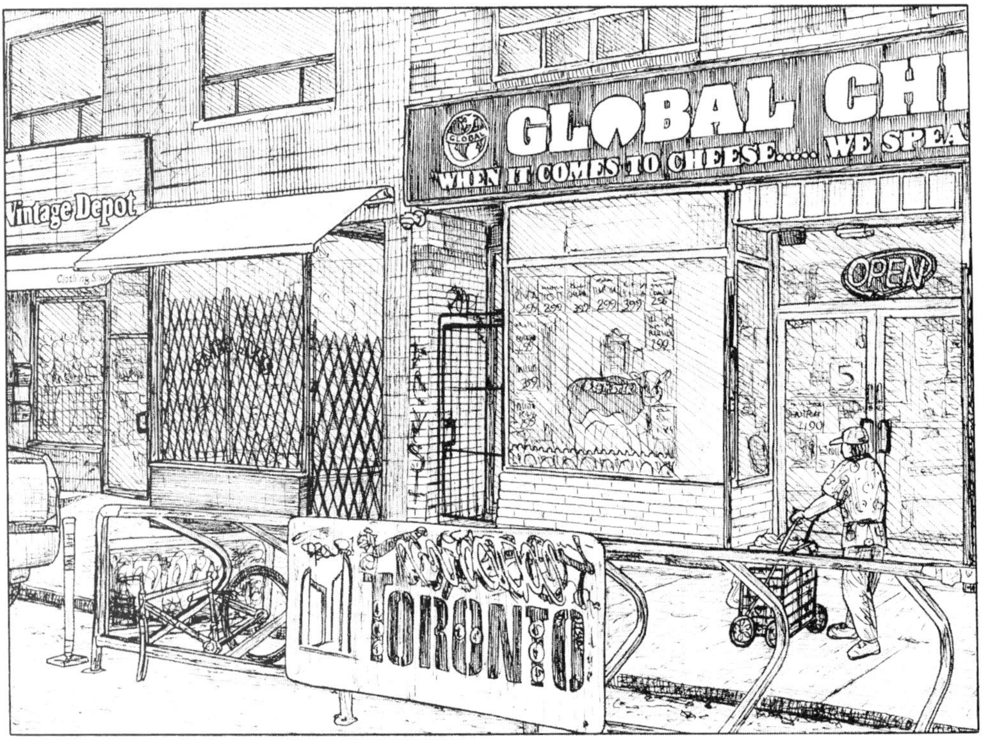
Vintage Depot
Clothing Shop
GLOBAL CH
WHEN IT COMES TO CHEESE..... WE SPEA
OPEN
TORONTO

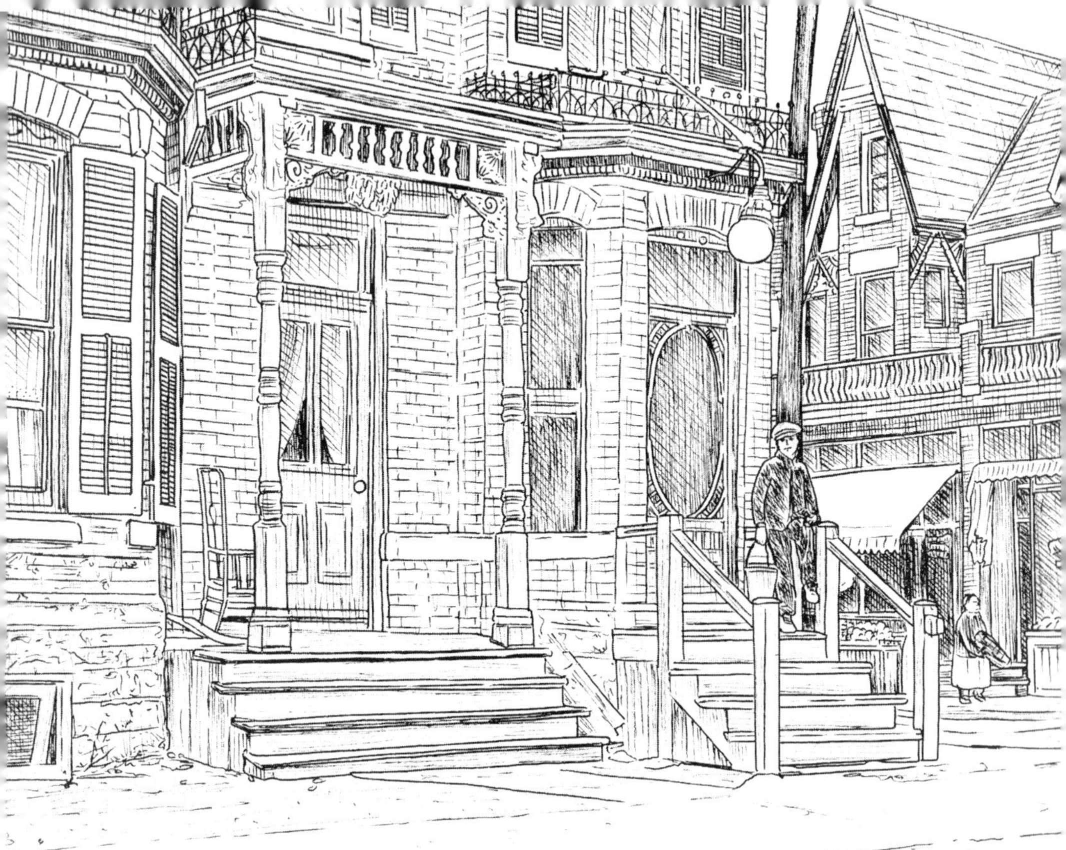

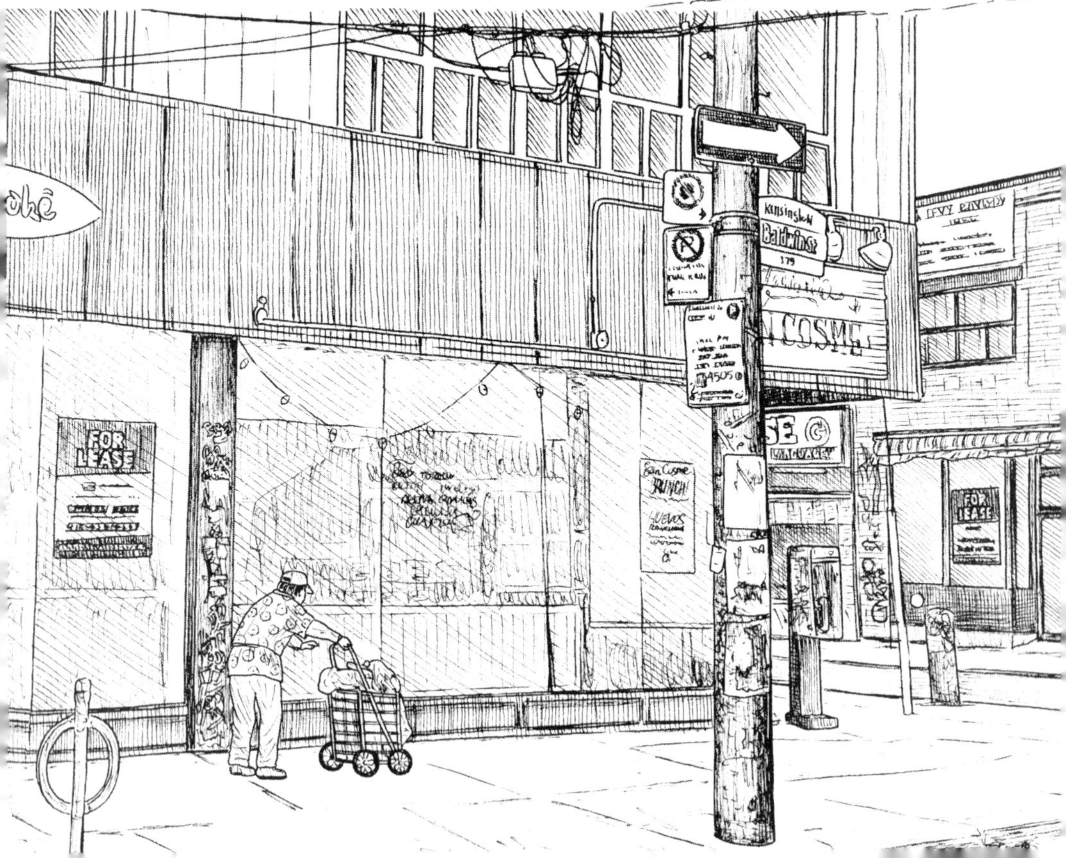

FOR LEASE
San Cosme
BRUNCH
HUEVOS
Kensington
Baldwin St
179
COSME
FOR LEASE

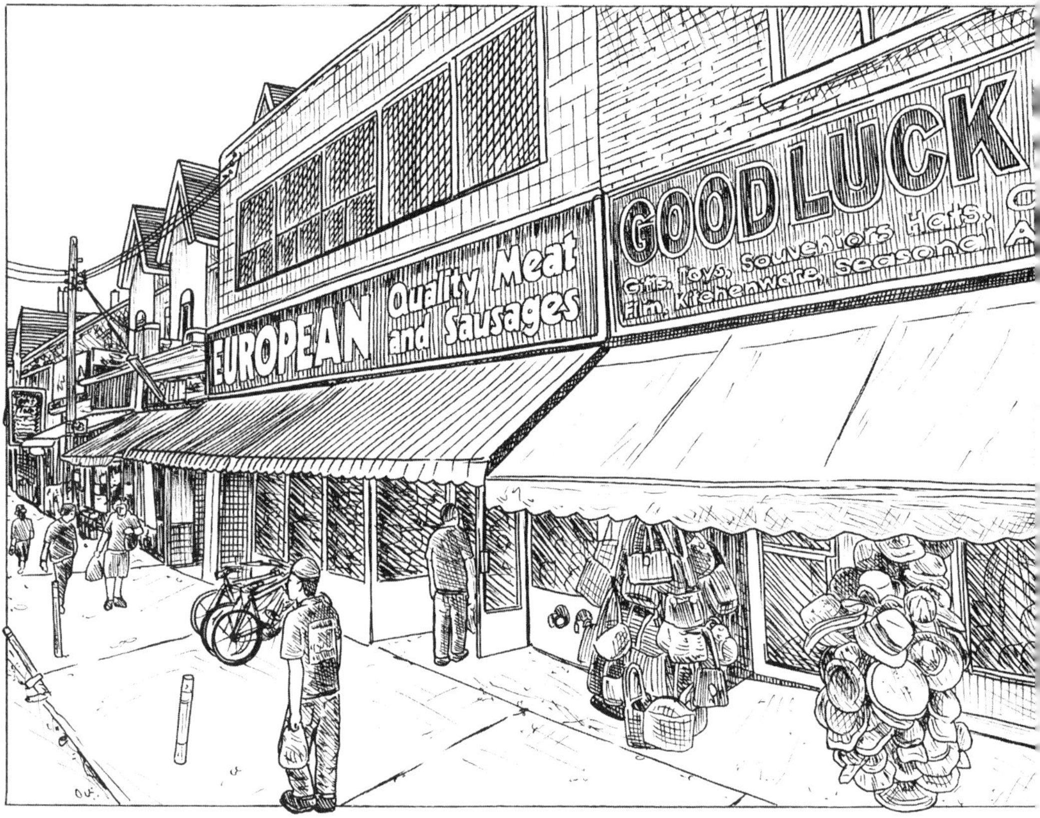
EUROPEAN
Quality Meat and Sausages
GOOD LUCK
Gifts, Toys, Souveniors, Hats,
Film, Kitchenware, Seasonal

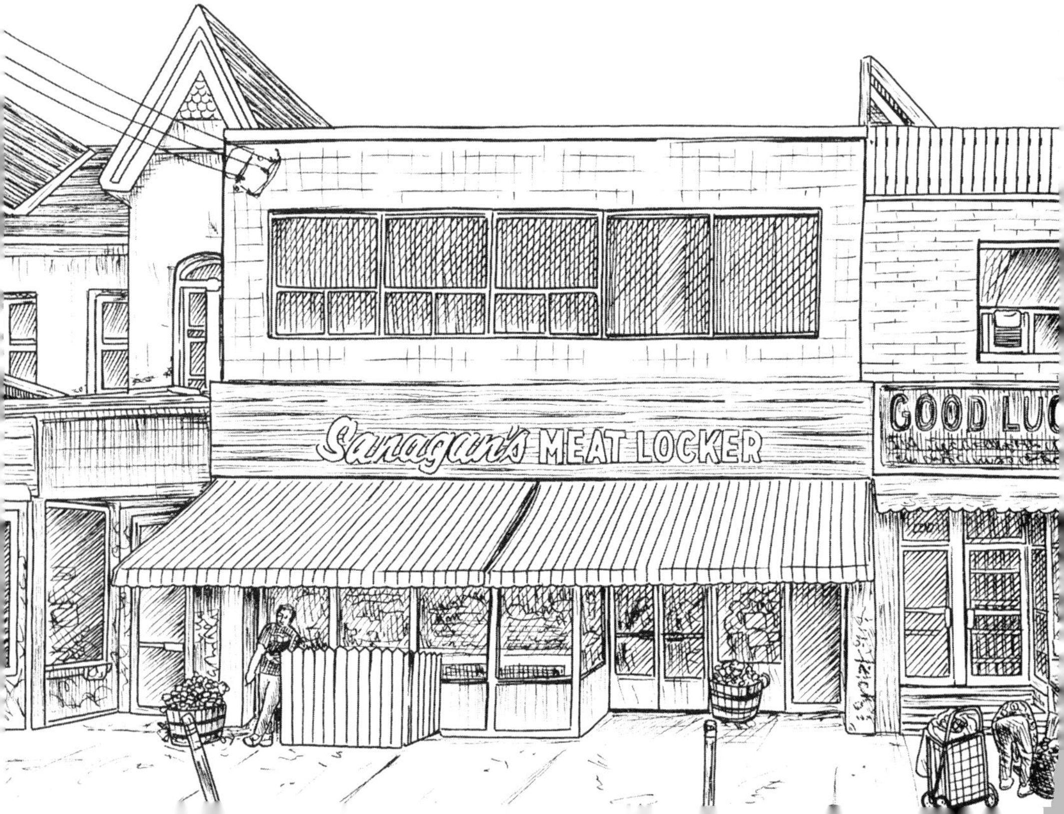
Sanagan's MEAT LOCKER

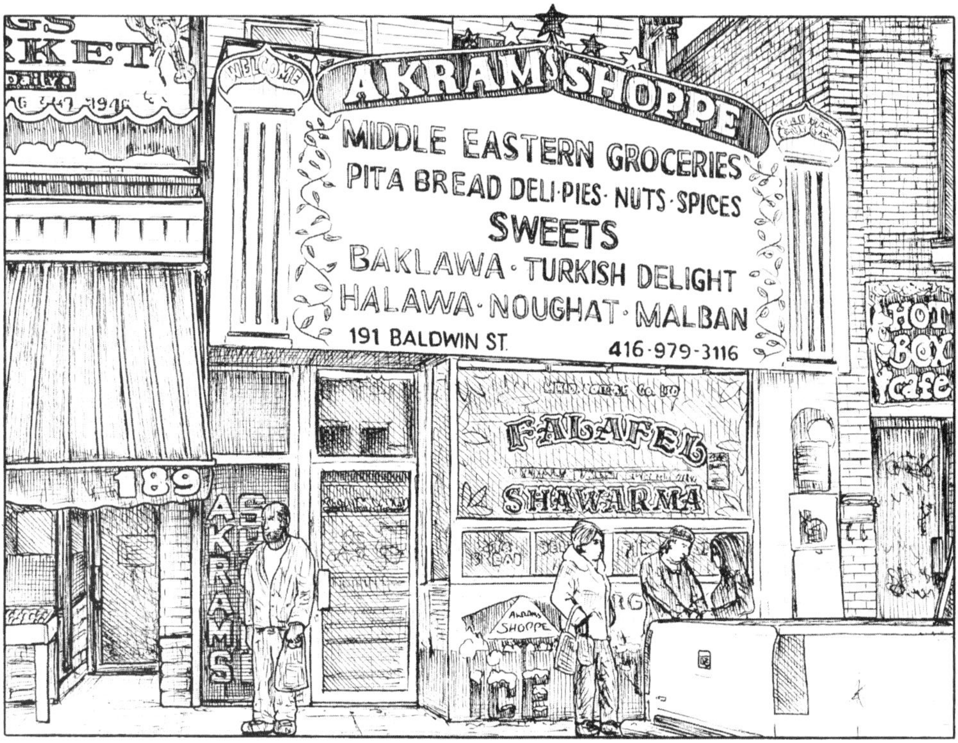
AKRAMS SHOPPE
MIDDLE EASTERN GROCERIES
PITA BREAD DELI·PIES· NUTS·SPICES
SWEETS
BAKLAWA·TURKISH DELIGHT
HALAWA·NOUGHAT·MALBAN
191 BALDWIN ST.
416-979-3116
FALAFEL
SHAWARMA
189
AKRAMS
AKRAMS SHOPPE
HOT BOX cafe

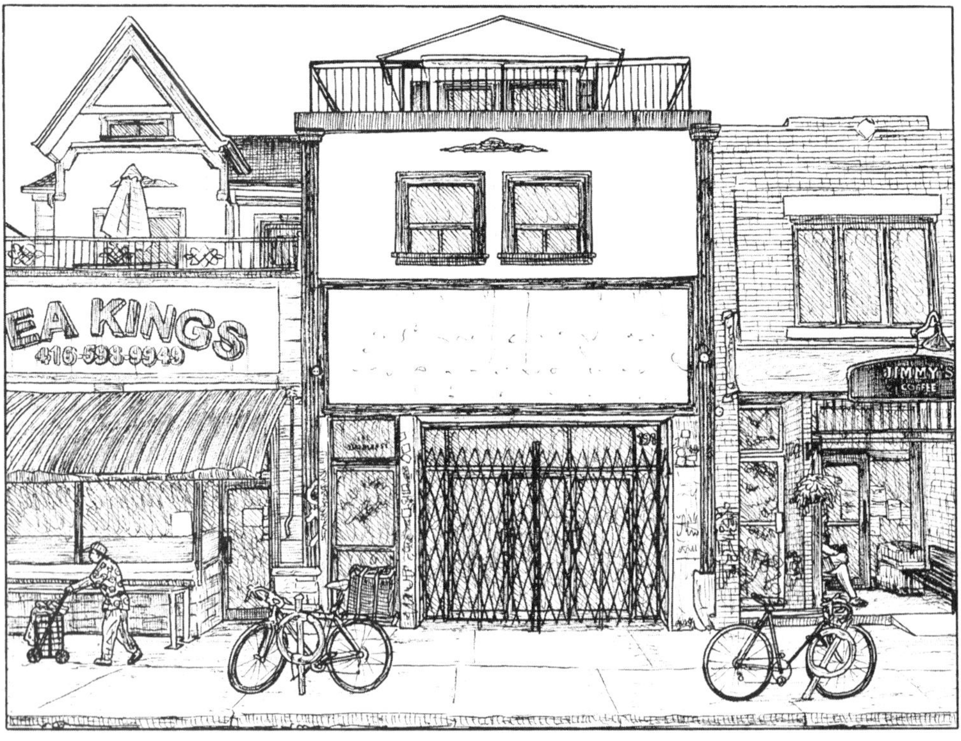
EA KINGS
416-598-9949
JIMMY'S
COFFEE

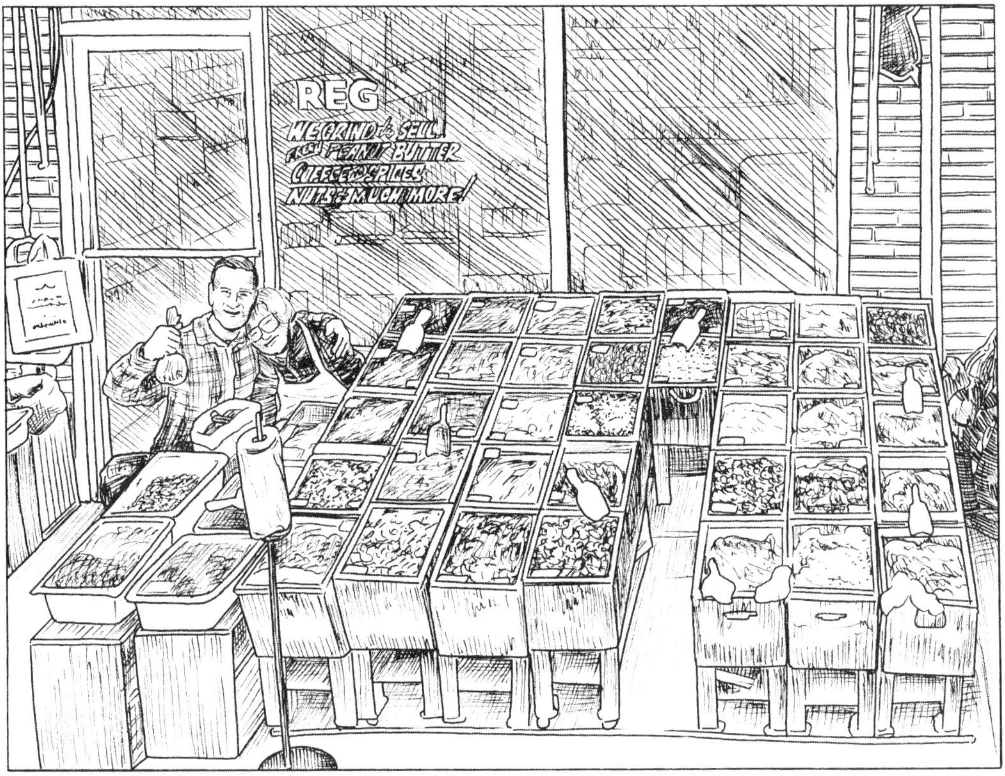
REG
WE GRIND & SELL
FRESH PEANUT BUTTER
COFFEE AND SPICES
NUTS & MUCH MORE!

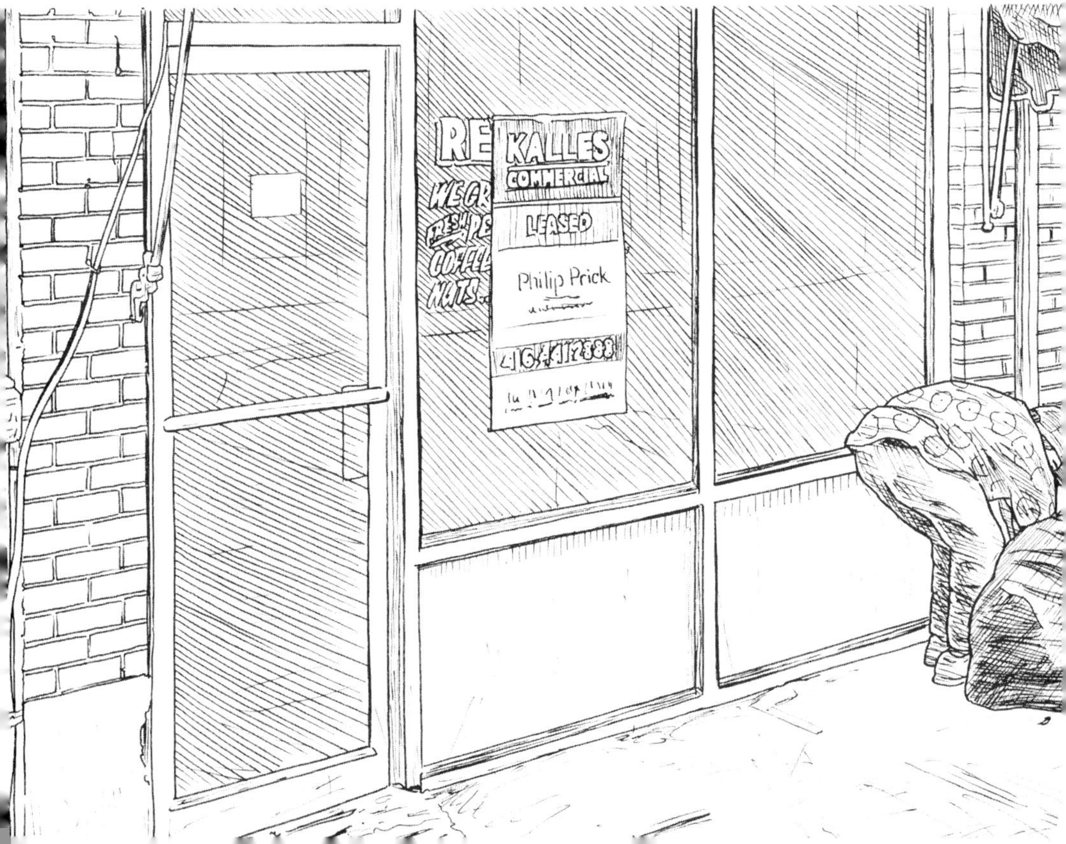
KALLES
COMMERCIAL
LEASED
Philip Prick
416-412-888

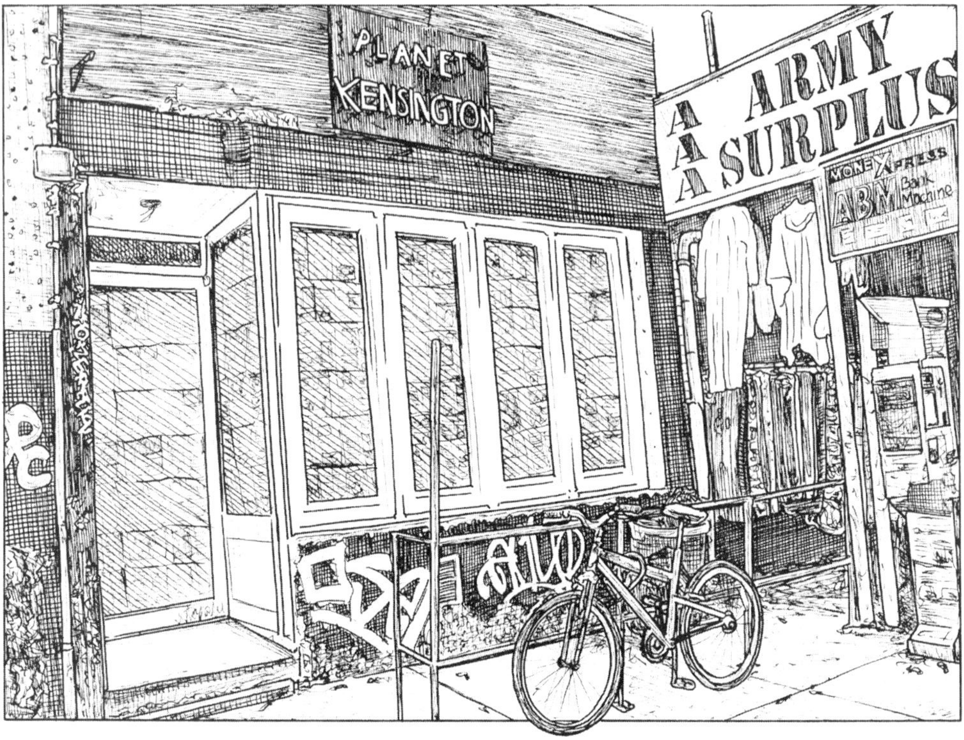
PLANET KENSINGTON
AAA ARMY SURPLUS
MONEXPRESS
ABM Bank Machine

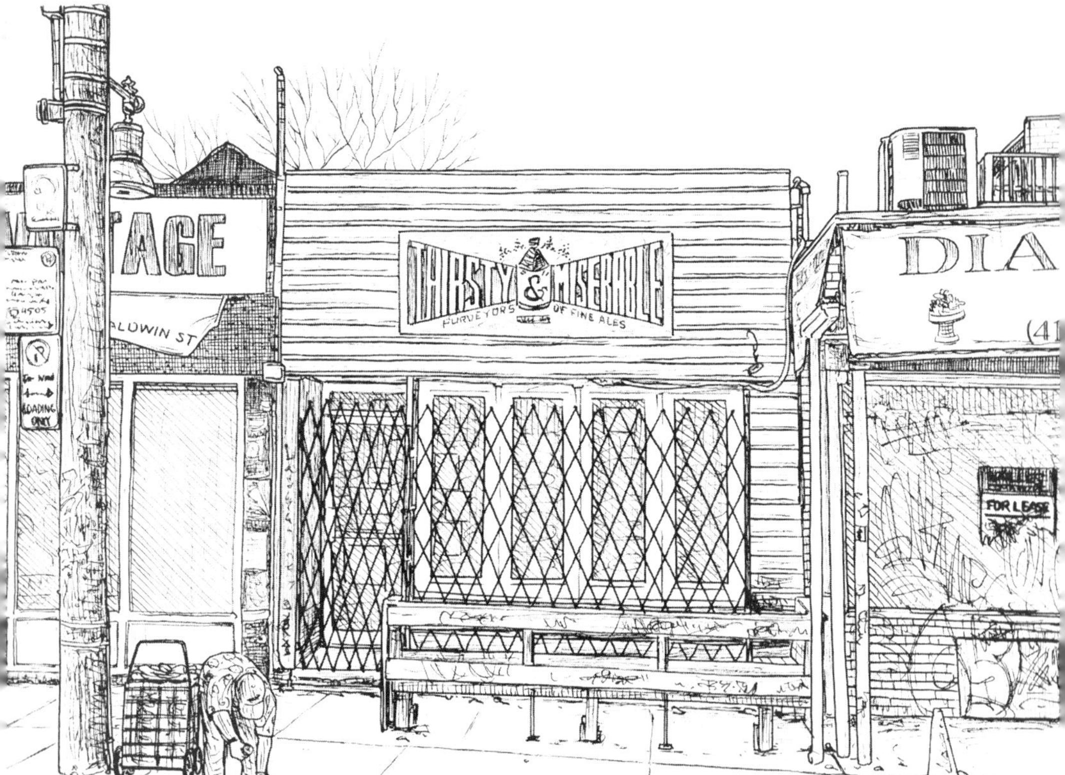
TAGE
ALDWIN ST
THIRSTY & MISERABLE
PURVEYORS OF FINE ALES
DIA
FOR LEASE
LOADING ONLY

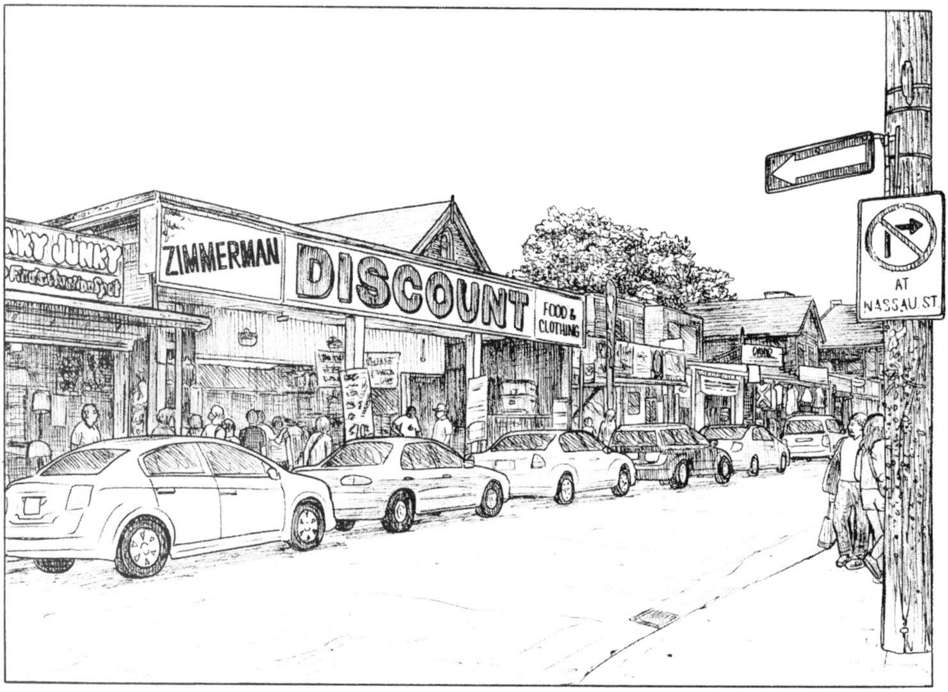
ZIMMERMAN
DISCOUNT
FOOD & CLOTHING
AT NASSAU ST

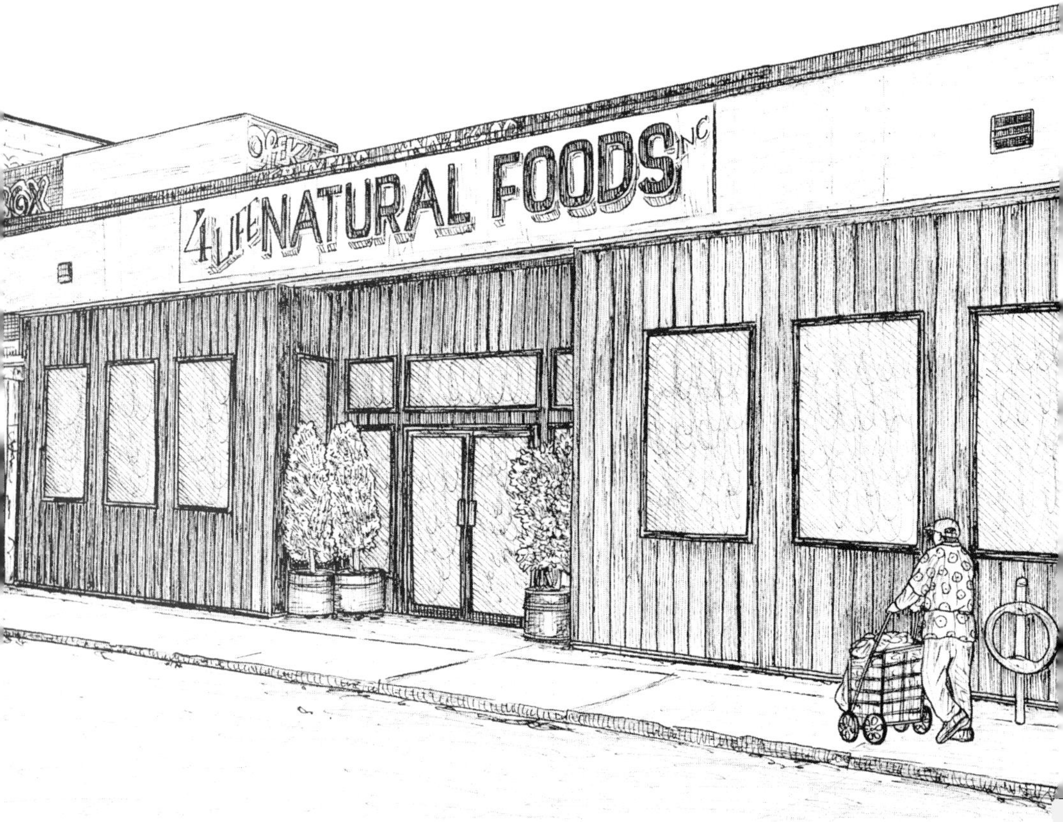
4 LIFE NATURAL FOODS INC

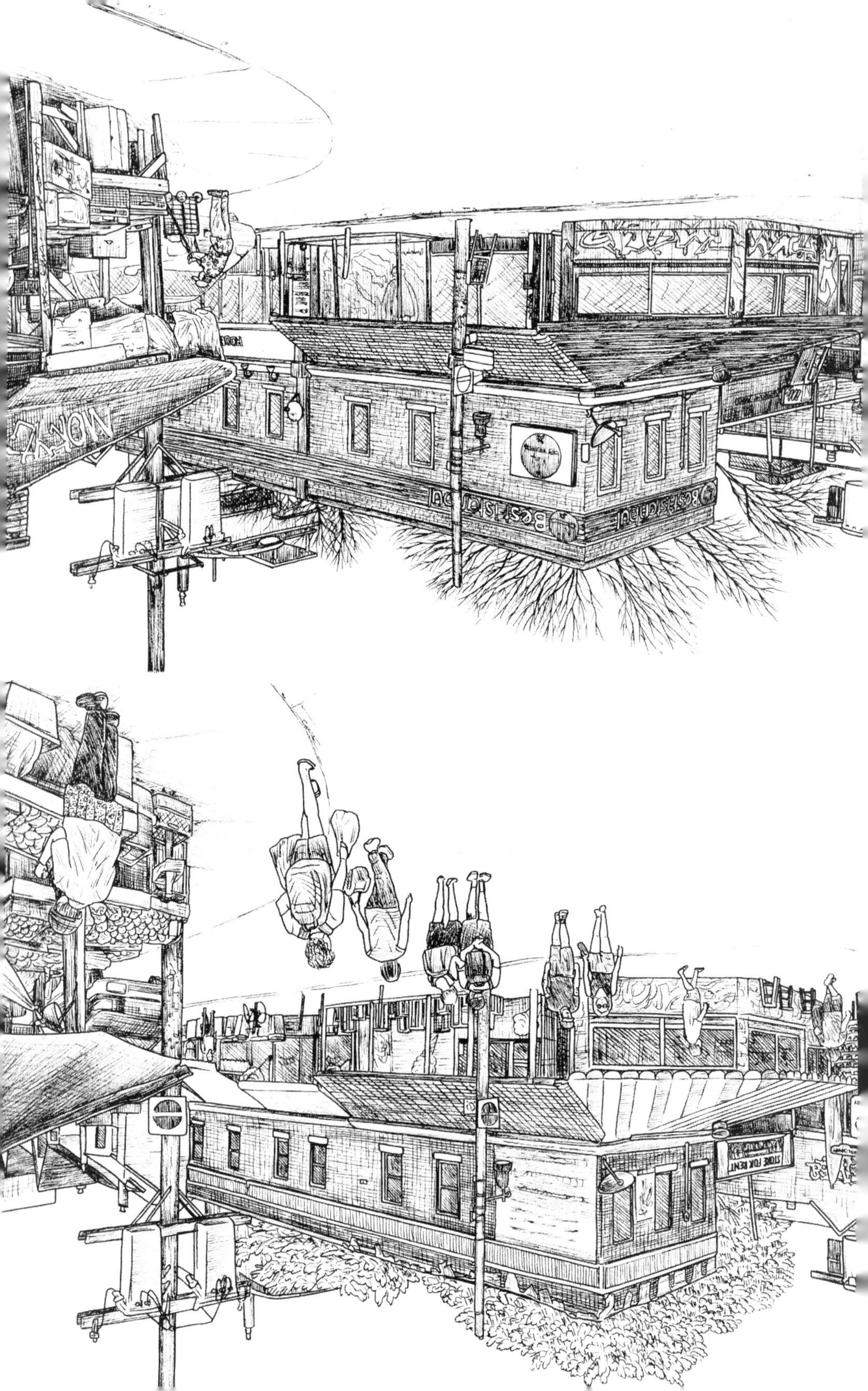
STORE FOR RENT

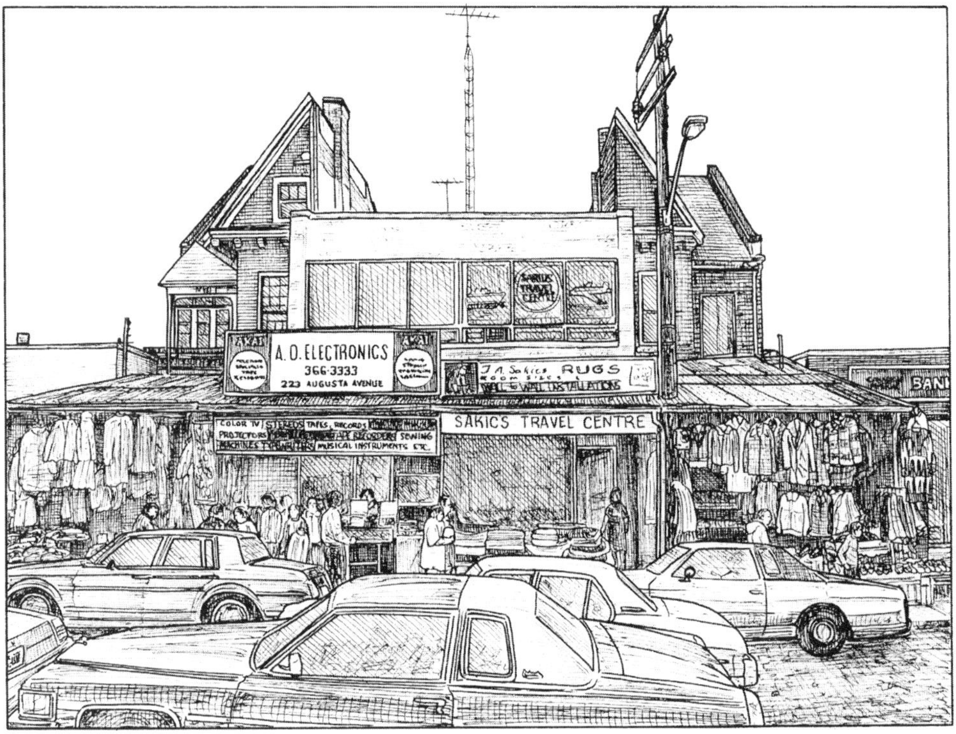
A. O. ELECTRONICS
366-3333
223 AUGUSTA AVENUE
AKAI
J.A. Sakics RUGS
WALL TO WALL INSTALLATIONS
SAKICS TRAVEL CENTRE
COLOR TV STEREOS TAPES, RECORDS
MUSICAL INSTRUMENTS ETC.
SEWING

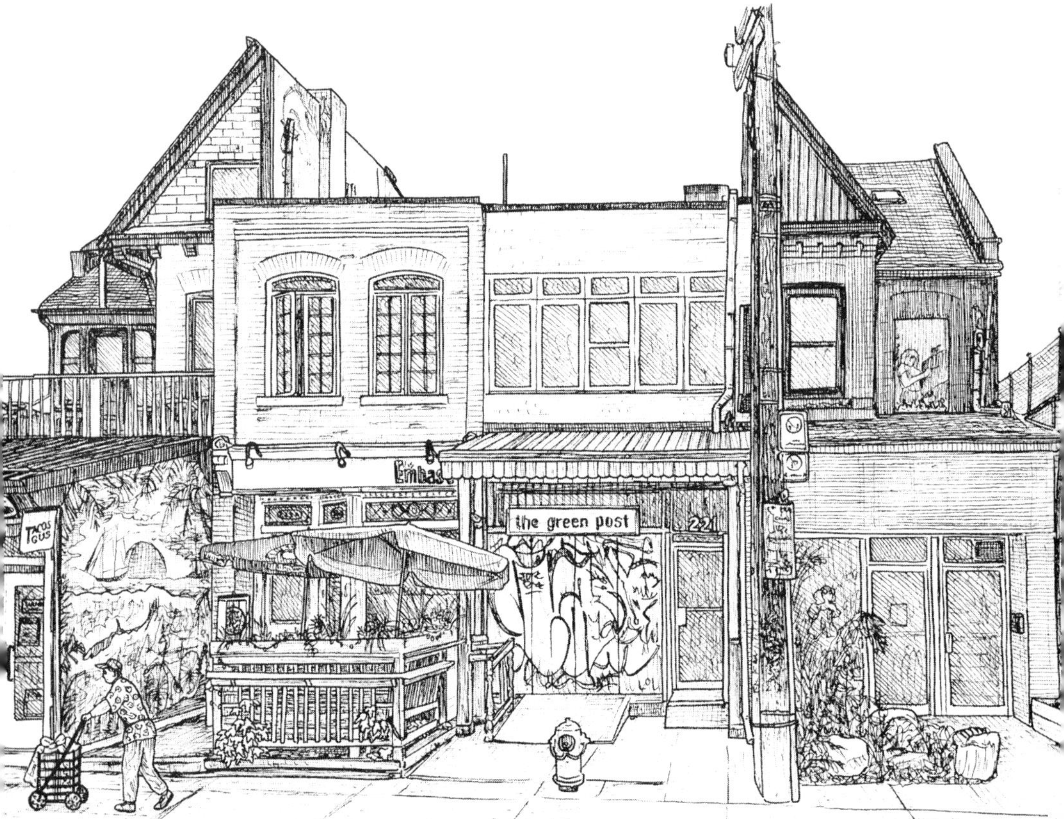
the green post
221
TACOS GUS

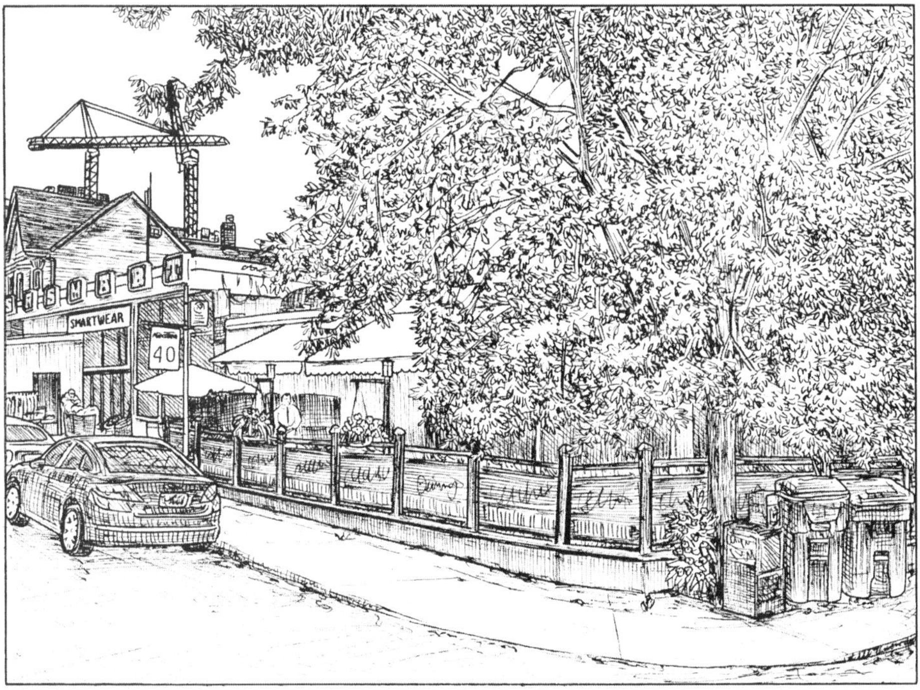
SMARTWEAR
40

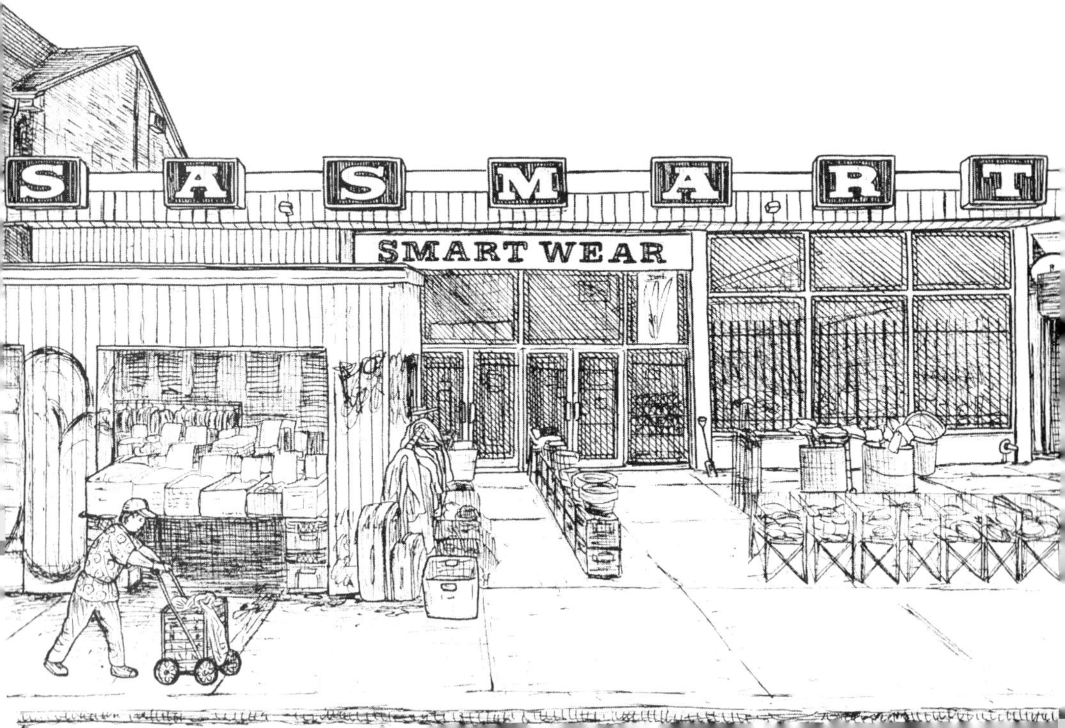
SASMART
SMART WEAR

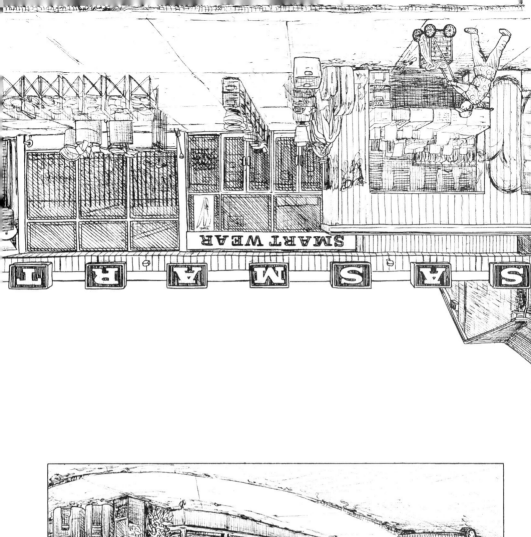

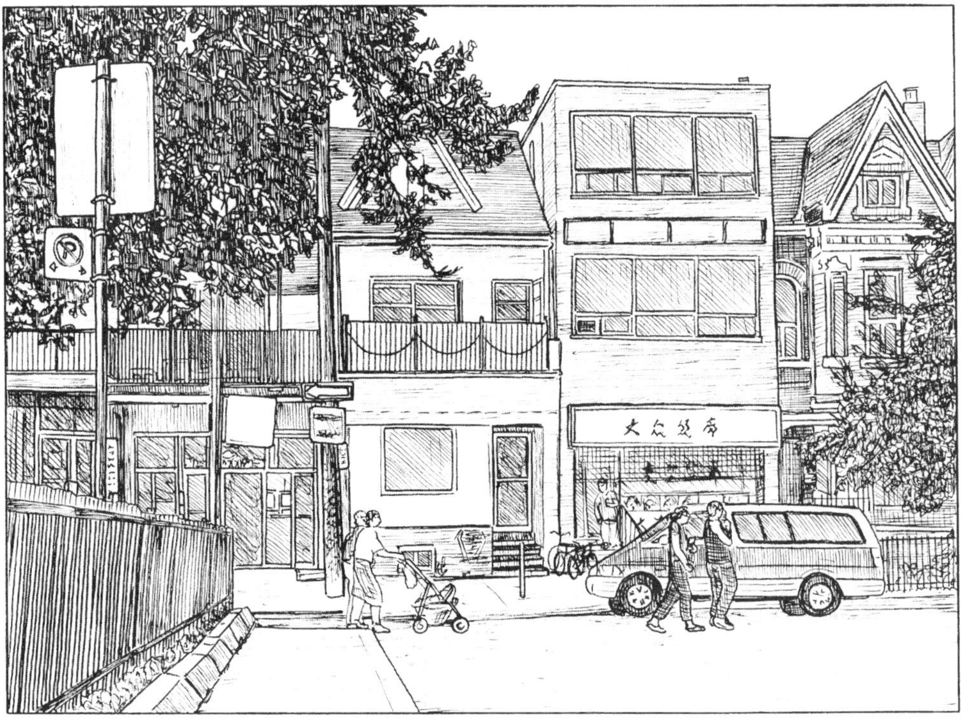

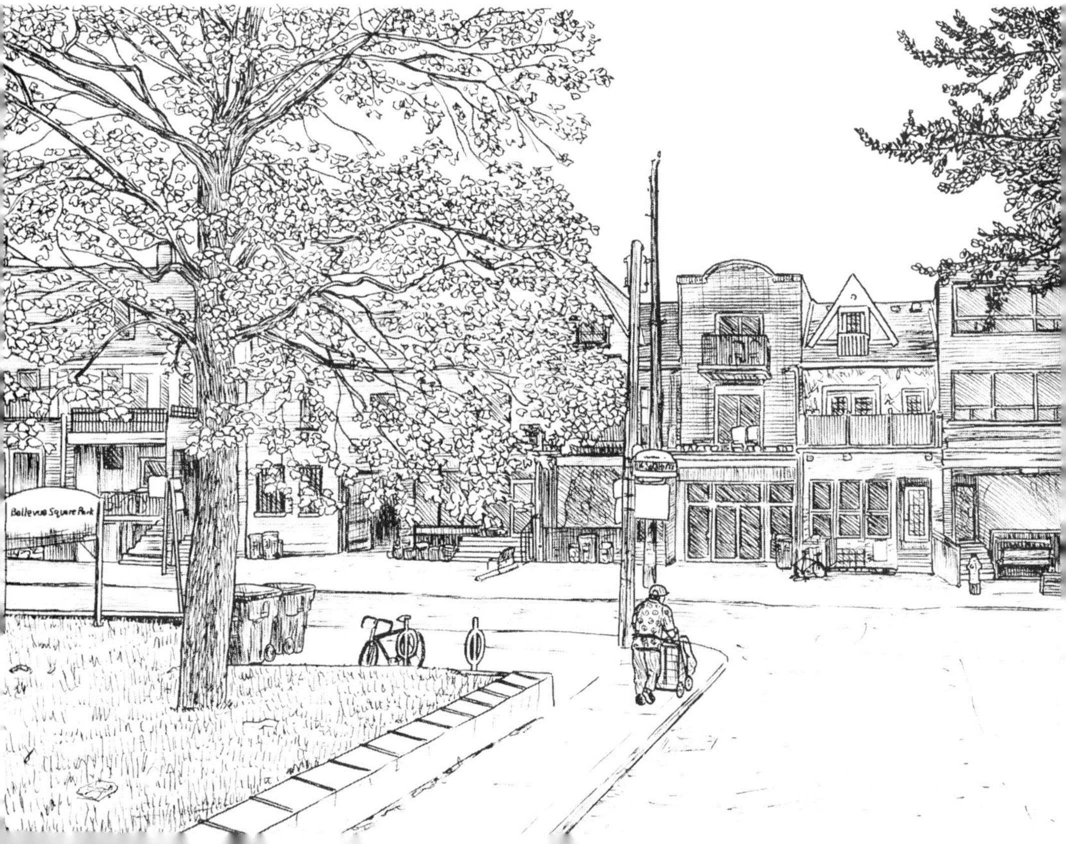
Bellevue Square Park

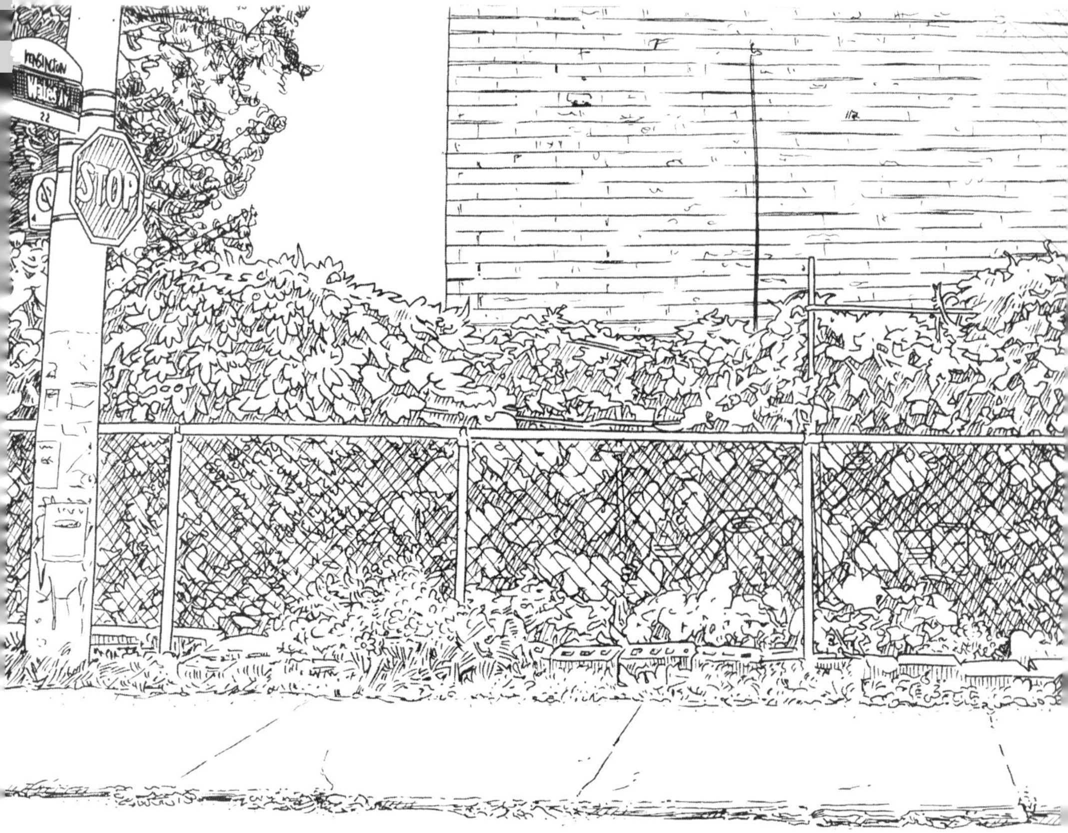
KENSINGTON
Wales Av
22
STOP

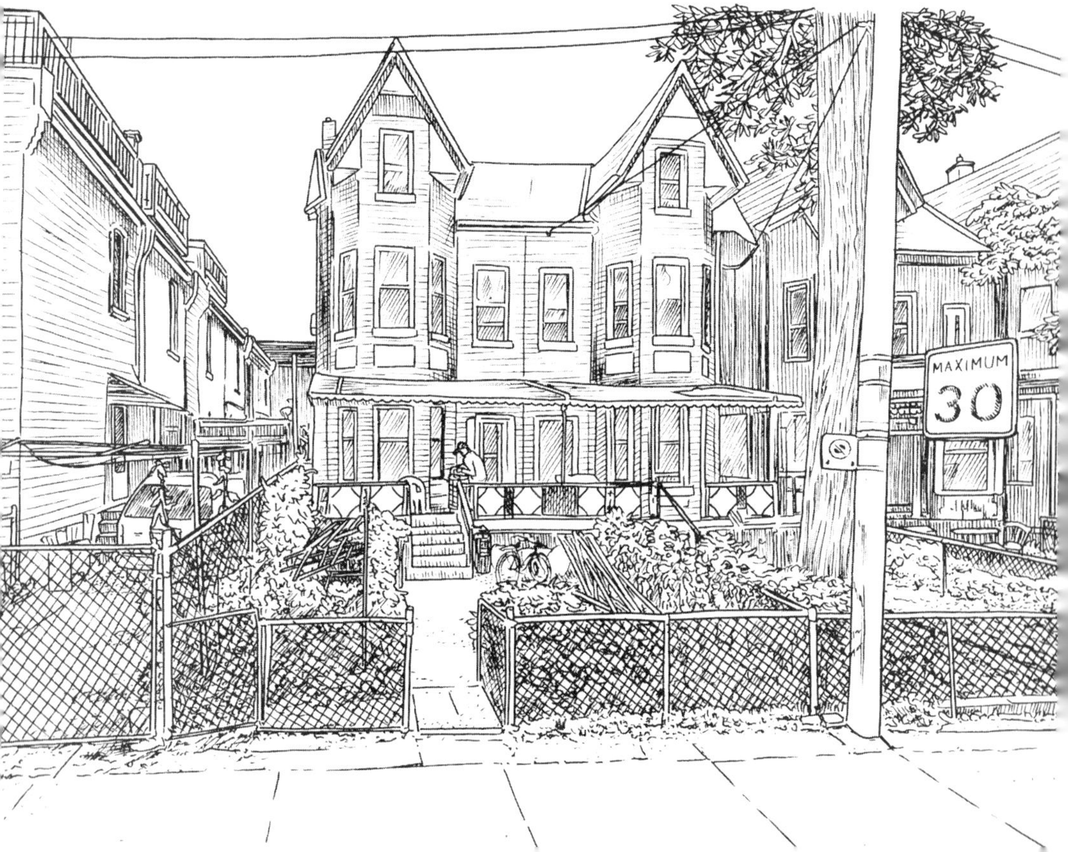
MAXIMUM
30

ILLUSTRATIONS BY DANIEL INNES

DENISON AVENUE